Donald ▓▓▓
07/18/98

The Winds Of Tomorrow

Donald Wilson

The Winds Of Tomorrow

DCW PUBLISHING COMPANY
Southfield, Michigan

FIRST EDITION

All rights reserved, including the right of
reproduction in whole or in part in any form.

All of the characters and companies in this book are fictitious, and
any resemblance to actual persons, living or dead, or
companies is purely coincidental.

© Copyright 1995 by Donald C. Wilson

Published by DCW Publishing Co., Inc.
19785 W. 12 Mile Road, Suite 601, Southfield, Michigan 48076

Printed in the United States of America
ISBN: 0-9648805-0-4

Library of Congress Catalog Card No.: 95-92559

THE WINDS OF TOMORROW is dedicated to my wife, Jane, the one person who motivated this writer with love, joy, passion and laughter as he tread through this literary endeavor. She was the everlasting force and impetus that carried this novel to it's completion ...thus, her love has touched each page, each sentence, each word and my heart...With my deepest love I dedicate this work to my Jane...

Preface

This novel was written to entertain, enlighten and to show that Black Americans, if given the opportunity, are no different than any other Americans of similar backgrounds, educations and home environments. Some are heroes and some are villains. Some are successful and some are failures. Black Americans are not a monolith...they do not think alike and they do not act alike. The negative image that many people have of African-Americans is the result of distorted truths, blatant lies, self-denigration, omissions in past history and the stereotypes promalgated by newspapers, movies and books that were purposely written with exaggerated truths degrading Blacks because the authors realized that was what the publishers and producers wanted...

Consequently, it is very seldom that we see anything on television, in the movies or in books that accurately depicts middle-class or wealthy Blacks on an equal level with their White counter-parts. Instead, we are shown mostly black buffoons on television, the drug pushers and thugs in the movies and poor, bedraggled, crime-ridden ghetto or plantation dwellers in books.

This kind of media racism sustains false stereotypes and is typical of the covert racism practiced in this country and culminates in major newspapers all across the nation sustaining this false assumption and television programs featuring Black actors which center primarily on comedy instead of portraying Black families in dramatic business environments similar to the "Dynasty" and "Dallas" television series.

In the 1990s Hollywood welcomed new, young Black filmmakers, provided they produced movies which were consistent and maintained the stereotype of Black urban ghetto dwellers involved with crime, drugs and prostitutes...Again this was typical of a racist media in establishing and maintaining the old opinion of Blacks that degraded an oppressed race. This was first done in the 1970s with the superfly movies which were the first attempt at Black exploitation by Hollywood.

This racist kind of thinking completely ignores the fact that two-thirds of the Black Americans in this country are now middle class or wealthier. Black Americans contribute over $400 billion annually to our nation's economy and most are not stuck in poverty as implied by these movies...Where are these middle-class and upper-class Black Americans being depicted in movies, television and books?..

Television again proved it was a tool of a racism of ignorance when Bill Cosby tried to get "The Cosby Show" on television in 1983. He had to argue with writers, producers and network executives who questioned whether the program's middle-class Huxtable family was really typical of Black family life. In truth, speaking from experience, most Black doctors I know live considerably better than the Huxtable family was portrayed on television, especially with a wife who is an attorney. The Huxtable family lived more on the scale of an auto worker, teacher or a civil service employee rather than a doctor.

In "The Winds Of Tomorrow" a wealthy Black family, the Stantons, is featured along with two equally wealthy White families. Some of the characters are good and some are just plain jerks. The storyline shows the interaction between the races as two major daily newspapers compete for dominance in the metropolitan Detroit area.

The families are faced with normal everyday problems from drug abuse and mid-life crisis to infidelity. The main character, Gene Stanton, begins a new thrust into the newspaper industry when he switches from publishing a Black weekly newspaper to an integrated daily newspaper with mostly White employees. His life is further complicated by a serious love affair that becomes a crushing climax in his life. Stanton's success with his daily newspaper draws the attention of local politicians who urge him to reach for higher political goals to save a city that is drowning in urban blight.

Because the entire topic is so broad, each aspect is given comprehensive and unbias coverage to clearly show how similar the races are when faced with a common problem such as child abuse, sexual orientation, breast cancer, violence, greed and racism...

Interestingly, as the storyline progresses, there is no definite line separating the good guys from the bad guys. Our complex lives are constantly changing. What is right today may be wrong tomorrow. This is an integrated novel that tells the story of the lives of many Americans. Their color and class status is irrelevant to their morals.

I have discovered in writing this novel an invaluable learning experience. My motivation for doing it arose out of the realization that there is no dramatic movie, television series or novel that features the ongoing lives of middle class and wealthy Whites and Blacks in an integrated environment that most Americans face daily as they struggle for influence, success and love.

Donald C. Wilson
March 1994

"Throughout our lives
as long as they may last,
we follow set ways
and the patterns of the past.

We fail to consider
the promises of the future,
holding on to old styles
and customs that we nuture.

Today as the sun rises
with new plans to arrange,
we know the winds of tomorrow
are the winds of change.

For though our hopes may scatter
in the shifting sands of sorrow,
our dreams will live on
in the winds of tomorrow".

The Winds Of Tomorrow

Chapter One

The rumble of thunder in the far off distance signaled the arrival of a long, black limousine when it pulled up in front of the old, closed down newspaper building in downtown Detroit just as the rain began pouring down. Two men, one White and one Black, both with their raincoat collars pulled up high around their necks, dashed from the car and towards the big, revolving door leading into the lobby of the building. A lone man patiently held an umbrella as he stood on the steps at the entrance to the building and directed the two men towards a separate door he held open for them. As soon as they entered, the real estate agent who had been waiting for them walked over to the white man and shook his hand, firmly. "Mr. Stanton...I'm Ollie Nathanson from Nathanson Commercial Realtors. I..."

"Hold it," the man interrupted, sarcastically, as he handed Nathanson his business card. "You got your people mixed up...I'm Roger Carlson, Mr. Stanton's attorney...He's Gene Stanton."

Nathanson looked from Carlson back to Gene Stanton with a puzzled expression on his face. "Wh...what?..I'm...I'm sorry, Mr. Stanton...I just assumed..."

"Forget it," Gene Stanton snapped. "What about this building?..You got a brochure and the architectural plans?"

"Yessir, I sure do," Nathanson replied, laying out a blue print of the schematics of the entire building on a wide counter in the lobby. "We'll start here on the fourth floor and work down. I'm sure you'll find the building satisfactory for your needs. That mechanic you sent over is inspecting the old presses now in the production department on the third floor."

Gene Stanton studied the blueprints for a minute and looked up at the real estate agent. "OK...let's check it out."

Nathanson handed brochures to Gene and Roger as he quickly led them towards the elevators just off of the lobby.

As the small group toured the old building, Gene remembered that day in the sixties when he first saw the inside offices of The Detroit Times Newspaper building. His father had sent him over to the Times to pick up some advertising material meant for the State Journal that had been mistakenly sent to an advertising account executive who handled the same account at the Times. When he first entered the building he had been impressed by the orderly presentation and excitement of a major daily newspaper. In the lobby he saw a classified ads counter, the personnel office and a large reception area furnished with huge leather sofas and chairs, a cocktail table and end tables stacked with out-of-state newspapers. A security guard sat at the desk just in front of two elevators and next to a wide marble staircase leading to the business offices near a hallway leading out to the newspaper docks. The guard stopped Gene and closely examined his identification, eyeing him suspiciously. When Gene explained that he was from the State Journal Newspaper and that he was there to pick up some advertising copy, the guard called the advertising department and verified it. He reluctantly gave Gene back his identification and directed him to the second floor advertising offices. Gene took the elevator up to the second floor and got off. He walked by the huge editorial offices which were crowded with employees rushing to meet the afternoon deadline. Many of the workers stared back at Gene, puzzled. Gene didn't quite understand why he was attracting so much attention until he reached the advertising staff offices which were located in an area about the size of a football field. There were approximately one hundred desks, all occupied, that were surrounded by slick, glass enclosed offices. The advertising staff was across the aisle from the bookkeeping section of busy employees and around the corner from the crowded circulation department. As Gene walked through the spacious offices he fully understood why he was drawing so much attention. Although he had observed a few blacks working as janitors and security guards, he was looking at a sea of White faces who all seemed to object to his being there. Gene was shocked!..This was the period directly after the enactment of the 1964 Civil Rights Bill, the deaths of John F. Kennedy, Martin Luther King and Robert Kennedy...A period that was still in the aftermath of the 1967 Detroit riots...Yet, here in this big, industrial northern city, the arsenal of democracy...racism was flourishing at a major daily newspaper!..It made Gene sick to his stomach!..

The account executive Gene was suppose to see had been summoned to a meeting. Gene sat next to his desk in the open offices and waited until a smiling man came over to him, apologized for the delay and offered to take Gene on a quick tour of the building while he was waiting. With his curiosity peaked, Gene willingly accepted the offer. They toured the entire four floors of the building. From the classified advertising department, women's editorial section, entertainment, television, and photography sections all on the fourth floor, the dispatch department, composing room and production departments on the third, retail and national advertising, editorial, bookkeeping, circulation and the cafeteria on the second floor to the personnel and business offices, and the newspaper docks on the first floor...The racial makeup of the employees remained consistent...almost totally White!..

As Gene was being led back up to the advertising offices on the second floor, the friendly man who was conducting the tour was stopped by some men returning from the cafeteria. Gene would never forget what one man asked his guide..."you breaking in another janitor?.."

Being born and raised in an integrated neighborhood and attending all integrated schools, Gene was startled to learn that discrimination in the news media was so extensive in his own native city of Detroit. He was determined to change it...He knew he couldn't do it publishing his family's weekly Black newspaper, The State Journal...only Blacks would see it...It was then that Gene decided he was going to own that building some day!..

It had been common with the demise of business in many urban areas across the country, that when the Whites left the inner cities they abandoned business that many Black entrepreneurs wanted to take over but the persistent, old time discriminatory practices on the part of banks and financial institutions denied the Black entrepreneurs commercial loans to finance these businesses. As a result, the businesses remained closed down and contributed to the blight and decay of most major urban areas all across the country. In Gene Stanton's case, a strong weekly Black newspaper and wise investments by the Stanton family enabled him not to rely solely on outside financing to purchase the old, closed-down, Detroit Times newspaper building.

Today, the small group slowly strolled down the darkened, wide hallways, stepping over and around debris, office furniture, and upturned chairs as they completed their inspection. Gene Stanton studied each room carefully, examining everything from the ceilings down to the floors. His facial expression remained stoical as the real estate agent nervously glanced back at him.

"You have any questions, Mr. Stanton?" the agent asked. "I think the brochure covers everything."

Gene Stanton shook his head thoughtfully. They had been touring the empty building for more than an hour. It was dark, dank and dirty. Most of the windows had been boarded up and the few that were not only showed the rain splattering up against the windows and coming down outside in drenching sheets. The sounds of heavy thunder echoed throughout the building.

Gene Stanton flipped the pages in the real estate brochure he held in his hands. "What's this room?..I didn't see it in the brochure..."

"That was gonna be the computer room," Nathanson answered. "Only it never go finished. They shut down before they got any computers in there."

Roger Carlson walked back towards Gene Stanton and peeked over his shoulder at the empty room. "What a mess!!"

Gene looked at Roger as a smile played at the corner of his mouth. "You're just prejudice, Roger," Gene said, smiling. "If this place was the Taj Mahal you'd object to it."

"No...this place...this whole building is just one big mess!" Roger exclaimed. "I don't even know why we're here...You can't be serious about this!"

"Oh, I'm serious alright."

"It'll take months just to clean this place up!" Roger argued.

"Oh, no," Nathanson interrupted. "The clean-up is part of the sale...anyone who buys it not only gets it cleaned up but they'll redecorate the whole building...all floors."

"That's fine...let's take a look at the presses," Gene said. "We might be able to salvage some of them."

"They're all working, Mr. Stanton," the agent answered. "And I got that information you wanted about the former newspaper employees...Names, addresses and phone numbers...I understand most of them are still available and they're anxious to come back."

Roger Carlson took the folder from the real estate agent and scanned the list quickly. "What's the date of this list?"

"It was just put together earlier this week," Nathanson answered, smiling broadly. "Those people are ready to get back to work."

Another man in the group walked over to Gene with a thoughtful expression on his face. Gene looked at him, puzzled. "What's the matter, Hank...is something bothering you?"

"I'm...I'm just wonderin', Mr.. Stanton," Hank replied. "Why'd this paper close down?"

"Bad management and terrible reporting," Gene answered. "In the final stages...they weren't even trying to produce a quality newspaper."

"And you want those people back?" Hank asked.

"They're experienced and seasoned journalists," Gene said. "With proper management, incentives and supervision...they'll be alright."

"I...I guess you're right, Mr.. Stanton," Hank said. "I checked out all of those presses...they're all workin."

The small group continued down the wide hallway leading out to the pressroom. Roger lagged behind as a grimace lined his face. Finally, he shook his head in disapproval, turned and walked away briskly, to catch up with the rest of the group.

By the afternoon it had finally stopped raining. The sun came out and people were enjoying themselves on the country club tennis courts. The sounds of a tennis ball being hit back and forth dominated the air as Roger Carlson tried to take out his frustration at Gene Stanton on the tennis court. The two middle-aged players grunted loudly each time they smacked the tennis ball, creating a groan from the sparse crowd sitting in the stands and watching them. In a short time the final point was scored and Gene Stanton walked slowly over to the net and gave Roger a high five handshake as they both roared in laughter. The two men, totally exhausted, continued laughing and slapping each other on the back as they walked away from the tennis court. They both placed a towel around their necks and dabbed at the perspiration rolling down the sides of their faces. They slowly made their way towards an outdoor cafeteria located near the tennis courts. As they walked under the large awning and plopped down at the small round table, they began to speak quietly, trying to catch their breath.

"Wow!..you're in some kinda shape!" Roger sighed.

"Me?..What about you?..I didn't see you givin' up."

"No way!"

"That's what I thought," Gene said, breathing deeply.

"You get my message before you got here?"

"What message?"

Roger wiped the perspiration from his face and caught his breath. "Merl Henderson...that woman from NEW."

"NEW?" Gene asked. "What the hell is NEW?"

"The National Equality For Women...She's been leaving messages for me all week...Probably wants my bod."

"Nobody but a hard-up undertaker would want that," Gene laughed. "Did she say what its about?"

"You know what its about," Roger snapped. "She wants to know if you've made up your mind about going to a daily newspaper."

Roger eyed Gene carefully as the waiter came over to their table and set two tall drinks in front of them. Both men relaxed and sipped their drinks. Roger sighed as he tested the first taste of his drink. "I told her I didn't think you were interested...After looking at that old building today...I told her I thought it was a dumb idea."

Gene glanced up and stared back at Roger. "Its not so dumb...I think it's got potential...a lot of potential."

"I don't believe it!"

"You better get use to the idea...We could earn each day what we've been grossing in a week!"

Roger quickly looked away. A frown appeared on his face a he wrinkled his brow. The two men drank in silence and stared out over the lush green grounds of the country club golf course nearby. In a few minutes more people crowded under the awning of the small outdoor cafeteria, pushing and shoving their way to the bar. Their loud laughter and shouting could be heard throughout the area. Roger finished his drink and signaled the waiter for a refill. He stared hard at Gene.

"You're not really dead-set on this are you?" Roger asked.

"Yeah...I am," Gene replied. "I've been thinkin' about this since the Times went belly-up. Most of the equipment is still in the building...a lot of their key personnel are still in the area, available and ready to go back to work...It's a natural."

Roger leaned back in his chair and studied Gene, thoughtfully. "You'd try something like that just because NEW and a few of those civil rights groups are urging you to?"

"Its not only that," Gene answered. "I think it's a helluva opportunity for us to develop a major daily newspaper. It'll provide hundreds of jobs. Detroit is a big city...it can easily support two major daily newspapers."

"Yeah?..So what happened to the Times?.."

"They simply provided a bad product. They didn't even try to compete with the Daily Press."

Roger leaned forward and lowered his voice. "But what about your family?..How do you think they'll react to this?"

"I dunno...probably mixed," Gene answered. "Pat's against it...She wants me to retire like I'm some old man...Well I'm not old and I'm not about to retire!"

"Then you haven't mentioned it to the rest?"

"No...not really...but they suspect something's up."

Roger glanced over his shoulder and moved his chair closer to Gene. "Look...let me get something off my chest," Roger whispered, anxiously. "I've been with your family since I got my law degree. Even though I was a White boy...your father treated me like a son...giving me my job back when I got out of the army."

"I know all that...What's your point?"

"Now...now you're heading the most successful Black weekly newspaper in the country. A multi-million dollar corporation."

"So?..What's this leading to?"

"Just this...I made a promise to your father I intend to keep," Roger said, firmly. "Since I'm part of the corporation and almost part of this family, I'm gonna speak my mind...I think it's ridiculous that you're even thinking about jeopardizing everything you and your family have gained just to go up against the Dugas family and all their money!..You can't compete with the Daily Press Newspaper...they'll smash you like a fly!"

"You just said the magic word, Rog," Gene shot back. "Why does it have to be a Black newspaper?"

"Because when your father started this newspaper he realized that was the only support he could get."

"And now?..Don't you think this city would support an integrated daily newspaper owned by a Black family?"

"I don't know, Gene...It'll be risky!"

Gene stood up to leave and Roger looked up at him.

"Can I give you a lift?" Gene asked.

"No!..I don't need a damn lift!" Roger fired back. "I just can't believe that you're even thinkin' about doin' something like that!"

Gene picked up his tennis bag and slowly turned as he walked away from the table. He suddenly stopped in his tracks and turned back to Roger with a determined look on his face.

"I'm not just thinkin' about it," Gene said, calmly. "I'm gonna do it!"

The Palmer Woods subdivision in the city of Detroit represents a combination of old, stately mansions that were built during the roaring twenties for wealthy automobile executives and contemporary plush estates constructed just after the second world war. Some of the mansions are as large as schools and hospitals. The entire area sets just across from the lush, green meadows of Detroit's Palmer Park. The homes are graced with wide trunked, towering shade trees that protect the beautiful area like proud sentinels and follow the winding streets throughout the panoramic landscape.

Today, the huge circular driveway in front of the Stanton mansion in palmer Woods was crowded with long limousines and expensive sport cars. The sound of the soft murmur of a sleek, black Cadillac interrupted the quiet scene as the car moved slowly along the driveway and stopped in front of the spacious porch. Roger and Janet Carlson got out of the car and walked up past the vine covered pillars and rang the doorbell. In a few moments the massive front door opened and the couple walked inside.

Earnest and Hattie Stanton had began publishing The State Journal during the mid-fifties. A Black weekly newspaper that brought local and national news about Blacks in society, sports and entertainment to the African-American population in the City of Detroit, the Journal avoided controversy, especially stories concerning racial conflict, until the mid-sixties when it became swept up in the civil rights movement. In reaction to the Journal's new hard core civil rights reporting and editorials, their mostly White advertisers, out of fear of offending their White customers, threatened to withdraw their ads from the Journal if the policy wasn't changed. Fervently committed to the civil rights movement, Ernest Stanton, his wife, Hattie, their teen-aged daughter, Gloria, and their newly wed son, Gene and their daughter-in-law, Patricia, all ignored the threats and charged ahead, printing stories fighting for equal rights for all Americans. When Martin Luther King, Jr. was assassinated in 1968, the State Journal was almost bankrupt from the advertising boycott. Ernest Stanton employed the services of a young, White attorney, Roger Carlson, fresh out of law school and a civil rights advocate, to file a federal lawsuit against the advertisers in violation of the 1964 Civil Rights Act which barred secondary boycotts in retaliation for civil rights activities. The lawsuit was finally settled out of court in the early seventies, but by that time Earnest Stanton, trying to keep the struggling newspaper alive, had suffered a paralyzing stroke, forcing him to turn over most of the management of the newspaper to his son, Gene.

With the influx of money from the court settlement and a loan from the Dugas family, owners and publishers of the city's largest daily newspaper, the Daily Press, the Journal survived the effects of the advertising boycott as the civil rights movement lost momentum and racial conflict stories decreased. Ernest Stanton died after a massive heart attack, leaving the daily running of The State Journal in the hands of his son, Gene. Hattie Stanton stepped aside and allowed her son, his wife and Roger Carlson to manage the newspaper.

Gene and Patricia Stanton developed into superb business managers while Roger Carlson perfected his job as the corporate attorney to the maximum plateau. Throughout the years, as the State Journal's circulation grew, Patricia Stanton played less of a role at the newspaper and became more prominent at home as the Stanton family expanded to six grown children. Gene II, Karen, Joe, Liz, Kim and Mel Stanton, who developed into a major basketball star at the University of Michigan in the early nineties.

This evening most of the Stanton family, including Roger and his wife, Janet, sat at the large dining room table and finished their dinner as they all joined in and calmly discussed the events surrounding the family newspaper. Constance, the long time family cook and maid, patiently and caringly waited upon each person, removing and examining their plates as they finished. Suddenly, she stopped and glared disapprovingly at the youngest Stanton daughter, Kim.

"You still don't know how to eat good food do you?" Connie exclaimed as she snatched Kim's dish from in front of her. "Struttin' around here lookin' like a broomstick!..All that education and you're still too stupid to know how to eat!"

Everyone in the dining room smiled and chuckled softly at Connie's admonishment of Kim. Kim looked knowingly at her oldest sister, Karen, shrugging her shoulders hopelessly.

"Connie...C'mon, give me a break," Kim pleaded.

"Leave her alone, constance," Karen interceded. "She's a grown woman now. It's too late to change her."

"Don't you say nuthin' to me!" Connie snapped at Karen. "You can't talk...you were just as bad as she is when you were that age!"

Karen ignored Connie's statement and turned to her father. "Speaking of changing, dad," Karen said, sarcastically. "What's this you're planning with the newspaper?"

Gene dabbed at his lips with a napkin and sipped a glass of wine. "That's why I wanted you all here tonight. I toured the Detroit Times building the other day and it verified that we're in a position to triple our profits and get both feet into the newspaper business" Gene stated optimistically. "With the demise of the Times it leaves this city with only one daily newspaper."

"Did it occur to you that this city can only support one newspaper?" Patricia asked. "After all, it's a known fact that most major cities are losing population to the suburbs."

"That's true, but it shouldn't effect our circulation," Gene answered, "When we go daily I plan to run special sections each day that'll feature rotating suburban communities."

"But how do you know they'll want to take our newspaper?" Patricia asked.

"We'll make 'em want our newspaper by creating new innovations, special fashion sections, beefing up local events like high school sports and neighborhood activities," Gene replied.

"And that'll cost money, Gene," Pat shot back. "That's something the Press has that we don't."

Gene's oldest son, Gene II, agreed with his mother. "That's why the Times failed, dad," Gene II argued. "They couldn't compete with the Press...the Daily Press just has too much money for anybody to compete with them. The word is getting around that they're planning to build a new, state of the art newspaper plant in the suburbs...How you gonna meet competition like that?"

"I wasn't raised to run away from competition and neither were you," Gene snapped. "I think the time is right for us to change from a Black weekly to an integrated daily!..Sometimes a man has got to stand up for what he believes in, son!"

"Do you really believe those readers and advertisers will look to us the same as the Press?" Karen asked, anxiously. "No way!..Some of those bigots don't want anything Black anywhere near them, especially to have a Black ran newspaper delivered into their homes everyday!"

Gene looked in Roger and Janet Carlson's direction as he calmly continued. "This is an integrated corporation that'll be publishing an integrated, daily metropolitan newspaper," Gene stated, firmly. "We'll be providing a voice for minorities who have never really been heard from before. We'll have women managers, both Black and White, working side by side with men managers...Black and White. Our newspaper will be designed to truly represent the make-up of the entire metropolitan community and we intend to produce the most modernly efficient major daily newspaper in the country!"

"That sounds good...but can it work?" Patricia asked, sarcastically. "We have to look at this thing more practical then idealistic."

"I think dad's right," Liz said. "We can beat the Press by producing a better newspaper."

"How?" Gene II asked. "By using more expensive newspaper stock?"

"No!" Liz replied, quickly. "I'm talking about providing comprehensive news stories on every important issue that television just touches on. We'll change the Sunday supplements and update them with a special four color fashion section each Sunday...The advertisers will love it!"

"You mentioned advertisers, Liz?" Roger retorted. "Well, the advertisers want paid circulation. They wanna know how many folks out there are gonna see their message!..On Sunday alone the Press has a circulation over 500,000!..We have a little over 100,000 now and we may lose some of that if we switch to a daily newspaper!..No...we can't win...the press will eat us alive!.."

"I can't believe this!..I don't understand you, dad!" Karen exclaimed. "Why the hell risk a successful weekly newspaper to chase a damn dream!.."

"Take it easy, Karen...your father's no fool," Patricia said, cooly. "I'm sure he'll do what's right for the family."

Gene II quickly interrupted the heated conversation.

"No, mom...I think Karen's right!" Gene II argued. "As managing editor of the State Journal, I think I have a better insight as to what's involved here...Right now we're only dealing with one little labor union. We've never had any real labor problems before... but if we go daily...we'll have to deal with as many as fourteen different newspaper craft unions...that alone could break us!"

"I'm afraid some of you may be missing the point," Gene answered, calmly. "The main reason the Daily Press will object to our going daily is because of the monopoly they now have over all of the advertisers in the six county area. When we come on board we could cut into their take...We could show a profit three times greater than we're earning now...even with those costly labor unions."

"What about our paltry circulation?" Kim asked. "We can't compare with the Daily Press."

"Since our circulation won't be as great as the Press' we can't charge as much," Gene explained. "But we'll still have our share of advertisers and there are thousands of people out there, both advertisers and readers, who prefer to have a choice of what newspaper they read...and I intend to provide them with that choice."

"If you're counting on organizations like NEW, the Hispanics, the NAACP and those other civil rights groups to boost our circulation you can forget it," Roger declared flatly. "They'll talk a good fight but when we fall off the cliff they'll just wave goodby!"

The argument continued throughout most of the evening until Mel Stanton, the youngest of the family, showed up late with his glamorous White girlfriend, Kelly Millard, a stunning young woman with flashing blue eyes and long, golden hair. Mel, tall and lean, over six feet-five inches, was a prototype of the major college basketball player who was projected to become a professional star and go early in the National Basketball Association's upcoming draft.

Mel smiled broadly as he greeted everyone in the dining room. "Hi, folks...sorry I'm Late...I had to pick up Kelly and I'd like you all to meet her...Kelly, this is my family."

Kelly smiled at everyone. She stopped and turned back to Mel when she noticed the Carlsons sitting at the table grinning at them. Mel quickly corrected himself. "And this is my special brother, Roger Carlson, with his pretty wife, Janet. Roger is our corporate attorney and he's been a member of this family longer than most of us have..."

Everyone acknowledged Kelly with big smiles as she escorted Mel to the head of the table, towards Gene. Mel stopped when he reached his mother and grandmother, kissing them both on the forehead. He spotted his sister, Karen, sitting next to a stranger he had never met. He leaned towards Karen, extending his hand to the stranger. "Who's your new friend, sis?..And by the way...how's Bob doin?"

Karen angrily ignored Mel's needling remarks. They were all aware of Karen's marital problems with her husband, Dr. Robert Whyte, who was Chief Surgeon at City Hospital. Karen quickly looked away from Mel as Connie leaned over to Liz and whispered in her ear. "Look who's coming to dinner."

Liz smiled broadly and welcomed Mel and Kelly with big hugs. The conversation quickly picked up again as Mel paused next to Janet and Roger.

"You decide what you're gonna do about the NBA draft?" Roger asked. "The papers say you're gonna be a number one selection."

"You've made us all so proud of you!" Janet exclaimed.

The stranger sitting next to Karen suddenly stood up and shook Mel's hand, excitedly. He turned back to Karen as he pointed at Mel. "Hey!..Is THIS your little brother?..I saw him in the NCAA finals with all them bad moves!..They couldn't stop him with a net!"

The excited man suddenly caught himself shouting as he noticed everyone staring at him. He shook Mel's hand again. "I'm Ron Harris, man," he said, trying to compose himself. "I'm the new sports announcer at TV-5...I was just transferred here from Saginaw...Your sister Karen is showing me around Detroit."

"Nice meeting you, Ron," Mel answered, politely as he turned back to Karen, smiling. "You still keepin' count, sis?"

"Yeah, that's my little brother," Karen replied, sarcastically. "Super Jock with a super big mouth!"

Mel turned back to Roger and Janet. "The draft is lookin' pretty good. Everyone seems to think I'll be drafted early in the first round...but it's just a gamble what's going to happen and it could mean big bucks...You know what I'm sayin?"

"What's the next move, Mel?" his mother asked.

Kelly excitedly interrupted before Mel could answer. "The Memphis Mustangs are REALLY interested!..They've already arranged for Mel to take a physical," Kelly blurted out. "I guess they wanna make sure they're not gettin' any damaged goods."

"You still havin' those headaches?" Gene asked, concerned. "You're probably just uptight about the draft...anybody would be."

Mel quickly glanced at Kelly. "Naw, pop...not anymore."

Just as Gene started to respond, Connie placed a cordless phone in front of him. He looked up at her, slightly annoyed.

"It's the black sheep," Connie said. "He's calling from Washington, DC."

Gene quickly picked up the telephone, grinning. "Joe?..How ya doin, boy?"

"Just fine, dad...How are you and mom?" Joe asked. "I'm gonna be out of the country for awhile on special assignment. I'll have a few days off before I leave...I'll be home by tomorrow evening."

"I was hoping you could make it," Gene replied, happily. "This is your newspaper, too."

"My flight should arrive at Metro at eight...Could you arrange for someone to pick me up at the airport?" Joe asked. "I gotta go now, dad...Give mom and everybody my love."

"I sure will, Joe...and don't worry. Kim's here and so is Mel. Someone will meet you tomorrow at eight at Metro Airport...it'll be good to see you."

Gene turned to Kim as he hung up the phone. "Your big brother will be here tomorrow...He wants you to meet him at Metro Airport at eight tomorrow evening."

"Secret agent 007," Liz quipped. "I wonder what's going on?"

"Who knows?..He's probably on his way to Bosnia," Kim answered as she turned to Gene. "I'll be glad to pick him up, dad."

Liz turned to Mel. "Hey, little brother...you're acting kinda strange...you alright?"

Mel put his arm around his father's shoulders and slightly chuckled. "I'm cool, sis...I just want everybody to know...I'm with my ol' man...no mater what he does with the newspaper. Even if it means I have to drop round ball!"

Kim smiled broadly at Mel. "Way to go!..If you can forego a million dollar NBA contract I guess I can let Hollywood cool it's heels for awhile until we can get this daily newspaper going."

"You two don't have to do that," Gene protested. "I don't want you and Mel leaving your careers...that's not right."

"Well, I don't know about the rest of you," Gene II spoke to everyone in the room. "But if you go daily, dad...you'll have to do it without me...I've got to think about my family"

Gene II's wife, Susan, placed a hand on her husband's shoulder in a gesture to back his decision. "Gene's been offered the editor-in-chief job at Newsmonth magazine."

"You'd move your family to New York?" Patricia asked, surprised.

"It's a great opportunity, mom," Gene II answered, proudly. "They're even willing to buy us a place in upstate New York."

"What about your newspaper stock?" Karen asked. "You plan on keeping it?..I may be interested in buying it."

"No...we'll hold on to it," Gene II replied. "It might come in handy someday."

Kim looked at her father and shook her head sadly. "Not if this conversion doesn't work," Kim said, quietly. "I'm sorry, daddy...you know I'm with you but there is a lot of risk involved. We could lose everything if this fails and we're forced into bankruptcy...our stock wouldn't be worth a dime!"

"Make up you mind, Kim!" Mel demanded, angrily. "Who's side are you on?"

Karen quickly stood up to leave with anger flashing in her eyes. "I hope you're satisfied, dad!..your selfish dreams are breaking up our family!"

"Now don't speak to your father in that manner, Karen," Patricia interrupted. "He may still change his mind...Just last week we were talking about retiring and going on a cruise."

"You were talking about retiring," Gene snapped at Pat, angrily. "Not me!"

"I don't believe he's even considering that," Hatti interjected in a calm voice.

"See what I mean?" Karen shouted. "The only person he ever considers is himself!"

"Now, Karen...you're shouting," Hattie said.

"I don't give a damn!" Karen screamed. "I'm sick and tired of this!..If he doesn't give a damn about us...I don't give a damn about him!..His own lawyer tells him not to do this stupid daily newspaper thing and he still won't listen!..His wife wants him to retire and that doesn't make any difference!..Now his oldest son is forced to uproot his family and move completely out of the state...and he doesn't even blink an eye!..Well, if he's that insensitive to everyone else maybe he'll change his ways when I sell my newspaper stock in the State Journal to the Daily Press!"

"Karen!" Hattie shouted.

"Big deal!" Mel muttered sarcastically.

Kelly turned to Mel, nervously. "Maybe...maybe we ought to leave," she whispered.

Karen stormed out of the room angrily! Her escort stood up and looked at everyone as he shrugged his shoulders, helplessly and began to stutter. "Sh...she's just upset...I'm sorry."

With that last statement, he turned and followed Karen out of the room.

Roger and Janet Carlson, feeling the mounting tension in the room, also stood up to leave. Roger slowly walked over next to Gene and stared down at him. "I'll ask you one last time," he said, softly. "If our friendship matters to you at all...don't do this!..Will you at least agree to discuss it further?.."

Gene slowly looked up at his old friend and business associate as his eyes filled with moisture. Everyone in the room remained silent.

"As long as my wife and I control 51 percent of the stock in this corporation," Gene said, emphatically. "You can make book we'll publish a daily newspaper!"

Roger swallowed hard without changing his facial expression. He had put their relationship on the line and lost. His shoulders slightly drooped in defeat. "Then I want to go on record as totally disagreeing with your decision," Roger replied, almost in a whisper. "I promised your father I'd stick with you no matter what...So count me in!"

The room remained quiet as the Carlsons quickly left. Gene looked up and carefully eyed his family as Gene II and his wife Susan prepared to leave. Gene shook his head in complete disappointment.

"C'mon everybody," Gene said, quietly. "Let's have dessert."

Chapter Two

The fashion department at the State Journal Newspaper had been headed by Liz Stanton for the last three years. Under her leadership, the State Journal had won several newspaper fashion awards, conducted several national fashion shows and had been credited for advancing the modeling careers of many world renowned models. As a result of these accomplishments, Liz Stanton's name became synonymous with sophisticated fashions and modeling worldwide. Liz has been recruited by New York fashion agencies almost continuously but her family's ownership of the State Journal newspaper, her strong relationship with her father, and her father's commitment to switch to a daily newspaper that will publish a full-color, glossy fashion section each week as a Sunday supplement, has kept her in the city of Detroit.

An exceptional artist in her own right and a conscientious and creative business woman, Liz managed to maintain a nucleus of top professional models and attract extravagant designers to enhance the State journal's weekly publications. Most models new to the field, clamor to be selected by the State Journal just to work with Liz Stanton. Liz established an excellent rapport with her staff and openly displayed a tender and understanding affection towards her models. This attitude was especially obvious with one of her top models, Ze-Ze LeBlanc, an imported beauty from Paris who was being besieged with offers from bigger agencies but always turned them down, preferring to stay with the State Journal.

Today, the fashion studio at the State journal buzzed with excitement as Liz supervised a photo session. Many cameras clicked in unison almost constantly as several smartly dressed models assumed a series of rapid poses at the audio commands of Liz's assistant. The women accentuated sexy moves at various angles as the beat of music enhanced the stylish scene.

Liz studied each model carefully until she noticed a skirt slightly askewed on one of the models. She moved over towards the woman and snapped her fingers to attract her attention before she realized it was Ze-Ze.

"Ze-Ze...your skirt," Liz said. "Hold still while I straighten the hem."

Ze-Ze stopped moving, holding her position as Liz quickly kneeled at her side and reached her arms around her voluptuous hips to adjust the skirt. Liz glanced up at Ze-Ze's face. She returned Liz's stare, expressionless.

"I believe you're gaining weight," Liz teased.

"I need to speak with you," Ze-Ze whispered.

After the skirt was adjusted Liz continued to stare at the glamorous model as the woman resumed smartly moving her body to different poses while her eyes remained fixed on Liz. Ze-Ze wetted her lips and stared at Liz seductively. Liz was almost hypnotized by the model's overt actions as she continued posing and tossing her long, black hair cascading over her slim shoulders. She silently moved her lips as she continued staring at Liz, first from one pose, then another. The room became deadly silent except for the sound of the background music and the clicking of the cameras as the two women become lost in a world of their own. Ze-Ze moved closer to Liz and whispered, huskily. "I said I have to speak to you...now"

Liz reached out her arm and Ze-Ze took her hand as she gracefully stepped down from the small stage.

"Is something wrong?" Liz asked.

"This damn director of photography!" Ze-Ze snapped, angrily. "He is not giving me the exposure you promised!"

"You'll be on the cover."

"But with three other girls!...Not by myself as you promised me!..And I refuse to be shot by this arrogant photographer any longer!"

"Please...just be a little more patient."

"I am going home!" Ze-Ze stated, flatly, as she quickly turned and marched out of the studio.

Liz started to follow her as the photographers continued shooting. Suddenly, the head photographer stopped as Liz turned back towards the stage.

"Hey!..What the hell's happened to Ze-Ze?" the photographer asked, angrily. "We still go an hour's worth of work to do!"

Liz walked slowly back towards Andre, the head photographer. She noticed the stares from everyone as Andre glared at her, furiously!

"Just calm down, Andre," Liz said, calmly. "She'll come back...relax."

"Damn!..Damn!..Damn!..Here I am straining my schedule to accommodate you and some ding-bat broad screws it all up!" Andre screams. "Doesn't she realize who I am?..Doesn't she know I just completed the updated portfolio of Leonette!..The greatest fashion model in all of Europe?"

"I know..We all know," Liz answered.

"This could ruin my reputation!" Andre shouts.

Liz quickly motioned for everyone to take a break and gather around her as she sat down on the corner of a desk at the front of the studio. The crew all poured coffee and sat down to relax as they waited for Liz to begin speaking. Liz turned to Andre who was still fuming.

"We recognize your accomplishments, Andre," Liz said "That is why I fought so hard to get you for this shoot."

"Then why did she walk out on me?" Andre asked.

"Ze-Ze...just has problems...bear with us," Liz answered. "I'll make it up to you...I promise."

"What's this meeting about, Liz?" a model asked.

Liz turned her attention back to the rest of the staff and smiled broadly. "I have some great news for you, boys and girls," Liz said, beaming. "I want you all to know that in the near future this newspaper will no longer be called the State Journal...and I am happy to inform you that my father has decided to begin publishing an integrated daily newspaper. We are buying the old Times building downtown and all of its equipment. As a result, all of your jobs will be expanded with a raise because we will be publishing a full-color, glossy fashion magazine supplement with each Sunday newspaper!"

Everyone in the studio became excited as the models all screamed and squealed in delight at the news. The photographers and artists began slapping each others hands. One of the models leaped from her seat, eagerly. "You mean we'll have our very own fashion magazine every Sunday?"

"Complete with editorial content," Liz replied. "And on slick, glossy stock."

"And in four color, too?" the model asked.

"You heard what the boss lady said," a second model responded. "Isn't this fabulous...I can hardly wait!"

"That Sunday supplement will be in addition to a daily black and white section on fashions that will be published every Monday, Wednesday and Friday," Liz added. "You're going to be busy girls so be prepared to bust your butts!"

"What's this daily paper gonna be called?" Andre asked. "And when is all of this supposed to happen?"

"Our new name will be The Detroit Herald...and I guess as soon as all of the details like personnel and remodeling are completed, we'll know exactly when we'll begin publishing," Liz replied, proudly. "My dad expects to have our plant in full operation and ready to go in a matter of weeks."

One of the artists walked over to Liz and hugged her, affectionately. He stared into her eyes as a tear ran down his cheek. "I's so happy for you and your family, Liz," the artist said, calmly. "You all have been so diligent in publishing this weekly. Now...to realize that you will have the opportunity to publish one of the first daily newspapers in this country ever published by Blacks..well...this is truly history!..I'm really proud of your entire family!"

"Yeah...we all knew something was going on," another artist said. "But we weren't sure if it would be good or bad with all these other companies cutting back...but this! This is just super!..I guess your dad's got more guts than we gave him credit for!"

"I never dreamed we'd go daily!" the first artist said, anxiously. "I'm gonna start on a dummy layout for that introductory supplement right away!"

As everyone began shouting and talking excitedly about the new newspaper and the first fashion section, Liz watched them and quietly smiled. She didn't say a word as she slowly turned and looked longingly back at the empty doorway...

It was almost dark when Kim met her brother, Joe, at Detroit's Metropolitan Airport in the suburb of Romulus. As usual, she immediately began teasing him about being a CIA agent and he neatly avoided any mention of his job. When they arrived at the Stanton mansion Kim slowly followed Joe as he wandered throughout the huge home, looked around at the familiar surroundings and slowly became more comfortable. The house was almost empty as they browsed from room to room. Finally, he stopped and turned to his youngest sister.

"How's dad handling the pressure about the newspaper?" Joe asked. "I know everybody's pulling his chain."

"You know it...but he's a bull...standing by his guns," Kim answered. "When he knows he's right...nothing can change his mind."

"What about mom...is she backing him?"

"No way!..Not this time. She wants him to retire."

"Retire?..Are you kiddin?"

"That's right...She thinks it's time for him to get out of the rat race and turn the business over to us."

"I can't go along with that," Joe said, irritated.

"Neither can I...Dad's not ready to retire," Kim said. "In the first place he's too young...but just because they've got a little money, mom wants him to retire...and dad is simply not ready for that...he may never be."

Joe chuckled softly. "Can you see him sitting in a rocking chair?..Not in this life time!"

Joe continued walking from room to room, closely examining each window and studying the surrounding outside areas. Kim became suspicious.

"Yessir," Joe said, calmly. "The old homestead looks great."

"You expecting someone?" Kim asked. "You're acting as nervous as a cat."

Joe ignored Kim's question and walked back towards her, still smiling casually. He pulled out a portable phone and quickly made a call. He smiled at his sister as he waited for someone to answer. A serious expression flashed across his face as he began to speak in hushed tones. "Foxtrot...Blue Dog has arrived and everything is a go," he whispered. "Yes..everything...I know...we're prepared."

Kim, surprised by the conversation, watched Joe impatiently until he finished the conversation. He looked back at her, still smiling, broadly.

"So what's happening on the west coast?" Joe asked. "How's your movie career coming?"

"What the hell's goin' on?" Kim demanded, angrily.

"What?"

"What's with this 'Foxtrot'?"

"Dammit, Kim!..That's none of your business!"

"I'll make it my business!"

"You know I can't discuss that!" Joe snapped at her. He noticed the hurt expression on her face. "I'm sorry...I didn't mean anything...I...this is a sensitive area."

"No...you're right. I should learn to mind my own business," she replied. "I shouldn't have asked."

Joe attempted to relieve the mounting tension between them. "What about the rest of the family?" Joe asked. "How are they reacting to the big switch?"

"What would you expect?..Karen's being a bitch and threatening to sell her newspaper stock to the Daily Press. That could kill dad's plans if she did. Liz is on our side as long as it includes a four-color fashion section every Sunday.'"

"What's grandma sayin?"

"That's the funny thing about this...all she did last night was shake her head...She never really said very much."

"I find that hard to believe," Joe said, thoughtfully. She must have something going on in that head of hers...I understand that Mel is suppose to be selected in the first round of the NBA draft...Is he gonna accept?"

"That's what he's been playin' for all these years," Kim replied. "You know he wants to...but...I think if dad asks him to stay here and work on the paper...he would...What about you?"

"What do you mean?" Joe asked. "You know I' backing dad. I think it's a great move!"

Suddenly they heard a loud crash in the next room and Joe quickly spun around towards the sound, crouching with a revolver in his hand!..Kim was startled by Joe's sudden Movement and at the sight of the gun!..She stood frozen, staring at her brother who was holding the gun with both hands as he waited for someone to come through the doorway!..

"Oh, my GOD!" Kim screamed.

"Who's in there?" Joe whispered, anxiously.

Connie suddenly walked through the doorway leading from the kitchen, holding the pieces of a broken vase in her hands. She stopped when she saw Joe and set the broken pieces down on the dining room table. Joe quickly stuck the gun in his belt and closed his coat. Connie was surprised to see Joe.

"Joseph?..Little Joey?..I didn't know you were already here!" Connie shouted happily. "Come here, boy, and give your Aunt Constance a big kiss!"

Joe put his arms around Connie and hugged her affectionately. Connie stepped back, admiring him. "You're too thin!.. C'mon in the kitchen so I can work on you!"

Kim still stared at Joe in bewilderment as he walked into the kitchen with his arm around Connie while they laughed and talked happily.

Later, Kim and Joe remained silent as they sipped coffee at the kitchen counter.

"I knew you'd be behind dad," Kim said. "I was concerned about your new assignment."

"What new assignment?" Joe asked, innocently.

"You know...that super-secret agency the CIA is involved with. It's kinda dangerous isn't it?..Is that what this Foxtrot is all about?"

"You been seein' too many movies, sis," Joe replied. "This Company isn't that mysterious...c'mon, lets drop that subject. Tell me about your Hollywood career."

Kim looked at her brother in total exasperation as he stared back at her and smiled. Connie placed a giant piece of cake on a plate in front of each of the.

"I...I might have a chance at a supporting role in a Chadwick film," Kim said, thoughtfully. 'I'm suppose to read for the part when I get back." She quickly looked at Connie and made a face. "If I'm not too fat by then!"

"Chadwick?..Isn't he the one who won the Oscar last year?..He's suppose to be the hottest director in Hollywood. What's the title of the movie?"

"Too Late To Run...action adventure and a lot of sex."

"I bet that sex part didn't go over too good with Steve," Joe said, chuckling. "What's he in to now?"

Kim hesitated and stared down into her coffee cup before she answered, thoughtfully. "Probably some rock 'n roll groupie!..I don't really know or care...It's all over between us...I haven't seen Steve in a month!"

"Has he called you?"

"Everyday...he can't seem to accept that its over...He just understands the groupie mentality."

Joe looked at his youngest sister and his heart sunk as he noticed the moisture welling up in her soft, brown eyes. He reached over and placed his hand on top of hers.

Downtown Detroit was crowded with afternoon traffic as workers hurried back and forth from lunch and shopping. The blare of car horns echoed throughout the wide avenues as giant policemen on horseback trotted along next to the automobiles and directed traffic. The sidewalks were filled with bustling tourists, street people, business people and wide-eyed school children. In the distance could be heard the low, moaning sounds of boat whistles on the Detroit river, which were intermittently cushioned by the ringing of church bells and the wailing of sirens.

A long, black limousine slowly separated from the heavy traffic and pulled up to a stop in front of the luxurious restaurant with a long canopy that extended across the wide sidewalk to the street. The doorman smartly opened the rear door of the limousine and Patricia Stanton quickly emerged and walked briskly under the canopy, over the thick, red carpet leading into the wide Gothic front doors of the establishment.

Inside the restaurant it was only sparsely occupied as a maitre d' proudly led Patricia to the rear of the softly lit and spacious dining area where a lone woman was sitting at a table, slowly stirring her drink. The woman looked up as Patricia arrived and smiled at her.

"Mrs. Stanton...I'm so happy you could make it," the woman said, graciously. "Please have a seat."

"Thank you," Patricia answered, sitting down. "But I think your business should be with my husband instead of me, Mrs. Henderson."

"Can I order you a drink?" Mrs. Henderson asked.

"White wine...Have you been here long?"

Mrs. Henderson looked at her now empty glass and smiled. "Long enough...I need your help, Mrs. Stanton. We believe your husband could become on of the most powerful men in the state...maybe the country."

"Oh?..How?"

"You're being coy...I understand that you have a law degree. You must know what I mean," Mrs. Henderson replied. "The minute he switches over to a daily newspaper his voice and his opinions will be heard by many people."

"What's that got to do with my having a law degree?"

"How do you feel about our organization?"

"The National Equality For Women?..I suppose they served a purpose."

"Served?..That's past tense," Mrs. Henderson said. "Don't you believe there's still a need for our movement?"

"Possibly...I've never given it much thought...I've been too busy fighting discrimination against minorities in schools, employment and voting rights...You got a problem with that?"

"No...I didn't mean..."

"How can I help you, Mrs. Henderson?" Patricia asked, impatiently.

"I've been trying to make contact with your husband but that watchdog attorney of his doesn't seem to like me."

"That would be Roger...Roger Carlson...He's also a very close friend of our family."

"I didn't mean to offend...He watches over your husband like a mother-hen," Mrs. Henderson said.

"That's his job. He's good at it," Patricia snapped.

"Look...I've been selected to represent several minority groups to insure that your daily newspaper really does speak for and to the people...We're meeting with your husband tomorrow and we need some leverage, Mrs.. Stanton...We need to know...What does your husband REALLY want?"

Patricia smiled as she slowly sipped her drink. "I think you picked the wrong person, Mrs.. Henderson...I don't want him to go daily. In fact...I want him to retire...slow down the pace. The hectic life of publishing a daily newspaper could kill him."

"Does he have a heart condition?"

"I don't want him to get one," Patricia shot back. "He's in great shape and I intend to keep him that way."

"Some people thrive on work...retirement could kill him. I always believed we should work as long as we want to."

Patricia suddenly stood up, preparing to leave. Mrs. Henderson quickly stood and reached for Patricia's arm.

"I'm sorry...please...don't go," Mrs. Henderson pleaded. "I didn't mean to..."

"Offend?..Don't worry about it," Patricia said, firmly. "Listen, if you want some leverage to make my husband respond favorably to your proposal, you'd better talk to him yourself...The only think he ever talks to me about these days is that damn daily newspaper...going daily and increasing the circulation...That's it!...Circulation!..You want some leverage?..Get all those groups to commit to subscribing to that damn daily newspaper and he'll jump through hoops for you!"

"I apologize, Mrs. Stanton...I really didn't mean to offend you."

"I'm not offended, Mrs. Henderson. I understand where you're coming from...You just gotta know where I'm goin...Good afternoon and good luck!"

Patricia quickly turned and walked rapidly out of the restaurant as both Mrs.. Henderson and the maitre d' stared after her, surprised.

Early in the morning, Karen Stanton Whyte had invited Ron Harris over to her home for breakfast. Her three children were off to school and she was anxious to get to know Ron better. They had met at a dinner/dance her sorority had given about six months ago, and as usual, Karen attended the affair by herself. Ron was introduced to her by an old sorority sister as someone who had just been transferred into the Detroit area as a TV sportscaster for the local TV station. She also implied that Ron could become the straw that stirred Karen's appetite for sex and make her life more interesting. Karen knew that this description meant that Ron was a potential lover who was temporarily between women. Karen didn't need any permanent relationship that may get out of hand and disrupt her marriage, but she did want a sexual partner who she could control. Her husband, Bob, hadn't made love to her in almost a year now and she was getting tired of waiting. When she danced close to Ron that evening she could distinctly feel the bulge in his trousers pressing against her. Ron was a stud that she had to have. This morning after he had accepted her invitation to breakfast, she had became excited with anticipation as she examined herself in her dresser mirror.

She knew she was an attractive woman. Not cute and petite like her youngest sister, Kim, or even glamorous and sophisticated like Liz. Karen was simply sexy. She had a beautiful body and a face with delicate, keen features, deep set eyes and a full, inviting mouth. Her peach colored complexion went nicely with her dark brown hair that framed her face and cascaded down to her shoulders. As she thought about Ron coming over this morning, she gently began to massage her breasts and stomach. She was ready... She felt a deep thrill go through her body when she heard the door chimes signaling Ron't arrival.

Dr. Robert Whyte had spent a frightful night at City Hospital. He was tired and beat. He looked forward to an afternoon of complete relaxation. Maybe even looking at the soap operas on TV and nodding off to sleep. The kids were still in school and he knew that his wife, Karen, would know what to do. As he drove through the winding streets of his luxurious suburban neighborhood he remembered those afternoons he and Karen use to steal when he was just an intern at Henry Ford Hospital. The thick corn beef sandwiches with Swiss cheese and mustard on an onion bun, the smooth taste of benedictine and brandy, and most of all, the sex... GOD, he thought, they would go at it like dogs in heat for four solid hours, fall asleep, wake up and start all over again... He smiled to himself as he remembered those days ten years ago... Had it really been that long?.. Nowadays when he came home it was usally late in the evening and the kids would dominate the household. By the time the kids went to bed, he and Karen were at each other's throats about his working at the hospital and not having any time for her or the family... But not today. Today would be different, he thought. He had tried calling Karen all morning but no one had been home... but he knew she would know how to respond when she saw the sandwiches and the bottle of B and B he had picked up. Yeah, he mused, just like old times...

Ron swallowed hard as he watched Karen prepare breakfast in the skimpy negligee. He tried to relax as she brushed against him, smiling and cooing every chance she got. The scent of her aroma mixed with her cologne was driving him nuts!... He sipped his coffee slowly as she continued to prance around the large kitchen. Finally, he got up from the table and walked up behind her, circling his arms around her slim waist and kissing her lightly on the back of her neck. Karen slowly switched off the oven and looked up into his eyes, smiling. "You don't want any breakfast?"

"Damn!.." Ron mumbled, huskily. "To hell with any breakfast!... I want You!"

Karen reached her arms around his neck and kissed him deeply, sticking her tongue deep into his mouth. Ron returned the kiss while she licked at the insides of this mouth and pressed her soft, firm body against his. Ron's arms remained locked around her waist, pulling her hips into him as he cupped her tight, firm buttocks. They continued the long kiss as she grinded her hips against his straining hardness. Slowly, she removed her mouth from his, kissing his cheeks and lightly nibbling at his neck. Her flickering tongue danced down to his now opened shirt which revealed his hairy chest. She opened the shirt completely and began to gently suck each of his nipples, tenderly. Ron sighed deeply as her thick, dark head of hair slowly moved down to his groin. She deftly unzipped his fly and slid her gand inside his trousers, beginning a slow and gentle massage... In moments his rigid member was released and lightly bobbed in front of her face. She looked up at him and smiled, wetting her full, red lips and shaking her long hair out of the way. He leaned back against the kitchen counter as his knees became weak in anticipation. He closed his eyes and waited for her warm, moist touch...

After fighting the lunchtime traffic it was late noon when Dr. Robert Whyte carefully drove his car up into the circular driveway and the garage door slowly lifted up. As he drove toward the garage he stopped his car and stared back at a strange car parked further down the winding suburban street. He thought about the several day-time robberies that had happened in the area recently and he quickly jotted down the license number. He then drove his car inside the garage, parking it next to his wife's Porshe.

It was early afternoon when Karen woke up in her bedroom, still laying in Ron's arms. He smiled at her and nuzzled her face, gently caressing her cheeks softly with his hand while he lightly nibbled at her earlobe. She sighed in deep response as his other hand roamed under the sheets.

"You're a beautiful woman," Ron whispered. "How come you're just now coming into my life?"

Karen pulled him closer, her arms encircled his neck as she kissed him long and hard, her tongue exploring his mouth. "Some women need more love and attention than others. If her man can't give her what she wants and needs... she has to look elsewhere... We can't do what you men do."

"Meaning?"

"You men can go out and pickup a woman at a bar," Karen replied. "Some men get high-class prostitutes... We can't do that."

"Is that what you think of me?"

"Certainly not... I knew you had the warmth and strength of a real man shen I first met you... A man who would appreciate the love of a responsive woman."

Karen began lightly kissing his neck, shoulders, and gently nibbling at the hairs on his chest.

"What about your husband?"

"Robert?... He's too busy at the hospital to take care of my needs," Karen sighed, kissing Ron flush on his mouth.

When they parted she clung to him, burying her face into his neck, excitedly.

"GOD, you're wonderful!" Ron said as he returned her kiss. He slowly moved to position himself on top of her as she held him tightly.

"Make love to me, baby!" Karen urged. "Make me feel it like I've never felt it before!"

Dr. Robert Whyte walked slowly through the large, luxurous ranch styled home. He turned on various lamps and lights as he picked up articles of clothing that were strewn carlessly all over the floor. In the kitchen he discovered a half-cooked breakfast and a broken plate on the floor in front of an upturned chair. He heard the faint sounds of music as he walked down the hallway leading to the master bedroom. He suddenly stopped in his tracks when he heard soft laughter and the tinkling of glasses coming form the bedroom. He silently eased closer to the closed bedroom door as he saw a light glowing from the crack at the bottom. Suddenly, he heard a man's heavy laughter which instantly stopped and was followed by the deep sighs of a woman... Dr. Whyte quietly opened his briefcase and pulled out a revolver. He released the safety on the gun and inhaled deeply before he turned and faced the door. He paused as he raised his foot to kick the door open!.. When he kicked the door open, Karen began screaming at the top of her lungs as Ron scrambled out of bed, frantically reaching for his clothes!.. Robert Whyte stood in the doorway in the dim light, holding the gun with both hands!..

"No!.. No!.. No!.." Karen screamed in fear. "Don't do it, Bob!... Don't SHOOT!"

Robert charged across the room towards the naked man and shoved him up against the wall as he jammed the muzzle of the gun against the man's throat!

"You ready to die, you damn fool?" Robert screamed, angrily. "I'm gonna blow you away!"

"No!.. please, man!" Ron pleaded as tears streamed down his face. "This was her idea... not mine! She asked me over here... I thought she was divorced!"

"Divorced?" Robert asked. "How in the hell could you think that?"

"She's been after me since I came in town!.. I'm the new sportscaster at TV-5!" Ron continued. "Your problem is her not ME!... Point that gun in the right direction!.. Killin' me ain't gonna end your problem... You'll just end up in jail!"

Robert slowly lowered the gun to his side as he glared at Karen in disgust. She stood next to be bed, clutching the sheets over her naked body and trembling!.. Robert turned back to the frightened man who was still sobbing, hysterically!

Ron harris quickly put on his trousers and shoes. He grabbed the rest of his clothes and cautiously edged towards the door where Robert stood, menacingly. The man was so frightened he was shaking!..He stammered as he tried to speak. "Can...can I leave now?"

Robert slowly stepped aside, leveling the gun at Ron's head. "I'll show you to the door," Robert grumbled as he followed Ron through the doorway.

When Robert returned to the bedroom he found Karen wrapped in a flimsy negligee and sitting on the side of the bed smoking a long, black cigarette. He stood in the doorway and glared at her. She nervously puffed on the cigarette, waiting for him to say something. Finally, she couldn't hold back any longer.

"Well...just don't stand there," she said. "What did you expect?..You leave me alone all week...and we haven't made love in almost a year!..What was I supposed to do?"

Robert slowly raised his arm and pointed the gun at her! "You bitch!" he shouted angrily. "I wish those haughty-taughty society friends of yours could see you now!...I oughta kill you!"

Karen stared at her hugband, smiled and slowly go up from the bed and sauntered directly towards the muzzle of the gun, challenging him with a smirk on her lips!

"Go ahead...shoot!" She commanded, blowing smoke in his face in contempt. "I might as well be dead...married to you!"

Robert backed down, reluctantly lowering the gun in disgust. "I want a divorce!..I can't stand the sight of you!"

"You can't afford a divorce, Robert," Karen said as she turned and walked away. "This is Stanton money that has got you where you are...Chief Surgeon at City Hospital...And if you want to stay there...You'd better stay here!"

"You go to hell!"

"Besides," she continued, sitting back down on the bed and blowing clouds of smoke into the air. "What about our children?"

"Don't you dare bring them into this!..And don't lie to me...I know this isn't the first time!" Robert shouted. "Maybe it would be better if the Daily Press gets this scandal and smears you and your family all over the paper!"

Karen quickly stood up at the mention of the threat to smear the Stanton family.

"You wouldn't dare!" she shouted.

"The hell I wouldn't!"

Robert walked away in disgust and stared out of the window overlooking the large backyard. He suddenly smiled to himself as an idea flashed across his mind. He slowly turned back to Karen who was still standing next to the bed, watching him.

"If you really want another chance...there is only one way that I would give it a try," he said, seriously.

"I think we could make a go of this marriage...if we both tried," she quickly responded.

"I've known about your filthy little escapades for some time now...Frankly I couldn't care less," Robert said, flatly. "But there is one way we can remain married...Of course...we'd both have to work at it, but there's one more condition I must have."

"Name it," Karen said, anxiously.

"Take your State Journal stock off the market and sign it all over to me."

"Wh..What?"

"You heard me!...Don't sell your stock," Robert demanded. "Sign it over to me and you'll keep your marriage...Refuse and we're divorced!"

"You can't prove what happened here today," Karen argued. "It'll just be your word against mine"

Robert reached inside his coat pocket and pulled out a driver's license. "I've got all the proof I need of what happened here today...an eye witness...A Mr. Harris...yes, that's his name...Ronald W. harris, TV-5 sportscaster!"

Karen walked closer to Robert and reached for the driver's license. Robert quickly moved it out of her reach.

"It seems your Mr. Harris was only too happy to leave his driver's license and his TV-5 identification with me when he left," Robert said, smugly. "I just might call his wife!"

Karen angrily reached a second time for the driver's license and Robert backhanded her, knocking her flying, head over heels, across the bed and landing hard on the floor on the other side!..She sat there, surprised and dazed, staring up at Robert as her eyes flashed with anger!..She dabbed at a trickle of blood coming from her nose!..

"I'll remember this day, Robert," she said, sniffling between sobs. "Because I've been thoroughly fucked!"

"Yes...you certainly have been, my dear...and in more ways than one!"

Robert turned and quickly left the room, slamming the bedroom door with a loud 'bang'...

Chapter Three

The State Journal weekly newspaper had served the African-American citizens of the City of Detroit and its suburbs for many years. The Stanton family had made sure that it was published with dignity and respect. During the sixties when the fight for civil rights was predominant throughout the country, the State Journal risked the wrath of their White advertisers but staid the course of seeking justice and equal opportunity for all Americans. The employees became proud of this heritage and stood behind the newspaper and it's owners from one generation to the next.

Today, as Gene Stanton stood at the end of a long conference table and addressed his managers and editors about the State Journal converting to a daily newspaper, many eyes were watery as they realized that although their jobs were being saved, it also meant the end of the State Journal...As Gene finished his short speech everyone was excited but still cautious.

"Ladies and gentlemen, we intend to produce the most modern and efficient daily newspaper in the country," Gene concluded. "This can only be accomplished with your professional guidance, expertise...and most of all...your continued loyalty ...because I know from years of working with you all in the past...that with your help...we can do it!"

Everyone in the large room began clapping enthusiastically as they stood up and shouted praise upon the Stanton family. Gene II sat next to his father, first subdued then surprised by the thundering applause and loud rejoicing. One man quickly stepped forward and began shouting proudly.

"We're with ya, Gene!" the man shouted loudly. "At last we're gonna get a chance to fight the Daily Press on even terms!..This company's growing and we're gonna grow with it!"

"We wanna thank the whole Stanton family, especially you two Genes," another man shouted. "We know you're probably taking a lot of flack from your stockholders for makin' this decision, but this'll not only save our jobs...it'll mean more jobs for a lot of folks out there that really need 'em.. GOD bless you both for investing in Detroit!"

All of the people crowded into the conference room gathered around the Stantons and shook their hands in gratitude. One robust woman grabbed Gene II in a bearhug and kissed him on the cheek. Gene watched his son's surprised expression and smiled as his secretary tugged at his sleeve.

"Mr. Stanton...have you forgotten that those civil rights groups are waiting in your office?" the secretary asked, anxiously. "They've been waiting almost a half-hour now...and Congressman Ghetts' office just called...He's on his way over here."

The coalition of various civil rights groups was headed by Merl Henderson of the National Equality For Women. The group represented all minorities in the metro Detroit area. They all crowded into the large paneled executive offices, waiting anxiously as Gene strided through the door and greeted them all warmly. He apologized for being late and everyone smiled and nodded with understanding and forgiveness as Gene shook each of their hands. Merl Henderson of NEW took the opportunity to introduce herself and began the meeting.

"Mr. Stanton, I'm Merl Henderson, president of the Detroit Chapter of the National Equality For Women," she said, proudly. "We'd like to know what some of your plans are regarding women and minorities."

"I appreciate your interest, Mrs. Henderson," Gene answered. "I feel women and all minorities should be granted the same rights at employment as all Americans."

"That's good...and I'm sure most publishers of daily newspapers would respond the same way," Mrs. Henderson replied. "However, at the present time, women and minorities comprise less then eight percent of management and supervisory positions in the media all across the country...and most newspapers have less than ten percent minority employees...How do you plan to overcome this?"

Gene stood behind his desk and addressed the entire group. "Our plans are to publish the best damn daily newspaper in this country...A newspaper that is truly representative of this metropolitan area...We intend to concentrate on actively seeking out and recruiting those who are not represented in key positions. Since fifty percent of this community are women, you can rest assured that they'll be given an equal opportunity at all positions from top executive positions to the lowest entry level positions."

"What about we Hispanics?" a man in the group asked. "Are we gonna be a part of this newspaper?"

"You're part of this community aren't you?" Gene asked. "Your citizenship papers are just as good as anyone else's. I certainly hope the Hispanics and Latinos honor our newspaper and join us."

"You really mean that?" the man asked.

"Look, I am deeply committed to civil rights," Gene replied. "Probably for longer and more involved than any of you have ever been. I respect the rights of all Americans. That includes all minorities, gays, the handicapped, women, people of all ages...They all will be welcomed at The Detroit Herald Daily Newspaper...Remember, the only way we can print the truth in its entirety is to know what's the truth and to practice it in our newspaper!"

The group quietly excused themselves and moved out into the outer corridor where they all huddled and talked in hushed tones. In a few minutes they somberly strolled back into the office. Merl Henderson stepped forward.

"Mr. Stanton, we are all impressed by your genuine sincerity," Merl Henderson said. "And we've decided to show you that we're willing to invest in your daily newspaper...we..."

Gene quickly interrupted her. "I'm sorry...but there's no stock for sale."

"No...I didn't mean that. We probably couldn't afford it anyhow," Mrs. Henderson said, smiling. "Before we decided to approach you, we arranged to have a little leverage to make you understand our positions. We each solicited our individual organizations for signed subscriptions to have The Detroit Herald Newspaper home delivered into each of our member's homes...Of course some of them refused...But considering that we didn't have too much time to get this operation Herald underway...I think we did pretty good."

Several men stepped forward carrying big cardboard boxes. Each box is labeled with the name of a civil rights organization. The Boxes were stacked in front of Gene's desk. Gene stared at them, dumbfounded!..

"Mr. Stanton, let me present you with over one hundred thousand paid subscribers to the Detroit Herald Newspaper before you even publish a single edition!" Mrs. Henderson said, proudly. "You're giving us a voice...and this is our way of showing our appreciation!..Your newspaper could play a major role in ending sexual and racial discrimination in the media!"

"Wh...What?"

"Of course you better remember...what the LORD giveth...The LORD can taketh away!" Mrs. Henderson said as she shook Gene's hand.

Gene was staggered by the subscriptions as everyone lined up to congratulate him, all smiling broadly. After they all had left the offices, Gene thumbed through the boxes of subscriptions and smiled to himself. He shook his head in disbelief. He realized how important this windfall was and that it represented the doubling of his current circulation at the most critical time. His advertising rates for the Herald could be escalated to reflect his larger circulation. He was sure The Detroit Herald would now be successful. His thoughts were interrupted by the ringing of the telephone. He quickly picked it up. "Yes, Mrs. Williams?"

"The congressman is here."
"Send him right in, please."

U.S. Congressman Charles G. Ghetts was one of Gene Stanton's oldest friends. The two had attended school together since kindergarten. They even went to college together and joined the same fraternity. Ghetts had turned out to be one of the Stanton family's biggest supporters and in turn, the State Journal had always supported his candidacy. Gene knew he could depend on Congressman Ghetts. When Ghetts quickly walked into Gene's office his arm were outstretched and he had a big grin on his face. The two old friends greeted each other warmly. The congressman broke the amenities and suddenly stepped back, staring at Gene with a disappointed expression on his face.

"What the hell's goin' on, Gene?..You gonna drop the Journal?"

Gene smiled and walked back behind his desk. He sat down and motioned for Ghetts to take a seat.

"Its good you dropped by, Charlie...I've been meaning to call you...I guess if anyone should be told first it should be you...I think you're about the only one of my grade school buddies still left in this town...How's politics?"

"The hell with politics," Charlie snapped. "Tell me this isn't true...We need that paper!"

"Now hold on, Charlie!" Gene protested. "We're gonna be bigger and better than ever before, only we're gonna do it everyday instead of just once a week."

Charlie quickly stood up, leaning over the desk closer to Gene's face "No good, Gene!..I want you to hold up before you go through with this," he warned. "This could destroy our constituency!..They got no place else to go!..Just do me a favor and hold up until that's over...We gotta stick together to advance our goals in this world!"

"I'm surprised to hear you ask me that...It doesn't sound like you, Charlie...Is there someone else behind this?"

"Look, Gene...You know how politics are," Charlie replied. "You do someone a favor...they do you a favor...then sometimes they call in their note and you gotta pay off."

"This is disturbing...I was planning on endorsing you if you don't blow it between now and the election."

"Gene, this is serious!" Charlie shouted. "If I can't deliver...I could lose my biggest supporter...and without him...I'm dead meat."

Gene stared hard at his old friend. Charlie's eyes avoided Gene's.

"Who is it, Charlie?" Gene asked, quietly.

"Someone's calling in his notes...and he means it," Charlie answered, embarrassed. "They told me to tell you not to go daily...if you do...I'm out of business!"

Gene got up and walked over to the window, turning his back to his old friend.

He stared down at the newspaper employees below as they drove off the parking lot. Gene didn't bother to turn around as he softly began to speak.

"Charlie...Charlie...Charlie!" Gene groaned in disappointment. "You've been bought and sold!...How could you stoop so low to compromise your office like this!.."

"Gene...just listen!"

Gene turned around and glared at the congressman, plainly upset. "I'm sorry, Charlie!..I just can't do it...too many people are depending on me!"

"But what about me?"

"I don't do business like that!"

"If...if you do this...you're gonna regret it, man!..I swear you will!..I tried to warn you but you're just to damn hard-headed!...Too hard-headed to listen!"

The congressman quickly turned and walked towards the door. He suddenly stopped and turned back to Gene. He glared at him angrily and shook his head in disgust!..He finally turned and stormed out of the office, angrily slamming the door shut!..

The National Basketball Association's draft day was a big event at the Stanton mansion. Mel Stanton had been projected as an early round draft pick because of the all-star reputation he had built as a point and shooting guard on the University of Michigan's National Championship team. Mel was considered a prototype of the NBA's shooting guard. He was tall, quick and a prolific scoring machine. In his senior year he had broke or tied most Big Ten and NCAA scoring records. He was a master at three-point range and he had earned the nick-name, "Bomber" because of the high arc, over near seven footers' heads, from outside the three point range. Today was to be Mel's day and many of the Stantons' family and friends had gathered at the family home in anticipation of a huge celebration. Mel had declined the NBA's invitation to be in attendance in person at the draft ceremony because he preferred being with his family when the magic moment arrived.

The loud chattering in the home's spacious great room was suddenly quieted, going down to a slight whisper whenever the TV annoucers mentioned Mel's name or his school. Kelly Millard, Mel's glamorous and blond girlfriend, would not move from his side. Her hand tightly squeezed his as the minutes grew closer to Mel's selection. Mel calmly relaxed back in a large leather recliner as Kelly sat on the arm rest, holding his hand nervously. The two TV announcers were passed a note which one of them quickly began reading aloud, excitedly. "We just got word from the NBA Commissioner's office, folks...that the Memphis Mustangs have declared Mel Stanton of the University of Michigan Wolverines...as their first round draft pick!"

Everyone in the room erupted into shouts and applause, turning to Mel in congratulations!..Mel calmly acknowledged the attention, smiling slightly with his eyes half closed. He fingered his chin, thoughtfully. Kelly stared at him, surprised by his inaction. She stroked his arm anxiously glancing back and forth from the people in the

THE WINDS OF TOMORROW

room, the huge TV set and back to Mel.

"Gee!..They picked you pretty high!" Kelly said, happily. "I didn't think you were gonna go that fast!"

"Why?...You didn't think I was good enough?" Mel asked.

"No...I mean...I thought," Kelly stammered. "This is unbelievable!"

"Don't get too excited...I still have to talk to my dad first."

"Why?...You know I want you to play," Kelly said, anxiously. "Doesn't it matter to you what I want?"

"You're just thinkin' about money," Mel snapped.

"I'm thinkin' about you...I want the best for you...We could be real happy!" Kelly said, squeezing his arm. "I know you say you already have money...You're talking about your family's holdings in the newspaper aren't you?"

Its not like I need the money," Mel said, thoughtfully. "I just wanna play ball."

"Well that's the same way I feel...I just want to play ball too...but what good is your family's money doin' you if its all tied up in the newspaper?" Kelly asked, whispering in Mel's ear. "You can't spend it...its all locked up in stock...This money you're gonna get from bein' drafted so early is alive and movin, honey!..Its all yours and you can spend it now!"

"You mean you can spend it now!" Mel chuckled.

"Don't you like the way I take care of you?"

Mel quickly looked around the room at the others. "Cool it, Kelly!"

"I only give you the best stuff don't I?" she asked, quietly. "Anything you want."

"I need time to think...Everything's moving too fast," Mel answered. "I'll wait on my dad and see what he says...If my family needs me...they come first."

Kelly angrily stood up and prepared to leave. "Well, I'm not gonna wait on your dad!..We got the whole world in front of us...all we have to do is reach out and grab it!"

She turned to leave, then suddenly stopped and turned backed to Mel. He stared at her, surprised. "Where in the hell do you think you're goin?" he asked.

"I'm going back to my apartment and pack," she answered. "If I don't hear from you in an hour...well...It's been nice."

Kelly turned and marched out of the house in anger. Mel watched her leave the room and didn't bother to get up. Every one else in the great room glanced at each other, knowingly and quietly chuckled as Mel continued watching the NBA draft.

Gene Stanton sat behind his wide desk in his office at The State Journal Newspaper, deeply engrossed in the Audit Bureau of Circulation quarterly reports. He realized that the circulation of the Detroit Herald, now potentially over two hundred thousand, didn't compare with the Daily Press' gigantic circulation of six hundred thousand, but he strongly felt that the Herald would at least provide readers and advertisers with a viable choice. He suddenly heard his office floor creaking and looked up to find Roger Carlson standing in the doorway, staring at him. Gene quickly took off his glasses and leaned back in his chair, surprised to see him.

"How long have you been here?" Gene asked.

"I just came in...you were busy reading," Roger replied, quietly. "I didn't mean to disturb you."

Gene got up and walked around to the front of his desk as Roger came all the way into the room with his hand extended. The two men shook hands warmly.

"I'm sorry about blowin' my stack the other night," Roger said, regretfully. "I shouldn't have sounded off the way that I did."

"Forget it...I understand how much you care about the newspaper and the family," Gene said. "We're old friends and this is a passionate issue...I appreciate your concern."

Roger turned his back to Gene and walked over to the window, staring outside at the traffic. "No...I'm no friend, Gene...Not until I tell you what happened to me and how it may have influenced my argument with you."

"What happened?"

"I was contacted last week by Roy Irving."

"The attorney for the Daily Press?..I think I know what that was about."

"It would be hard for me to prove...but...they tried to buy me off!..They offered me a lot of money, Gene...A lot of money!" Roger said, nervously. "They...they wanted me to sabotage your efforts to switch to a daily newspaper!"

"Never mind!..I don't wanna hear anymore!" Gene responded quickly. "You're here and that's good enough for me...I've missed you the last few days. I knew something was going on."

"It wasn't easy," Roger said.

"You still on the Stanton team?"

"If you still want me," Roger replied. "Aren't you interested in finding out WHEN they made me this offer?"

"It probably came directly from Dugas."

"I'm sure you're right...it probably was from F. Walton Dugas."

"Well I don't wanna know when they made you the offer. You're back and that's all that counts...You've always been a good and loyal friend."

The two men shook hands again, firmly. Gene stepped back and looked Roger in the eyes. "It'll take a helluva lot more than Dugas and his money to break up this team."

"You're a heck of a guy, Gene!" Roger said, relieved. "I wasn't sure how you would react...Maybe you'd throw me out of your office."

"Nonsense...You're a man of high principle," Gene said, smiling. "You told me didn't you?"

"I'll begin the paperwork on the changeover right away," Roger said. He turned and started to leave the office. When he reached the door he stopped and looked back at Gene.

"You know something?..You're a lot like your ol' man."

Gene smiled to himself when Roger left the office. He realized he'd have to be more like his father if this conversion was going to be successful...There were certainly a lot of people hoping that it wouldn't be...He knew he was undertaking a monumental task by converting to a daily news paper...He just hoped he hadn't bitten off more than he could chew.

Chapter Four

The marriage of Gene Stanton II and his wife, Susan, has been on the rocks for years. The promise of a new start as editor of Newsmonth Magazine offered them an opportunity to repair their unstable union and began a fresh new life. Gene II had suspected his wife of being unfaithful to him and that feeling had weakened their relationship. The facts that no "lover" ever materialized to support his suspicions and the couple's three children, were the only reasons the marriage had survived as long as it had.

Today, Gene II thoughtfully sipped a cup of coffee at the kitchen table while his wife prepared dinner. He shuffled through several papers scattered on the table in front of him and smiled to himself. His wife slightly turned in his direction as she glanced at him while she busily continued working. She began to speak without looking up.

"You're having second thoughts aren't you?" Susan asked, angrily. "Well forget it!..We're going to New York!"

"If you had seen the way those people were acting at that meeting...they actually gave ME credit for saving their jobs and trying to create more employment in the city...You would've thought I was some kind of celebrity!" Gene II said, still overwhelmed. "They really thought I was somebody important...And I was the guy who was trying to talk dad out of the idea!"

"Well...you didn't know," Susan replied. "And besides, it doesn't make any difference now."

"I should have known it was the right thing to do," Gene said. "It will bring more jobs into the city...GOD knows we need that."

"Well, nobody really knew...so drop it."

"Those civil rights groups knew."

"I don't care about those civil rights groups."

"I do...Those groups are providing The Detroit Herald Newspaper with a guaranteed paid circulation of over one hundred thousand!"

"Gene!...Gimme a break!"

"We haven't published a single daily newspaper yet and already we've got a circulation of more than twice the size of the State Journal!" Gene II said, excitedly. "Hell...with that kind of beef, the advertisers will come to us!"

Susan stopped and walked over to her husband, angrily!

"What about me and the kids?" she shouted in anger. "You may never get an opportunity like Newsmonth is offering you again!"

"If this daily newspaper works..."

"If!..If!..Dammit, Gene!" she screamed. "Why don't you stand up like a man for once in your life instead of hanging on to your father's coattails!..And don't fool yourself into thinking your father needs you!..He doesn't need you!..you need him!"

Gene II Quickly stood up, staring hard at his wife!..

"That may be true, Susan," Gene II said, firmly. "But this time I am standing up like a man...and we're STAYING!"

"I thought we had an understanding!..We both agreed what this move to New York meant to our marriage!" She argued. "Now...if you're willing to risk all of that to stay here...it'll be your last chance...and I mean it this time!"

Susan stared face to face with her husband!..Gene II slowly shifted his stare and avoided looking her directly in her eyes...

Hattie Stanton, the matriarch of the Stanton family, was disgusted with the way her son's family was reacting to his converting from a weekly black newspaper to an integrated daily. She had expected them to show more support in his decision. The same way she had supported her husband when he began publishing The State Journal. To Hattie, loyal support was to be expected from your family if not earned. Her son, Gene, has certainly earned both his family's respect and support. He had stood behind his children in every endeavor they had ventured into and she felt they should reciprocate. Especially when the newspaper's success would be profitable for all of them and it would signal the first time in the country that an African-American had successfully published a major, integrated daily newspaper.

This evening, the entire Stanton family along with Roger and Janet Carlson, had gathered in the great room of the Stanton mansion at Gene's special request. Everyone knew what the meeting was about. They were somewhat surprised at Gene's warm demeanor in face of the past family conflict about the conversion. Gene stood in the center of the room studying them all while they chatted and laughed in good nature with each other as drinks and food trays were passed around. When Connie removed the last tray Gene began speaking in a calm and controlled manner.

"I'm glad you could all be here tonight," Gene began. "I think it shows that big families like ours...and true friends like the Carlsons...can have a serious disagreement and still survive intact...but before I go any further, my mother has a few words she would like to say...Mom?.."

Hattie Stanton stood up and walked slowly over next to her son in the middle of the spacious room. She eyed each and every person as she began to speak. "I just wanna talk about how me and your grandfather managed to start a Black newspaper during the depression and how we were able to survive despite being young, stupid, poor and Black," she said, in a stern but calm voice. "We survived because of two things...love and loyalty...We backed each other to the hilt!...No matter how much we may have disagreed in private...We backed each other in public. That's why this newspaper is where it is today...We stuck together!..And when your grandfather had his first stroke and your dad took over...We backed him, too...just like always...Today, we are living in a different world. Man has conquered space, the Soviet Union has collapsed, and many major cities in the United States have Black mayors...We are fortunate to be living in a country where no matter what your color is...you still have more opportunities than most people in the world have!..It is up to each one of us to take advantage of living in the best country and do something about it!..Our family has outgrown publishing a little weekly newspaper for Blacks only...Now, we are ready to publish a daily newspaper meant for everybody!..One that can give the people the real news and help form opinions and endorse candidates for public office...A newspaper that will give every citizen a voice...instead of just a few of the elite who have privvy to the publisher's stock of expensive booze!..Now, we can become powerful and help move the act of free people forward!..Your daddy has the brains, drive and nerve to put this daily newspaper together...And all of you should be proud and work with him, support him, and back him to the hilt!..That's all I wanted to say...Maybe it will help you form the right perspective on this conversion...Sometimes we all get confused...can't see the forest for the trees...But deep in your hearts...You know your place should be with him!"

Everyone in the room remained quiet as Hattie slowly made her way back to her chair. Her words lingered in the air, penetrating their minds until Gene II broke the silence.

"Grandma's right!..I don't know why I couldn't see it in the first place," Gene II said, turning to his father. "I'm turning down that offer from Newsmonth, dad...My place is here...with my family!"

Karen impatiently puffed on a cigarette a she felt everyone's eyes shift towards her.

"I've already withdrawn my stock from the market," Karen said, nervously glancing at her husband. "I'm not selling anything...I figure the least I could do is wait and see what happens."

Gene relaxed as he saw his family coming back together. He smiled at Gene II who winked back and silently toasted his father. Karen would not look in her father's direction. Liz immediately started passing around dummy copies of the layout of the first color fashion section for The Detroit Herald Newspaper's first Sunday edition. Roger Carlson moved to the center of the room and toasted Gene.

"This is just great!..It seems some of us were off base the other evening, but we're all on the same page now!" Roger said, smiling broadly. "My wife and I plan on staying with this corporation and this family...as long as you'll have us!"

"I've offered to stay, too...Dad says he really doesn't need me, but I'm gonna hang around a few weeks and see what happens," Kim said, smiling. "They're casting a film that I'm really interested in but my agent feels we'll be in a better negotiating position if I'm not too available...I might be here for a few months...So, like it or not, dad...you've got me, too."

"I know we're gonna make it now!" Gene laughed. "I guess I'm one of the luckiest guys in the world to be surrounded by friends and family like I have...Tomorrow afternoon...I've scheduled a news conference at The Journal...I'd appreciate it if you all could be there...It would show that our entire family is behind The Detroit Herald...But right now...Connie, bring out the champagne!"

"Its already here!" Connie shouted happily. "I knew this family would get their act together!"

As everybody enthusiastically discussed the Detroit Herald Newspaper, Joe Stanton walked over to his father grinning broadly from ear to ear and firmly shook his hand.

"Wow!...This really makes me wanna stay here and work with you, pops!" Joe said. "I'm just sorry I can't...You understand don't you?"

"Yeah, sure son...I understand," Gene answered.

Patricia walked over and grabbed Joe's arm, leading him over towards Hattie. Gene stared after Joe, thoughtfully as he intermingled with the rest of the family.

Later that same evening, as he was practicing his speech for the news conference, Gene walked into the library with several sheets of paper in his hands. He found his son Mel, slouched dejectedly in a huge leather chair with his hands covering his eyes. Mel looked up at his father with dilated pupils. Gene could see that he was upset and distraught as he gripped his favorite high school basketball trophy. Gene went over to him, showing great concern.

"Mel...you alright, son?" Gene asked, quietly. "How'd the physical examination go?"

Mel barely moved as he answered in a low, soft voice. "Dad...How ya doin?.." Mel asked. "You all set for your big speech?"

"Never mind that," Gene replied. "What's wrong with you?"

"Dad...remember when we won the State Championship?"

Gene relaxed and slightly laughed. "Yeah...we damn near didn't make it!..All that snow!"

Mel chuckled softly. "Talk about March Madness!..The way we were slippin' and slidin' tryin' to drive on all that ice!..I thought we were goners!..But you were determined to get me there...and I knew it was important to you too."

"Yessir, that was really something," Gene said, still laughing. "As soon as we get there Coach Robinson slips and breaks his ankle."

Gene stopped suddenly and stared at Mel. "Is everything alright, son?"

Mel sighed deeply. His anguish came to the surface as his eyes filled with tears. "All I wanted to do was make it to the NBA...I wanted to play with the best...I wanted to show the world, dad!"

"I know...I know, son." Gene said, sensing the pain in Mel's voice. He waited silently for Mel to continue.

"I blew it, pops!" Mel said, dejectedly.

"Why?..What'd they say?" Gene asked, anxiously. "There's nothing wrong with you is there?"

"Nothing I can't wash out of my system!..It looks like I am gonna be here to help you start that daily newspaper after all."

"What'd they find?"

"They won't let me play this season, dad," Mel answered sadly. "I can't play until I can get a clean bill of health...I'm suspended from the NBA for a whole year!"

"Suspended!..Why?..You haven't done anything to be suspended for!"

"Yes...Yes I did, dad."

"Like what?"

"I did coke, dad," Mel mumbled, ashamedly. "I did coke!"

Gene was shocked!..He looked down as his youngest child, slouched in the deep cushioned leather chair with tears streaming down his cheeks. He could see that Mel was in obvious pain and anguish!

The following evening Gene sat in the family room in his robe and pajamas with papers scattered all over the cocktail table. He busily jotted in a small notebook and listened to the late news on television. Patricia pretended to read a book as she sat across from him, until she glanced at Gene as he suddenly began intently watching TV. She looked at the TV and laid the book down. Gene turned and watched her closely, tryin to determine her reaction.

"I think the news conference went off good today, don't you?" Gene asked.

"Yes, I agree." Patricia replied.

"You're still upset about Mel, I can tell...well, you're not alone...so am I...I just wish there was something we could do to help him over this hurdle."

"The drug problem is like a giant octopus...it's all over the country and in all walks of life," Patricia said. "I guess it wouldn't be fair to come down on him too hard...He's already been knocked off his pedestal...How do you think he got started?"

"I dunno...You know how it is in sports nowadays," Gene answered. "Some of these kids don't stand a chance."

Patricia stared hard at Gene before she continued. "Well, at least this conversion to a daily newspaper seems to be bringing our family back together...That ought to help Mel...It could even help you and I."

"Uh, huh," Gene answered, writing in his notebook.

"You're not listening to me."

"What?"

"I said you're not listening to me," Patricia answered, irritated by his nonchalant response. "Would you reconsider taking the cruise after the newspaper changeover?" She carefully placed her hand on top of his.

Gene looked up at her, surprised. "That's not practical. In fact it's stupid!"

"Stupid?"

"Yes...You think I'm gonna start an enterprise as vast as this and stop to take a damn cruise?..You're not thinking straight, Patricia, but I'm sorry...I expect to be deeply involved in this newspaper for quite sometime."

Patricia angrily removed her hand from his and leaned back on the sofa in disgust. "You're pretty determined about all of this aren't you?"

"You know I am."

"And us?..Are you just as determined about us?"

"Meaning what?"

Patricia hesitated before she answered. "Never mind...forget it."

"No...If you feel you have something to say...Say it."

"What good would it do?" She asked, angrily. "You're so wrapped up in that damn newspaper you don't care what I do anymore."

"Are you going to go through that tirade again?"

"Is that what you think I'm doing?"

"Get off my back and get a life, Patricia!..I'm only middle aged and I'm not ready to chuck it all in just because we've accumulated a little wealth," Gene said, fed up. "I wish you'd stop trying to make me retire and get a life of your own!..You got a law degree...use it!"

"Is that what you want me to do?"

Before Gene could answer his attention was suddenly diverted to the TV screen as the voice of the announcer continued. "...History was made in our city today as Gene Stanton, publisher of our city's only Black newspaper, The State Journal, announced the end of The Journal and the beginning of The Detroit Herald Daily Newspaper. This switch is expected to provide over fifteen hundred additional jobs in our community as well as giving our city the proud distinction of having the country's only major daily and integrated newspaper published by African-American. The mayor and several dignitaries were on hand to congratulate the Stanton family. This is indeed an honor, folks...From a meager, small weekly Black newspaper in the forties to what could possibly become...one of the top major daily newspapers in the country!..Only in America, folks...Only in America!"

Patricia watched as Gene smiled to himself and nodded his head in confidence. He put the notebook down and slowly lifted up his drink from the cocktail table and toasted the TV set. "Only in America!" Gene mumbled.

Suddenly the phone on the end table began ringing. Gene, still smiling, quickly picked it up.

"Hello." Gene answered.

"Stanton?" a gruff voice asked. "This is F. Walton Dugas."

Gene smiled to himself again. This was the first time in many years that he has even spoken, person to person, to the publisher of the state's number one major daily newspaper, The Daily Press. It felt like he was talking to infamous royalty. Gene thought that he must be important to warrant a call from F. Walton Dugas.

"F. Walton Dugas?" Gene said, surprised. "I haven't talked to you in years...What brings this on?"

"I was just sittin' here watchin' TV...Saw your news conference, " Dugas said. "It reminded me about old times...The way your old man use to sweat and hustle each week to get that newspaper out...He was a helluva man!"

Gene paused before he answered. "What can I do for you?..I know you didn't call just to reminisce."

"No...I didn't. I'm calling to refresh your memory," Dugas replied. "You remember in the early seventies when your father was about to lose that newspaper?..If it had closed down then it would've killed him...You realize that don't you?"

"Of course I do...and you're probably right."

"You remember who stepped in and save your family's little newspaper don't you?" Dugas asked. "Nobody else would lend him a dime...but my father did...He lent your daddy fifty thousand dollars and that's what kept that newspaper goin...remember?"

"Yes, I remember...what's your point?"

There was a long pause before Dugas answered. "Just this!..Do you really think that after we saved your family's newspaper from goin' bankrupt way back then, that I'm gonna sit back and let you become my chief competition is this city?" Dugas shouted, angrily. "This city is mine...The Daily Press...You and that rag of a newspaper won't stand a chance against us!"

Gene grimaced as he spoke into the phone, visibly upset by Dugas' outburst! "There's room for two daily newspapers in this city!" Gene snapped.

There was another long silence on the other end of the line before Dugas' voice came back on, deeper and more menacingly! "You might be right!...There may be room for two daily newspapers in this city...but not yours!..You listen to this, Gene Stanton...I'm building a state-of-the-art newspaper printing plant in the suburbs that'll put you out of business in a hot minute!..So I'm gonna say it just this one time...Don't do it! Don't do it!.. Cause if you do...I'll spend every penny I got and every breath in my body to destroy you!..Do you hear me?..I swear I'll totally destroy you!"

"Are you serious?" Gene asked, angrily. "You really have the nerve to feel that because of that loan we're committed to you for life?..The only thing threats like that will get you is stronger competition!..You go and build your new plant...that's alright with me!..Because we're going to publish our daily newspaper and if I needed any reason to push me to do it...You just gave it to me!..Face it, Mr. F. Walton Dugas...This city has two daily newspapers as of now!..The fat's in the fire...let's see who gets burned!"

Dugas slammed down the telephone angrily and turned to a man who sat across from him at his desk in his study. The dim light from the small lamp on the desk cast an eerie shadow across the man's smiling face when he saw the hatred blazing in Dugas' eyes as he glared at him...

"I want him stopped!" Dugas shouted, angrily. "If you have to wipe out his whole family...I want them stopped!..Do you understand?"

DONALD WILSON

Chapter Five

White supremacist groups such as Skinheads, Neo-Nazis, the Ku Klux Klan and others who subscribed to racial theories, were growing in America during the nineties. Nationally, such groups rose to 346 in 1991 from 273 in 1990, an increase of 27 percent. After years of stagnant membership, Ku Klux Klan groups alone increased from 28 to a total of 97, according to Klanwatch, which monitors hate group activity in the United States. During the same period cross-burning more than doubled to 101 in 1991, up from 50 in 1990.

Some northern states had at least 17 White supremacist groups. These groups were fueled by a perceived threat to White dominance by Black progression...They vented their anger toward racial and ethnic minorities and thrived on racial tensions and scapegoating sustained by a sagging economy as well as anti-minority messages from desperate conservative politicians. When those hate group members looked for answers they heard "reverse discrimination, quotas, unqualified minorities taking the jobs of qualified Whites under affirmative action programs."

When the news that an African-American family was going to own and publish a major daily newspaper in the City of Detroit reached the hierarchy of a major hate group, its leaders vowed that something had to be done to stop this from happening.

Today, in a remote compound in the heavily wooded hills in a northwestern state, an enormous gathering of Neo-Nazis and the Ku Klux Klan members held a rally at a White supremacist church. Loud cheering erupted from the overcrowded open arena as a gruff, male voice, laced with a deep, southern accent echoed from the loudspeakers throughout the surrounding forest. As the man's voice boomed over the huge crowd the audience shouted and jeered in a loud and fervent response to each point the speaker emphasized as he screamed into the microphones. Armed guards stood around the wide stage as the flushed and excited faces of the people, all with serious, angry expressions, revealed their insidious determination to hate!...Some of the audience, including small children, were dressed in camouflage military uniforms and waved flags, guns and rifles. Huge banners of the Aryan Nation's flags depicting a swastika along side of the Ku Klux Klan's flags and a burning cross covered the walls behind the podium. The speaker, a Ku Klux Klan Grand Dragon, was dressed in a white robe complete with decorative Ku Klux Klan headdress. The large rotund man was sweating profusely as he shouted into the microphones.

"It is time for the White people of this country to unite and form a White only nation for our own kind!" the Grand Dragon shouted. "We must stop the advancement of the Black mongrels and non-Whites who are slowly trying to gain control of our news media in order to infect the minds of young and innocent White boys and girls all across the country!"

The audience erupted in loud shouting and foot stomping with a volley of applause as the Grand Dragon paused, waiting for the response to quiet down. He carefully eyed his audience as he lowered his voice and continued.

"Today, we even have a Black man in Detroit who is about to start publishing his own daily newspaper to spread the lies and distort the truth that could eventually destroy us!"..the Grand Dragon continued. "But I assure you all...as my blood runs pure the same as yours...He too will be stopped!"

The crowd screamed, shouted, and applauded with a standing ovation of approval as they gave his final words the Nazi salute and shouted racial epitaths!..The speaker was quickly escorted from the stage by stern faced guards dressed in combat gear, boots, helmets and armed with rifles and automatic weapons.

A lone man, impeccably dressed in a dark Ivy league suit and carrying a slim briefcase, sat patiently in front of a wide executive desk and waited for the Grand Dragon to return to his office just off stage from the noisy rally. The man, conspicuously out of place, was startled when the office door was flung opened and two heavily armed guards stepped inside and took their places on each side of the doorway. The two guards were quickly followed by the Grand Dragon who strided briskly through the door and ignored the man sitting at his desk. The Grand Dragon disrobed, carefully hanging his costume inside the closet. He took off the decorative headdress and placed it on a shelf in the closet. He slowly walked behind his desk and sat down, eyeing the man waiting for him. He lit up a long black cigar and dabbed at the sweat running down the sides of his heavy jowls. He glared at the man who sat across from him and scowled.

"You Damien?" the Grand Dragon asked, gruffly.

"Yessir," the man replied as he reached inside his briefcase and pulled out a single sheet of paper which he gave to the Grand Dragon. "I hope this is satisfactory."

The Grand Dragon scanned the sheet briefly and laid it down on his desk in a disinterested manner. "I ain't impressed with that!..I know all about you...We got hundreds of people who can do the job...probably just as good!"

"Maybe," Damien replied.

"No maybe about it!..I know it!..You sure and hell ain't my choice!"

"I was told you wanted to confirm my selection, sir," Damien said, respectfully. "Is there some additional information you need?"

"I wanted to meet you face to face...to see if you're a man I can trust," the Grand Dragon snarled. "I don't want this thing to get screwed up...too many of our people are in prison now!..That's why we failed in 1984."

"In 1984?"

"Yeah...a lotta folks we didn't really know...who were suppose to be on our side...turned out to be somebody else!"

"You have my credentials, sir."

"To hell with your credentials!"

The Grand Dragon glared at Damien as he reached inside his desk drawer and pulled out a large manila folder he tossed on the desk in front of Damien. Damien opened the folder slowly as he kept his eyes on the Grand Dragon. He cautiously lowered his gaze down the opened folder. Several photographs of members of the Stanton family lay spread out on the desk. The Grand Dragon picked up a photo of Gene Stanton.

"Start with this one first," the Grand Dragon said. "Get rid of him...you won't have to worry about the rest of 'em!"

Damien nodded thoughtfully as he took the photograph from the Grand Dragon's hand. When he looked back up the Grand Dragon was standing over him, glaring at him suspiciously!

"We want it done as soon as possible!" the Grand Dragon commanded. "With no mistakes!"

The two men stared hard at each other as the roar of the noise and the sounds of stomping feet of the audience in the arena caused the shelves in the office to vibrate and shake!

The months passed quickly as Gene Stanton completed all of the necessary details to purchase The Detroit Times Newspaper building. At last the first day of business had finally arrived and Gene began the bright, autumn day in good spirits. People had called him from all over the country congratulating him and wishing him well. He had received telegrams, faxes and gifts from politicians, celebrities and business associates he had never heard of before. His name had been mentioned on practically every TV news program. It was indeed his day.

Gene proudly parked his car in the spot reserved for the publisher in the executive garage next to the newspaper building. He was greeted warmly by a grinning black guard at the entrance of the garage when he stepped off the elevator.

"Its good to see ya, Mr. Stanton," the guard yelled, proudly. "Thanks to you I'm back on the job."

"Hang in there," Gene beamed. "We're gonna be here for a while."

"At least I don't have to duck anymore," the guard laughed as Gene walked across the street to the main building.

It was early on a brisk fall morning as Gene strode towards the front steps leading to the large revolving doors of the building. Many people hurriedly went in and out of the doors. Most of them failed to recognize Gene and that suited him just fine. As Gene neared the front of the building he as forced to slow to a stop as workmen attached a hoist to a large sign that read, "The Herald", the building's new name. The huge sign went up directly in front of Gene as it was slowly lifted up high above the sidewalk into the air. Gene looked up, following the movement of the giant sized sign as it was lifted completely to the top of the four story building. Gene smiled broadly as crowds of people continued to move through the revolving doors leading to the lobby. Some of the people noticed him and smiled. After a while, when the sign was safely secured on top of the building, Gene walked briskly through the revolving doors and into the crowded lobby. People were lined up in several rows in front of the employment office. The lines stretched completely across the spacious lobby. Before he could reach the elevators at the rear of the lobby, a woman working behind the want ad counter noticed him.

"Good morning, Mr. Stanton," the woman shouted across the crowded lobby. "And congratulations!"

Gene smiled and nodded to the woman. "Morning, Irma," Gene replied. "Kinda crowded isn't it?"

All of the other people in the lobby suddenly realized who Gene was and they began shouting at him in congratulations. Gene smiled back and graciously accepted their congratulations as the elevator door slid opened and he stepped inside, relieved as the door slid closed.

The employment office at The Herald was packed with people applying for jobs at the newspaper. One young woman who was neatly dressed in a business suit, sat nervously in front of a desk as the personnel officer read her application and resume. The man suddenly looked up at the woman with a surprised expression on his face.

"Dugas?...Are you related to The Dugas family?" the personnel officer asked.

"Yes...I'm their daughter, Marcy," the woman answered.

"But...they...they own The Daily Press!"

"I'm aware of that."

"Then...then what are you doin' here?" the man asked, whispering. "Why don't you work for The Press?"

"Because I don't agree with their editorial policy," Marcy replied. "You have a problem with that?"

"I don't know about this," the man answered, nervously. "I'd better clear this with my boss."

The man quickly got up and left the room, still clutching Marcy's application and resume. In a few minutes he returned followed by another, much older man who was now holding Marcy's papers.

"Ms. Dugas?..I'm Mr. Hartwell, Personnel Director here at The Herald," the older man said. "I think we've got a little problem here."

"We?..I don't have any problem...I've got my masters in journalism...three years experience at The Times...No...I'm sorry, but I don't have a problem...You might...According to your new publisher, Mr. Gene Stanton, I thought I'd be welcomed."

"Well...er...ah...that's true," Hartwell stammered, nervously. "What Mr. Stanton said... he meant...only this is a unique situation."

"You mean you're gonna turn me down?" Marcy asked.

Hartwell hesitated before he answered. He looked nervously at the other man who shrugged his shoulders, helplessly. "Just give us a few minutes, Ms. Dugas," Hartwell said. "We'll see if we can straighten this out."

"Please do," Marcy said, sarcastically.

Gene II was managing editor at The Detroit Herald and unofficially the assistant publisher. This was a responsibility he had inherited at The State Journal because he was the oldest Stanton child and it carried over to The Herald without any questioning or fanfare when he turned down the offer from Newsmonth Magazine to continue working with his father. Gene had welcomed his son's decision to stay and he and his namesake had worked closely together during the changeover, sharing the complicated conversion only with Roger Carlson, the corporate attorney. Together, the three of them had worked long hours negotiating with the newspaper unions and arranging to re-hire almost sixty percent of the personnel who had been employed with The Times. The re-hired employees, who were more than 95 percent all white, were grateful to the Stantons for restoring their chosen livelihoods and fully realized that their futures were tied to the success of The Herald regardless of the new owners being African-American. Gene Stanton had always protected Gene II from being forced to make difficult decisions and as a result, he was reluctant to do so without his father's knowledge. He fully realized that once his father was made aware of the difficulty he was facing, his father would ultimately make the decision for him, leaving Gene II in a no-win situation.

Today, the first full day of operation for The Detroit Herald Newspaper, had Gene II deeply involved with going over the editorial schedule with several editors in the long editorial conference room, while just outside of the glass enclosed conference room, the spacious newsroom was crowded with new and old employees being trained on various projects. The buzzer on the phone alerted Gene II and he quickly snatched up the phone. "Yes, Ms. Cunningham..."

"Personnel on two, Mr. Stanton."

Gene II quickly switched to the right line. "Stanton speaking."

"Mr. Stanton...This is Archie Hartwell in personnel."

"Yes, Archie...how can I help you?"

"I hate to bother you at such a hectic time," Hartwell said. "But something's come up down here that I think you oughta know about."

"Go on...What's this all about?"

"Marcy Dugas...F. Walton Dugas' daughter," Hartwell stammered, cautiously. "She's down here in my office, now...said she wants a job!"

Gene II was startled!..He switched the phone from on hand to the other, nervously. "A job?..Are you serious?"

"As serious as a heart attack!" Hartwell answered. "Can I send her up there to talk to you?"

Gene pondered the question for a moment. "No...No...I don't wanna talk to her...She's probably just bird-doggin' for her old man, anyway!..No...wait a minute...I'll call you right back."

Gene II nervously hung up the phone and quickly dialed another number. His father's rapid fire response surprised him. "Stanton here."

"Dad, we got a problem...Marcy Dugas is in personnel...She's applying for a job."

"You're kiddin!"

"No...What shall I do with her?"

"What's her qualifications?"

"Gee...I don't know, dad...She's probably just a plant for her father anyway."

Gene laughed at his son. "Naw...I don't think so...That would be too obvious. Send her up to my office...I wanna talk to her."

Gene Stanton carefully studied Marcy Dugas' resume and application as she sat across the wide executive desk from him, smiling and watching him closely.

Marcy was a beautiful young woman. She had her soft blond hair tucked neatly into a ponytail. She wore a pin striped gray business suite and matching pumps. She sat patiently as Gene scanned her resume. He took off his glasses when he was finished reading and smiled back at her.

"With your background and qualifications...you're exactly what I want here," Gene said. "How come you've never worked for your father?"

"A long, standing family feud," Marcy replied. "He disagrees with the way I live and I disagree with everything he stands for...its been like that for a long as I can remember."

"Join the club," Gene laughed. "I hope this doesn't add more fuel to the fire...your father's furious with me you know."

"I can imagine," Marcy answered quickly. "He's furious with me, too...He has been for a long time."

Gene chuckled for a moment, then became serious as he stared at Marcy. "Look, Marcy...I'm trying to run a major daily newspaper here and I need the best professional talent I can get...hey, if you want the job...I'll be happy to have you here?"

"The I'm hired?"

Gene stood up and walked around his desk, holding out his hands to her. She firmly grasped both of his hands as she stood up, delighted.

"You bet you are!" Gene answered, grinning. "Welcome aboard, Marcy Dugas!"

Marcy became more excited as she squeezed Gene's hands, gratefully. "Thank you, Mr. Stanton!" she exclaimed. "I promise you...with all my heart...You'll never regret this!"

"No...I don't think I will," Gene said as he began to escort her towards the door of the office.

When they reached the outer office, Gene was surprised to see his youngest daughter, Kim, waiting for him.

"Kim...I didn't know you were out here," Gene said. "What's going on?.." Gene's attention was quickly diverted to a woman sitting in the receptionist's office and smiling at him...He couldn't take his eyes off of her and she knew it. The sunlight streaming through the office window enhanced her beautifully sculptured and delicate features with shadows that blended in with her long, black hair that created a feminine mystique that touched his heart with a soft, warm glow...He finally managed to move his eyes from her inviting smile back to his daughter who was trying to get his attention...

"Dad...Dad!..Over here..." Kim laughed. "We had a lunch date, remember..I made the reservations." Kim suddenly looked over at Marcy and stopped..."Marcy!..Marcy Dugas!" Kim shouted...The two women quickly embraced as they began screaming and hollering, happily!

"You two know each other?" Gene asked, startled.

"We went to college together," Marcy shouted, grinning.

"So that's why you came here," Gene said, smiling.

"That's one reason," Marcy laughed. "If it hadn't worked with you...Kim was next on my list."

"It is so good to see you, Marcy!" Kim said. "What have you been doing?"

"I thought you were still in tinsel town, Kim."

"I came back when I heard dad was going to switch to a daily newspaper...What are YOU doing here?"

"This is just fabulous!" Marcy replied. "Your dad just hired me!"

"Really?" Kim squealed in delight. "Adrian was just hired, too." Kim motioned to the beautiful woman with the long, black hair who was sitting in the receptionist's office watching them with a big smile on her face. She was impeccably dressed and moved like a model as she got up and walked over towards them. Gene was taken by her striking appearance...

"I just finished taking her on the grand tour," Kim said. "Adrian...this is Marcy Dugas...It looks like you two are gonna be working together."

"Nice meeting you, Marcy," Adrian said, softly. She slowly turned to Gene, staring up at him with her big, brown eyes. "And this must be your father, Kim."

"Oh...I'm sorry...Dad, this is Adrian...the woman I spoke to you about," Kim said, apologetically. "You remember...beauty and the brains...Ms. PHD...She was one of my professors at State."

"Your daughter's one of my biggest fans," Adrian said, smiling at Gene. "Its so nice meeting you, Mr. Stanton...I've heard so much about you...I didn't think you really existed."

"I exist...believe me," Gene replied.

"I just went on a tour of your building," Adrian said. "I'm really impressed...with everything..."

"Oh!..That's too bad!" Marcy said sadly. "Its been so long since I worked here...I wanted to see it, too."

"No problem," Kim said. "I'll take you on the tour now."

"I thought we were going to lunch," Gene protested.

"I'll take a raincheck," Kim replied. "I haven't see Marcy in ages...Why don't you take Adrian?..She's your employee now...Maybe you can bring her up to date on what's been going on around here."

Gene turned to Adrian who was smiling, broadly. "If you don't mind having lunch with an old man, Adrian...I'd be honored."

"So will I," Adrian answered "You're the man of the hour in this city today."

"Not really...just tryin' to make a buck," Gene said, as he turned back to Marcy. "Marcy...I'll arrange for you to talk to my son right after lunch. My secretary will take you up to his office."

"Thank you again, Mr. Stanton," Marcy replied. "I'll make you proud of me."

"I already am," Gene said, smiling. He quickly turned back to Adrian. "Shall we go?"

Adrian smiled, proudly and placed her hand on Gene's arm. Gene turned to his secretary who was staring at them both, dumbfounded! "We're going to lunch, Katie," Gene said. "We'll be at Joseph's if anyone wants me. Set up a one-thirty appointment with my son to interview Ms. Dugas. Tell him I hired her...reporter...medium level."

Katie nodded her head and stared after them, disapprovingly, as they left the office arm in arm!

The sports department of The Herald was located down the wide hallway from the main editorial offices and near the front elevators on the second floor. Gene had assigned his son Mel, to work as a reporter in the sports department until his suspension from the National Basketball Association was lifted. Mel hadn't seen or heard from Kelly since she stormed out of the Stanton home during the NBA draft proceedings on television, and he felt it was just as well since he was determined to stay away from drugs.

This afternoon, Mel sat back in his swivel chair with his feet on his desk and studied several typewritten sheets of paper in his hands thoughtfully. Most of the sports department desks were vacant during the middle of the day with the exception of several glass enclosed offices located in the rear where the editors and supervisors worked. A few secretaries were scattered throughout the spacious office as the sounds of their typewriters echoed across the room. Mel suddenly stood up and threw the papers on his desk in disgust! He walked angrily down the endless rows of desks towards the glass enclosed offices. Just as he neared the offices several people walked out of one, ending a meeting. They stared at Mel, startled by the angry expression on his face. Mel stopped the first man out of the office.

"Is Pete still busy, Ray?" Mel asked.

"What's the matter?" Ray asked. "You look upset about somethin."

"It's that story on Walker's retirement," Mel answered angrily. "That's not what I wrote!"

"Relax...that happens a lot in this business. You'll still get the byline...don't worry about it. That's what re-write people are for."

"But that's NOT what I wrote!" Mel argued. "They made him sound like an alcoholic!"

"Well, isn't he?..He's been dried out so often they got his picture on the wall in the DT's section at City Hospital!"

"Don't talk about him like that!" Mel shouted angrily. "Glenn Walker was one of the greatest fighters of this century!..This makes him sound like some skid row bum!..If they were gonna do that they should've put somebody else on that story...not me!"

Ray glared at Mel with a sarcastic sneer on his face. "Whatsa matter?"..Daddy's little boy don't wanna do the bad stories?..You just wanna write about Golkilocks and Little Orphan Annie?..Or doped up basketball players?"

"You cruisin' for a bruisin?" Mel snarled. "You better lay off, Ray...I don't take on old men!"

Ray angrily braced himself, ready to take on the much younger, bigger and taller Mel! "Anytime, buddy boy!..Don't let my age stop you!..It ain't my fault you got bombed out of the NBA!"

Other men quickly moved in and separated Mel and Ray before fists started flying!..The two angry men continued yelling and screaming at each other until a secretary moved in between the group of men and tried to attract Mel's attention!

"Mel!..Mel!.." the secretary shouted. "There's someone here to see you!"

The woman motioned across the open office to the wide double doorway where Kelly stood, waiting nervously. Mel quickly turned away from the men, snatching his arm from the grasp of one of the men in anger. He walked over to Kelly and quickly ushered her out into the hallway as everyone stared at the tall black man and the glamorous White girl. Mel and Kelly spoke in hushed tones as people walking by glanced at them, curiously.

"Wow!..That was gettin' pretty hot and heavy in there!" Kelly said, still shocked at the scene. "What's going on?"

"That's just part of the garbage you get when your ol' man is the publisher!..Everyone wants to put the boss' son in his place!" Mel replied, staring into Kelly's eyes. "It's good to see you and you're looking great...How have you been?"

"Miserable!..I miss you terribly!"

"Isn't this what you wanted?..It'll be a year before I can play in the NBA...You said you couldn't wait."

"No!..That's not true!" Kelly protested. "I was upset because you were leaving it up to your father to decide...and it was our future...not his!..I didn't learn about the suspension until almost a week later!"

"Then why didn't you call?"

"I didn't know what to say!" Kelly sobbed, loudly. "I felt so terrible for you!..Like it was my fault!..I'm just no good without you, Mel!..Please!"

Mel quickly glanced over his shoulder back into the sports department as Kelly raised her voice, sobbing loudly. He slowly moved her further down the hall away from the inquisitive stares of the people in the sports department. People walking by continued to stare at the couple as Mel tried to comfort Kelly.

"Take it easy, baby!" Mel pleaded in a whisper. "Everyone's staring at us!"

"I don't care if you NEVER play that damn game again!..I love you, Mel!..I love you so much!"

Mel put his arms around her and pulled her closer to him. She buried her face into his chest and sobbed hysterically!

"Where are you staying, honey?" Mel asked, softly.

"I'm in the same place...Will you come by tonight?..Please!"

Mel quickly hugged her, brushing her cheeks with his lips, lightly. "I'll be free about seven," he answered with tears welling up in his eyes. "Maybe we'll have dinner or something."

Kelly looked up at Mel, still crying as tears streamed down her face, smearing her makeup. She reminded Mel of a little girl in trouble at school and his heart went out to her as he remembered their wonderful times together.

"Yes...that'll be great," she said. "I'll fix a special dinner for you."

"You alright now?" he asked, concerned. "No more tears?"

"Uh, uh," she sobbed.

Mel turned to go back into the sports department. He stopped and turned back to Kelly. She hadn't moved from the spot where he had left her. She stared at him, motionless.

"And Kel?" Mel said, quietly. "Don't make it too special."

THE WINDS OF TOMORROW

Chapter Six

At noon everyday the plush downtown restaurant is crowded with businesspeople enjoying extended lunches in the atmosphere of sophistication and resolving grandiose business transactions. The big three of the auto industry, exclusive law firms, advertising agencies, city politicians and newspaper executives all found their way into the jammed bistro in order to be seen and heard amongst Detroit's business and political elite.

Gene Stanton sat with Dr. Adrian Grant at a prominently placed table and slowly sipped his drink as he nodded at various people walking by. Several others stopped to congratulate him and wished him luck with The Herald. Adrian smiled at Gene when they finally had a moment to talk without any distraction.

"I see you are a very popular person, Mr. Stanton," Adrian said.

"Don't pay any attention to that," Gene replied. "Most of these guys are stoppin' because they see an old man like me with a beautiful young woman."

"Oh, c'mon now...don't be modest," she said. "You know you don't really believe that."

"They probably think you're one of my daughters."

A large man with a flushed face walked over to the table, leaned over and shook Gene's hand. The man was obviously excited.

"Gene...I got great news!" the man said, anxiously.

"Adrian...this is our advertising director, Al Cronin," Gene said. "Al...this is Dr. Adrian Grant...She's a member of our editorial staff."

"Nice meeting you, Ms. Grant," Al said, impatiently. "Gene...listen to this..."

"What's happened?" Gene asked, interrupting.

"I didn't want to bother you at lunch," Al said, "But when I saw you over here

I couldn't resist the temptation!..Something fantastic has happened!"

"C'mon, Al...what is it?"

"The fashion section!..It's all sold out...for the next three issues!" Al said, gleefully. "We had to start up a waiting list for advertisers who want to get in!"

"You mean they're coming in THAT fast?"

"It was because of that slick dummy the fashion department mailed out. They're eatin' it up!" Al beamed. "In fact, I'm gonna tell you right now...don't be surprised if editorial asks for an increase in size!..It's the color on that slick, glossy stock...It's working for those highclass women's stores...they love it!"

"That's great," Gene answered. "I thought it might eventually become a success...but this...this is unbelievable!"

Al grinned broadly as he straightened up and began to leave. "Well, I gotta get back to the paper...Nice meeting you, Ms. Grant."

"That's Doctor Grant!" Adrian corrected, firmly.

"Oh?..I'm sorry, Dr. Grant," Al quickly apologized as he backed away. "Gene...I'll see ya later."

Gene smiled at Adrian as Al left the restaurant. "You're pretty proud of that, aren't you."

"Shouldn't I be?..It was a lot of hard work. I earned it...but most men seem to forget it."

"Should I call you doctor?"

"I wish you'd call me Adrian."

"Then you call me Gene," he said. "Tell me something about yourself...How'd you meet Kim?"

"I met her at Michigan State. When she first came in I sorta took her under my wing...Like a little sister."

"You're not that much older than Kim"

"I think older...There's a difference you know. I lost both parents when I was twelve and I've been on my own for a long time...even through a lousey marriage."

"You've been married?" Gene asked. "You have any kids?"

"No...I was married to one," she snapped. "After the divorce I realized I preferred older men...much older men."

Gene hesitated before he slowly brought his glass up to his lips. He stared at Adrian over the rim of his glass. She returned his stare with a seductive smile playing at the corners of her mouth.

"How'd you happen to come to the Herald?"

"Max Jenkins...one of your editors, called me," she answered. "When he told me what you were doing and what your plans were...I became intrigued with the idea of working on a major daily newspaper."

"What about your career as a journalism professor?"

"Like so many of those of us who teach it...most have never actually done it. I decided it was time to test some of the theories I advocated."

"Is that the real reason?"

"Part of it."

"What's the rest?"

"A persistent dean who was going through a middle-age crisis and thought I was the cure."

"You had an affair?"

"Not really...He thought it was," she replied, thoughtfully. "I thought we only had a good, intellectual friendship...that is...until one day I discovered my car in the faculty parking lot with all of the windows smashed out?"

"He did that?..It must've scared you to death."

"No...he didn't do it."

"Who did?"

"It seems he had confessed to his wife that he was in love with me...without bothering to tell me," she answered. "He told her he wanted a divorce and she decided she wanted a head...mine."

"What happened?"

"After the car incident, word spread that I was breaking up his family...Then it became open season on one Dr. Adrian Grant."

"They gave you a hard time?"

"Everyone did...Listen...I know how I look and it attracts a lot of attention," she said, seriously. "But I have never flaunted my looks...I didn't have to."

"I can understand that," Gene said, smiling.

"Thank you...but when the scandal broke out I couldn't walk across the campus without dirty cracks, jokes, innuendos, and students and faculty on the make."

"That's too bad."

"And I really didn't deserve it...I hadn't done anything. I had never encouraged him...... It was all in his imagination."

Gene could see the moisture welling up in her eyes. He could feel her pain. He reached across the table to gently pat the back of her hand. She turned her hand up and firmly clasped Gene's hand as she stared into his eyes, searching...

Liz Stanton's downtown luxury apartment represented the latest in fashionable urban living. The highest of the high rise apartments in rent and altitude, Liz took pride in it's seclusion and security. The scenic view her penthouse suite provided overlooked downtown Detroit's Renaissance Center and the Detroit River. Her eastern view covered Belle Isle in it's entirety.

Liz sat impatiently on her living room sofa in the expensively furnished apartment as soft music drifted from the stereo. It was early evening and she was dressed in only a small bathrobe. She wondered what was so important that her brother, Gene II, just had to see her about this evening. She was irritated when her buzzer rang and he pressured her into seeing him without calling her beforehand. In a few minutes she heard a soft knock at her door. When she opened the door her brother stood there with a big smile on his face. He looked her up and down as he walked into the apartment.

"What's the matter, Liz?..You're in bed kinda early."

"What are you doing here and why didn't you call?"

"Your secretary said you weren't feelin' good so you went home a little early...You alright, sis?"

"Just a slight headache...I'm alright."

"I've go some news that might cheer you up...I wanted to see your face light up when I told you...I knew you'd be pleased."

"Pleased?..Pleased about what?" Liz asked, irritated at his attitude. "What's happened?"

Gene II sat down on the sofa with a smug expression on his face as he slowly poured himself a drink. Liz stared at him impatiently. "Gene!"

"Alright...alright...take it easy!..Al Cronin called me this afternoon...Drury's Department Store bought the center spread in the fashion section for the next six months?..Hartman's wants the back page for the next YEAR!..And listen to this, Liz...The advertising staff has sold out the fashion sections for the next three months!"

"Sold out!..So soon?" Liz said, stunned. "I wasn't prepared for that!"

"That dummy section you put together was dynamite!" Gene II beamed, proudly. "The advertising staff is setting up a waiting list...first come....first served. It looks like you've come up with a winner, Liz!..This could revolutionize the newspaper industry all across the country!"

"I...I don't know what to say...I didn't think it would happen this fast!...Does dad know?..What'd he say?"

"He's proud of his daughter!...You've made him all smiles today...couldn't be happier!"

Liz quickly turned towards the bedroom, then suddenly stopped, abruptly. Gene II saw the expression on her face and glanced at the closed bedroom door, then back to Liz. He quickly stood up to leave, downing his drink in one gulp.

"Hey...I'm sorry, sis...Did I come at a bad time?"

"You should've called."

Gene walked over to the door. "I guess I wasn't thinking...but it WAS good news wasn't it?" Gene II asked, smiling. "You get your rest, Liz...You've earned it...I'll see you at the paper tomorrow morning."

Gene II quickly left the apartment. Liz closed the door gently behind him and leaned back against the door smiling to herself, confidently. She balled up her fist and shoved it high up into the air in triumph!..

"YES!" she shouted, proudly.

Liz slowly turned down all of the lights in the living room and slipped quietly into the bedroom, softly closing the bedroom door. She smiled at Ze-Ze, laying in the bed, stretching liesurely.

"Why were you so long?" Ze-Ze asked, huskily.

"That was my brother, Gene," Liz answered. "He had some good news for me."

"What's happened?"

Liz walked closer to the bed and stared down at Ze-Ze, smiling at her with a twinkle in her eyes.

"It's our fashion section...The ads are all sold out for the next three months!..It's working, Ze-Ze, it's gonna be a success!"

Ze-Ze smiled and held out her arms to Liz. "Oohhh!..I'm so happy for you!..Come here to me."

Liz's short bathrobe fell to the floor as she silently slipped into bed next to Ze-Ze. The two naked women embraced as they kissed. Ze-Ze's tongue explored Liz's mouth hungrily as she pushed back the covers revealing their smooth, well proportioned bodies. They undulated in perfect coordination as Ze-Ze's head slowly moved down to Liz's neck, kissing and nibbling as she mouthed her breasts. She lightly nibbled at Liz's small, firm breasts, licking from the underside of each arm, across the stiff nipples, as her tongue expertly circled and traced the outline of each breast. She whispered to Liz in French with a low, heavy voice as she continued to kiss and worship her breasts and neck. Liz responded by slightly whimpering and pulling Ze-Ze closer to her, crushing their breasts together. Slowly, Ze-Ze began moving downward, kissing and licking Liz's stomach and the insides of her thighs. Finally, her head nestled between Liz's long, shapely legs as they spread further apart to allow Ze-Ze more access. Liz responded by placing both of her hands behind Ze-Ze's head and thrusting her hips into the air as the slurping sounds of Ze-Ze's quickly moving tongue and Liz's deep sighs filled the room.

The curtains at the bedroom window slightly moved from the soft caresses of the autumn breeze as the lonely sound of distance thunder rumbled in the sky.

The Dugas Estate in Grosse Pointe, Michigan, was on one of the largest estates in suburban Detroit. Built in the 1920s by an auto magnate, it became a tourist attraction known all across the country. The Dugas family bought the estate in the 1960s as their newspaper, The Daily Press, grew in circulation, surpassing the previous number one city newspaper, The Detroit Times. By the mid-eighties the Dugas Estate had grown to almost twice the size it was when John Dugas originally purchased the property. His son, F. Walton Dugas, had taken over the newspaper and his family's estate in the late seventies when his father died. As the newspaper grew in circulation the estate had expanded in acreage. The Daily Press put a stranglehold on the Detroit Times, forcing it completely out of business in the early eighties. F. Walton Dugas considered the metropolitan Detroit area the personal property of The Daily

Press and he resented the intrusion of Gene Stanton's Detroit Herald newspaper. Dugas had initiated plans for the construction of a new, multi-million dollar, state-of-the-art newspaper printing plant in the eastern suburbs of Detroit in order to quickly smother the chances for success of any new publisher because they would lack both the ability and the facilities to compete with The Daily Press.

Today, as he drove his car down the long, winding private road leading to the Dugas Estate, his fury for his daughter and his son nagged at him, forcing him to screech the car to a halt in front of the home, march inside and sling his briefcase on the desk in his library. When he joined his wife and daughter in the spacious living room of the museum-like home, he eyed his daughter suspiciously as his wife, Julia, greeted him with a drink. He snatched the drink and ignored his wife's pleasantries as he settled down on a deeply cushioned sofa. His eyes remained fixed on his daughter, Marcy.

"How was your day today, Marcy?" Dugas asked, calmly.

Marcy nervously bit her lip and looked down at the drink in her hands. "It was alright...nothing special...How was yours, father?"

"Oh?..Is that right?..nothing special, eh?" Dugas snapped. "I had a strange day...Funny things have been happening all day."

"That's too bad, Walt," Julia said. "I hope it was nothing serious."

Dugas ignored his wife's remarks and continued staring at his daughter as he spoke. "No...It's nothing serious," he answered. "Just disloyalty that's all!"

Marcy quickly got up and nervously fixed herself another drink as she felt her father's eyes follow her movements.

"What kind of disloyalty?" Julia asked.

"The worst kind, Julia," Dugas snarled. "When your own blood knifes you in the back...it hurts!"

"Wh...What are you talking about?" Julia asked.

"Why don't you ask your darlin' daughter," Dugas said. "I'm sure she'll be glad to fill you in!"

Julia looked from her husband to her daughter and tried to figure out exactly what was going on. She turned to Marcy, completely confused. "Do you know what your father's talking about?"

Marcy slowly sipped her drink and frowned at her father. "Yes...I think I do," Marcy replied.

"You know DAMN well you do!" Dugas snapped, angrily.

"What's this about, Marcy?" Julia asked, nervously.

"I was hired as a reporter for The Herald this morning."

"What?..You mean you're going to work for the Stantons?" Julia asked, bewildered. "They're your father's competitors!..Why would you do that?"

"Because she hates me that's why!" Dugas shouted, angrily. "We put her through college to become a top reporter at The Daily Press and look what she does!..That's why she worked for The Times...to get back at me!..Here, I had a job for her on our own family newspaper as City Editor and she turns it down for some night reporter's job at The Times, duckin' pimps and chasin' whores for that human interest bull!..Then, after I force The Times out of business. Well, now she goes to my worst enemy and works for him!..My own damn dauhgter!"

"That's not true!..I don't hate you!" Marcy protested. "I just disagree with your editorial policy of bigotry and sexism!..I dislike everything you and your newspaper stand for!"

"You're just like your brother, Douglas!" Dugas raved, angrily. "I get him a job with the biggest law firm in the state and he blows it by getting caught screwing some secretary in the conference room!"

"Oh, daddy!..I don't want to hear you ranting and raving!" Marcy said, disgusted. "Why don't you just let us lead our lives without trying to control us?"

"Well, if you think you're gonna be able to write that liberal dribble for Gene Stanton...you'd better think again!" he warned.

"Walt!..What do you mean?" Julia asked.

"There's no telling what he may mean, mother!" Marcy shouted. "That's what's wrong with him!..He has no respect for his fellow man, whatsoever!"

"Fellow man?..you think Gene Stanton is my fellow man?" Dugas argued. "The way my father helped finance that Black sonofabitch's father...and he pays me back like this?..You better get your priorities straight, young woman!..The only reason Stanton hire you was to get back at me!"

"I'm a qualified journalist!" Marcy screamed.

"You're my daughter first and its damn well time you started behaving like one!" Dugas shouted. "What you did today is showing no respect for your father!..It's damn right embarrassing!"

"I'm sure she didn't intend to embarrass you," Julia said, softly.

"Dammit, Julia!..Will you stay out of this and shuddup!" Dugas angrily shouted. "I know what she intended and I'm tellin' you now, daughter dearest...If you don't quit that job tomorrow and join me at The Press..neither Gene Stanton or The Detroit Herald is gonna be around too much longer!"

"You can threaten me all you want," Marcy replied. "But this is my last word...I will not quit The Herald and I will never work for your newspaper until it's racist and sexist policies are changed!"

Dugas glared at his daughter with his eyes blazing in anger!..He threw his empty glass into the fireplace and stormed out of the room!..Julia turned to Marcy who calmly got up and poured herself another drink!

Gene Stanton worked late every night. He sat behind his wide, executive desk in his library and slowly thumbed through The Daily Press Newspaper. His eyeglasses rested low on his cheeks as he carefully studied each page. Hearing a slight noise, he looked up to see his daughter, Karen, standing in the library doorway. Gene was momentarily surprised. "Karen...I didn't know you were here," Gene said.

"I was with mom," Karen answered. "I've been waiting for you."

Gene took off his glasses and rubbed his eyes. "What can I do for you?..And how's my grandkids?"

"The kids are fine...You look tired, dad," Karen said, showing concern. "Is this too much of a grind for you?"

"No...not really...It's just getting my blood moving."

"I'm surprised to see you reading the competition," she said, motioning to the newspaper Gene was reading.

"That's the only way I can find out what they're doin...No use reading ours...I know what we're doing."

"I hear Liz's fashion section is a big success."

"Yeah, it is...She's worked hard on it."

"You know, dad...since I changed my mind about selling my stock...Bob has kinda talked me into taking a more active role in the newspaper. He thinks I have too much time on my hands."

"You mean you want a job?" Gene asked.

"Something like that...only I'm not as creative as Liz," Karen said. "I think I'm more suited to be on the business end instead of..."

"Look, Karen," Gene interrupted. "I know you and I haven't always agreed on everything...In fact it's gotten to be downright nasty sometimes...but this is your newspaper, too. Your grandfather wanted us all to become part of it...So if you want a job..."

"I want to be on the board of directors."

"What?"

"Don't you think I'm qualified?"

"No...It's not that...I'm just surprised to find out you're that interested, that's all," Gene said. "Let me think about it...I'll see what I can do."

"I've already spoken to Roger...He says it can be done," Karen said, smiling broadly.

Gene looked up at his oldest daughter, surprised. She continued to smile at him with a knowing glint in her eyes.

• • •

It was in the dead of night and the city of Beirut, Lebanon was in shambles. Sirens screamed as ambulances raced through the streets of Muslim West Beirut where many people lay wounded in the Shiite slums as the result of a skirmish between the pro-Iranian Hezbollah and the mainstream Amal militia allied with Syria. Mysterious shadows moved with caution as each unknown sound could signify an angry attacker.

Joe Stanton, completely dressed in Arab attire for this covert operation, was leading a group of Amal militia down a lonely, dark road which led to an Iranian terrorist headquarters. The men took cover in the shadows of the giant crates and boxes which were recently unloaded from a French frigate in the harbor and delivered to the rival Shiite Muslims in exchange for kidnapped prisoners. A few hundred yards down the road Joe and his men saw a brightly lit office building with several military vehicles parked in front. They suddenly heard loud shouting as several men were marched out of the building and into the middle of the street where they were shoved back against the walls of an old, partly shelled building. The men were all bound, gagged, and blindfolded when they were kicked and punched repeatedly by their captors as they waited for the French officers to come out of the building to complete the exchange.

Joe Stanton motioned for his men to gather around him as he knelt on one knee, covered by a long shadow of the surrounding warehouses. Joe whispered secretively as the men crowded around him.

"Alright...we're in time!..They haven't completed the exchange yet!" Joe whispered. "You guys got any questions?"

"We're all set," a man replied. "What's the plan?"

"I want five of you to set up automatic fire on top of that highest building to provide us with cover if this doesn't go down right," Joe said. "And you other five will set up charges in these other buildings to attract their attention while we release the prisoners."

"I thought they had agreed to swap the prisoners for the supplies," a second man snapped.

"They did," Joe answered, quickly. "But sometimes they've been known not to keep their word!..The minute we see anything wrong we start our action, got it?..Our job is to get those prisoners and those French officers back to that frigate safe and sound!..We won't have too much time to move in...On a hand signal from me...we go into action!"

The men quickly moved out to their designated areas. Joe and his men checked their weapons and stealthily moved out to position themselves on top of a building near the bound prisoners. They hid in the shadows and waited. In a few minutes, Joe and his men heard more shouting and hollering as the French officers from the frigate were roughly shoved outside into the street next to the surprised and frightened prisoners! The terrorists kicked and spat on the French officers!..They laughed harshly as they began beating them with the stock of their rifles!..

Joe realized that the terrorists were not living up to the agreement to free the prisoners and he quickly began waving his arm to signal his men to ignite the explosives in the buildings lining the street. At the first sounds of the explosions the terrorists froze and their attention was diverted from the prisoners. At the same moment,

Joe and his men on top of the building began repelling down the wall and into the streets, surrounding the surprised terrorists at gunpoint!..They efficiently disarmed the terrorists and quickly marched them back into the building!..They tied and bound the terrorists while they released the French officers and the relieved prisoners. Joe, his militia, the prisoners and the French officers immediately evacuated the area as the smoke from the fires caused by the explosions filled the black night!..

Joe and his militia escorted the French officers and the freed prisoners to the French frigate waiting for them in the Beirut Harbor. In gratitude for the actions of Joe and the militia, the French officers praised them for their brave rescue. As they waited to board the ship, the ranking French officer, Captain Trudeau, gratefully shook Joe's hand. "How did you know we would be there?" Captain Trudeau asked. "If it hadn't been for you and your gallant men...why...we would all be prisoners now...or...possibly...dead!"

"We received word from our command staff yesterday afternoon that this was supposed to go down," Joe answered. "We suspected a double-cross might happen after they received the supplies...We've dealt with those people before."

"But what about the supplies we gave them?..They have guns, ammunition, rockets and food!..That could last them for months!"

"We've taken care of that, too," Joe replied, smiling and glancing at his watch. "We should know in about thirty minutes."

Captain Trudeau glanced back at his men and then back to Joe. "Oh, I see!..You have thought of everything!.." he said, proudly. "I am glad and most grateful that you are on our side!"

Suddenly their attention was drawn to a lookout aboard the frigate who was pointing excitedly beyond the harbor and shouting and screaming frantically!..Everyone looked in the direction the man was pointing at and they saw a large truck speeding directly toward their cluster of militia, ex-prisoners, and French officers!..As the truck descended down upon them at a terrific speed the men all began to scatter, running in different directions for their lives!.. As the truck bore down on them Joe snatched a grenade launcher from the shoulder of one of his men!..He quickly knelt down on one knee with the launcher on his shoulder and aimed at the oncoming truck!..Joe fired when the vehicle was only about one hundred yards away!..The truck exploded in a shower of flames and debris!..

Everyone breathed a sigh of relief as they came back together again, shaking hands and embracing after such a near-death experience. When the French officers and their men boarded the ship they waved goodby to Joe and his militia as they began their long march towards the mountains.

As Joe and his group of Amal militia were scaling the treacherous mountains, leaving the war-torn Beirut area, they were suddenly attracted by an array of flashing lights in the area where the terrorists' headquarters was stationed. They heard a series of loud explosions!..The men turned in time to see the entire area ablaze!..

Chapter Seven

The Detroit Community Committee, Inc. was founded after the Detroit race riots in 1967. It became a committee of community leaders, Black, White, Asian and Hispanic, who were all impeccably dressed, well heeled, over-educated and especially adapt at talking intellectually and friendly over expensive lunches and teas where they exchanged business cards each week and privately tried to advance their own personal careers instead of sincerely trying to contribute something to help the Detroit community. In most cases commissions and committees derived from civil unrest are doomed from the moment of conception for the simple reason that governments do not form committees or commissions to blame responsibility on governments or civic institutions. There is an automatic tendency toward the whitewash to the extent that riot commissions minimize criticism of the public officials to whom they must look for primary implementation and underwriting the committees or commissions. Another draw-back of these kinds of organizations is that, invariably, the personnel are selected from the elite of the dominant society and lack the ability to understand the lives and the mind-set of the people who ignited the street action in thefirst place. Founded on false racial assumptions leading to predetermined conclusions, committee members set off on a mission to confirm, not to discover. As a result, most post-riot committees do little more and accomplish considerably less than serving lunches and boosting personal and political ambitions.

Patricia Parker-Stanton had been an active member of the Detroit Community Committee, Inc. for many years. In the past, because she was an attorney and the wife of the publisher of the only Black weekly newspaper in the City of Detroit, her presence at these weekly meetings legitimized the authenticity of the committee's diverse membership and was considered a nice representation of the feminine Black elite. Now, since her husband became one of the country's first Black publishers of a major daily newspaper that circulated in the entire six county metro Detroit area, her active presence at these meetings signaled an opportunity for entrepreneurs and aspiring politicians to establish a viable social connection that could advance their careers.

Patricia was elegantly dressed in an expensively tailored business suit and wide brimmed hat when she arrived late at the committee meeting and walked briskly into the executive conference room on the top floor of a downtown skyscraper. Everyone in the crowded room turned to admire her. The spacious room was jammed with important community people. Patricia smiled politely and graciously sat down at the long, glistening table. The conversation in the room picked up again as the low chattering resumed. One of the women sitting at the table reached over and tugged at Patricia's arm.

"You're late again," the woman said. " Everyone's been asking about you."

"Why?..Was I suppose to do something?" Patricia asked. "Really, Sonja...I think you're exaggerating again."

"He's been looking for you, too," Sonja said. "I think you're late on purpose."

"What he?"

"You know who I'm talking about, girl...That's why he wants you to chair that sub-committee."

"Bill Clark?..He just wants my husband's newspaper to endorse him...tryin' to butter me up, that's all."

"Hhhmmph!" Sonja smirked. "Never seen no butterin' up like that!"

"What's on the agenda today?" Patricia asked, quickly looking around the room. "There's certainly a lot of folks here."

Sonja glanced towards the front of the room. "You can try to change the subject if you want to," Sonja continued. "But there he is...standing down there staring at you...I don't think he's lookin' for any endorsement from The Herald, either...not with that hungry look on his face."

"Sonja, will you stop!" Patricia protested. "This entire organization was set up to better race relations not to start up illicit romances!..Bill Clark wants my husband's endorsement...not his wife!"

"Who you kiddin?..He's been after you for a year!" Sonja shot back. "Before he decided to run for city council... and the way you been dressing lately... I think you're about ready to get caught!"

Patricia couldn't stop herself from laughing out loud. "You are a NUT!" Pat replied, still laughing. "And besides, he's too young for me. I don't think he's too much over forty."

"So?..What difference does that make?..He's a hunk and he digs you...Live a little." Sonja said as she glanced to the front of the room. "Here he comes now...like a damn homing pigeon!"

A handsome man in his early forties slowly walked towards the two women, making his way through the heavily crowded room , shaking hands and smiling broadly. As he neared them, Sonja quickly got up and moved away. The man sat down next to Patricia and handed her a cup of coffee.

"Hi...I've been wondering where you were," he said. "We missed you."

"Our family has been kinda busy," Patricia replied. "I guess it was later than I thought."

"You're referring to the newspaper changeover?"

"Yes, of course...That and a few other things."

"Have you given any thought to chairing that sub-committee?..I wanted to nominate you tonight. You ought to be good heading a sub-committee to fight racism in the media."

"Maybe."

"I was wondering," Bill whispered. "After tonight's meeting... could we stop downstairs at Lou's and have drink?"

"My car will be waiting for me."

"It won't take long...I just wanna let you in on a few things I think your sub-committee should be doing."

"Oh...I don't know if I'll have the time to run a sub-committee like that." Patricia said, thoughtfully.

"It shouldn't take too much of your time. We need people like you to help organize drives to hire more minorities like your husband is doing at The Herald. Just think about the jobs you could help create...That's why I'm running again for council."

"Don't get me wrong...I think that's a great attitude to have," Patricia said. "On second thought...If you can do that...well, I guess I could chair that sub-committee."

"That's fine!..I'll place your name in nomination today...After the meeting...we'll have that drink...I'll see you later."

Bill Clark smiled warmly at Patricia and gently squeezed her hand. Patricia felt she had just got herself involved in more than just the sub-committee. Just as Bill walked away, Sonja slipped back into the chair Bill had vacated. Her eyes caught Patricia's and she winked, knowingly.

"Some endorsement!" Sonja muttered.

Gene Stanton had not seen his sister, Gloria, in almost a year. When he heard she was arriving at the Stanton home that afternoon he had arranged for Roger Carlson to assist him at home on several projects. He remembered how Roger had always been infatuated with Gloria and he knew he'd be surprised by Gloria's sudden and unexpected appearance.

The success of The Detroit Herald Newspaper the last few months had vaulted the entire Stanton family to a current news status that warranted personal television and radio interviews for each member and Gloria wanted to be a part of it, too. Gloria lived in Wisconsin and she was Gene's younger sister and only sibling. When her husband died a few years ago, Gene and their mother, Hattie, had hoped Gloria would return to Detroit and join them at the Stanton mansion. However, in deference to her son, Willard, Gloria decided to remain in Wisconsin until her son received his degree in mass communications. With the success of The Detroit Herald and her son's graduation from Wisconsin University, Gene hoped that her visit was a prelude to moving back to Detroit.

Gene and Roger worked diligently that afternoon, going over several corporate ledgers in the library. As soon as they heard the front door chimes Connie rushed into the library doorway!..

"Alright!..Get off of it!" Connie shouted, loudly. "They're here!..C'mon and greet your sister and her son."

Roger was shocked!..He looked up from the stack of ledgers with a surprised expression on his face. He stared at Gene, startled!

"Gloria!..Your sister, Gloria?" Roger asked. "I didn't know she was coming!"

Gene looked at Roger and smiled, knowingly. "You still carrying that crush aren't ya."

"So that's why you wanted to work at home!"

"Surprise, surprise, surprise!" Gene said, laughing.

"Gee!..Gloria!..I haven't seen her years!"

Hattie walked into the library smiling as she peeked out of the library windows. "Oh, my GOD, Gene!..Here they are!" Hattie screamed in delight. "And Gloria is as pretty as ever!"

Gene stood up and put an arm around his mother's shoulders. "Well, c'mon, mamma...let's go see your baby daughter," Gene said, chuckling. "Before Roger has a heart attack from seeing his old flame."

They all quickly headed for the front door with Hattie walking between Gene and Roger as they all laughed happily.

Later that afternoon, after lunch, everyone sat around the dining room table discussing the newspaper. All eyes were on Gloria as Roger stared at her, hypnotized by her beauty. Gloria looked back at Roger and smiled.

"Roger!..Please stop staring at me!" Gloria said. "You make me feel uncomfortable."

"I'm sorry...I just can't get over it!' Roger replied. "You're as beautiful as ever!"

"Well you know us Black folks," Gene teased. "We never look our age."

"You do!" Roger shot back, laughing.

Patricia looked at Gloria and smiled. "Oh, those two!..Still arguing like teenagers...They'll never change."

"Roger started it," Gene argued.

"I did not!" Roger protested.

"Oh, hush!..Both of you...and grow up!" Hattie refereed. "It's a wonder we still have a newspaper."

"Well...from what I've been hearing back home...it's doing pretty good, "Gloria said. "Everybody's talking about it all over the country!.. It was mentioned on the national TV news last week!..Big time!..Tell me, big brother...Are you still hiring?"

"Why?..You lookin' for a job?"

"Not for me...For Willard. He's anxious to get started in the newspaper business."

Gene turned to his nephew. "Is that so, Willard?"

"My degree is in mass communications," Willard answered. "I'd love to be part of The Herald!"

"That's swell...I'll take you to the office with me tomorrow and you can look around, "Gene said.

"Is Dugas giving you any trouble?" Gloria asked.

"What would you expect?" Gene asked. "He's done everything to stop us except have us locked up!"

"Why?..Detroit is big enough for two daily newspapers." Gloria said. "This is a big metropolitan area."

"Dugas says we betrayed him," Patricia said.

"Betrayed him?" Gloria asked, surprised. "How can be say that?"

"He's hot because of that fifty thousand dollars his old man lent dad in the seventies," Gene answered. "Dugas claims that without that money we would've lost The State Journal way back then."

Gloria suddenly got up and began pacing back and forth, visibly upset. "Maybe it's time for you to know what really happened...way back then."

"Gloria!..No!..This is not the time!" Hattie said, firmly.

"Willard...leave the room for a minute," Gloria said. "Isn't Mel home?..Go visit with your cousin, Mel, for awhile."

"What?..Mother, what is wrong with you?" Willard asked, irritated. "I am not a child!"

'Willard!' Gloria raised her voice.

Willard quickly got up and angrily left the room. Roger also stood up, searching everyone's eyes. "If...if this is something you'd rather I not be involved in..."

"Sit down, Roger," Gene said.

"No...please, Roger," Gloria said, calmly. "This is strictly family...I'll talk to you tomorrow."

"Now just a minute!" Gene protested.

"No...Goodby, Roger...This is family," Hattie agreed.

Everyone waited patiently as Roger left the home. When they heard the front door close, Gloria continued...

"No one knows the real reason Mr. Dugas was so willing to lend dad that fifty thousand dollars except daddy, mamma and me," Gloria said, angrily. "And believe me it was not a damn loan!..It was more like a pay-off!"

"A pay-off?" Gene asked. "A pay-off for what?"

"It was a pay-off so we wouldn't reveal the father of the baby I was carrying," Gloria answered.

"Baby?..What baby?" Gene asked.

"Are you talking about Willard?" Patricia asked. "What's that got to do with the Dugas family?"

Gloria stopped nervously pacing the spacious dining room floor. She leaned on the dining room table with both hands and stared at everyone closely. "Willard's father was not my late husband," Gloria explained, carefully. "He was already conceived when I met Ben Thompson...Willard's real father is...F. Walton Dugas!..And that's why Dugas' father gave daddy that fifty thousand dollars!..It was hush money...not a damn loan!"

"You...you mean you and Dugas?" Gene asked, unbelieving. "I can't believe that!"

"You didn't believe in anything in those days," Gloria snapped.

"But when?" Gene asked. "How did he ever get the opportunity?"

"Just take my word for it, big brother, " Gloria answered, angrily. "You don't owe that bastard one red cent!"

"Does he know?" Gene asked, still shocked. "Does Dugas know he has a son?"

The room was dead silent as Gloria sat down at the head of the table and stared at everyone with her eyes blazing in anger! "No he doesn't ," she answered solemnly, "But if he keeps giving you a problem...he will!"

It was late in the evening at The Detroit Herald Newspaper offices as Gene prepared to leave. He took one last look at the latest ABC circulation figures laying on his desk and smiled. The daily newspaper business at The Detroit Herald had been going great for the last two months!..Circulation had increased by twenty percent and advertising revenue was doubled what had been projected!.. Gene Stanton was feeling great as he waved goodby to the janitors cleaning up his office suite and stepped to the rear of the waiting elevator. The elevator quietly descended to the next floor where it stopped and the door slid open. Adrian Grant stepped on and saw Gene standing by himself. A big smile crossed her face.

"Hi, Adrian," Gene said, grinning. "How's the job coming?"

"Just fine," she answered. "How have you been?"

"I'm alright...it's a fast pace but I love it."

"I can tell."

"You're here rather late tonight."

Adrian glanced at her watch. "I was trying to wait for the mechanic to deliver my car...I just called his shop and they're closed!..Now I'm in a mess!"

"You need a ride?" Gene asked. "I'd be happy to take you anywhere you want to go."

"Really?" Adrian asked, surprised. "I just might take you up on that offer...I have a townhouse on the other side of downtown."

When the elevator stopped in the lobby they both quickly stepped off and turned to each other.

"My car's in the executive garage down the street." Gene said. "It's just a block down, but it's raining a little...Do you mind?"

"Oh, that's OK...I'll walk with you. I like the rain."

They walked outside of the building and were greeted with an increased amount of rain. They both laughed and quickly headed towards the garage, partly running and walking briskly.

It was raining in a downpour when Adrian and Gene reached her townhouse. She opened the door and they quickly went inside. They both were soaking wet!..Adrian looked at Gene and smiled.

"Oh!..You're all wet!" she exclaimed. "I'm so sorry!"

Gene quickly took off his wrinkled suitcoat. Adrian took the coat from him and hung it up on the back of the door.

"I'm soaked!" Gene groaned.

"Why don't you take off that shirt?" she asked. "Let it dry a little and I'll iron it."

"I don't wanna put you through a lot of trouble."

"Nonsense...You got wet doing me a favor," Adrian said, taking the shirt from him. "It's the least I can do...I'll be right back. Why don't you fix us a drink?..I'll have the brandy."

Adrian quickly disappeared into the rear of the home. Gene went over to a small portable bar and began fixing the drinks. He started to look for some scotch but he couldn't find any. Adrian shouted from the back room.

"It's in the bottom cabinet...lower right corner."

Gene opened the lower right cabinet door and found a new unopened bottle of his favorite and very expensive scotch.

"Hey!..I'm in luck," Gene said. "You got my favorite scotch...Old Lighthouse."

Adrian came back into the room with a small bathrobe loosely wrapped around her.

"I know it's your favorite." she said, huskily. "That's why I bought it."

Gene turned around at the sound of her voice. He didn't realize she had walked back into the room. She stood there, smiling at him with the soft light in the room embellishing her gentle beauty as her long, black hair cascaded over her shoulders.

"Why did you buy it?..You didn't know I was coming over."

"I was hoping you would."

Gene handed Adrian her drink and slowly sipped his. He stared at her thoughtfully and shook his head.

"I like your hair like that," Gene said. "You make me feel like I was twenty years younger."

"I've been trying to see you."

"About what?"

"Us."

"Us?"

"Yes...I tried to work up the nerve to go up to your office in the ivory tower...but I couldn't think up any excuse that would make sense."

"Why did you want to see me?"

"You know I'm after you," she said, quietly.

Gene smiled. "What would you do with an old man like me?"

"I'd make love to you...that's what I'd do."

"There is a considerable age difference, you know."

"Age is a state of mind...And you know that as well as I do...Right now I'd say you're about thirty years old."

She paused, still staring at him. Waiting for a response.

"Adrian...as lovely as you are...I can't do anything about it...I'm married."

"That's your problem...I'm not."

She slowly set her drink down on the portable bar and moved closer to him. She put both of her arms around his neck and pressed her soft body against his. She could feel his hardness pressing against her as she stared into his eyes.

"Adrian...no...You don't know what you're doing."

Gene tried to step back but she continued to hold him, moving even closer and grinding her hips against him. She tilted her head up to his. Before he could react, she kissed him flush on his mouth, her tongue meeting his. Gene's arms quickly embraced her. They held the kiss, barely moving their heads as they savored each other for many moments. When they parted he stared at her, still holding her.

"Damn!..I like the way you make a point, lady!"

"I hope you enjoyed it as much as I did."

Gene gently placed his hands on her hips, slowly moving her back away from him.

"You better get my shirt," he mumbled.

"No...I want you to stay."

"I can't do that."

"Why not?"

"You better get my shirt."

"Am I moving too fast?"

"My shirt...please..."

Adrian stepped back and stared into his eyes. "Ok, Mr. Stanton...I'll get your shirt, but I'm not giving up... You're gonna think about that kiss tonight... you're gonna remember how it felt and...how it tasted...You're gonna think about it a long time...And remember...when you do...I'll be thinking about you, too!"

Gene stared at her and smiled as she slowly backed away, her eyes never leaving his!..

The building directly across the street from The Detroit Herald was formerly a local radio and television station that the Times Corporation had to diverge itself of in accordance with Federal Communications Commission's regulations. When they sold the building the new owners moved the radio and TV stations to a new, more modern complex a few blocks away. Most of the building remained vacant when the Times stopped publishing and with the exception of a few offices occupied by The Detroit Chamber of Commerce, it was virtually closed down.

Today, Damien quickly followed the caretaker down the long hallway of the office building. He waited patiently as the man fumbled with his large ring of keys and tried to open the door to a suite of vacant offices. Finally, the door opened and the two men walked inside the empty office. The caretaker quickly rushed over to the front windows and raised the shades allowing bright sunlight to flood into the rooms.

"This is one of our finest suite of offices. It was formerly used by an insurance company," the caretaker said, proudly. "Since it is a front office...if we do the painting and clean the carpet and drapes...you could get it for one thousand per month...As I said before, front offices are a bit higher."

"That'll be fine," Damien said as he walked from office to office. I'll pay the thousand...What's that building directly across the street?"

That's The Detroit Herald Newspaper...Are you in the newspaper business, Mr...?"

"Long...Mr. Long," Damien lied. "And no...I'm not in the newspaper business... I'm in personnel."

"You got an employment agency?" the caretaker asked.

"Yes...Something like that," Damien replied. "only we do mostly contract work."

Damien walked over to the front windows and looked out. He saw several large red trucks with the name, "The Herald", stenciled on the sides of the trucks in big, yellow block letters. The trucks were almost blocking the street.

"You understand, sir," the caretaker said, "We're only allowed to accept a one year's lease."

"I understand," Damien said as he motioned towards the front windows. "Those trucks always block up the street like that?"

Damien lifted up his briefcase, opened it and pulled out a pair of binoculars. "Do you mind?" Damien asked the caretaker. :"I just wanna survey the area."

"Those trucks are pickin' up the morning edition of The Herald," the caretaker said. "They'll be gone soon. You take your time and look over the area... I wanna make sure you're satisfied before we set up the lease."

Damien continued looking through the binoculars. He closely examined The Herald's building, each floor and each window until he stopped at a group of windows on the third floor. He saw Gene Stanton standing inside a large conference room addressing a group of people sitting at a long, gleaming conference table. Damien smiled and placed the binoculars back inside the briefcase and pulled out a large roll of bills. He quickly peeled off several large bills and handed them to the caretaker.

"This will do fine, friend!" Damien said, anxiously. "It's exactly what the doctor ordered!"

The caretaker looked from the windows back to Damien, surprised. Damien turned back to the windows and smiled broadly.

The luxurious Los Angeles hotel suite seemed to be exceptionally large and spacious to Kim Stanton, but it was the only space available to her and it was important to get this problem with Steve Dents finally settled, once and for all. She stood in front of the dresser mirror and finished dressing. Her partly unpacked luggage laid open on the huge bed. She applied the last touch of make-up as the sound of a soft knock on the door attracted her attention. She quickly opened the door and Steve Dents stood there leaning against the door frame, smiling... He strutted into the suite and reached out his arms to Kim. She angrily turned away, ignoring him.

"Hey!..What's goin' on?..Aren't you glad to see me?" Steve asked, surprised. "It's been almost two months...Don't I at least get a hug?"

"Get your hugs from your groupies!" Kim snapped.

Steve chuckled as he closed the door behind him and followed Kim into the suite.

"C'mon, Kim...can't you forgive and forget?" he pleaded. "It's all part of the job...I love you, baby...everybody knows that...Don't you remember what we've had together all these years?"

"It won't work this time, Steve!" Kim replied. "It was nice while it lasted but as soon as you cut that side with The Empress...everything changed!"

"Changed?..How?.."

"You were big time with a following of groupies that had to put you in bed every night and you loved it!..Everything changed after that...including us!"

"But that's all part of the job!..That's what they expect from rock'n roll stars!"

"I didn't expect it from you!"

"Then why did you come back?" Steve asked. " I know you still love me!"

"My agent called...I came back to read for a role...not to see you!"

"Then why call me?" he asked, smiling knowingly.

"To finally end this thing!" she answered as she tossed a ring at him. "It's over,

Steve!..Please don't make this any more difficult than it already is!..Stop calling me!..Stop sending me those damn flowers and leave me and my family alone!"

"I didn't have to come here for this!" Steve said, angrily.

"It seemed this was the only way you'd believe me," Kim shot back. "Face to face!"

"Is it that two-bit actor?" he asked. "I'll break his damn neck!"

"That's none of your business!"

"Word is out that he's been cast for the lead in that new Chadwick film...Is that what you're here for?"

"Drop dead!"

Steve quickly grabbed Kim by both shoulders and began shaking her violently with his eyes blazing in anger!

"So you think you're gonna drop me just like this, eh?..So you can start layin' around with Vic Martin...big time movie star!" Steve shouted, angrily. "Well, you listen to this, bitch!..No woman is gonna dump me like this and get away with it!..I don't care how many big-shot brothers you got!..I'll kick your ass and theirs, too!"

Steve roughly pulled Kim into his arms and forcibly kissed her, smearing her make-up!..She struggled with him until he suddenly released her with a sneer on his face!

"You're disgusting!" Kim cried. "I can't understand what I ever saw in you in the first place!..Get the hell outta here before I call security!"

Steve didn't move. He stared at her, still smiling. He slowly began unbuttoning his shirt and unzipping his trousers. "I'm gonna leave you with a little something, bitch!" he smirked, angrily. "Something you won't ever forget!"

He moved towards her as she backed up, frightened!..He quickly began slapping her face, knocking her back on the bed. Blood seeped from the corner of her mouth, dripping on to the bedspread!..He began laughing hysterically!..He jerked off his shirt and pounced on top of her, grabbing her blouse and ripping it in half!..

"No!..No!..Don't do this!" Kim screamed, loudly.

"Shuddup, you dumb bitch!" he snarled as he pulled at her skirt. "I'm gonna give you a screwin' like you've never had before!"

There was suddenly a loud knock at the door of the suite.

"Go away, goddammit!" Steve shouted angrily.

"Kim!..Kim!..What's goin' on in there?" a muffled voice shouted. "It's me...Joe...Let me in!"

Steve quickly froze!..He slowly got up off of Kim and backed up, frightened!..He began to put his clothes back on as he looked at Kim with fear in his eyes!..She glared at him smiled as the knocking became louder!

"Don't tell him anything!..He'll kill me!" Steve pleaded.

"I think you better leave, Steve," she said, composing herself. "And you're probably right...he would kill you!"

"Kim!..Kim!.." Joe shouted, angrily. "Open this damn door, Steve or I'm comin' through it!"

Kim quickly got up and opened the door. Joe stood in the doorway, furious!..He looked from Kim to Steve, angrily!

"What the hell's been goin' on in here?" Joe demanded.

"St...Steve was just leaving," Kim stammered.

Joe noticed the trickle of blood in the corner of Kim's month and her torn blouse. His eyes flashed in anger and he completely lost control when he realized what had almost happened to his sister!..He slowly turned to Steve who was cowering against the wall!..

"You hit my sister?" Joe shouted, disbelieving. "You sonofabitch, you!.. You tried to rape my sister, didn't you?"

"Now wait a minute, big brother," Steve pleaded, backing away from Joe! "Don't lose your cool!"

Joe moved like a flash of lightning with a spinning reverse kick to Steve's throat!..Steve staggered backwards as Joe followed with a front kick to his groin that bent him over, setting Steve up with a perfectly timed reverse punch to Steve's head. His eyes rolled back in his head and blood gushed from his mouth as he crumbled to the floor! Joe lifted him up and propped him against the wall as Steve tried to beg for mercy!..Joe began pummeling his body, slugging him like a heavyweight boxer, over and over!..Kim pleaded with Joe to stop as Steve fell to one knee with blood dripping from his mouth!..Joe was in another zone as he kicked Steve directly in the face, sending him sprawling towards the doorway! Joe pushed Kim out of his way as he grabbed Steve by the nape of his neck as he was crawling out of the doorway!..Joe easily threw Steve down the hallway as Kim continued to scream!..Doors to other suites were opened and quickly closed as Joe calmly followed the crawling Steve as he tried to get away from Joe!..Everytime Steve would manage to get to his knees, Joe would kick him in his butt, sending him sprawling on his face again!..Joe was cursing and shouting with each blow!

"You were gonna rape my sister, eh?" Joe continued to shout as he delivered blow after blow!.."You gonna rape my sister?..You gonna rape my sister?..You think you're a big man...beatin' up on women!"

Joe kicked him again!..When they reached the end of the long hallway, in front of the elevator, Steve's face was a grotesque, bloody pulp!..The elevator door slid open and the occupants froze in terror at the grisly scene!..

"If I ever hear of you botherin' my sister again... I'll kill you!.." Joe shouted angrily as he threw Steve into the elevator!..

The people standing in the elevator looked on in horror as Joe dusted off his hands!..He stared back at the people as Steve groaned in pain.

"Take care of this garbage for me!" Joe said, just before the elevator door slid closed!..

Chapter Eight

Over the last six months The Detroit Herald Newspaper had continued it's phenomenal success!..The circulation had increased to almost 300,000 home delivered newspapers! The advertising throughout the entire newspaper had almost doubled with the introduction of the slick, four color, Sunday Fashion Section. The Fashion Section was so successful, The Herald had started carrying a smaller, black and white, self-contained fashion section on Wednesdays and the advertisers who couldn't wait to get into the Sunday fashion magazine, jumped at the chance to be included in the weekly edition!..In addition to those innovations, Gene had pursued other ideas to increase the Sunday circulation. He had enlarged the size of the Sunday TV magazine to the size of the average movie magazine to accommodate more different sized ads. He increased the size of the entertainment staff and used slick, glossy stock.

The meeting that Gene had called today was to introduce another innovation to stimulate the Sunday circulation and increase advertising accounts. Although The Herald published the regular Sunday comics that every major daily newspaper across the country published, Gene had came up with the idea of a self-contained comic book as an additional bonus with each Herald Sunday Newspaper with advertising directed towards teenagers such as jeans, tennis shoes, sports equipment, music videos, motion pictures and fast food franchises. Gene projected that with this latest innovation, The Detroit Herald could rapidly become a model for other daily newspapers from coast to coast!..This new change would also be sure to boost The Herald's Sunday circulation!

Many of The Herald's corporate executives, department heads and editors sat calmly at the long conference table, talking quietly as they waited for the publisher's arrival. In a few minutes there was a commotion out in the hallway as Gene Stanton, followed by Roger Carlson, Gene II and several members of the publishing staff, quickly marched into the spacious room. The staff members began setting up presentation easels and placing covered charts on aluminum stands. Gene took his place at the head of the table while Roger sat on his right and Gene II sat on his left

Gene smiled, acknowledging several people as he waited for the polite chatter to die down. When he had everyone's attention be began.

"Ladies and gentlemen...I called this special meeting because of two important developments that have recently occurred. These events could insure the ultimate success of our newspaper as well as revolutionize newspaper publishing in this country...First, Mr., McConnell, our Circulation Director, has a few words...George?.."

A small bald headed man, neatly dressed in a gray pinstriped suit, quickly walked to the head of the table and proudly stood next to Gene, smiling.

"Thank you, Mr. Stanton," Mr. McConnell said as he turned and unveiled one of the charts. Using a pointer, he began his presentation. "As you all can plainly see, this represents the latest Audit Bureau of Circulation figures. When we first began publishing The Herald, we were estimated as having approximately 208,000 paid circulation...compared with our chief rival, The Daily Press' circulation on Sunday of 604,000...Two curious changes have taken place since that time..."

McConnell turned and uncovered the other side of the chart. "Our circulation has grown almost 90,000 while the Press' Sunday circulation has dropped considerably...over 50,000...And our records indicate that the only thing we have done during that period that The Press has not done, is publish the Sunday Fashion Magazine and the fashion section on Wednesdays...That alone seems to be responsible for this surge in our circulation and the decrease in circulation for The Daily Press!.."

Several people began applauding and spontaneously started chattering as the excitement permeated the large room. Gene stood up and shook George McConnell's hand, firmly. He waited for the noise to subside and for George to return to his seat at the long table.

"Thank you, George...That was a fine job," Gene said, directing his attention to the rest of the people. "And not only are our customers happy to be receiving these sections...the advertisers are lining up for it!..We now have a two year waiting list of advertisers who want to get into both fashion sections!..I think this shows that those readers out there, the public, wants new innovations in newspaper publishing!.. But I think we can expect to be copied by The Daily Press...They have access to the same information we have...but we're gonna stay a jump ahead of ' em!"

"How can we do that?" someone shouted.

Gene smiled knowingly and eyed everyone closely as he continued. "The comic sections in the Sunday papers all across the country are all the same...Some haven't changed much since the turn of the century! We've gone through two world wars, the atomic age and the space age...but we're still publishing the same old, tired comics!..I am proposing...

Just as Gene spoke those last words there was a loud sound of a volley of rifle fire and the shattering of window glass as shots ricocheted throughout the conference room!..Everyone jumped up and some dove for cover as they all began screaming and hollering for their lives!..Gene's body was spent around in mid-air and hurled across the room from the impact of the bullets!..Chaos was everywhere as people began scrambling back and forth, hysterically shouting, while Gene II and Roger knelt down and held Gene's limp body in their arms!

"Oh, my GOD!.. Somebody call 911" Gene II screamed! "My father's been shot!..Hurry!..Godammit, Hurry!"

In a few minutes the sounds of sirens wailing in the distance could be heard as the frightened people all crowded around their fallen publisher, in shock and bewilderment!...

An ambulance with it's siren screaming, squeeched to a halt in front of City Hospital's Emergency Entrance as doctors and attendants flung open the rear doors of the vehicle and quickly removed the patient, placing him on a waiting gurney. As the crew moved quickly and efficiently into the emergency room entrance, Gene II, his suit splattered with blood, climbed out of the ambulance and followed the crew. Gene II was dazed and shocked as they rushed through the swinging doors!..Several doctors, nurses and attendants, on both sides of the gurney, worked feverishly and shouted orders, trying to save Gene's life!..Gene II watched, unmoving, as nurses cut away his father's clothing. Another doctor rushed over to the busy scene!..

"Is this the gunshot victim?" the first doctor asked.

"Yes...just above the heart...massive bleeding!" a second doctor answered.

"JESUS!..What'd they use...a cannon?"

"This doesn't look too good!"

"Get him ready!..They're waiting for him!" the first doctor ordered. "We don't have too much time!"

Gene II was shoved away from his father's side as the crew sped up the procedures. Gene II watched from across the room until they finally wheeled his father away. In a few minutes the first doctor came out of the operating room and walked over to Gene II.

"Mr. Stanton..I'm Dr. Woods," the doctor said. "All I can tell you is that they're operating right now!..They'll do their best to save him...How did this happen?"

"We don't really know...We were having a staff meeting and then all of a sudden...those damn shots were everywhere! This is awful!..He's got to make it!" Gene II began crying.

"It's too early to say," Dr. Woods said, sadly. "He was hit twice...just above the heart...A little lower...and it's all over!.."

"Oh, my GOD!" Gene II sobbed.

"Aren't you...Is that Gene Stanton in there?" Dr. Woods asked. " The newspaper publisher?"

"Yes...I'm his son."

"We just started taking The Herald," Dr. Woods said. He looked at Gene II's clothes. "Wow!..You're a mess!..You wanna clean up somewhere?..I could get you a coat or something."

Gene II turned away in disgust, just in time to see Roger bursting into the emergency room!..The two men embraced, warmly.

"How...How's he doin?" Roger asked.

"It's too early to tell," Gene II answered. He was hit twice...just above the heart...they're operating now!"

"I called your mother...They should be here any minute."

"They find out who did it?"

"It came from a vacant office across the street," Roger replied. "Looks professional. The police are still there. They think he's still in the area."

Gene II couldn't hold back his anguish any longer!

"The Bastard!" he shouted angrily, pounding his fist against the wall. "The dirty bastard!"

"Take it easy!.. The rest of the family will be here soon," Roger whispered. "They'll be looking to you for strength...compose yourself!"

"I'm Dr. Woods, one of the attending physicians," Dr. Woods said to Roger. "I was on duty when they brought Mr. Stanton in...You are?.."

"Carlson...Roger Carlson...I'm the corporate counselor and a very close friend of the family."

"I was just telling Mr. Stanton, here, I could get him a coat," Dr. Woods said. "Find him a place to clean up...it won't look so bad when the family gets here...Besides, that operation might take three or four hours."

"I understand, doctor...Thank you." Roger replied. "Is there a waiting room where we could take the family?"

"Yes...I'll have someone show you where it is."

Roger turned back to Gene II who just leaned back against the wall with his eyes closed.

"You alright?" Roger asked, concerned. "Can you handle it?"

"Yeah...I'm OK," Gene II mumbled. "I'll just clean up a little...before they get here."

• • •

The entire Stanton family except for Joe and Kim, sat in the family waiting room as the surgeon, Dr. McBride, and Dr. Woods, spoke to them explaining Gene's grave condition."

"Mr. Stanton has just undergone a quadruple bypass operation," Dr. McBride said, calmly. "The two rounds went completely through his body, but there was massive damage to the arteries...We replaced the damaged arteries with veins from his legs...As far as we're concerned...the operation was a success...however, we're far from being out of the woods."

"How are his vital signs?" Dr. Robert Whyte asked.

"Oh...Hi, Bob...I've been so busy... I forgot this was your family," Dr. McBride said, apologetically. "His vital signs are all stable...We're in good shape there...but your father-in-law has lost a lot of blood...As you know, Bob, normally we wouldn't have operated on a patient that weak from the loss of so much blood...but...in this case...we simply had no choice."

"I understand." Bob replied.

"Just be honest, Doctor," Karen said, firmly. "Will my father make it or not?"

"If he survives the next forty-eight hours...He'll stand a good chance."

"Oh, My GOD!" Patricia sobbed as Mel placed an arm around his mother's shoulders, comforting her.

"He'll make it, mom," Mel whispered, softly. "Dad is strong...he's a fighter!"

Your son's right, mam," Dr. McBride said. " He is in excellent condition...He's in recovery now...As soon as we get him up in Intensive Care I'll arrange for you to see him. He'll still be out...but I think you may feel better if you saw him."

Dr. Robert Whyte turned to Patricia. "I'll arrange for you to stay here...as long as you want...You can use my office."

"My poor boy!..Who could have done this to him?" Hattie cried out, loudly. "Everything was just coming together. The paper was doing so well!"

Liz looked at her grandmother and began crying also. She quickly got up and left the room. Gene II just laid back on the deep cushioned sofa and straight ahead as his wife, Susan, dabbed at the moisture filling his eyes. At the rear of the room, Roger Carlson's eyes met Gloria's. She quickly turned her head and stared out of the window down at the slow moving traffic. Roger slowly made his way over to her.

"Has anyone called Kim or Joe?" he asked her.

"Yes...Kim's on her way...She said Joe just flew back to Washington two days ago," Gloria answered, huskily.

"Joe was in L.A.?"

"He had to testify in a federal case out there."

"Has anyone contacted him?"

"We left word with CIA headquarters in Washington...They said they'd take care of it."

Gloria turned and looked Roger directly in his eyes, searching for an answer. "You any idea who's responsible for this?"

"No...The police are still checking...It looks professional...but they really have no idea who could have done this."

Gloria turned back to the window with a determined look on her face as she nervously bit her bottom lip. "They don't, eh?" she mumbled. "Well...I Do!"

The Central Intelligence Agency's building in Washington, D.C. was dark in most of it's offices as night fell. With the exception of a few lights scattered throughout the upper floors, the building was closed down for the night.

Joe Stanton used his identification card in the slit provided at the side entrance of the building and the door slid open. He stepped on the elevator in a calm manner, wondering what was so important that he was ordered back downtown at this late hour. When he walked into his commander's office he was greeted by a large man sitting behind a wide desk. The man took off his bifocals, rubbed his eyes and stared at Joe thoughtfully as Joe sat down in front of him.

"What's the matter, Walt?" Joe asked. "You don't look so good."

"We're gonna change your assignment for awhile," Walt replied. "The chief wants to keep new blood in the middle east."

"They weren't happy with the action at the supply depot?"

"No complaints...we were commended by the French government. You did more than we could've expected...A very fine job."

"So?..What's this about a new assignment?" Joe asked, visibly irritated. "You said when I got back from L.A...I could take a few comp days."

"It's the Neo-Nazis...We gotta put a net on those nuts before they start some kinda war!"

"What'd they do now?"

"We got passage for you to return home right away," Walt said, glancing at his watch. "I'd say you got about thirty minutes to catch your flight."

"What?..You're sending me home?" Joe asked, surprised. "I thought you just said something about the Neo-Nazis?"

"I did...we're not sure yet...but all evidence points to them trying to assassinate...your father!" Walt continued quickly, putting up his hands. "Now hold on!..just listen!"

Joe quickly stood up, angry and startled by Walt's words "My father!..What happened to my father?" Joe demanded, angrily. "What the hell is this all about?"

"Your dad's been shot, Joe," Walt answered, calmly. "Our reports say he's in bad condition...but he's holding his own...I want you to join your family at City Hospital in Detroit...right away!..One of the guys has a limo downstairs waiting to take you to the airport!"

"What?..How the hell did..."

"No more questions," Walt interrupted. "You know as much about it as I do...Just call us as soon as you get there!..And good luck, Joe...I understand you got one heck of an old man!"

Walter stood up, reached across his desk and shook Joe's hand with a firm grip. Joe, still stunned by the news, hesitated, nodded back at Walter, then quickly turned and left.

    The two police officers carefully walked across the top of the building directly across the street from The Herald. They moved cautiously with guns drawn. They searched every vent hood and behind each air conditioning unit. Below, down in the streets surrounding The Herald building, police cars blocked the intersections as sirens could be heard off in the distance. The police had been ordered to search and research every square inch of the vacant building. They still believed the gunman was somewhere in the area.

    Officers Delaney and Mack became disgusted in turning up any evidence of the assassin. Everytime they reported that they didn't find anything, they were sent back up on top of the roof.

    "This is the third time we been sent up here," Delaney groaned, "And we still ain't found a rat's ass!"

    "Yeah...after all this time...I think he's probably long gone," Officer Mack said.

    As the two policemen walked near the edge of the roof they suddenly heard a slight scratching sound!..They stopped and stared at each other!

    "You hear that, Mack?..Where's it comin' from?"

    Mack began walking along the edge of the roof slowly as he closely examined the concrete molding decorating the top of the building's Gothic design. "I'm not sure, Art...sounds like it might be a little further down," he whispered softly. "You still hear it?"

    "Nah...can't hear anything now."

    Suddenly they heard the sound of a loud moan, deep breathing, and a weak, faltering voice, pleading!..The two policemen froze and tried to figure out where it was coming from!..

    "OOoohhhh!..Help me!" a voice cried, weakly. "Please...help me!"

    "You hear that?" Mack shouted, excitedly. "Where the hell is it comin' from?..I still don't see anybody!"

    Art Delaney quickly walked over to the corner of the building. He pointed to an object laying in the shadows beneath the decorative molding running along the outside edge of the roof. "What's that over there?" Art asked. "It wasn't there before!..Well I'll be damned!..It's a rifle!"

    The two policemen carefully picked up the rifle and closely examined it, being careful not to disturb or destroy and fingerprints.

    "I'm sure this wasn't here before!..You think this is it?" Mack asked.

    "It smells like it's just been fired...I'd bet my weekly paycheck on it!" Art answered. "Listen!..There it goes again!"

    "Over here!..Please!.." the voice pleaded, louder than before. "I can't hold on much longer!"

    The two policemen looked in the direction of the sound of the voice in the corner of the building where they saw the back of the heads of two gigantic, concrete lions that were facing the street. In between the two heads they saw two bloody hands clinging to the concrete molding and slowly losing their grip as they began to slide off!..Before the policemen can reach the corner and grab the hands, they see them disappear from the edge leaving a smear of blood!..The policemen stopped and stood in terror until the silence is broken by a sickening thud!..They rushed over to the edge and stared down into the street! They saw several newspaper trucks and police cars, some parked at odd angles, blocking the streets. The wide, open bed newspaper trucks were lined up in front of the building, waiting to be inspected by uniformed policemen and waved on to deliver their newspapers. The two policemen standing on the roof carefully perused the entire area, then stared at each other, unbelieving that they couldn't find a body!..

"Where the hell is he?" Art asked, shaking his head. "I swear he fell from this ledge!..Look at the blood smeared all over the molding!..That's why we didn't see 'em...He musta been hidin' between those two lions, hangin' from that molding for a long time!"

Mack continued carefully looking over the street before he spoke. "This is weird!..The only thing I can figure is that he fell into one of those newspaper trucks that's what happened!..Our man is probably on his way to be delivered!..C'mon...we'd better alert the sergeant!"

The Teamster's Union and The Detroit Herald's management agreed in the union contract that each newspaper delivery truck must have a driver and a jumper deliver each truck load of newspapers. The suburban shopping centers always received the first editions of The Herald for street sales at the newspaper boxes. When the large Detroit Herald Newspaper truck pulled up in front of a suburban newspaper sub-station it was lightly raining. Two muscular men quickly climbed down out of the cab of the truck, laughing and joking as they sipped coffee from styrofoam cups and casually walked back to the rear of the vehicle to began unloading the newspapers. The two men tossed their coffee cups into a trash bin nearby, removed the rear gate on the truck and began tossing off stacks of newspapers. Suddenly, both men froze as they stared at the blood stains all over the newspapers!..

"Hey! These papers are ruined!" the driver shouted, angrily. "There's blood all over 'em!"

"JESUS!..How in the hell did that happen?" the jumper asked. "We can't deliver this mess!..You think this has somethin' to do with ol' man Stanton's shooting?"

"I don't think it!..I know it!" the driver snapped, anxiously. "That's why they were inspectin' our trucks!"

"Then why didn't they spot this mess?"

"Cause he wasn't here when they inspected," the driver answered. "He probably climbed up here after they Ok'd our truck. When we pulled away he was probably back here...and as soon as we were far enough away...he jumped off!"

The jumper nodded his head, thoughtfully, and climbed up into the truck, staring at all the blood smeared on top of the newspapers. His eyes followed the huge globs of blood until he saw a crumpled figure laying between and partially under several stacks of newspapers near the front of the truck bed! "I got news for ya!..He didn't jump off!"

"Wh...What?"

"He's still here... and it looks like he's dead!..This man ain't breathin!..You better call the cops, Dennis!..Tell 'em we got the guy who shot Gene Stanton!"

Gene Stanton was hooked up to several instruments, tubes and machines. He was breathing with great difficulty as Patricia sat next to him and held his hand while she sobbed quietly. The ominous sounds of the life support systems and the slow, constant beeping of the heart machine dominated the room as the nurses and attendants moved about noiselessly and efficiently. Liz comforted Patricia and gently wiped away the moisture from her mother's cheeks. Hattie sat calmly on the other side of the bed and stared down at her son, silently. Liz whispered in her mother's ear.

"Don't worry, mom...he's strong," Liz whispered, softly. "Dad's gonna make it...I hear Joe and Kim are here...They're outside in the hall...Don't you want to see them?"

"I...I guess I better, hon," Patricia said, thoughtfully. "I know they're worried about their father...Yes, you're right...I guess I should."

Liz led her mother out of the room slowly. Just as they reached the hallway Kim and Joe rushed over and tenderly embraced their mother. Kim, crying loudly, buried her face into her mother's bosom as Joe's arms encircled them both!

"Oh, mamma!..mamma!.." Kim cried. "Is he gonna be alright?..oh, please LORD!"

"Hey...Dad's gonna make it, mom," Joe said, calmly. "Just hold on...he's a strong man...it'll be alright!"

"I'm so glad you're both here...You better go see your father!" Patricia cried, softly. "We don't know how much...You better go see him now...Let him know that you're here!"

Kim and Joe followed their mother back into intensive care while the rest of the family remained in the hallway, waiting patiently and sadly as they quietly sipped endless cups of coffee...

Later that evening the entire Stanton family sat in Dr. Robert Whyte's office at City Hospital. As Chief of Surgery, Robert was in a position to answer all of their questions and render professional advice on Gene's condition. Everyone listened attentively as Robert explained.

"His condition has improved a little, but essentially it's still the same," Robert said, slowly. "We won't be able to give you a clear reading until the next twenty-four hours. The operation was extremely successful. His blood pressure is good...No signs of clotting...no signs of any pneumonia. If we can make it through the next twenty-four hours...I think we'll be out of the woods."

"When do you expect him to regain consciousness?" Karen asked.

"Anytime now," Robert answered. "He was heavily sedated but I expect him to wake up anytime, hon."

"Will he have any pain...or permanent damage?" Joe asked.

"No signs of any brain damage or paralysis...They got to him fast...there was no stoppage of blood circulation."

"If he continues to recover...how long will he be...You know, Bob...incapacitated?" Patricia asked. "He hates laying in bed for any length of time."

"Knowing your husband, Pat...It won't be too long," Robert said, smiling. "And again...I can't overstate the one fact on our side."

"What's that?" Mel asked.

"He's in excellent condition!"

"Thank GOD for that!" Kim whispered, softly.

"Do they have any lead on who might have done this?" Robert asked, anyone.

"The police tracked him to the roof of the building across the street from The Herald," Joe answered. "They think he may have fallen or jumped off the building...They've recovered the rifle that was used...but so far...they haven't found any sign of his body...I'm sure they'll get him."

Suddenly a blue light on Robert's wall started flashing as an excited female voice came on the public address system. Robert quickly stood up behind his desk!..

"Code Blue!..Northwest I.C.U.!..Code Blue!" the voice shouted urgently. "Northwest ICU!..Code Blue!..Northwest ICU!..Code Blue!..STAT!..STAT!..STAT!"

Robert stared at the Stantons and quickly turned, headed for his office door!..He stopped and turned back to the startled family!

"We'd better go!" Robert said, anxiously. "I think that's him!"

The entire family, all with worried and concerned expressions on their faces, quickly followed Robert out of the office!..

Several doctors and nurses rushed in and out of the Intensive Care Unit as a group of doctors crowded around Gene's bed and worked ferverishly!..The Stanton family, all nervous and tense, stood anxiously in the hallway, waiting for some word. Liz and Kim stood next to Patricia and comforted her as she leaned back against the wall and trembled in fear!..Hattie, Gloria, and Karen paced back and forth and kept their eyes glued to the doors of ICU. The three Stanton brothers huddled with Roger Carlson and spoke in quiet, hushed tones. Finally, several doctors, nurses and attendants walked out of the unit, expressionless. Dr. Robert Whyte slowly walked out of the unit and over to Patricia. By the time he reached her, everyone in the family crowded around them. Bob looked Patricia directly in the eyes and smiled.

THE WINDS OF TOMORROW

"Is...Is he alright?" Patricia asked.

"He's alright!..He just regained consciousness," Robert said, smiling broadly. "I think we're out of the woods!"

"Wh...what happened?" Liz asked. "Why all the excitement?"

"He's coming and going," Robert replied, chuckling. "He woke up and disconnected his life support systems and slipped back into unconsciousness!..He's unbelievable!"

Thank GOD!.."a relieved Patricia sighed. "Can I see him?"

"Is he conscious now?" Liz asked. "Can I see him, too?"

"Alright!" Mel shouted to the world. "My ol' man's gonna make it!"

"Yeah, Mel...I think you're right!" Robert said, losing his professional mannerism and grinning broadly. "Sure you can see him, Liz...You can all see him...but just a few at a time...please."

Joe Stanton sat in the hospital cafeteria at a large table, by himself. He sipped a cup of coffee and pondered his father's condition. In a few minutes he was joined by his sister-in-law, Susan. She sat down across from Joe and stirred her coffee, thoughtfully.

"Wow!..That's a relief!" Susan said, sighing. "It looks like your dad's gonna be OK!..It's good you and Kim could be here."

"Yeah...We damn near lost him." Joe said.

"It's good to see you again, Joe...I've really missed you," she said, placing her hand on top of his. "This is terrible!..What are we going to do?"

"We don't have any choice...You shouldn't be here, Susan. I thought you and Gene were going to New York."

"He still refuses to leave," Susan snapped. "Now he's deeply involved with The Herald...When I saw you last night...I almost broke down."

"I know...I felt the same way," Joe said. "But don't worry...I'll stay away as much as I can."

"But I don't want you to stay away!' she protested. "I can't handle this thing any longer!"

"You've got to handle it!..As soon as I'm sure dad's OK...I'm outta here!"

"That won't help!..Each day...each night...you're constantly on my mind! All those afternoons in your arms...I can never forget!"

Joe quickly stood up, preparing to leave. "We've got to forget it, Susan!..It was a mistake..He's my brother...and I'll never forgive myself!..You stay here until I go back up to dad's room."

"Joe!..Please...just a few more minutes!"

Joe ignored her pleadings as he turned and quickly walked out of the spacious cafeteria. She stared after him, longingly!..

Gene Stanton laid in his hospital bed with his eyes partly closed as Patricia, Hattie and Gene II stood nearby, watching him. Patricia reached out and gently stroked his forehead. Gene's eyes blinked as he tried to focus. A big smile creased his face as he recognized his family.

"Gene!..Gene!..Can you hear me?" Patricia asked.

"Uh, huh...I'm OK," he whispered, weakly.

"You have any pain, son?" Hattie asked.

"I don't feel a thing," Gene replied. "What day is it?"

"It's Friday, dad," Gene II answered. "Three A.M."

"We all set for the Sunday edition?" Gene asked, sleepily.

Gene II was surprised. "Er...ah...well, no, dad," he stammered. "I haven't been at the office for a few days."

Gene closed his eyes. "You better!..Gotta put that Sunday paper to bed!" He suddenly opened his eyes again. "And another thing, Gene...there's something else."

"What's that, dad?"

"The next time you write a controversial editorial," Gene said, sleepily, "give me a warning so I can duck!" With that last statement he closed his eyes and drifted off to sleep.

Gene II, Hattie and Patricia looked at each other with big smiles on their faces. Hattie wiped the tears from her eyes and held Patricia's hand as Gene II walked proudly out into the hallway to the rest of the family.

All of the Stantons were relieved that the crisis was finally over. They sipped coffee and relaxed as Gene II snapped his briefcase closed and prepared to leave.

"Where you going?" Mel asked, surprised.

"I'm going back to the office...We got a Sunday paper to put out...remember?"

"Mind if I go with you?" Liz asked.

"Kim and I would like to tag along, too," Joe said. "I've never even seen the building."

"Count me in," Karen said, cheerfully. "I've got some work to catch up on."

"Good idea...Why don't we all go together?" Gene asked, smiling. C'mon, Mel...You guys can help me...Mamma and grandma will keep an eye on dad...You know what dad just said?..We got a Sunday paper to put to bed!"

The six Stanton brothers and sisters happily walked down the hospital corridor smiling broadly, arm in arm, as everyone passing by ... stared at them in amazement!

Chapter Nine

It was an early fall afternoon and the chattering of squirrels was only inter mit-tently interrupted by the rustling of leaves as they were gently rearranged by a soft autumn wind. The huge trees surrounding the Stanton mansion stood like protective sentries as the multi-colors of the season enhanced the beauty of nature's gradual change.

An automobile slowly drove down the long, circular driveway, coming to a stop in front of the wide, pillared, vine covered front porch of the great home. Gene II, his wife, Susan and their three children climbed out of the car, walked upon the porch and rang the doorbell. In a few moments, Connie answered, smiling, and they walked inside the massive front door as the three children scampered down the wide hallway. Susan quickly tried to restrain the children as Connie grinned broadly.

"Now don't make too much noise," Susan cautioned her children. "Remember, your grandfather is very ill."

Gene II turned to Connie with great concern. "How's he doin?.. Is everything alright?"

"No problems... He was screaming for his coffee early this morning," Connie answered. "It won't be long before he's back to normal."

"Can we go see granddaddy?" Gene III asked, anxiously. Patricia walked into the hallway and happily hugged her three grandchildren. "I thought I heard you three out here!" Patricia gushed, happily. "Give your grandmother a big kiss!"

She hugged and kissed the three children as they laughed and giggled. Gene II and Susan watched proudly.

"Hi, mom," Gene II said. "How's he doin?"

"He's doin' just great!.. He's been lookin' forward to this visit."

"Are you sure the kids won't be too much?" Susan asked. "He just got home and I didn't want..."

" If he didn't see his grandkids he'd really throw a fit!" Patricia interrupted. "Go on up, kids!.. He's waitin' for you!"

The children quickly ran up the stairs as Patricia turned back to her son and his wife. They all began to laugh as they followed the children up the wide, winding staircase.

"That jerk who shot him isn't doin' too good," Gene II said, thoughtfully.

"I hope they throw the book at him!" Patricia said, angrily. "Where'd he come from?..What's his grudge against your father?"

"The police think he's a professional hit man," Gene II answered. "He hasn't regained consciousness...still in a coma, so they haven't been able to question him."

"They haven't even identified him yet," Susan said, in disgust. "He might die first...then we'd never find out who was behind this!"

When they walked into the spacious master bedroom they found the three children sitting on the bed and talking to their smiling grandfather. Gene II walked over to the bed and shook his father's hand, grinning broadly. " Hey, big guy...you're lookin' pretty fit...wanna go a couple of rounds?"

"Naw...I might hurt you," Gene answered, chuckling. "I feel like I've been hit in the chest with a bulldozer!"

"You look great," Susan said. "Is everything alright?"

"If I could get them...to stop treating me like an invalid, everything would be OK," Gene answered. "They'll probably try to potty train me next!..How's our newspaper doin?"

"Don't worry about the newspaper, your kids are taking good care of it," Patricia replied, looking at Gene II and Susan. "The doctor said he shouldn't be too active or even talk about the office...That was a terrible ordeal he went through."

"C'mon, Pat!..Lighten up," Gene protested weakly. "I don't have to be babied...I can still stand up and pee!"

The three children began laughing loudly.

"Mom's right...maybe the kids should go downstairs now so you can get your rest," Gene II said. "They just wanted to see you to make sure you were OK."

"AAaawww, daddy!" Arielle complained. "We just got here!"

"Me, too!" Gene III protested.

"Hey, wait a minute!" Gene responded. "I haven't had a chance to tell 'em about my adventure."

"Granddaddy play horsey?" Kevin asked, jumping up and down on the bed.

"I'd better take them downstairs before they upset you," Susan said, leading the three children towards the door. "We'll just stop in and say hello to Hattie."

"Granddaddy play horsey?" Kevin, the youngest cried.

"No...Granddaddy can't play horsey for a long time," Susan answered as they went down the hall.

Gene looked at his son with a serious expression on his face. "What did you get on the shooter?..Who's he working for?"

"Dunno, yet...He's still out of it...in a deep coma."

"Damn!..It's been more than a week!..What are the police sayin?"

"They suspect he was hired by some right wing terrorist group," Gene II answered," to stop you from publishing a major daily newspaper...and to serve a warning to any others who might try!"

Gene turned his head in anger, staring out of the window. "Hell!..That wouldn't stop The Herald from being published!..Don't they know how many we are?"

"And that's not all."

Gene looked up at his son, studying his face closely.

"What else?"

"They haven't identified the man yet...They have no idea who he is or who hired him."

"What about his fingerprints?" Patricia asked.

"That's just it, mom," Gene II answered. "The man has no fingerprints...they have all been surgically removed. A real pro...whoever hired him wanted the job done right!"

"He came close," Gene said.

"The police are very concerned, dad...They feel that if they, whoever they are, went through all of this trouble to hire a professional assassin to stop you...they'll try it again!"

"Oh, My GOD!" Patricia choked, putting her hands up to her mouth in fear!

The Intensive Care Unit at City Hospital was busy. The public address system paged several doctors as nurses, attendants and patients walked up and down the wide hospital corridor. A policeman guarded one room particularly close, even peeking through the small window in the door every now and then. Inside the room, Damien laid on the bed unconscious and handcuffed to the railing on the side of the bed. He was hooked up to several life support machines and devices. The policeman opened the door to the room and allowed a nurse and two male hospital attendants into the room. After the policeman removed the handcuffs, the two attendants methodically turned the patient over, under the watchful eyes of the nurse who managed the disconnecting and reconnecting of the I.V. and other devices. The policeman placed the handcuffs back on the patient and walked out of the room. When the nurse and the attendants were about to leave the room, the sudden loud moaning of the patient attracted them back to his bedside.

"Hey!.. He's coming out of it!" an attendant said.

"It sure looks like it," the nurse answered, excitedly. "One of you stay here and I'll get the doctor...Let me know if there's any change...I'll be right back."

The nurse and one attendant quickly left the room as Damien began moaning again. The remaining attendant watched him nervously.

"Hey, mister...can you hear me?" the attendant asked.

Damien groaned louder. His eyes slowly blinked opened. He glared at the attendant and searched his surroundings, suspiciously. He tried to move his arm until he realized he was handcuffed to the bed railing. He stared at the attendant in anger!

"Wh...Who the hell are you?" Damien asked, weakly.

"I'd better get the doctor!" the attendant replied. Just as he turned to leave. Damien grabbed his wrist!..

"Where am I?"

"City Hospital...Intensive Care Unit," the attendant replied, frightened. "You're a police prisoner."

Damien let go of the man's wrist and tried to rise up from the bed until he realized his leg was handcuffed too!

"I got to get the hell outta here!" Damien snarled, as he wiggled the handcuffs. He froze when the uniformed figure of the policeman filled the doorway!

"Forget it!" the policeman growled, angrily. "You ain't goin' nowhere, buddy!"

Gene II, his wife and children were getting ready to leave after the visit with his father. Hattie and Patricia walked with them down the hallway leading to the front vestibule. Gene II anxiously glanced at his watch.

"We'd better get goin," Gene II said. "I've got an editorial meeting scheduled this afternoon."

"Did your father speak to you about your cousin, Willard?" Hattie asked.

"Yes, he did, grandma," Gene II answered. "He said he has a degree in mass communications."

"He wants to work at The Herald," Hattie said.

"I know...Aunt Gloria had mentioned it before the...before dad's accident."

"And?"

"What?..Why are you looking at me like that?"

"So?..What are you going to do?" Hattie was growing impatient with her eldest grandson.

"I told him to put in an application."

"Oh, c'mon, Gene!" Patricia said, disgusted. "He's your cousin, for GOD's sake!"

"I told you...No nepotism!" Gene II snapped. "That's what's wrong with this industry now and I'm not going to be a part of it!"

"Well, who the hell are you to suddenly become so self-righteous?" Patricia shot back, angrily. "Would you be an officer in the corporation and managing editor if it wasn't for your father?"

"That's not the point, mom!" Gene II protested.

"That is the point!.. We must look out for each other!"

"The Herald is not The State Journal!.. This is a nationally recognized major daily newspaper and ..."

"Oh, can it, Gene!" Susan angrily interrupted. "Willard is your cousin...your aunt's only child!"

"That doesn't mean I have to hire him."

"Maybe I should speak to your father instead," Patricia said, calmly.

"No...don't bother dad."

"Meaning?" Hattie asked.

Gene II walked over and put an arm around his grandmother's shoulders, smiling broadly. "OK...OK...I'll check out his qualifications and see where we can place him."

"He wants to work on the advertising staff," Hattie said firmly.

"C'mon, grandma!.. We've got half the family working at the newspaper now...I'll find something for him...don't worry about it."

"When...today?" Patricia asked.

"Tell him to meet me in my office first thing tomorrow morning...I'll find something."

"You hard of hearing or something?" Hattie asked, louder.

"I said he wants to work on the advertising staff!"

"OK!..Alright!..I'll put him on the advertising staff, OK?" Gene II gave in, reluctantly. "Where is he anyhow?..I haven't seen him since the hospital...I thought they were staying here."

"They are...Willard went to the newspaper this morning," Patricia said.

"He's probably looking for you...Your Aunt Gloria had to take care of some mysterious business she's been upset about...Something extremely important."

The tall, massive iron gates guarding the Dugas Estate were closed when Gloria's small foreign car pulled up and stopped, facing them.. Gloria got out of the car and peered through the iron bars down the long, winding private road leading to the Dugas mansion. She looked for a buzzer or doorbell. Finding nothing, she angrily marched back to her car, got inside and began blowing the horn. She was momentarily startled when she heard a distant voice coming from an intercom system fastened high above the gates. Looking at the intercom, she also noticed several television monitors mounted higher on each side of the gates that were rotating back and forth, scanning the entire area.

"May I help you, miss?" the voice asked.
"Yes...yes you can," Gloria replied. "Who am I speaking to?"
"The butler, mam," the voice answered.
"Good...I am Gloria Stanton Thompson...I'd like to see Mr. F. Walton Dugas, please!..Tell him it is extremely important!"
"Ma'am?"
"I said I'd like to see Mr. F. Walton Dugas," Gloria said, impatiently.
"Do you have an appointment, ma'am?"
"Just tell "your highness" I'm here and I'm angry!"

There is silence at the huge gates as Gloria got out of the car an began pacing back and forth, angrily. Finally, she heard static over the intercom as the butler came back on.

"Mr. Dugas says he does not know you, Mrs. Thompson," the butler said. "Please leave the premises or I'll call the authorities!"
"Go back and tell him Gene Stanton's sister want to speak to him...right now!"

Gloria walked back to her car, got inside and angrily slammed the door shut!..A few minutes passed before the huge gates silently slid open. Gloria's car slowly followed the winding road past the heavily wooded foothills guarding the vast estate with it's majestic mansion setting far beyond the long, rolling green lawns. When she reached the Gigantic mansion and walked upon the wide, spacious and tiled porch a haughty butler met her at the front door and led her to a large, expensively paneled library. As soon as she was seated the butler left the room. In a few minutes F. Walton Dugas slowly walked into the room with a big grin creasing his deeply tanned face. He was tall, slim and immaculately dressed in a grey business suit. The craggy lines in his face failed to hide his handsome features. His hair was slightly sprinkled with gray which added an intellectual appearance to his businessman posture. He looked

Gloria up and down with admiration filling his eyes.

"My GOD!..Gloria Stanton!..What a lovely vision you are!" Dugas whispered, startled by her beauty. "Why I haven't seen you in...what?..Twenty...twenty-five years!...You look marvelous!..Just as beautiful as ever!"

"Twenty-two years to be exact," Gloria replied, sarcastically.

He stared at her thoughtfully and tried to determine why she was there. "How...How is your brother?" he asked politely. "Is he going to be alright?"

Gloria carefully studied his face, watching his eyes searching for any signs that would reveal that he knew much more about the shooting. "Yes...he'll be alright...despite nearly being blown to hell!.. But he'll make it."

"Would you like a drink...or anything?"

"I'm not in the mood to drink."

"Then...how can I possibly help you?..You look upset...Do they have any clue to who tried to kill your brother?..I understand that the assailant is still in a coma."

"That's right...they don't have a clue...but I do!"

Dugas ignored her last remark and poured himself a drink, nervously glancing at Gloria over the rim of his glass. "To think that a man was almost killed right in his own offices and in broad daylight...that's frightening!"

"It's more that frightening, Frank...It's attempted murder!"

Dugas sat down behind a wide mahogany desk and stared at Gloria, thoughtfully. "You seem to think I had something to do with it!"

"You got that right!" Gloria shot back, angrily. "I've heard about the way you've been harassing him...ever since my family bought The Times building."

"That's preposterous and a lot of rubbish!" Dugas said, angrily. "I'm a newspaper publisher not a gangster!"..Your brother only represents token competition to me and that's all!"

"Is that why you threatened him?"

"You remember how my father helped your dad with that loan during the seventies?..It stopped your old man from going bankrupt and closing down your family's newspaper...It just doesn't seem right for your brother to show his appreciation by becoming my main competition in this city!..You gonna blame me for getting angry at him?..Now he's hired my daughter just to rub salt in the wound!"

"Now just a damn minute!" Gloria shouted. "Let's start with the truth and work forward...forget the fairy tales!"

"Fairy tales?" Dugas asked, surprised. "What the hell are you talking about?..Are you telling me my facts aren't straight?"

A stunned Gloria stared at Dugas in surprise! "You...you mean you really don't know why your father let my dad have that money?"

"Look, Gloria...I'm sorry about what happened to your brother, but I had nothing to do with it...There's a lot of people in this country that simply are not ready for a Black man to own and operate a major daily newspaper!..Gene knew what the risks were!..My father admired what your family was doing with the Black weekly you were publishing, that's why he was willing to help...Your father knew how to stay in his place instead of trying to tread ground where he shouldn't be!..But not your brother!..Oh, no...not him!..He's gonna try and compete with me on a level playing field! Well you can tell him for me that'll I break him and that damn newspaper before I let that happen!..Especially after we helped your family with that fifty thousand dollars in the seventies!"

Gloria began laughing right in Dugas' face. "Help?..Is that what your father told you?..That he was actually helping my father?"

"If it wasn't help, then what was it?..Your family stayed in business didn't they?"

"I wonder how many other families your father has helped."

Dugas quickly glanced at his watch and looked at Gloria, impatiently. "If you have something to say, come on out and say it!..It's been good seeing you again and I'm sorry about your brother's shooting, but I don't have too much time left."

"You better have time for this!"

"That sounds like a threat."

Gloria slowly stood up and walked over to the large window that overlooked a spacious golf course with an unending and rambling lawn. Her back was to Dugas when she began speaking, softly. "Remember about some twenty-three years ago when you and a few of your business associates coaxed my sorority to join a little party you were throwing aboard your new yacht?"

"It was harmless..nobody got hurt."

"Not hurt.. just drunk...If you remember ...you came on to me pretty strong that night."

"You were then as you are now, a stunning beauty."

"Didn't it bother you to come on to a Black girl?"

"Is that what this is all about?"

Gloria slowly turned and faced Dugas with fire burning in her eyes! "You raped me, you bastard!"

Shocked, Dugas quickly stood up behind his desk!..He looked over towards the library door to make sure it was closed. "Are you out of your mind?..You can't prove a charge like that!" Dugas shouted, angrily. "Not after all these years!..You don't have any proof!"

"The hell I don't!.. My proof is a twenty-two year old, six footer who's probably at home right now, wondering where in the hell I am!"

"You...you're a liar!"

"That's what that fifty thousand dollars was all about, Frank!..It wasn't a loan or a gift!..No, not by long shot!..That money was a pay-off to keep your butt out of jail!"

Dugas glared at Gloria, unable to speak as she calmly turned away and strutted to the door. She stopped and turned back to Dugas. "I want that harassment to stop, Frank, and I mean now!.. If I ever find out that you did have something to do with that shooting...Your ass is grass!"

Gloria quickly turned and marched out of the room, slamming the door behind her!..Dugas stared after her in shocked silence!..

Chapter Ten

Al Cronin, Advertising Director of the Detroit Herald, was ecstatic with the gains in circulation the paper had made in the last few months. The new innovations the Stantons had implemented had made advertisers fight to get their messages into those supplements. The fashion sections on Sundays and Wednesdays were both extremely successful and the expanded sized TV magazine along with the adult adventure comic book in each Sunday newspaper, offered something to The Herald home delivery customers that they couldn't get anywhere else. All of this made Al Cronin's job a lot easier as advertising accounts line up on waiting lists.

Today, Al Cronin escorted Willard Thompson around the wide, spacious and glass enclosed advertising offices. Several employees stared as the two moved from desk to desk. Al proudly introduced Willard to various staff members, most of whom were white and somewhat surprised to see a black person in the advertising department. Finally, Al took Willard into the large executive office of the advertising manager, Jerry Seiner, who looked up in surprise as the two men walked into his office. "Jerry, I'd like for you to meet Willard Thompson," Al said, cheerfully. "The newest member to your staff...Willard...meet your new boss, Jerry Seiner, our retail advertising manager."

Jerry Seiner quickly stood up and extended his hand, reluctantly to Willard who grasped it firmly. Jerry looked from Al to Willard, puzzled. "Er...ah...good to meet you, Willard...You have any experience in newspaper advertising?" Jerry asked as he searched the top of his desk. "I must've missed seein' your resume...just a minute."

Jerry pressed his intercom button as he looked around his desk. He remained puzzled as he spoke into the intercom.

"Julie...Do you have Mr. Thompson's resume?..I can't seem to find it."

In a few moments his secretary, Julie, walked into the office and handed Jerry the resume. He glared at her disapprovingly. 'Why am I just getting this?"

"A messenger just brought it up from personnel. Sorry," Julie said as she quickly turned and left the office.

Jerry scanned the resume while Al Cronin became nervous and impatient. Suddenly, Jerry looked up at Al and then back to Willard, thoughtfully. "I dunno..." Jerry mumbled. "You don't have any experience, Mr. Thompson."

"I think we can waive the experience factor, Jer," Al said, confidentially.

"I graduated first in my class," Willard said, proudly. "I'm an artist and a writer, Mr. Seiner...I was also advertising manager and editor of my college newspaper."

"That's not the point," Jerry snapped back. "We require extensive experience in newspaper advertising before we bring anyone on our staff. Maybe we can find a spot for you in our dispatch department...The pay isn't as much but it'll give you some experience in dealing with our advertisers and ad agencies...at the entry level."

"I didn't go through five years of college to become a messenger!" Willard replied, angrily.

"Jerry...I think you should reconsider in this case," Al said, calmly.

"No...I'm not gonna do it!" Jerry shot back, stubbornly. "You tellin' me my job?..You may be the director, Al, but the publisher has set firm rules and regulations...Sometimes it's just not practical to try to implement affirmative action in certain highly skilled positions."

"Listen...I'm not asking for any kind of affirmative action," Willard said. "Just take a look at my portfolio."

Willard opened up a large leather portfolio he had been carrying under his arm. He spread it open across Jerry's desk. Jerry glanced at the slick looking ads which were professionally laid out neatly on each page of the portfolio. He looked back up at Willard, shaking his head in a negative manner..."This is fine, Mr. Thompson...but you still need on-the-job advertising experience before we place you on our advertising staff," Jerry said as he waved his arm to the people sitting at desks just outside of his office. "See all those people out there?..Most of those employees have been in advertising while you were still in grade school. They're not putting together some high school or college yearbook...This is the pros...They're putting together a major daily newspaper!"

Al Cronin nervously began pacing back and forth in the office, visibly irritated by Jerry's attitude which clearly caused Al's growing impatience. "I think you should make an exception in this case, Jerry," Al said, angrily. "It would be best for all concerned."

"No!...I'm sorry...that's my final word!" Jerry said, adamant in his decision. "It's either dispatch or nothing. I can't change the rules just to suit an unexperienced applicant who had never worked a day in newspaper advertising!"

Willard smiled and began folding up his portfolio. Jerry handed him back his resume.

"Thank you for your time, Mr. Seiner," Willard said, politely.

"Take your resume back down to personnel and fill out an application for dispatch clerk," Jerry said. "That's where I started...They may be able to put you to work as early as next week."

Willard walked towards the door as Al stood in the middle of the office, frustrated and speechless. Willard stopped and turned back to Jerry. "I'll discuss this with my uncle, Mr. Seiner," Willard said, still smiling. "My mother and I are having dinner with him tonight. He's been home from the hospital a few days now...I'm sure he'll know what I should do."

Jerry walked around his desk towards Willard and shook his hand while he simultaneously ushered him towards the office door. Al remained seething, standing in the center of Jerry's office with a frown on his face.

"Yeah, that's best...talk it over with your uncle," Jerry said, victoriously and relieved that Willard was leaving. "I'm sure your uncle will agree with me...You know the old saying..."you've got to crawl before you can walk" ...Your uncle's just been released from the hospital?..Anything serious?"

"You're damn right it was serious!" Al retorted, angrily. Jerry sensed something was wrong. He quickly looked back at Al and then back towards Willard.

"Who's your uncle?" Jerry asked.

Willard smiled broadly as he continued through the office door. He slowly stopped and turned back to face Jerry Seiner.

"Gene Stanton," Willard said, softly.

Startled, Jerry quickly turned back to Al Cronin who stared back at him with a big grin slowly creasing his face!

Damien laid in bed stiffly as a doctor finished examining him. A nurse and a policeman stood in the background. When the doctor was finished he turned to the nurse.

"I think he's doing just fine," the doctor said. "He should be ready to be moved to the Wayne County jail in a few days."

"Good!..That's where he belongs!" the policeman growled.

"Shall we maintain the physical therapy?" the nurse asked.

"Yes...continue the same program as long as he's here with us," the doctor answered. "Massage his legs at least four times a day... but it's really no big deal...Get him out of bed...let him sit in a wheelchair and walk around the room."

Damien moved his wrist that was handcuffed to the railing on the bed. "How am I suppose to do anything like that with these things on, doc?"

The policeman stepped closer to the bed an unlocked the handcuffs. "Don't worry...I'll be here. He's too weak to give me any trouble!"

"You can just cuff him to a wheelchair...Let him sit up awhile," the doctor said. "It'll get the circulation moving."

An attendant walked into the room just as the doctor left. The attendant began helping Damien out of the bed and into a wheelchair. The policeman handcuffed Damien to the wheelchair while the attendant strapped him in the chair and secured him. The nurse and the policeman left the room. Just as the attendant was finished, Damien began speaking to him in a soft whisper.

"Aren't you the same guy who's been turnin' me over everyday?" Damien asked.

"Yeah, that's me...I got this whole wing," the man answered.

"What's your name?"

"Call me Dave," the attendant replied. "Is there something I can get for you?"

Damien looked up and studied Dave's face carefully, then slowly looked him up and down. "How big are you, David?"

"Five-ten...two hundred pounds...Why?"

"We're about the same size," Damien answered. "You wanna make a few bucks?"

Dave stopped and glanced over his shoulder at the door. He could see the back of the policeman's head through the small window in the door. He turned back to Damien and shook his head as he lowered his voice.

"No way!..I don't wanna get involved in anything!...I'm just doin' my job and mindin' my business," Dave replied, nervously. "I lose this job and I'm in deep do-do!..Besides, the cops are watchin' you like a porno movie!"

"OK!..OK!..Don't blow a gasket!" Damien said, smiling. "My mistake...I just thought you might be interested in earning a fast five thousand."

Dave started to leave and then stopped suddenly and turned back to Damien. He walked over closer to him and quickly glanced at the door. He looked at Damien, nervously biting his lower lip before he spoke.

"Five thousand dollars?" Dave asked in a whisper.

"Five thousand smackeroos!"

"What do I have to do...kill somebody?"

Damien smiled confidently and glanced at the door. Dave was taking the bait!..

"Naw...nothing like that...maybe just a phone call and a little cooperation with some friends of mine...They'll tell you what to do."

"Who do I have to call?"

"You sayin' you'll take the job?"

"For five grand?..You're damn right!" Dave exclaimed. "Who do I call?"

"Uh, uh!..No names!" Damien replied. "I like you, David, but you could be a police plant."

"Not with my record!..That's why I can't afford to lose this job or turn down that kind of money!..As long as I don't have to do anything illegal...you got your boy!"

"A phone call ain't illegal."

"When do you want me to do it?"

"As soon as possible...Just call a certain number and say you're callin' for a friend of theirs that needs their help," Damien said. "Tell 'em where I am and that I will change clothes with you, but I need to get out of these cuffs and get some wheels so I can get away from this hospital."

"I didn't say I'd change clothes with you."

Damien looked up at Dave and smiled. "You mean you wouldn't sell me those rags you're wearin' as part of a five thousand dollar deal?"

"Is that all I gotta do?" Dave asked, reluctantly. "I could get you a complete set"

"See...I knew you'd figure it out."

"What about the cuffs?"

"Don't worry about that...You just make the call...Tell 'em what I told you to...They'll take care of the small stuff."

"What's the number?"

"Dial four-nine-one-zero-five -five -zero...And oh, yeah, tell 'em to bring the five thousand...in cash."

The two men stared at each other as Damien smiled, broadly!

Kelly walked into the plush apartment staggering with both arms full of groceries. She placed the bags of groceries on the kitchen table and began to scan her grocery list, thoughtfully. She walked back through the apartment to make sure she had closed the front door. She casually glanced into the bedroom as she walked pass the open bedroom door. She saw two empty suitcases

THE WINDS OF TOMORROW

laying open on the bed. At the same time she heard the shower running in the bathroom and saw Mel's naked figure behind the fogged up shower door.

"Hey!..What're you doin' home so early?" Kelly shouted. "And what's with the suitcases?..The paper sending you out of town on an assignment?"

Kelly paused, waiting for a response.

"I'll be out in a minute," Mel replied, solemnly.

Kelly pondered the situation for a moment and stared at the two empty suitcases. She quickly went back into the kitchen and began putting away the groceries. In a short time, a dripping wet Mel appeared in the kitchen doorway with a towel wrapped around his waist. His tall, bronze, muscular body gleamed from the moisture running down his skin. He wore a somber expression on his face as he stared at her.

"You've done a lot of shopping," Mel said. "You planning a big dinner or something?"

"Hi, honey," Kelly answered, smiling. "What a nice surprise."

"You let me down, Kel," Mel said, bitterly.

Surprised at the solemn tone in his voice, she turned to face him, nervously. "Why?..What's the matter?"

"You promised to stay off the junk!"

"I have!..I wouldn't lie about that!" Kelly protested, vigorously. " I haven't touched anything since you came back! You know that!"

"You're a liar!"

"What the hell are you talkin' about?"

"Your friend Otto called while you were out," Mel said, angrily. "He left a message on your machine."

Kelly stared at Mel with a worried expression on her face. He slowly turned away from her in disgust. She rushed past him to the phone and snapped on the answering machine. While she listened to the messages, Mel watched her, intently until Otto's voice came on.

"Kelly, baby...I got your mess...Let me know when and where and I'll drop it off...I can be reached at the club. You know the number...Luv ya, hon...Bye."

Kelly angrily snapped off the machine and turned back to Mel who was leaning back against the doorway, staring at her, sarcastically.

"I'm leavin!" Mel muttered. "I should've known better!"

"No!..No!..This isn't fair!" Kelly shouted. "I haven't done anything!..honest!"

"Then why is that creep still callin' you?" Mel asked, angrily. "I'm tryin' to keep a clean slate!.. That's the only way I can get reinstated in the NBA...and you got this jerk on the line...still supplying you!"

That's not true!..I haven't seen or heard from him since we got back together!"

"Then why is he calling you?"

"Because he's a racist bastard who's tryin' to break us up!"

"Maybe he's right."

"Is that what this is really all about?" Kelly asked, angrily. "You're lookin' for a way out because your rich, Black family doesn't want you to marry a White girl?"

"That doesn't even deserve an answer...They all love you," Mel replied, calmly. "I just wanna get reinstated in the NBA...and I never will be if you're associating with known drug dealers!..And leave my family out of this. They've already accepted you!"

"Well they don't act like they have!" Kelly sneered. "Big deal...Your dad's been home from the hospital more than a week and you STILL haven't taken me over there!"

Mel turned and walked out of the room. Kelly closely followed him, fuming in anger!

"Forget it, Kelly!.. This just isn't working!"

"That's because you don't want it to work anymore!" she argued. "It was different before when you couldn't play ball without looking up in the stands to see if I was there!" Mel stopped and turned back to Kelly, staring into her eyes. "We've made some big mistakes in the past...both of us...but throughout everything that has happened...I've always loved you...and you know it!"

Then why are you leaving me?..I made you a promise and I've kept my word!" Kelly cried. "It's been hard sitting in this apartment all day waiting for you to come home...but I've done it...clean and sober!..Dammit, Mel!..I've done it because I love you so damn much!"

Mel turned to walk away and Kelly suddenly jerked off the towel from around his waist and shoved him roughly back against the door!..Before he could stop her, she pushed up against him, pressing her body to his as her hands roamed all over his naked body!..Her mouth gently kissed his chest and slowly moved up to his face as her tongue darted lightly over his lips until she plunged it into his open mouth!..She raised her thigh and wrapped it around his upper leg!..

"No!.. It's no use!.. It's ..." Mel gasped as he tried to resist.

His voice was soon smothered by her feverish kisses all over his face. She furiously began jerking off her clothes and throwing them on the floor!..His arms encircled her small waist as his passion overcame his senses. In a few minutes they both were breathing heavily as they collapsed on the bed, completely naked and wrapped in each other's arms in a heated embrace!..

Her body was soft, firm, shapely, smooth and White, contrasting sharply with Mel's as she gently moved on top of him. Her long, blond hair flowed down her back as she straddled Mel's body and slowly began positioning herself with her long, shapely legs on both sides of his body. He fondled and worshipped her beautiful, pointed breasts, mouthing each one patiently, trying to stuff the entire mound into his mouth as Kelly's head rolled from side to side in deep pleasure. His erect member found her wet opening almost automatically, as she slowly began moving up and down on his stiff shaft. They pressed their bodies together, forcing him deeper and deeper inside her as the pace of their movements increased to the point of a thundering convulsion, after which they both collapsed, into each other's arms!..

Dave, the hospital attendant, walked casually into the intensive care unit carrying a towel over his arm. He smiled at the policeman on duty who was sitting in front of the door to Damien's room and slightly nodding. The policeman suddenly looked up, surprised, as Dave approached him. He returned Dave's smile and relaxed back in his chair.

"Take it easy and relax... you deserve it," Dave said, smiling. Been a long day, eh?..How about your prisoner...is he awake?"

"Gee, thanks, Dave," the policeman grinned. "The prisoner...Er...ahh...I dunno...He's been mighty quiet. What's up?"

"Leg message...got to get him ready to be transferred to the county jail tomorrow."

"Yeah...that's where he belongs," the policeman sighed. "That guy is weird...gives ya the creeps!"

Dave calmly strolled into the room and found Damien laying on his side. He propped himself up on one arm when Dave walked in.

"How'd it go?" Damien whispered.

"Like clockwork...You all set?" Dave asked, softly.

"Your transportation is waiting right outside the front doors...Just get in it and drive away."

"The question is, my friend...are you all set?"

Dave reached over and quickly unlocked the handcuffs as he grinned, broadly. He handed Damien a set of keys and a gun. "That answer your question?" Dave asked.

Damien rubbed his wrist and looked up at Dave. "My friends take care of you?"

"Big time...Just like you said they would."

The two men moved quickly and silently. When Damien slipped into the bathroom to change clothes, Dave climbed into the bed and handcuffed his wrist to the bed rail. In a few minutes, Damien came out of the bathroom dressed as a hospital attendant. He calmly sat on the side of the bed facing Dave and grinned. Before he could say anything, the policeman opened the door to the dimly lit room!..

"You about finished?" the policeman asked.

Damien cooly continued sitting on the bed, unmoving, with his back to the policeman and blocking Dave from the policeman's view. Damien winked at Dave and fingered the gun...

"Just a few more minutes," Dave mumbled.

The policeman hesitated before slowly closing the door. Damien got up and moved in closer to Dave, staring down at him, smiling.

"You did a good job, David," Damien whispered. "I'm gonna hate to do this...but it'll get you off the hook, ol' buddy."

Dave looked up at Damien with a confused and puzzled expression on his face as Damien's fist smashed into his nose, knocking him unconscious!..Damien grunted as he continued pummeling his fists into Dave's bloody face!..When he was finished, he calmly walked back into the bathroom and washed the blood from his hands. He placed the gun in one hand and covered it with a towel over his arm. He casually strode out of the room through the door, past the nodding policeman and down the long hospital corridor!..

A little while later, a nurse slowly walked down the hall pushing a medicine tray on a cart. As she neared the policeman, he looked up and smiled at her. The nurse smiled back, looked at the paper cup in her hand and checked a list on clipboard.

"You need any help?" the policeman asked.

"Yes, please..Can you come into this room with me?" she asked. "It says he could be dangerous."

The nurse followed the policeman into the dark room. She quickly selected the medicine and poured a glass of water. The policeman stood in the background, waiting and watching carefully. The nurse gently shook the figure as it lay on it's side facing the wall...

"Sir...Sir...It's time to take your medicine," the nurse said, softly.

Getting no response except a slight moan, she motioned to the policemen who stepped forward and turned the man over. The nurse suddenly dropped the medicine and screamed in horror at the bloody face!..The policeman quickly turned on the ceiling lights and he was shocked by the man's battered face!

"What the hell!..He's all beat up!" the policeman shouted. "Who the hell beat up this prisoner?"

"Oohhh!..Help me!" Dave moaned, weakly. "That sonofabitch tried to kill me!"

"Dave !..Dave, what happened?" the stunned nurse asked.

"You...You gotta get him!" Dave shouted. "I came in here for the leg message...and just as I finished...he got loose and jumped me!"

The nurse quickly turned to the befuddled policeman who stood frozen in disbelief!..

"This isn't the prisoner, officer!" the nurse shouted. "This is Dave...our attendant!..The prisoner has escaped!"

Chapter Eleven

It was slightly raining when a station wagon drove into the motel parking lot. Susan Stanton quickly got out and opened her umbrella as it suddenly began raining harder. She hesitated while she tried to read the numbers on the door of each unit through the heavy downpour. Finally, she ran over to one unit and gently knocked.

"Who is it?" a man's voice asked.

"It's me, " Susan answered. "Open the door...it's pouring out here!"

In a few moments the door opened and Susan quickly went inside. She closed the umbrella and shook the rain from her dark, red hair. She quickly took off her raincoat as Joe Stanton walked over to a leather arm chair and sat down, eyeing Susan, carefully. She walked over and sat on the bed directly in front of him, crossing her legs seductively. She looked at Joe and smiled.

"Aren't you happy to see me?" she asked, coyly.

"No...You shouldn't be here," he answered, somberly.

"I know...I've tried...I've really tried, Joe...but I had to see you. These past weeks at the hospital, worrying about your dad and seeing you every day...but not able to touch...It's been very hard on me!"

"Why didn't you move to New York?" Joe asked. "It would've been so much easier."

"You know why...Once he became involved with the paper he was hooked. Now, with you dad getting shot...he's determined to stay here and run the newspaper! ..It's like he's addicted to that damn job!"

"That's why we've got to stay away from each other."

"No!..I love you!..What can I do about that?"

"I can do something. I can stay out of your life."

"Do you want me to leave my husband?"

"He's my brother!..I can't ask you to do that...break up his family!"

"Why can't we be together?..You're my whole life...each day and each night...you're on my mind!"

She got up and walked closer to him. Her hand rested on his as as he looked up into her eyes. Her touch electrified him, her fragrance entranced him and her deep brown eyes infatuated him...and she knew it...She could feel him tense up when she moved nearer.

"Susan...nobody knows I'm back in town," Joe said, softly. "I had planned to arrive this evening...I wanna stay home until they recapture that killer."

"I know...I heard about his escape from the hospital and I know that's why you came back so soon...but can't we have this time together before you let them know you're here?"..

"How much time?"

"Like...like the rest of the day?"

She slipped onto his lap and began kissing his neck, loosening his shirt and tie...

"Dammit, Suan!...How can you stay away from your children that long?"

"After you called last night...I made arrangements."

"Where does Gene thing you are?"

"He thinks I'm in school...We've got the whole day, baby."

She kissed him flush on his mouth, her tongue searching out his. He gently lifted her up to her feet. They both stood facing each other as she put her arms around his neck and slowly grinded her pelvis against him. He pulled her to him, holding her tightly!

"GOD, I love you!..I never should've let this happen," Joe grumbled, kissing her neck. "Look at the mess we're in now!"

"Oh, Joe!..Hold me!..Make love to me!..I've missed you so much!"

He began kissing her hair, her ears and her mouth as she sighed deeply with each caress.

"I've missed your smell..your softness...and that wonderful laugh," Joe said. "When we're around the family and I hear that laugh...it goes right through me."

She stepped back and stared at him, smiling sexily. "You DO love me...don't you."

He reached for her as she continued moving backwards away from him, teasingly.

"Of course I do," Joe answered. "If I hadn't been so damn stubborn...we'd be married today."

"But you wanted to Agency...It was all you ever talked about...the CIA was the only thing on your mind then...You dropped me for the Company and it tore my heart apart."

"I know...it was the biggest mistake I've made in my life!..But you didn't make it easy for me...You and your ultimatums."

"You can have me now...Just say the work and I'll divorce Gene."

"I couldn't do that...think what it would do to your children," Joe said, thoughtfully. "It would rip my entire family apart...and...I'd lose a brother...A good brother."

"Your good brother knew how we felt about each other before he asked me to marry him," Susan snapped.

"You didn't have to say yes," Joe said.

"And you didn't have to join the CIA!"

She stared at him with her eyes burning with desire as she slowly began unbuttoning her blouse. She continued undressing while he watched her, admiring her golden and voluptuous body. She knew he liked to see her undress so she purposely made a show of it. Her large erect breasts stood out full and round, lightly bobbing in his face over an extremely thin waist and wide hips that tapered down to long, shapely legs.

"You've got to make up your mind, baby," she whispered huskily. "Life isn't easy...we can't go on like this...I'm willing to sacrifice everything to have you...I always have!"

When she was finished undressing she slowly walked over to him, completely naked, and looked up into his eyes. Her closeness to him increased his desire as he quickly embraced her and kissed her sensually on her mouth. they clung to each other as the months of being apart are dissolved by their heated passion!..Each kiss, each caress increased their love as the room seemingly began to swirl around them and they began their day long journey to reconsumate their love!..Joe quickly stepped back away from her and pulled off his clothes. She came back into his arms and kissed him hard as his erect member pressed against her stomach. She kissed all over his chest, lightly nibbling at his nipples while her small hand slowly massaged his groin. She led him to the bed where she turned her back to him as she laid face down. He climbed over her, straddling her firm, smooth buttocks. He kissed the back of her neck, burying his face in her hair. He lightly nibbled her ears and neck. His tongue danced over her back, down to her narrow waist. She slightly protruded her bottom, arching her back when she felt his legs moving next to her upper thighs, waiting for his first thrust into her body.

The storm outside was at it's peak now as the rain continued to pour down with loud thunder cracking and rumbling as darkness descended and lightning flashed across the skies, momentarily knocking out the lights in the room as the two lovers moved in perfect coordination, their moist bodies locked together as their deep breathing blended in with the rain against the window pane...

F. Walton Dugas sat in his spacious office at The Daily Press Newspaper in a large executive armchair behind an oversized desk. He thumbed the top of his desk thoughtfully as he pondered the fact that he and Gloria Stanton may actually have a twenty-two year old son. How would he look?..Would he be White or Black?..Maybe have his features and Gloria's color. No..maybe it would be best to have her features and his color...Gloria Stanton was still a beautiful woman and this child offered him a chance to have a real son instead of that drunken whimp that lived in his home...Of course, maybe the son wouldn't want to have anything to do with him...since no matter what his color was or how he looked, he would still be considered Black...That's not fair, Dugas mused. What the hell was he, chopped liver?..His thoughts were interrupted when the intercom on his desk buzzed...

"Yes, Agnes," he snapped.

"Mr. Wilder from personnel is here, Mr. Dugas."

"Fine...send him in."

In a few minutes a middle aged, bespectacled man slowly walked into the office with his hands nervously clasped behind his back. He looked at Dugas with a meek expression on his face. Dugas greeted him warmly.

"Hello, Ed...How's things going in personnel?"

"Er...ah...It's all going fine, sir," Wilder replied, timidly. "Is anything wrong?"

"No...everything's just fine...Why?...did you think anything was wrong?"

"No...er...It's not every day that I'm summoned to the publisher's office," Wilder said, relieved.

"I want you to do me a favor, Ed," Dugas said in a somber tone. "I want you to locate a young man for me...He's about twenty or twenty-one years old...This is personal."

"I'll do whatever I can, sir."

"He may be working at The Herald."

"In what capacity?"

"I don't know...I'm not even sure he's working there," Dugas answered. "You'll have to find out. He's only been in town a few weeks but I know he has some connections over there."

Wilder immediately pulled out a notebook and pen, preparing to write down some information. "What's his name, sir?..I'll put someone on this right away."

"No...no...this is extremely confidential...I want you to handle this personally."

"I see...Then I will handle it personally...You can count on me, sir."

"Fine...I knew I could...How long have you been with the paper now, Ed?"

"Twenty-two excellent years, sir," Wilder answered, proudly.

"Good...I'd like for you to remain here until you retire," Dugas warned. "Do you understand?"

"Perfectly, sir...What's the young man's name?"

"His name is...His last name is Thompson...I don't have any first name...but he's only been in town a few weeks and he may be working at The Herald."

"Is there anything else I should know about this young man?"

"No...I'm sorry...that's all I have...except he's supposed to be around six feet tall."

Mr. Wilder turned to leave. Just as he reached the office door he stopped and turned to Dugas. Dugas stared at him with a puzzled expression on his face.

"Is there anything else?" Dugas asked.

"You have no description?"

"No...No I don't."

"Is this man Black or White?"

Dugas became irritated by the question and he glared at Wilder in contempt. "I really don't know!" Dugas snapped, angrily. "You got a problem with that?"

"Oh, no sir...I have no problem with that," Wilder replied, nervously. "I'll get on this right away, Mr. Dugas...As soon as I get some information I'll get back to you."

"I expect to hear something from you within the next twenty-four hours, Ed...Don't let me down."

"Yessir...Within the next twenty-four hours."

Ed Wilder quickly left the office as Dugas got up and began pacing the floor, impatiently.

Gene Stanton was tired of being sick. Dressed in his pajamas and robe, he sat in a deep cushioned recliner on the wide veranda just off of the master bedroom and read The Detroit Herald Newspaper. The long, rambling lawn next to the Stanton mansion, offered viewers a perfect picture of a beautiful fall day complete with towering trees topped with multi-colored crowns, standing on acres of deep green meadows partially sprinkled with leaves as the soft winds of autumn scattered them around the busy squirrels and intruding birds.

Gene took a sip of his orange juice when he heard the sounds of laughter coming closer as Kim swept into the bedroom. Surprised that her father was not in the bedroom, she began calling him, concerned.

"Daddy!..Daddy...where are you?" Kim shouted.

"I'm on the veranda.....C'mon out."

Kim rushed out to the veranda with an anxious look on her face. Gene took off his glasses and stared at her, smiling broadly.

"Daddy!..Isn't it kinda dangerous sittin' out here with that nut runnin' around loose?" Kim asked, concerned. "What are you doin' out of bed anyway?...Honest, daddy, if you..."

"Hold on!..I'm not worried about him, here in my own home!" Gene answered, laughing. "No one can even get back here. I'm minding my own business, reading my paper and relaxing like my doctor ordered me to...You know that...besides, Mel just called...he and Kelly are coming over tonight...Joe is due in from Washington and Roger's on his way over here now..Hell, I'm a popular guy."

Kim grinned at her father, quickly bended down and kissed him on the cheek as she hugged him, affectionately.

"I'm glad Mel and Kelly have worked things out...I really like her a lot," Kim said. "And you, dad...you look great!"

"I'm gaining back my strength each day. I ought to be back on the job in a week or so."

"Don't rush it...I don't think you should try to come back too soon," Kim cautioned. "I'm gonna be here for a while so I can help you recuperate."

"Recuperate?..How can you help me do that?"

"Remember the walks we use to take over the back grounds?...We'll be able to do that again while you're off work."

"I thought you were due back in Hollywood."

"They've given me more time to take care of my daddy...Besides, I got fabulous news today!"

"What kind of fabulous news?"

"You know...about the film."

"Well?.."

"I got the co-starring role!" Kim screamed in delight. "Can you believe it?"

"Fantastic!" Gene exclaimed. "I 'm really proud of you!..I guess those stiffs out there in La-La Land must be pretty sharp after all!"

"I'm playing opposite Vic Martin!..This is better than I could ever wish for!"

"What's the shooting schedule...and when do you start?"

"They're doing re-write now...I should get my draft of the revised script in a few days."

"Then you'll get the schedule?"

"As soon as the "Suits" approve it we'll go into rehearsal," Kim answered. "I'd say we won't begin principal shooting for at least another ninety days or so...Which means I'll have a little more time to spend with you.

They were suddenly interrupted when Roger Carlson stuck his head through the open French doors leading from the bedroom. "Is this a family meeting or can anybody join in?" Roger asked, smiling.

"Hi, Roger," Kim said, smiling. "Is Janet with you?"

"I thought you were coming over earlier," Gene said. "I've been waiting for you."

"Yeah, I bet you have," Roger said to Gene as he turned to Kim. "Janet's downstairs talking to your beautiful young friend...Wow!...Is she a living doll!"

"Well, I'll let you two discuss your business," Kim said as she kissed Gene on the forehead. "I gotta talk to Janet."

Kim stood up to leave.

"Who's your beautiful young friend that Janet's talking to?" Gene asked.

"Adrian...You remember Adrian Grant," Kim replied with a twinkle in her eyes. "She called me today. She wanted to know if she could come over and see you...I told her it was alright...OK?"

"Yeah, sure," Gene said as a big smile crossed his face. "She'll certainly make any man's day a lot brighter."

"She is one pretty young thing!" Roger drooled.

"You better not let her hear you refer to her as that "pretty young thing"...she wants to be known as Doctor Grant," Kim said.

"Doctor?" Roger asked, surprised. "She's a doctor?"

Kim started to leave again as a big smile flashed across her face. "PhD...She works for The Herald...and I think she's infatuated with my dear, dear father," Kim said, quickly kissing Gene on his forehead again. "See ya later, tiger!"

Kim laughed as she walked back through the French doors and into the bedroom.

"And if you believe that...I got a bridge I wanna sell you," Gene laughed.

Roger waited until Kim was out of earshot and he suddenly became serious. "We got big prolems!..I didn't want to say anything in front of Kim...Where's Pat?"

"She's attending a Community Committee meeting downtown," Gene replied. "I think they're gonna vote her to the chair of a sub-committee against racism in the media."

Roger plopped himself down in an armchair across from Gene and rubbed his forehead in frustration. Gene stared at him, puzzled.

"Pat's a good choice for that spot," Roger muttered. "She's an attorney and she knows what she's doing."

"What's the matter?" Gene asked. "You look upset."

"This is exactly what I was worried about...Who went with Pat?"

"Nobody...She drove herself."

"Listen, Gene...We've got to re-assess you and your entire family's security," Roger whispered, dead serious. "Someone has just tried to blow you away and you and your family act like it was nothing!..Now, with this maniac escaping from the hospital...who knows what he'll try next!"

"They'll get him in a day or two," Gene said, thoughtfully. "He can't do too much...the guy was just in a week long coma."

"How do you know that?" Roger shot back, angrily. "You're the publisher of one of the major daily newspapers in the country and a multi-millionaire...you and every member of your family are not safe until they capture that sonofabitch and the bastards who hired him...and throw 'em all in prison!"

"We don't really know if anyone did hire him."

"Oh, they know...The police claim he's a professional hit man."

"The police?..They don't even know who he is!"

"And you know why they don't.."

"Yeah...I know all about the missing fingerprints," Gene said. "He's not the first felon to do that."

"That's not the point!" Roger argued. "The missing fingerprints indicate that he's done this before, which could mean that he was working for some organization that has been contracted to stop you!..And if they tried once..."

"...They'll try again," Gene interrupted. "I know...that's what Gene II has been preaching to me every day. He probably got that idea from you...But I can't let something like that possibility control my life."

"What about security guards around your home?"

"That would scare the hell out of everybody!" Gene snapped. "I appreciate your concern but lets wait and see if anything else happens...The cops are watching this place constantly. They've stopped by here so many times the last couple of days I believe Connie's got a boyfriend...if something does happen a second time...then we'll react...agreed?

"If it's not too late!" Roger sighed, disappointed, as he stood up, dejected. He looked down at Gene and shook his head. "You must be getting better...you're just as stubborn as ever...When do you plan to return to work?"

"I'll start spending a few hours there each day next week," Gene answered. "I'd better do something before you and my family put me in the poor house..."

Roger smiled and started to leave. "I'll send up your gorgeous visitor...poor girl...You'll probably ruin her day, too...But you better be careful with her and don't do anything I wouldn't do...We've got enough problems without you adding any more."

Gene smiled and took another sip of orange juice as Roger left. He picked up the newspaper and tried to continue reading as birds chirping in a nearby tree attracted his attention. In a few moments his attention was drawn to the slight creaking of the bedroom door. He looked through the French doors leading to the bedroom and saw Adrian Grant standing in the bedroom doorway, smiling at him. He felt a deep surge of emotion swell up in his chest as he was shocked by her striking beauty. He hadn't realized how badly he wanted to see her...but she knew. Neither said a word as she wet her lips and slowly walked across the wide room towards him, swinging her purse by the strap and accentuating her hip movements with each step while she stared directly into his eyes. She stopped when she reached the veranda.

"You thought you could get away from me, didn't you?" she whispered softly.

Gene smiled broadly as he took in her glamorous appearance. Her long black hair framed her delicate features like a work of art. Her hair draped down over her shoulders to an expensively tailored and deep cleavaged blue suit which firmly covered the contours of her voluptuous figure. The hemline of her skirt stopped about six inches above her knees, revealing a pair of long, slim shapely legs and stylish pumps. Gene could feel his heart respond as her complete image filled his eyes.

"GOD!..You are gorgeous!" he whispered in awe. "I forgot how extremely impressive you are!..Why would any man want to get away from you?"

"I haven't slept since this thing happened to you." she said, concerned. "I've been very worried...I've missed you so much!"

She slowly walked over to him, graciously bent down and kissed him flush on his mouth...Her tongue explored and lingered in his mouth for a long moment. Her eyes opened and she stared into his. She slowly stepped back, smiling.

"Orange juice," she whispered, faintly. "I didn't mean to smother you...Feel any better, now?"

Gene remained speechless as he watched her gracefully sit down in the chair facing him and cross her legs, revealing her smooth, creamy thighs. She glanced from his eyes to her legs and back to his eyes as he stared at her, hypnotized by her sexuality. She slowly uncrossed and crossed them again, switching their position and then moving one leg slightly and rhythmically as she inched the short skirt up higher on her thighs!.."You see anything you like?"

"You trying to give me a heart attack?" Gene asked, watching her carefully.

"You've been shot," she replied, huskily, "and I'm trying to make love to you...without touching you...or hurting you."

"You have...I won't lie to you ," Gene said. "I've been thinking about making love to you every night...and every day..."

"I want you...I want to feel you inside of me...making love to me...If I thought it wouldn't hurt you...I'd climb into your lap right now and put you inside of me...right here on this veranda!"

"What a lovely thought...I've never wanted a woman...any woman...as bad as I want you!..I don't know how much longer I can wait!"

"Just hurry and get well," she said. "That's why I had to come...I had to see you and tell you that...I feel...I think...we've been together before..."

"Before?.."

"Yes...When I heard about the shooting I was devastated! It was as if someone had shot me in the heart!..Like I was reliving an experience that had separated us before!..I cried and cried!..I couldn't stop crying!"

"I know...I know...I just kept thinking about you during this whole ordeal...as if you knew how I felt."

"I did."

"But we still must be careful...and wait a while." he said.

"I...I think Kim suspects how I feel about you...Your daughter is very sophisticated, you know."

"She's always been deeply perceptive." Gene said, thoughtfully, "a very precocious child...a daddy's little girl."

Adrian seemed relieved. "I know you think it's bold of me to come over here...but I couldn't help myself...I want you so badly!..I'm just that way...when I see what I want...I go after it...I've never felt this way about any other man. Maybe I'd better leave now...I don't want to raise any suspicions by staying too long."

Gene watched her as a big tear ran down her lovely cheek. She stood up and slowly walked back over to him. She kissed him again, long and sensuous!..He was almost breathless as she stood up straight and backed up to the French doors.

"I love you," she whispered. "When can I come back?"

"Kim's plans have changed and it looks like she's going to be here for awhile," Gene answered, thoughtfully. "I think you two should become closer friends and you should visit her here more often...I expect to be up and about in a week or so..."

"About?"

"In a week or so."

"I'll be looking forward to your early recovery," she said, smiling, "and I will make it a point to visit Kim more often...Remember...when you get well...I spell the word "sex" with a capital "S"..."

Gene watched her with a big smile on his face as she sexily sauntered back across the spacious bedroom. When she reached the doorway, she turned and blew him a kiss!..

Chapter Twelve

The enormous conference room in the Westin Hotel of Detroit's Renaissance Center was crowded with city leaders, politicians, news media and local celebrities as the Chairman of The Detroit City Community Committee pounded his gavel on the podium to attract everyone's attention.

"The vote is unanimous, "he shouted gleefully. "The new chairperson of our Community's Anti-Racism Sub-Committee is Mrs. Patricia Parker-Stanton!"

Everyone stood up, applauding and cheering as the people standing near Patricia began to shake her hand and hug her. She was quickly led up to the speaker's podium as the chants of "speech!"..."speech!"...could be heard throughout the enormous, overcrowded conference room. As Patricia stood behind the podium the shouting and hollering of the exuberant crowd quieted down as she began to speak...

"I am humbled by your vote," Patricia began, "and I intend to do the most honorable job I can do, to make this subcommittee an effective tool to eliminate all racism in our city...Today, the despicable legacy of racism haunts our country in all walks of life and it eats at our nation's infrastructure like a cancer attacks the human body...Racism is spreading with the determination and destruction of a loose cannon, recklessly over-running our cities and suburbs, invading our local, state and federal governments, all branches of the media, our schools, professions, the military, sports, entertainment and all parts of American life...We must stop this racism by structuring an effective committee that will reach out and halt this insidious social perversion that is threatening the lives, rights, safety and welfare of all Americans!"

The crowd erupted in a tremendous applause as everyone surrounded the podium, congratulating Patricia on her acceptance speech. City Councilman Bill Clark stood next to Patricia and grinned broadly. As the crowd slowly dispersed and the excitement subsided, Bill Clark managed to pull Patricia aside.

"You were terrific!" Bill said, grinning.

"Thank you...It's not difficult when you're fighting for something you've always believed in," Patricia said. "The problem is that most people don't really know how to resolve this problem of racism or what the real answer is."

Bill looked at her admiringly as her eyes sparkled in excitement!..

"And what is that answer?" he asked.

"I believe it's a whole series of social changes that must take place. Our priorities must be re-assessed. As an example, Whites, Blacks, Hispanics and Asians...know so little about each other it's amazing...I have always felt that our public schools, from kindergarten through high school, should have a mandatory curriculum on race relations and brotherhood that dispel some of the myths that have been propagated by ignorant and racist parents, relatives and friends."

"That's interesting," Bill said, thoughtfully. "They seem to have classes on everything except how to get along with each other."

"Exactly...this could become one of the primary causes our committee could research and promote," Patricia said. "Remember, when a child is born it doesn't have any prejudices or racist notions in their body...Racism and hate have to be taught..so why not teach them how to love...and not to hate?"

"That's good...That's very good," Bill said.

"Thank you again...I'm glad you understand how I feel about chairing this subcommittee and this subject...I've always been very passionate when it comes to human rights. That's why I got my law degree."

"I know...and that's why I nominated you," he said. " I still can't understand why you never practiced law. The civil rights movement needed a person like you to fight for minorities' and womens' rights...What happened, Pat?"

"Gene Stanton happened...We met when I was a senior at college. I got caught up in the State Journal Newspaper as an editor...I was so fascinated with what the whole Stanton family was trying to do with that newspaper that I became a part of it...fighting for civil rights causes and exposing crooked politicians...We were married shortly after the Viet Nam war began and we started having our children. When Martin Luther King and Bobby Kennedy were killed and Watergate hit the headlines...Gene and I thought we were the Woodward and Bernstein of Detroit...Two idealistic kids who really thought the moon was made of cheese and we could make a difference!..Before we knew what was happening, our home was full of children...exit law career."

"That's too bad...You would've made an excellent attorney. I...We all need people like you."

"I've thought about it often."

"It's not too late, you know...This committee could be your launching pad to a successful law career," he said, anxiously. "I could help you in many ways...You could begin a whole new life...Patricia Parker-Stanton, Part Two."

Patricia laughed. She turned to look up at Bill who was deadly serious. "Why should you help me?" she asked.

"You're important to me, Pat...I'm sure you know that."

"But you're a popular city-councilman, Bill...I don't think we should..."

"You know how I feel," Bill said, interrupting her. "After all these years...I want to see you ,Pat."

Patricia took a sip of her coffee, refusing to look him in the eyes. He stared at her, waiting for a response. In a few moments, other people crowded around them, congratulating Patricia...

The home that Gene Stanton II and his wife, Susan, shared with their three children was located in the North Rosedale Park area on the far northwest side of Detroit. A mixture of stately Tudor mansions, English colonials, ranch and Cape Cod architectures represented the style of single family homes that lined the well-manicured neighborhoods, and were graced with giant maple trees, evergreens, white pine and birch trees that shaded large front porches and spacious driveways...

Gene II was tired when he pulled into his driveway and walked across the front porch, into his home. He walked into the library and set his briefcase on the desk. He picked up the mail laying neatly on the corner of the desk and thumbed through it casually. He looked up when he felt Susan's presence and nodded at her as she stood in the doorway.

"Hi...I didn't know you were home," Gene II said. "You pick up the kids yet?"

"I told you this morning they were spending the day with my mother," Susan answered. "She hasn't seen them in a month."

Gene II looked back up at his wife as he remembered their early morning conversation. "Oh, yeah...You said you had something you wanted to speak to me about this evening," he said, slowly. "If it was so important, why didn't you tell me about it this morning?"

"It is important...It's something we have to discuss at some length and I didn't want to ruin your day."

"Since when did you start worryin' about ruining my day?"

"Oh, Gene!"

"I hope it's not about moving to New York...I told you, I am not about to leave my family in a lurch with my ol' man just released from the hospital...So don't even try it!"

"This isn't about us moving to New York," Susan said, solemnly. "It's about me and the kids moving to New York."

"What?..You're talkin' about some kinda vacation or somethin?"

Susan slowly walked completely into the room and faced her husband with her eyes locked to his. "We can't go on like this...when you decided to stay here and work on your family's newspaper...you virtually resigned from our marriage."

Gene II threw his hands up in disgust. "I hope we don't have to go through this again!..Look, my father almost died!..The nut that shot him has escaped from the hospital and the police think he might try something again!"

"I realize that!..I'm not some insensitive twit!"

"Then get off my back!..If you wanna go to New York for a while...until things cool off...it's alright with me. Just stop naggin' me by beating a dead horse!..This just isn't the right time!"

"I'm sorry about your dad...and I'm sure he'll be alright," Susan said. "But I can't let what happens to your family constantly take priority over what I want in my life."

"And what the hell is that, Susan?..What do you want so damn bad?"

"I want a divorce!..I want out of this marriage!"

He stopped and stared at her, disbelieving!..He slowly walked closer to her. "Is there...Is there someone else?" he asked her, calmly.

"Why do you always ask me that?..We should've been divorced years ago!"

"Then what suddenly brought this on?"

"It's not sudden...our marriage has been over for a long time," she replied angrily. "We don't even touch each other..."

"I've been involved in this changeover...You know that," he said, thoughtfully. "It hasn't been easy switching from a weekly to a daily. Now, with this thing happening to dad...maybe I haven't given you the attention I should have...but..."

Susan walked past him, over to the window. She watched her children playing in the yard. "But what?" Susan shot back. "Do you really believe that's why our marriage has failed?"

"It's probably a contributing factor...I know I've been gone most of the time...I understand how you must feel."

"No you don't...You don't even know me!"

"But we have three children and...a marrigae that can still be saved," he pleaded. "Look, I'm even willing to try a marriage counselor if you think that will help...but we just can't throw all these years of marriage out the window!"

"You can try marriage counselors or anything you can think of!" Susan said, angrily. "It won't make a damn bit of difference!..I'll still want a divorce!.."

Gene II walked up behind her and placed both hands on her shoulders, spinning her around furiously as he glared at her!.."Then there must be someone else!" he shouted in anger. "Who is it, Susan?..Tell me who the hell is it?"

F. Walton Dugas worked at his desk in the publisher's office at The Daily Press newspaper. When he heard the buzzer on his intercom system he quickly picked up the phone.

"Yes, Agnes...what is it?"

"Mr. Wilder on line two."

Dugas quickly pressed another button and sat back in his large, executive chair and crossed his legs. "Yes, Ed...Do you have any information for me?"

"Yessir...I sure do," Wilder replied.

"That was fast work...How'd you do it?"

"There's a few people at The Herald who are still friends of mine."

"Good...Let's have it."

"A Mr. Willard E. Thompson was hired on the advertising staff of The Detroit Herald Newspaper yesterday. He is twenty-one years old...Has a masters degree in Mass Communications from the University of Wisconsin...His mother's name is Gloria Stanton Thompson and his father's name was Benjamin T. Thompson...He's a six footer and he was born in Milwaukee on March 3rd, 1972...That's about all, Mr. Dugas."

"You've done a fine job, Ed...I won't forget it...There is one more thing...I'd like for you to arrange for me to see this young man."

"You want to meet with him?"

"I didn't say I wanted to meet with him," Dugas corrected. "Just get him over here...Have him make an appointment with you in your office...I'll just happen to drop by at the same time."

"But...How am I suppose to do that?"

"Just get him over here under some pretext of offering him a job on our advertising staff...Hell, offer him anything....Just get him over here!"

"But...but, Mr. Dugas...there's one other thing that you ought to know about Mr. Thompson..."

Dugas became irritated at the hesitancy in Wilder's voice. "Well, c'mon, man...out with it!" Dugas demanded.

"Mr. Dugas...he's black!"

Gene Stanton sat in a deep, cushioned chair next to his bed and watched television. He could hear Connie call him from the hallway. She stuck her head into the partly opened doorway.

"Mr. Stanton...you awake?" she asked, softly.

"No, I'm asleep."

"Huh?"

"If I had been asleep...you would've woke me up."

"The hospital just called."

"What did they want?"

"Some Doctor Hathaway," Connie replied. "He wanted to know how you're doin...I told him you were doin' just fine. But, he wouldn't take my word for it...they're sending over a Doctor Thorpe to examine your wounds to make sure they're healin' right...said it's normal procedure in these cases."

"That'll be the day," Gene said, disgustedly. "When is he comin' over?"

"A little after five this afternoon," Connie answered. "Dr. Thorpe will stop by here on his way home from the hospital...And you've got some company comin, too."

"Who's the company?"

"Your daughters...Karen and Liz."

"Good...maybe they'll break up the boredom around here." Connie came further into the room and glared at Gene with her hands on her hips, angrily..."You callin, me boring?" she snapped. "I feed you all the food you want...give you your medicine on time...take your calls...make your calls...and you say I'm boring!"

"Now wait a minute, Connie!.."

"Naw!..You wait a damn minute!" she growled. "I am not your nurse and I sure ain't nobody's secretary!"

Connie marched out of the bedroom in a huff, angrily mumbling under her breath as Gene chuckled to himself. In a few minutes he heard the voices of his two oldest daughters out in the hallway. They both came into the bedroom with big smiles on their faces. They kissed Gene playfully and sat down on both sides of the bed.

"What'd you do to Connie, dad?" Karen asked, smiling. "She's so angry smoke's coming out of her ears!"

"Nothing," Gene answered, innocently. "She's just too sensitive."

"Connie?..Sensitive?" Liz asked, laughing. "C'mom, dad...'fess up...what'd you do to her?"

"I told you...nothing."

"Looks like you're recuperating pretty fast," Karen said. "When are you going back to the office?"

"Yeah, please hurry back, dad, before it all falls apart," Liz urged. "Gene and Karen don't know what they're doin!..We need you!"

"Not half as bad as I need to get out of here and go back to work," Gene moaned. "This sitting around is drivin' me nuts!"

Karen rolled her eyes at Liz. "So me and Gene don't know what we're doin, eh!..Thanks a lot!"

"Well you don't," Liz laughed. "Karen thinks a "double truck ad" is a truck with two trailers!"

Gene began laughing loudly, holding his chest.

"You alright?" Karen asked. "Has the doctor told you when you could go back to work?"

"No...not yet," Gene answered, still chuckling. "They're sending a Dr. Thorpe over here this evening at five to see how the wounds are healing.

"Dr. Thorpe?" Liz asked. "You know him, Karen?"

"Nope...never heard of any Dr. Thorpe," Karen replied. "What happened to Dr. Hathaway?"

Liz turned to Karen, thoughtfully. "Maybe you should call Bob and find out who this Dr. Thorpe is..."

"I appreciate your concern but I'm sure he's alright," Gene said, smiling. "Probably just some friend of Hathaway's."

"No...I think Liz is right," Karen said. "We can't be too careful and it's not gonna hurt to check..."

Karen picked up the phone from the nightstand and quickly dialed her husband's office at the hospital. In a few moments she was speaking to Bob's secretary.

"Dr. Robert Whyte, please...I'm his wife." Karen spoke into the phone, impatiently. "Yes, it's very important!"

"Dr. Whyte speaking..."

"Bob...I'm with dad...He just got a call from the hospital," Karen said, nervously. "He said Dr. Hathaway called and said he was sending a Dr. Thorpe over here this evening to examine him."

"That's bull!..Carl Hathaway is on vacation and we do not have anyone on our staff called Dr. Thorpe!" Bob said, anxiously. "You better call the police!"

Karen's eyes widened in fear as she stared at Gene and Liz!..

It was late in the afternoon when the door chimes rang clearly in the shadowy Stanton mansion as the autumn sun began to set earlier. Connie quickly walked to the front vestibule. She opened the door and faced a distinguished looking, bearded gentleman carrying a small, black medical handbag in his hand. The man smiled broadly at connie...

"Yes...can I help you?" Connie asked, politely.

"I'm Dr. Thorpe from City Hospital," the man said. "Dr. Hathaway called and said I was coming to examine Mr. Stanton."

"Oh, yes, Doctor," Connie said, calmly. "Mr. Stanton is expecting you ...Follow me, please."

Connie closed the door behind the doctor and quickly led him up the wide, winding staircase. The entire hallway was shrouded in the long evening shadows as the doctor followed Connie to the master bedroom. She stopped and turned to the doctor. He looked at her, puzzled...

"Is Mr. Stanton sleeping?" he whispered.

"He was awake a few minutes ago," she answered, whispering. "Just go right in..."

Connie turned away and hurriedly walked back down the long hallway, disappearing down the staircase. The doctor slowly opened the door and walked into the spacious and dimly lit master bedroom. He saw a figure laying in the bed, under the covers. There was a small lamp lit on the nightstand next to the king-sized bed. The doctor smiled and quickly unzipped the medical bag. He reached inside and brought out an Uzi machine gun!..When the doctor looked back up he found himself staring directly into the barrel of a 357 Magnum revolver which was pointed at his head by a man sitting up in the bed, grinning at him!..

"You're...You're not Mr. Stanton!" the doctor shouted in surprise! "Who are you?"

"I'm your worse NIGHTMARE!" the man said, softly.

A second man suddenly stepped out of a closet, leveling a shotgun at the doctor!..

"Freeze!" the second man shouted! "Police!"

"Fuck you!" Damien screamed as he threw the Uzi at the man sitting on the bed and tossed the medical handbag at the man standing in front of the closet!..Several shots were fired as Damien sprinted across the room and hurled himself through the huge picture window, shattering the glass and landing with a resounding "thump" in the bushes next to the mansion!...

Chapter Thirteen

Liz stood in the kitchen of her plush apartment sipping a cup of coffee and carefully watching Ze-Ze direct the two men who were moving in her belongings. Everytime the two men would bring in a box or a piece of furniture, they would eye the women suspiciously and slightly smile at each other in a subtle manner. Liz could feel the anger swelling up inside her and managed to control it with intellectual patience and understanding. When they were finished, Ze-Ze quickly wrote them a check. The men took the check but seemed hesitant to leave. Ze-Ze glared at them, angrily.

"Is there something else?" Ze-Ze asked, impatiently.

The men looked from one woman to the other, smiling broadly. "Are you two actresses or something?" the first man asked.

"That's none of your business!" Ze-Ze snapped, angrily. "Please leave!"

"Unless you're doin somethin' illegal," the second man said, staring at her, hungrily...

Liz overheard the men talking to Ze-Ze and she quickly put down her cup and marched into the living room, visibly irritated!

"These two giving you a hard time?" Liz asked Ze-Ze.

"They're just leaving," Ze-Ze answered.

The second man stared hard at Liz, looking her up and down and licking his lips...He glanced at the first man and smiled knowingly, before he turned back to Liz...

"Wow!..What kind of work do you do, lady?" he asked Liz.

"I don't think that's any of your damn business, mister!" Liz shot back, angrily.

"If you're not doin' anything abnormal," the first man said, "you must be highclass...er...professionals...if you know what I mean."

"That's it!..Get out!" Liz shouted, angrily. "Get the hell out of my apartment before I call security!"

The two men, surprised by Liz's outburst of anger, backed up to leave, slowly turning to go out of the door.

"Unless you two are hook..." the second man stammered, as Liz slammed the door in their faces!..

Liz turned around towards Ze-Ze and they both began laughing...

"They wouldn't know what to do with it if we gave it to them with bread and butter," Liz laughed. "Two ignorant gorillas who think they're GOD's gift to women!"

"So it begins...You sure you can handle this?" Ze-Ze asked. "There's going to be a lot of flack."

"I'm not worried about it, are you?"

"Of course not."

"Most intelligent people will understand," Liz said. "Those two bozos would screw a mannequin if they could figure out how to open up her legs."

"What about your family, Liz?..Aren't you concerned about how they're going to react?"

"That's the least of my problems," Liz answered, thoughtfully. "I happen to be blessed with very intelligent parents who believe everyone has the right to live their lives the way they want to."

"Do they all feel that way?"

"The only person who might have a hard time with this is my grandmother, Hattie...She's from the old school...She'll never accept or understand our relationship."

"Have you told them I was moving in with you?"

"No...not yet."

"I detect some lack of confidence," Ze-Ze said, smiling.

"No...it's not that...So much has been going on since we switched to a daily newspaper," Liz said. "When my father was shot we were all worried...everything came to a screeching halt...It didn't seem to be so earth shattering then...and I just haven't bothered to tell anyone."

"I hope we never regret this decision. It's like putting all of your cards on the table...We both are coming out of the closet."

"Not necessarily," Liz said. "There are plenty of men and women who share an apartment with the same sex."

"Not like we will."

Liz walked over to Ze-Ze and held both of her hands in hers as she studied her face intently. "This is how I want it...These nights apart were becoming too difficult...besides, you forced this decision when you said you were thinking about taking that modeling assignment in New York...You knew how to push my panic button..."

"I didn't want to leave you...but you gave me no alternative...I love you, Liz...I want to be with you"

"This is why I took off today. I wanted to make sure you moved in...Well we're together now...for better or for worse."

The two women embraced, pressing their slim bodies together and holding each other tightly as they kissed, with their tongues plunging passionately in the other's mouth...

The wide, spacious editorial offices of The Detroit Herald Newspaper was crowded with editors, reporters, copy people and secretaries who were all rushing to meet the upcoming afternoon deadline. Copy people walking briskly back and forth, shouting excitedly!..Telephones rang incessantly as each minute to deadline neared. The noisy, uncarpeted and enormously spacious room was filled with an assortment of beat-up and battered desks, mis-matched chairs and old, worn-out and tired typewriters amid a background of ceiling high windows framed by huge finely carved oaken walls.

The receptionist's area just outside of the editorial offices was jammed with visitors and messengers as the harried receptionist tried to deal with them all as politely as she could. A small disheveled man sat across the room from the receptionist's desk, patiently waiting. The receptionist looked over at the man and smiled...

"I'm sorry you had to wait so long, sir," the receptionist said, politely. "Can I help you?"

The little man calmly picked up his briefcase, stood up and shuffled over to the receptionist's desk. He fumbled in his pocket and brought out a dirty, crumpled piece of paper that was a newspaper clipping. He studied it for a moment while the receptionist and the other people in the room waited, impatiently.

"I would like to speak to Mr. Brock about this here article, ma'am," the little man said, softly.

The receptionist quickly scanned the article and handed it back to the man. "I'm sorry, sir...Mr. Brock is busy trying to meet a deadline," she snapped. "Why don't you call back tomorrow and set up an appointment?"

"But...but whut he printed about my deceased daddy is not true, ma'am," the man persisted, "my daddy was no gangster like he said in the paper and I want a retraction!"

"Oh, geez!" the next man in line groaned, loudly.

The receptionist noticed how upset the little man was becoming and she tried to clam him down as he dabbed at the perspiration running down the sides of his face.

"Mr. Comstock was your father?" she asked, calmly. "Then you're Mr. Comstock, too..."

"That's right, ma'am...I'm Wilbur Harvey Comstock and I wanna retraction to set the record straight!"

While the receptionist continued to try to explain that Mr. Brock was not available, several more people crowded into the receptionist's area and began showing their impatience over waiting for the little man to complete his business. The receptionist felt the growing tension as the deadline crept nearer and the little man refused to listen to reason. The next man standing behind him was a beefy truck driver type who towered over Mr. Comstock. He began to openly berate Comstock for holding everyone else up...

"C'mon, Mac!" the next man shouted, angrily. "She said the man wasn't available so beat it!"

The little man slowly turned around and stared up at the huge man, with an angry expression on his face. "I wasn't addressing you, sir!" Comstock replied in an even voice. "Will you kindly stop interfering in my conversation!"

"But Mr. Comstock," The receptionist pleaded, "Mr. Brock is going to be tied up for quite some time!"

Mr. Comstock wouldn't budge as he continued to explain further when the beefy man behind him shoved him aside, angrily!..Comstock calmly went back to the chair he had been sitting in and casually sat down. He quickly snapped open his briefcase and began to assemble a machine gun!...Suddenly, a woman in the area looked at what he was doing and began screaming!

"Oh, my GOD!..He's got a gun!" she shouted.

Before anyone could stop him, Comstock stood up with the machine gun leveled at everyone in the receptionist's area!..He shot the beefy man who had shoved him first as they all began running and screaming, throwing themselves on the floor!..The receptionist tried to run out of the office door and he shot her in the back!..He quickly moved over to the doors of the spacious editorial office and began firing across the long rows of desks at anything that dared to move!..As he wandered aimlessly through the maze of desks in the enormous office, he jerked off his dirty army jacket, revealing sticks of dynamite strapped to his chest!..

Satisfied that he was in complete control of all of the editorial offices as well as the large gymnasium sized office he was standing in, he remained in the center of the room looking from wall to wall. The only sounds that could be heard were the incessant ringing of the telephones and the back and forth swinging of the now empty swivel chairs!..he slowly moved back over to the doorway leading back to the receptionist area. Again, he searched carefully for anything that moved as he walked gingerly into the receptionist's area...Hearing voices murmuring excitedly back inside the editorial room, Comstock paused on the receptionist's side of the doorway, leaning back against the door frame, waiting patiently and grinning...He slammed another magazine into the chamber of the machine gun and began singing in a little child's voice...

"Last night, the night before, twenty-four robbers at my door...I got up and let 'em in...Hit 'em in the head with a rollin pin!..All hid?..Ready or not...here I come!.." he shouted loudly. "Mr. Brock!..Mr. Brock!..Come out, come out...Where ever you are!"

All of the many people in the spacious editorial offices remained frozen, hiding under their desks and behind filing cabinets!..A few people behind Comstock quickly managed to escape through the doors of the front office, stepping over the bodies of the receptionist and the beefy man!..As they ran out of the door, Comstock sprayed the front doorway with machine gun fire!..Finally, everything had quieted down when Comstock sat in a large executive swivel chair in the center of the large room, and shot out all of the windows in the glass enclosed offices!..

He spun around in the chair with his short legs spread out like a small child while he held the machine gun and waved it back and forth, ready to fire!..

In the distance, the sounds of alternating sirens coming closer and closer to the newspaper building, screamed in the background as Comstock, seemingly oblivious to all the sounds, sat in the swivel armchair in the middle of the vast room, spinning around with the machine gun leveled and his two feet sticking out in front of him as he laughed hysterically!..

Gene II sat behind his father's desk in the publisher's office and conducted a meeting with several local business-people who were directors of their respective companies and were considering opening offices in the Detroit area. The meeting was serious and tense when suddenly, Gene II's secretary barged into the office, obviously upset!..He was most annoyed by the bold, unannounced intrusion!..

"What's the problem?" Gene II asked, annoyed.

"Dean Montrose in editorial is on the line!" she replied, excitedly. "He says it's an emergency!"

Gene II quickly picked up his phone. "Montrose?..What's the problem?..I can barely hear you!"

"I...I can't talk too loud, Gene!" Montrose whispered, nervously. "There's a madman down here shooting up the place!..I'm under my desk right now!"

Gene II quickly stood up, completely unnerved! "Has anyone been hurt?"

"I'm afraid so!" Montrose shot back. "At least two people have been shot...they may be dead!..Get the police, Gene!..This guy is completely NUTS!"

Detroit Police cars blanketed the area surrounding The Detroit Herald Newspaper. Several ambulances stood by just down the street in the next block. Hundreds of onlookers crowded the street in front of the building and at both intersections on each end of the block as police tried to hold the crowd back. Several police brass huddled together around a police command car that was parked directly in front of the revolving front doors leading into the lobby. Police sharp shooters were placed strategically on top of the buildings on all sides of the Herald's building.

A SWAT team commander boldly walked towards the police command car with members of his team following behind him. The commander moved to the middle of the group and quickly became the center of attention. In the background, TV crews interviewed various bystanders...The SWAT team commander was soon asking most of the questions of the police brass.

"What do we have, Judson?" the SWAT commander asked. "Are all the exits secured?"

"Some waco's in there with an automatic weapon, shootin' up the place...looks like an Uzi!" Captain Judson explained. "He's killed two people and he's got the entire editorial department, about thirty people, as hostages!..Everytime somebody sticks their head up from under a desk. ...He shoots at 'em!"

"What's his gripe?" the SWAT commander asked. "Anybody know?"

"Yeah...he's after some reporter named Brock," a second police commander replied. "It seems this Brock called this guy's daddy a gangster in an article he wrote and the shooter didn't take too kindly to it!"

"Have you deployed any sharp shooters?" the SWAT commander asked.

"Oh, yeah...but it ain't gonna do any good," the first police commander said, "not with this joker."

"Why not?"

"I put the binoculars on him," Judson answered. "You can see him through the windows in the second floor...He's loaded with ammo and he's go his upper torso completely strapped in with dynamite sticks!..You pop him and he takes half the building with him!"

"Holy smoke!..That ends any ideas about picking him off," the SWAT commander grumbles. "Has anyone established contact with him?"

"Yeah...he's a cool cucumber," Judson replied. "He either wants to talk to Brock or the publisher...He wants that retraction on that story!"

"Geez!..Why didn't he just send a damn letter to the editor!" the SWAT team commander groaned. "Anyone get in touch with the publisher yet?"

Gene Stanton was still dressed in his pajamas and bathrobe as he sat behind his desk in the library, desperately concerned as he talked to Gene II on the speaker phone. Patricia, Hattie, Joe and Roger Carlson, along with several policemen, all stood anxiously in the background, waiting and listening...

"How many employees are in the editorial offices?" Gene asked his son.

"About thirty-five, dad," Gene II replied. "I arranged to have the gunman hooked up here and to the police outside in the street."

"What does he want?"

"He's upset about an article that John Brock wrote, calling his father a gangster...He wants us to print a retraction to clear up his father's name."

"Where's Brock at now?"

"He's in the editorial offices...probably hiding under his desk like everyone else!"

"Does the gunman know he's there?"

"I'm not sure...but he said he would only negotiate with Brock or the publisher...We don't have too much more time, dad...he's got about twenty-five sticks of dynamite strapped to his body!"

"What are the police doing?"

"I spoke to Captain Judson...He's got the SWAT team standing by, but he's prepared to wait him out to avoid any more bloodshed...too many lives involved."

"Can you put me through to Brock?" Gene asked, thoughtfully.

"Gosh!..I dunno, dad...Brock knows that if he answers his phone the gunman might find out where he is!"

"I thought you said most of them were hiding under desks...he ought to be able to answer his phone without anyone seeing him."

"OK...I'll try it," Gene II said, "I'll ring his number...Stay on the line, dad."

Gene waited patiently while the rest of the people in the room nervously watched. In a few minutes Gene II was back on the line. "Dad...you still there?"

"Yeah...did you reach Brock?" "I'm on the line now, Mr. Stanton," Brock whispered, hoarsely, "you gotta do something to get us out of here!..This guy's a psycho!"

"Just take it easy, John," Gene said, calmly. "I want you to answer a few questions first...Was your article completely authentic?"

"What?..Of course it was!..I wouldn't lie!"

"Did his father have a criminal record?"

"Well...no...but he associated with known criminals."

"Was he ever arrested?"

"No...Not that I know of."

"OK, John...you can get off the line now," Gene said, still calm. "We'll have this resolve in a short time...just stay under that desk until we can get him out of there...Try to be patient a little while longer."

Gene waited until Brock was off the line before he continued speaking to Gene II.

"Dad?..Dad?..You still there?" Gene II asked, nervously.

"Yeah, I'm still here...Have we gone to press on the third edition yet?"

"We were just getting it ready when this happened...Why?"

"I wanna talk to this...this Wilbur Harvey Comstock first," Gene said, thoughtfully, "but have the composing room on standby."

"OK...I'll get Comstock on the line."

There is the sound of ringing on the line while Gene waited, nervously.

"Editorial Department," Comstock sang jovially as he answered the phone. "May I help you?"

"Mr...Mr. Comstock," Gene II nervously stammered. "I've got my father, the publisher, on the line...He wants to speak to you."

"A big time newspaper publisher wants to talk to little ol' me?" Comstock shouted, laughing loudly. "Well I'll be damned!..I must be somebody important!..Is he on the line now?"

"Yessir...he's on the line now."

"Whut can I do fer you, Mr. Stanton?"

"What can I do for you, Mr. Comstock?" Gene asked, calmly. "I understand you've go a complaint with our newspaper."

"You're damn right I do!..And I want a retraction on that false article you ran about my daddy!.. He wasn't no crook!"

"If we print the retraction...will you surrender?"

"You gonna print the retraction?"

"You have my word."

"How do I know you're tellin' the truth?" Comstock asked, suspiciously.

"You'll see the retraction on the front page of the next edition," Gene assured him, firmly.

"Ah, hah!..I think you're tryin' to set me up for some dummy newspaper trick, Mr. Stanton!"

"No tricks...this is serious business. You hold the lives of fifty of my employees in your hands!..This is no time for tricks...We'll present you with at least ten newspapers with the retraction on the front page."

"You listen to me, Gene Stanton...the only way I'll agree to surrender is if you, yourself, come down here and show me at least fifty newspapers with that retraction on it!..And if you do try to pull any stuff...you'll be history!"

"I'm sorry...I would if I could," Gene said, "But I'm being honest with you...I'm still recovering from an attempt on my life and I am not physically able to do that."

"Oh, that's right...I remember...You were almost killed." Comstock said, apologetically. "I'm truly sorry about that, Mr.. Stanton... but I'll accept your son...unarmed!..And it better be your son and not some cop!..You got thirty minutes or our deal is off...My watch says four-twenty...I'll give you until five...Then I'll start usin' your employees for target practice and shovin' bodies out the window like ping-pong balls!"

Comstock slammed the phone down, angrily!

"You still on the line, son?"

"Yes...Yes, dad...I'm still here."

"I'll clear this with the police...I want you to get with the composing room supervisor right away...Set up a five column wide by five inch deep, retraction on the front page of the next edition on the fold...put a big, black, heavy border all around it..."

"I can handle the composing room, alright," Gene II said, hesitatingly.

"You got a problem with taking it down to Comstock?"

"It's...it's too dangerous, dad?..He's already killed two people!...I'm...I'm not going down there!"

Gene quickly turned his back to everyone in the room and switched the speaker phone back to private. He looked at his son, Joe, who had moved over towards him and now stood over his desk, staring down at him.

"What's the matter?" Joe asked in a whisper. "He doesn't want to do it?..I will!"

"Just a minute, Gene," Gene said into the phone. He placed a hand over the mouthpiece and turned to Joe. "You'd be willing to do that?..it's really not your responsibility and he's right...We're dealing with an unstable person...It will be dangerous as hell!"

"It's the kind of job I've been trained to do, dad," Joe replied, smiling, "besides, it's my newspaper, too!..Didn't Comstock say he would only deal with your son?"

"You can get downtown that fast?" Gene asked.

"We'll take him down in a squad car!" a police commander volunteered. "You ready, son?"

Patricia grabbed Joe's arm as he turned to leave. "Joey!...Be careful...please!"

"Don't worry, mom," Joe said, smiling. "You know...at first I really thought that this whole thing was a sham...a diversion to draw security away from dad...I don't anymore...But don't worry...this is a piece of cake...I've been in a lot worse situations than this."

"Don't be concerned with my security," Gene said, "you be careful...that guy has lost his marbles!"

"You'll still have your security guards, dad," Joe replied. "And I'll get back here as soon as I can."

Joe quickly turned and left the room, followed by the police commander and two uniformed policemen. Gene waited until he heard the wailing sound of the siren going away from the Stanton mansion. He turned his attention back to the phone...

"OK, son...we're all set. You get the composing room started on that retraction...Your brother, Joe, is on his way down there...he'll take it down to Comstock."

"Yes...that's probably best," Gene II whispered. "You understand don't you?"

"Yes...I understand...don't worry about it...You're doing a fine job."

Gene hung up the phone and looked at Patricia who was standing next to his desk with her arms folded as tears streaked down her cheeks...

Joe Stanton stepped off of the elevator on the second floor of The Detroit Herald newspaper building. He was pushing a small dolly stacked with freshly printed newspapers just off the press. Two other men on the elevator nervously slid a wooden pallet stacked with hundreds of newspapers fresh off the press, behind him. The two men deposited the pallet near the quiet editorial offices, nodded at Joe and quickly got

THE WINDS OF TOMORROW

back on the elevator and closed the doors.

Joe looked at the large clock on the wall in front of the editorial offices' receptionist area. it was one minute to five. He looked up and down the long hallway. No one was in sight. It was unusually quiet as he slowly wheeled the dolly towards the receptionist's area. He saw the two bodies laying sprawled across the floor in huge puddles of blood. As he slowly moved forward he could feel the eyes of the hiding employees following every move he made...

"Hey!..Get down, you fool before he kills you!" someone whispered.

Joe merely nodded, looked straight ahead and continued wheeling the dolly into the spacious editorial offices. He sensed movement behind him and suddenly stopped!..

"Freeze!..Just hold it right there!" Comstock ordered. "If you move I'll kill you!"

Comstock walked up behind Joe and began searching him carefully. Soon, he stopped and sat on the edge of a desk with the Uzi machine gun pointed at Joe's back! "OK!..You can turn around now!"

Joe slowly turned around facing Comstock. Comstock's face turned a bright red with anger as he stared at Joe!..

"I told that Gene Stanton not to try anything foolish!" Comstock screamed in Joe's face. "Who the hell are you?..You ain't his son!"

"The hell I'm not!..You said you'd accept his son," Joe argued, strongly. "Well, dammit!..I'm his son!..His second son...and if you don't believe me, check my driver's license!"

Comstock quickly slid off the desk and pulled Joe's wallet out of his back pocket. He fumbled through the wallet for a few moments and then put it back in Joe's pocket, while he still jammed the muzzle of the Uzi into Joe's back.

"OK...so you're his son...How many newspapers do you have?" Comstock asked, "I said at lease one hundred."

"You said fifty!..I got one hundred...check it out."

Comstock backed up towards the dolly, cautiously, keeping his eyes on Joe. He motioned to Joe with the Uzi.

"Alright, Mr.. Stanton...put your hands behind your head and get over there and face the wall while I check out these newspapers."

Joe did what he was told as Comstock went over the newspapers, counting them carefully. He stopped and read the retraction with a big grin on his face..."Well, one thing's for sure...Your ol' man keeps his word."

"What about your word...you plan on keepin' it?"

"How do I know these ain't the only newspapers you intend to print with that retraction?"

"I thought you might ask that," Joe replied. "I got a whole skid out in the hallway with more than five thousand newspapers stacked on it...You wanna check that out first?"

Comstock was stunned. "You...you have?..OK...If that's true...let's take a little walk out there and see."

Joe marched in front of Comstock, out through the editorial offices. They stepped over the bodies in the receptionist's area and out into the hallway. Comstock was overwhelmed by the pallet of newspapers stacked high up into the air and banded with steel cables. All of the newspaper had the retraction notice on the front page, visible on the fold...

"Well I'll be damned!.." Comstock exclaimed, surprised.

Before he could regain his composure, Joe moved like lightning and had Comstock in a deadlock hold with both of his arms and his chin bent backwards and Joe's knee in his spine!..Comstock immediately dropped the Uzi as Joe applied the pressure needed to disarm him!..

"AAaagh!..AAagh!.." Comstock managed to sputter, choking on his own blood! "What're you tryin' to do...kill me?"

"You got that right!" Joe replied, angrily.

"I told you I would surrender, didn't I?"

"Yeah, but this way...I knew you wouldn't change your mind!"

The sounds of shouting and applause could be heard inside the editorial offices as employees suddenly began to emerge from their hiding places. They seemed to come from everywhere!..They crawled out from under desks, behind filing cabinets, closets and just about anywhere they could possibly hide!..Women began crying hysterically when they saw the two bodies!..The entire area was suddenly filled with police and members of the SWAT team. Four policemen quickly handcuffed Comstock, read him his rights, arrested him officially and marched him away. Joe smiled at everybody as he calmly stepped on the elevator...

When Joe walked into the publisher's outer office he was surprised by the silence that greeted him. He realized most of the employees had been cleared from the building for their own safety but the soundless offices were eery in the dim shadows. He noticed a light shining from his father's office. When he walked in the office he found his brother, Gene II, sitting behind his father's desk, drinking and staring out of the window, thoughtfully. He didn't bother to turn around when he heard Joe walk into the room...

"It's all over, big brother," Joe said, quietly. "They've taken Comstock away."

"Yeah, I know...Little Joey to the rescue," Gene said, sarcastically.

"You alright?" Joe asked, surprised by the tone in his brother's voice.

"Yeah, I'm alright...just get the hell outta this office!"

Joe stared at Gene II, stunned by his angry response. He started backing out of the office, bewildered...

"Well?..Are you leavin' or not?" Gene II shouted, angrily. "What the hell are you standin' there for?"

"Yeah...I'm leaving," Joe spoke, calmly. "I just like for it to be my idea."

Chapter Fourteen

Roger Carlson sat in his living room deeply engrossed in reading the evening Herald as his wife, Janet, walked into the room. He put down the newspaper and stared at her with a puzzled expression on his face. Janet was obviously upset.

"I something wrong?" Roger asked.

"No...not really...I was just thinking about that madman at the newspaper," Janet replied. "You could've been caught up in that...You're on that floor everyday."

"Well, it's all over now...it's just sad those two people were killed...Such a waste!..I guess we're lucky more people weren't hurt."

"But don't you see. It shows how fragile our lives really are," Janet lamented, sadly. "It can be taken away at the blink of an eye."

Roger put the newspaper down and studied his wife, carefully.

"I guess life offers only so many opportunities at happiness," Janet continued. "We should take it when we can."

"Exactly what is all of this leading up to?" Roger asked, suspiciously.

"I think we should try to adopt again."

"C'mon, Janet...You know that is not going to work for us." Roger said. "The minute they discover you were hospitalized for mental depression they'll turn us down."

"There's other ways we can adopt. It may be more expensive...but at least we could try."

"Where did you hear about this?"

"Our minister suggested it...He said he couldn't vouch for it, but he had heard that several childless couples had successfully adopted a child through this organization."

Roger got up and walked across the room, pondering the situation. "What's the name of the organization?"

"It's called "The Forgotten Child Foundation"...These are babies who have either been abandoned or who have lost both parents and have no known living relatives," Janet answered, anxiously. "In some cases it might be better for us because there would never be any interference from a biological parent or relative."

"You're excited about this aren't you?" Roger said, thoughtfully. "Don't get your hopes up too high...Let me check it out first."

"We have an appointment for our preliminary interview...tomorrow morning at ten."

"Oh, Janet!..You shouldn't have done that without discussing it with me first!"

"But Mr. Chabot said it would only be an interview and I knew you'd be available since Gene Stanton is still off sick."

"Who is this Mr.. Chabot?"

"He's the mid-west director," Janet replied. "They have a full medical staff, a small clinic where they maintain new born babies...Roger, it sound just wonderful!"

"What are their fees?"

"Just minimal...but the great thing is...they can process our application in only thirty days instead of six months!..We can actually have our very own baby in one month!"

Roger saw the excitement in his wife's eyes and his heart melted. He walked over and embraced her, tenderly.

"OK...OK...We'll check it out tomorrow...only promise me something...don't get your hopes up and become disappointed. It'll only break your heart..."

Janet looked up at Roger and dabbed at the tears in her eyes as she nodded her head in agreement...

Patricia Parker-Stanton worked at her desk in the downtown offices of the City Community Committee. She was deeply involved in a report she was studying. She looked up as Councilman Bill Clark strolled into her office, grinning broadly.

"Hi, Bill...I'm surprised to see you this early in the day," Patricia said, returning his smile. "How'd you manage to get away from the City-County building?"

"I just got off the phone with Washington," Bill replied, anxiously. "The President's Committee To End Racial Injustice is meeting next week."

"I know...it's all in the press and on television...and it's about time!"

"The Vice-President is chairing the meetings...it's gonna last for six consecutive days," Bill said, beaming. "Senator Holden's wife was appointed to the committee last January, but she's seriously ill and can't make it."

Bill walked around her desk and leaned down, closer to Patricia. She looked up at him, startled, when he placed his hand on top of hers...

"So?..How does that effect me?" she asked.

"I recommended that you be named to replace her on the Michigan staff and Washington approved it!..I told 'em about some of the things you've done and they were overjoyed!"

Patricia was speechless!..She got up and walked to the front of the desk. She turned back to face Bill as he sat on the edge of the desk and smiled.

"What a great opportunity!" she exclaimed, thoughtfully. "I'd love to go...but I can't...not now!"

Bill walked around the desk and placed both hands on her shoulders. "Why not?"

"Gene's not completely recovered," she answered, "And that shooting at the newspaper has everyone up tight...I...I don't think I should leave now."

"Why not?..You told me Gene was doing just great and that he planned to go back to work next week."

Patricia stared up into Bill's eyes, searching. "Who else is going to Washington from here?"

Bill quickly embraced her, kissing her squarely on her lips before she could resist. He felt her body relax and her tongue softly met his...Suddenly she stepped back and tried to compose herself, visibly upset.

"You...You shouldn't have don that," she said, quietly.

"You know how I feel about you," Bill said, "this is nothing new...I've been in love with you ever since we met."

"You haven't answered my question...Who else is going to Washington from Detroit?"

Bill stood in the middle of the office, staring intently at Patricia.

"I am," he replied.

Gene Stanton sat in the wide family room in the Stanton home surrounded by his mother, wife and his daughter, Liz. He was clearly out numbered as he persisted with his decision to return to work at The Herald...

"I told you all once and I'm telling you for the last time," Gene said, determined. "I am going back to work next Monday!"

"Did your doctors say it was OK?" Liz asked. "I bet you can't answer that one!"

"They didn't say I shouldn't!" Gene shot back.

"Oh, for heaven's sake," Hattie argued, "you're the most hard-headed man I've ever known...except for your father!"

"Aw, ma!..Lighten up...I know what I'm doin," Gene groaned. "Pat's gonna be in Washington for a week...and I'm goin' back to work...I've been cleared by my doctors, so knock it off!"

"What's my going to Washington have to do with your going back to work?" Patricia asked.

"You must feel I'm doin' OK," Gene snapped. "You're not gonna be here."

"What's the matter?" Liz teased. "Mommie's little boy jealous?"

"And Liz is tied up with her new roommate," Gene chuckled. "Nobody cares about me."

"What new roommate?" Hattie asked.

Liz rolled her eyes at her father, disapprovingly. "One of my models moved into my apartment."

"Is it that French girl?" Hattie asked, suspiciously.

"Yes, it's Ze-Ze...Why?" Liz asked.

"I disapprove of that and you know it!" Hattie replied, angrily.

"C'mon, Hattie...it's Liz's life," Pat said.

"It's not right," Hattie argued. "Two young women being that way!"

"That's none of your business, mamma!" Gene interrupted, furiously. "Liz and Ze-Ze are two grown women and they do not need nor want your approval!"

"It's against the bible!" Hattie shot back, angrier.

"It's not even mentioned in the bible!" Liz retorted. "And if you can't understand it, that's...that's just too damn bad!..it's people like you with those old fashioned ideas that are responsible for so many teenagers committing suicide...Society tells them one thing and their minds and bodies are telling them something else!..It's time to wake up and smell the roses, grandma!..Everything is not just black or white...male or female!..There's a whole lot of folks in between!..Have a good trip, mamma...and...and goodnight!"

Liz angrily stomped out of the house and slammed the front door loudly!..Gene looked at Hattie in disgust as he shook his head slowly.

"Sometimes, mamma...you gotta give a little," Gene said, sadly. "Liz is a wonderful daughter and you've hurt her very deeply...for no reason."

Hattie angrily turned and marched out of the room!

It was Gene Stanton's first day back on the job. He sat behind his desk in his office at The Herald as the editors and supervisors from the editorial department all crowded in his large office. They all individually welcomed Gene back with big smiles and handshakes. The chattering and loud laughter began to settle down as Gene prepared to speak...

"Well, ladies and gentlemen," Gene began, smiling. "As I was saying before I was so rudely interrupted..."

Before Gene could finish his sentence everyone in the room began laughing as they recalled that Gene was shot as he was speaking in the conference room. All of the laughter quieted down as Gene, still smiling, continued...

"What's happened at this newspaper the last forty-five days is a grim reminder of our government's lack of a viable gun control law," Gene said, seriously. "Two completely unrelated events that could've caused the deaths of many innocent people...Considering the amount of bullets that were flying through the air, the death rate could've been much higher... This has greatly sharpened my opinion on a strong federal gun control law...While I was laid up I did a lot of research on this issue and one of the main facts that impressed me more than anything else...is that the second amendment of our constitution, which supposedly grants each citizen the individual right to bear arms...is the most ambiguous amendment to the U.S. Constitution..."

"What do you mean?" an editor interrupted. "It does grant the right for every citizen to bear arms."

Smiling broadly, Gene picked up a typewritten sheet of paper from his desk and waved it in front of the staff...

"This is a copy of the second amendment," Gene said, "once I read it to you, I'm sure you will understand why those opposed to gun control are reluctant to argue for it in federal court...Listen carefully..."A well regulated militia being necessary to the security of a free state, the right of the people to keep and bear arms shall not be infringed..."

Gene calmly laid the paper back on his desk as he studied the faced of the people sitting in his office...

"The key phrase is "A well regulated militia"...At the time that the second amendment was written, there was a great mistrust of the standing armies, as a result each state granted the right for it's "militia" to bear arms...What it was really referring to is what we call today...The National Guard!..There is NO MENTION of any individual citizen having the right to bear arms...

"I don't understand," a second editor said. "Why would those against gun control be reluctant to take a case to federal court?"

A third editor turned to the second editor with a slight smirk on his face. "Because if they went into federal court and lost, then a clear precedent favoring gun control would be set and soon more gun control laws would dominate the market...substantially decreasing the purchase and manufacturing of guns!"

"And that may not be such a bad idea," Gene said, anxiously. "In 1988, handguns killed seven people in Great Britain, nineteen in Switzerland, twenty-five in Israel, thirteen in Australia and eight across the border in Canada...These are all strong gun control countries... For that same period of time in the United States, eight thousand, nine hundred and fifteen Americans were killed as a result of handgun violence!"

Everyone in the room became quiet as those figures sunk into their minds. They looked at each other, stunned by the news!..

"Wow!..Those are some scary statistics!" the first editor said. "What are the latest figures you have?"

Gene pulled out another long sheet of paper and began to speak..."First, before I give you these figures, I want you to know that a copy of these figures and the source of this information will be on your desks when you go back to your offices...I wanted you all to understand why this newspaper is going to launch a strong drive for a federal gun control law!.."

"What year do these latest figures cover?" a fourth editor asked.

"The latest figures the FBI had were for 1991," Gene said. "The country of Japan had the best record of any country along with the most stringent gun control laws. For a country of 123 million people...approximately half the population of the United States, they only had 137 deaths by firearms. Great Britain, a population of 57 million, had 80 deaths by firearms, Canada, population 26 million, had 271 deaths by firearms, Germany, population 78 million, had 943 deaths by firearms..."

"Gee!..We got some cities with more deaths by firearms than some of those countries!" the third editor exclaimed. "I'm afraid to ask...what about the good ol' U.S. of A?"

"It's not good...and keep in mind," Gene said in all seriousness, "all of those other countries have strong gun control laws...Another factor you must be made aware of is that many people only look for deaths by handguns when they are gathering statistics...As a result, they get misleading information...However, if one should research the deaths by firearms, their figures will be much more accurate...You see, machine guns, AK-47 automatic assault rifles...are not considered as handguns while many of these weapons including sawed-off shotguns and deer-rifles, have been used in drive-by shootings and contribute greatly to the homicide statistics."

"What are the figures for the United States?" another editor asked. "I know we won't be proud of them."

"We certainly will NOT!" Gene snapped, angrily. "We should be ashamed of them!..To allow the wanton murdering of our citizens merely to support the gun industry is insane!..And every member of our congress and senate should hang their heads in shame as this carnage continues!..The United States, with a population of 253 million, had 14,265 deaths by firearms for 1991!..And THAT figure does not include accidents and suicides by firearms like the figures for the other countries which did include accidents and suicides but were no where near the unbelievable figures of the United States!..The state of California, with a population of 30 million lost 2,690 citizens, Illinois with a population of 8 million lost 830 people, and Michigan with a population of 9 million lost 676 citizens... New York, a population of 16 million lost 1,653 Americans, and Texas with a population of 17 million lost 1,840 citizens!"

"That's absolutely disgusting!" the first editor said. "It's sick!..If a foreign country had killed 14,265 Americans...we'd nuke 'em!"

"Why don't you have the suicide and accident statistics for the United States?" the fourth editor asked.

"You won't believe this," Gene answered, "the U.S. Consumer Product Safety Commission is barred by statute from collecting data on gun accidents!"

"Oh, now I smell a rat!" the first editor sneered. "I guess it doesn't take a rocket scientist to figure out what organization was behind that little gem of manipulation!"

"What are you proposing, Mr. Stanton?" the second editor asked. "Are we goin' after 'em?"

"Over the last five years this country has lost over 60,000 American lives due to deaths by firearms!" Gene replied, angrily. "You're damn right we're goin' after 'em!..it would be un-American if we didn't!..We, at this newspaper have had first-class examples of the results of the lack of effective gun control laws!..It's our responsibility to bring these gruesome facts to our readers...they've got to know what's going on with firearms in this country!..Our political leaders are not doing their jobs!..According to the National Education Institution over 100,000 American school children get up every morning during school semester, pack their lunch, pack their schoolbooks, and pack a gun to go to school!.."

"No wonder these teachers are intimidated by their students," another editor said, "Some of 'em are packin' iron!"

"In addition to this loss of life in our country," Gene continued, "the absence of an effective gun control law has caused some of the most notorious and dangerous criminals in the world to flock to the United States because of the easy access to firearms. These thugs and killers strut through our streets armed to the teeth, knowing that there are no effective laws to stop them!"

"What's your plan, Gene?" the third editor asked.

"Yeah!..How do we stop this murder?" the second editor asked, angrily.

"We will launch the strongest editorial attack against the lack of gun control that this country has ever seen!..We, here at The Detroit Herald, have seen the bloody results in the form of our colleagues...We read about murder by firearms everyday!..Now we're losing more young American lives as the death rate by firearms escalates each year!..From the desert to the sea...from coast to coast and border to border...to all of the United States of America...We must stop the violence!"

Chapter Fifteen

The offices of The Forgotten Child Foundation were located in the heart of downtown Detroit in the former offices of The Michigan Department of Social Services, which implied an officially sanctioned organization, the perfect endorsement for a baby selling operation. This was one of the main factors Luther Chabot had considered when he and his wife, Edna, and their gang of confidence cohorts were forced to leave Miami to avoid being arrested. After setting up their antiseptic appearing offices, joining and becoming active members of the local Right-To-Life Anti-Abortion group, and making large cash donations to major churches in the metro Detroit area, they quietly began soliciting young, pregnant suburban teenagers to help them avoid abortions. Within a matter of weeks they had references from important religious figures of professional couples eager but unable to adopt for various reasons, which Luther and his group planned to match with the growing list of young, unwed and pregnant women who jumped at the opportunity to avoid abortions while their pre-natal care was being paid for by the foundation.

Roger Carlson and his wife, Janet, felt uncomfortable as they sat in the waiting room of The Forgotten Child Foundation. Although the offices were clean and well maintained, they both felt an uneasiness that usually accompanied unfamiliar and suspicious business transactions. In a few minutes a woman dressed in a nurse's uniform stepped out into the waiting room and greeted them with a warm smile.

"Good morning," the nurse said, "are you Mr. and Mrs. Carlson?"

"Yes, good morning," Janet replied. "We have a ten o'clock appointment with Mr. Chabot."

"Yes, I know...I'm Edna...Mr. Chabot's wife."

"Nice meeting you, Mrs. Chabot," Roger said. "Are we too early?"

THE WINDS OF TOMORROW

"No, you're right on time...My husband will be with you in a few minutes."

"Have you been established here in the Detroit area long?" Roger quickly asked, casually.

Edna looked at Roger with a puzzled expression. She ignored his question. "What profession are you in, Mr. Carlson?"

"I'm a corporate attorney."

"I just asked because our clients must be in good financial status with a clean credit record," she said as she handed Janet an application. "Will you please fill out this application first?..Mr. Chabot will be right out and he'll answer any other questions you may have about our organization."

Edna quickly walked out of the room. Roger looked at Janet, confused and perturbed. "Did you see that?..She completely ignored my question!"

"Stop being so suspicious," Janet replied. "She's probably only doing what she's been told."

Just as they completed the application Mr. Chabot walked out into the waiting room and extended his hand to Roger with a big smile on his face.

"You must be the Carlsons," Chabot said, "I'm Luther Chabot...the director here. Glad to meet you both...Let's go into my office so we can talk...Did you have enough time to complete the application?"

Chabot reached for the application and quickly led them down a hallway to his office at the rear of the suite. His office was large, spacious and expensively decorated. He motioned for the Carlsons to have a seat as he scanned the application, thoughtfully. He sat behind his desk and continued perusing the application until he looked up and stared at Roger, peering over his glasses.

"You a lawyer for The Detroit Herald?" he asked, surprised. "Then why are you here?..You shouldn't have any problem adopting a child."

"My wife had a...a nervous breakdown a few years back," Roger replied, reluctantly, "and none of the adoption agencies would consider us beyond that..."

Chabot turned to Janet and smiled. "You alright now, Mrs. Carlson?..Have you had any recurrence of the problem since then?"

"No...I'm fine...That mental depression was caused by a plane crash that took the lives of both my parents," Janet explained. "It was an extremely traumatic experience."

"I can certainly understand that," Chabot said, turning back to Roger. "What I can't understand is why a man with your connections would have trouble adopting a child regardless of what happened to your wife."

"The State laws are very stringent," Roger answered. "They have to be protective against any potential child abuse by an unstable characteristic...I don't think my position was that important in that case."

"Well it seems to me that a severe reaction like your wife had was perfectly logical in considering the effects of such a drastic accident," Chabot said, thoughtfully.

"Thank you for being so kind," Janet said.

"What about now?..You feel you're up to dealing with an infant?" Chabot asked. "Many people think they are until they're confronted with the daily ritual of feeding and maintaining a baby...A lot of us just aren't meant for that, you know."

"Yes...I'm sure I'm ready...I've been working every day at The Herald as a supervisor in the business offices," Janet replied, confidently, "so I feel that I could handle the caring of a baby with no problem...In fact...if I could have had a baby on my own...I'd have at least three by now."

"Well, you certainly seem to have the right attitude," Chabot said, smiling. "Our foundation takes great pride in bringing parents and babies together...These are infants who are born out of wedlock to young mothers who cannot and do not want to raise the children...They come from all over the country to be adopted by our pre-selected parents...people such as you two...Some of the mothers are high school and college students, runaways, homeless...they come from all over."

"What are your fees?" Roger asked.

"We do not sell babies, Mr. Carlson...that's illegal," Chabot quickly replied, staring Roger directly in the eyes. "Other than the infant's maintenance cost and the mother's pre-natal care, we only ask for a small donation so we can continue to pay salaries to our personnel in order to place these infants with loving parents with substantial incomes who can assure the child a good and secure future...We are a non-profit organization."

"How much is the donation?" Roger asked.

"I wouldn't worry about that right now," Chabot answered. "We'll begin our investigation of you and your wife and if you are approved by our board, then we will ascertain the total amount of your donation fee."

"How soon will that be?" Janet asked, anxiously. "I was told we could have a baby in thirty days."

Chabot got up from behind his desk and walked around to Janet and Roger, smiling broadly. "That all depends on your investigation...Dr. Morton's physical examination of you both, and the availability of the kind of infant you may want...Right now, everyone seems to want a blond, blue eyed little girl...But just be patient. I'll contact you in a few days and we'll get this show on the road...if it's feasible...Goodbye for now...I'll be in touch..."

Roger looked at Janet and they both turned to leave. Roger carefully looked at all of the offices as they walked back down the hall. Janet frowned at the suspicious look in Roger's eyes...

Later that afternoon, Roger and Gene II sat in front of Gene's desk at The Herald, in a serious discussion about The Forgotten Child Foundation. Gene listened attentively.

"So you and Janet are going to try to adopt again?" Gene asked. "I thought you gave that up."

"Janet's becoming obsessive about it..," Roger replied. "She came up with this Forgotten Child Foundation and she really thinks she can get a baby in thirty days or so...Personally, I think it's a rip-off!"

"Why?" Gene II asked.

"The minute you walk into the place you can sense something's not right," Roger answered. "When I asked the director what the fee was...he evaded my question and said they only charged for the maintenance of the infants."

"That sounds reasonable," Gene said.

"Plus a small donation that will be determined after they complete their investigation," Roger added, sarcastically.

"You mean once they find out how much you're worth!" Gene II said, grinning. "They're gonna sock it to you, Rog, you ol' skinflint!..You still got the first dollar you ever earned!"

Gene chuckled, softly. "Maybe we ought to look into it. Have you contacted the police?"

"They haven't committed any crime that I know of and there's been no complaints filed against them," Roger said. "I checked with the Better Business Bureau...they're clean."

"If they are crooked...I'm sure they'll turn you down because of your connection to The Herald," Gene said.

"I know...I tried to prepare Janet for that," Roger said, sadly.

"Look, dad," Gene II said, "why don't we put a couple of our best investigative reporters on this?..They might uncover something."

"Who do you have in mind?" Gene asked.

"I think we ought to use two women instead of a woman and a man," Gene II said, thoughtfully, "this way, one could pretend to be pregnant and the other could be her caring best friend...If the pregnant woman appears desperate enough...they might tip their hands."

"Ok...go for it," Gene said, thoughtfully, "only after all the trouble we've had here recently I wanna make sure we take all the necessary precautions and I want to sit in when you interview whoever you select..I don't want anyone else getting hurt!"

"They'll have to have phony medical records to verify that one of them is pregnant," Roger said. "Chabot has some doctor on his staff."

"No problem...I'll arrange that with my son-in-law, Dr. Bob Whyte," Gene said, "as Chief of Surgery at City Hospital he ought to be able to set that up...What reporters are you planning to use?"

"I've got two excellent choices," Gene II replied. "One has been doing a fantastic job reporting on prostitution along the downtown corridors."

"You mean Marcy Dugas?" Gene asked. "Good choice...Who else?"

"Kim's ex-college professor," Gene II answered. "She's sophisticated and all business enough to mislead anybody...You met her, dad...Adrian Grant...She's been assigned to the City-County building."

"Ok...get 'em both up here," Gene said, thoughtfully. "Roger and I will sit in on your interviews."

Gene and Roger sat quietly as Gene II calmly interviewed the two women separately for the assignment of going undercover to investigate The Forgotten Child Foundation. When they were finished, Gene II called both women back into the office. They were both calm on the surface, but excited to learn they were going to be entrusted with this kind of responsibility.

"Remember, this assignment is strictly voluntary," Gene II warned. "It could become dangerous...But if these people are really in the baby selling business...we want to expose them!"

"When will my medical records be ready?" Marcy asked.

"As soon as you give me the word, I'll set it up," Gene II answered. "We'll switch your last names...Marcy Grant and Adrian Dugas."

"I'm ready," Marcy said quickly. "If I'm acceptable, order my medical records."

"Me too," Adrian said, anxiously. "When do we start?"

"Not so fast!..I want you both to thoroughly think this over during the weekend," Gene II said. "If either of you decide to change your mind, we'll understand...You can reach me here at the newspaper all weekend if you have any questions...The rest of my family's gonna be out of town this weekend so you won't be able to reach anyone else...Kim's gone back to the west coast, my dad's gonna be spending a few days on his special island in upper Michigan, and my mother's in Washington, D.C...So I'll be the only one available."

Adrian slowly turned to Gene and smiled. "That sounds wonderful, Mr. Stanton...Do you have a place up there?"

"We've got a little log cabin lodge on this island near Lake Superior...Grand Island," Gene replied, smiling. "Nothing's up there but pine trees, wild berries and black bears...And a lot of fishing...This time of year it's beautiful up there...quiet and peaceful...waiting for the first snowfall...I'll go up there and relax for a few days...Write a few editorials on gun control."

"You deserve it, Gene," Roger said. "Go up there and forget the rest of the world."

"He can sure do it up there," Gene II said. "The entire island is twelve miles long and five miles wide...It has a summer population of about fifteen hundred...and they seem to disappear in the woods...In the wintertime, I don't think there's more than fifty people on the whole damn island!"

"Wow!..That sounds enchanting!" Adrian exclaimed. "A whole big island...a piece of the world...almost all to yourself!"

"That would be a swell place for a honeymoon," Marcy laughed.

"There are a few spartan motels on the island," Gene said, "and two small restaurants and boat houses...but they're all closed during the winter months...It's a great place to hide-out."

Gene stood up, signaling an end to the meeting. The two women quickly left and Gene II and Roger retreated to their offices. Gene sat back down and relaxed back in his executive swivel chair. He studied an editorial outline on gun control he had written earlier. He shook his head thoughtfully and quickly jotted down a few changes. Suddenly his intercom buzzed and he picked up his phone.

"Yes, Flo."

"Mr. Stanton...Dr. Grant on line one."

Gene depressed the button for the first line. "Gene Stanton."

"I like pine trees, wild berries...and black bears, too," Adrian cooed over the line, slightly chuckling. "So when are we leaving for your mysterious Grand Island?..It sound absolutely delicious!"

"You really want to go up there?" Gene asked, smiling broadly. "It's kinda rustic and cold...Big, old fireplace and a pot belly stove...We may have to chop some logs...and really rough it!"

"I'd love it!" Adrian quickly answered. "I'll protect you in case that crazy person shows up again."

"We won't have to worry about him...He could never find that place...But you...I'd love to have you with me!" Gene said, laughing. "I don't know how much writing I'll be able to do...but I think you might be better project."

"I might, eh?..Thanks a lot!"

"You buy enough groceries for two days and I'll pick you up at your place on Friday around five...We'll get the corporate helicopter at City Airport...I'll be looking forward to sharing this experience with you."

"I will too...as I have been...ever since I first met you," she said, softly.

"It's gonna be cold up there."

"I'm not concerned about that...I'll have you to keep me warm."

"You're delightful!..Do you realize what you do to me?"

"I know what I'm going to do to you..This will be one weekend you'll never forget...And it will be incredibly sexy!"

The personnel director's office of The Daily Press was secluded at the rear of a wide office area with rows of desks and computer monitors. The sounds of office machines clattered efficiently in the background as many employees turned their attention to the rare Black man who walked confidently back to the director's office. Ed Wilder stepped out of his office and greeted Willard Tompson, shaking his hand, firmly. Wilder invited him into his office and quickly offered him a seat as he gingerly closed the office door.

"Glad to meet you Mr. Thompson," Wilder said, "let me thank you for making yourself available on such short notice."

Willard glanced around the office, suspiciously. "What's this all about, Mr. Wilder?"

"Before we start...there's someone else who wants to sit in on this interview," Wilder said, smiling, "if you don't mind."

"Oh?..Who is that?"

"Let me explain a few things before I identify this person," Wilder continued, nervously. "The Daily Press is about to launch an Affirmative Action Program to hire more African-American employees."

"That's very surprising...My understanding was that your newspaper was firmly against any kind of Affirmative Action Plan."

"Oh, no...Not completely...Our conservative stance has been largely exaggerated. We're searching for qualified minorities to join our company...especially on the advertising staffs...Since you're one of the first candidates to be interviewed..."

"Hold it right there, Mr. Wilder!" Willard quickly interrupted. "I am not a candidate!..I was just hired on the advertising staff of The Herald...My uncle is the owner and publisher...I'm not about to leave there!..How'd you guys even know about me?"

"Just be patient and listen to our offer," Wilder said, calmly. "The person who wants to sit in on this interview is our publisher, Mr. F. Walton Dugas!"

"The publisher?" Willard asked, surprised. "Are you serious?"

"Mr. Dugas believes in the "hand-on" approach...This is a delicate issue and he wants this program to be successful," Wilder replied. "He's waiting for me to let him know that he would be welcome to sit in on our...our little talk. Shall I call him in?"

"It's his newspaper," Willard snapped. "His building, too...It's OK by me."

Willard sat back in his chair and crossed his legs while Wilder spoke to his secretary over the phone. In a few minutes, F. Walton Dugas walked into the office. He slowly closed the door, not taking his eyes off of Willard as he quickly stood up and shook Dugas' hand. Dugas sized Willard up and looked him over carefully. Dugas tried to be subtle as he checked Willard's facial features, his build and his height...Finally, obviously satisfied, Dugas proudly stood facing Willard, eye to eye and smiled broadly.

"Yes...you're the genuine article," Dugas quipped.

"Wh...what?" Willard responded, looking from Dugas to Wilder, confused.

"I'm happy to meet you, Mr. Thompson," Dugas said. "We've checked out your qualifications and we are all impressed...You are the prototype college graduate we were looking for."

"Thank you, sir...but I just explained to Mr. Wilder that I was not available...I'm working for my uncle, Gene Stanton...Blood is thicker than water."

Dugas smiled. "My daughter works for The Herald, too. That's not unusual in this business...If she can work for your uncle, why can't you work for her father?..I'd like for you to come up to my office so we can discuss this matter further."

Willard picked up his briefcase and followed Dugas as they quickly left the confused Wilder sitting behind his desk with a puzzled and bewildered expression on his face. Dugas and Willard walked through the maze of desks among the astonished stares of the employees.

After they had settled in Dugas' plush office, Dugas sat behind his desk and studied Willard, thoughtfully. Willard sat in front of the desk in obvious discomfort.

"Tell me about your parents, Mr. Thompson," Dugas asked, respectfully.

"My dad died just before I was born...I never knew him. My mom married Ben Thompson when I was only three. He adopted me a few years later. He died when I was fifteen...and he was a very decent and caring person."

"You don't know this...but I know your family quite well," Dugas said. "Your grandfather and my father had a good business relationship...I know your uncle, Gene, and your mom...I've been knowing them both for more than twenty-five years."

"I...I wasn't aware of that," Willard said, surprised. "They've never mentioned your name."

Dugas got up and slowly walked over to the window overlooking downtown Detroit...

"Detroit is certainly a beautiful city," Dugas said, thoughtfully. "I'm gonna hate leaving here."

"You leaving Detroit?"

"We're building a state-of-the-art newspaper plant and business offices in Troy. We're expanding and the future looks great for all of our employees...and that could include you, Willard," Dugas said, grinning broadly as he reached behind several filing cabinets and brought out a scaled down miniature display of The Daily Press' new newspaper plant and general offices made up in styrofoam. "I just saw your mother about a month ago...right after your uncle was shot."

"That's just after we got here," Willard said, stunned.

"Look...I have a son and a daughter...My daughter is a reporter with The Herald...She's never agreed with me on anything," Dugas said in disgust. "My son's not worth a dime!..I know how important it is to have children who can live up to the image a parent projects..."

"What's all that got to do with me?"

"If you come over to the Press...I'll double your salary and give you a piece of the action...You could own part of all this!..I can make you a rich man!" Dugas said, indicating the miniature display sitting on top of his desk.

"Wait a minute...something's not right here!" Willard said, angrily. "What's going on?..Why would you do something like that?..You don't even know me!"

"When I met with your mother last month...she told me something that was difficult for me to believe...until now."

"What was that?"

"And I'm depending on you to keep this information confidential...for your mother's sake and mine...Of course it can be verified by your mother and a DNA test...I'll cooperate anyway I can."

"You've lost me, Mr. Dugas," Willard said, still confused. "Just what the hell are you talkin' about?"

Dugas turned around and faced Willard directly. He walked over behind his desk and leaned on the desk with both hands and stared directly into Willard's eyes..."Your biological father didn't die!..According to your mother...I'm your father!"

Willard was shocked when Dugas spoke those words!..He sat stunned, paralyzed to the chair!..

Kelly Millard sat in a medical examination room, partially dressed. In a few moments her doctor stepped into the small room with a big smile on her face. Kelly casually looked at the woman and smiled back.

"How am I doin, doc?" Kelly asked. "Am I still clean?"

The doctor, a middle aged woman, proudly patted Kelly on her back. "You've kept your word," the doctor replied. "There is no evidence of any drugs in your system...I'm so proud of you!..You must really be in love!"

Kelly got up from the examining table and began to put on her clothes. "I could've told you that...Mel and I are finished with that kind of life style...We just get high off of each other...I think it's a matter of growing up and accepting responsibility...It's not hard if you have the right kind of support system."

"Has Mel heard anything from the NBA?" the doctor asked, concerned. "It must be difficult for him being closed in at the newspaper...especially with all that violence!..How's his dad doing?"

"Just great...He was in such marvelous condition he's already gone back to work...He's been teasing us about getting married."

"I think that's a good idea...Especially now."

"Now?..What does that mean?"

"It means you're pregnant, Kelly!" the doctor beamed. "You're going to have a baby!"

Kelly was speechless when she plopped back down on the examining table, completely stunned!..

Roger and Janet Carlson sat in Dr. Robert Whyte's office in City Hospital. In a few minutes Robert walked in.

"I'm sorry you had to wait," he apologized. "There was a little emergency I had to look after...Would you care for some coffee?"

"No thanks, Bob," Roger answered, seriously. "I'm here to see about two things...You know we weren't able to adopt a child."

THE WINDS OF TOMORROW

"No...I'm sorry...I didn't know."

"The first thing we want to discuss is this...We went through a group called The Forgotten Child Foundation," Roger said. "They're suppose to be able to help couples who haven't been able to adopt through normal channels. We checked them out and I'm kinda suspicious of the whole outfit."

"He's suspicious, Bob," Janet said. "I'm not."

"Is this the same place that Gene II called me about?" Bob asked.

"It is...The Herald's gonna investigate 'em to see if they're on the up and up," Roger replied. "He said he was going to call you."

Robert began to search the top of his cluttered desk until he located a medical report. "He did...I've got a complete medical history for a Ms...Ms. Marcy Grant, twenty-four years old, White Caucasian and very, very pregnant."

"That's it...After the Foundation found out I was corporate attorney for The Herald, they suddenly became cautious...so I suspect they'll turn us down."

"What can I do for you?" Robert asked, handing the medical report to Roger.

"Bob...we'd like some information on the in vitro fertilization program," Janet said.

Robert looked at them both as a big grin creased his face. "You mean in which there is a surrogate mother involved?"

"Yes...I understand they are sometimes referred to as "host mothers"...Janet said.

"That's correct...There are two different types of surrogacy," Robert explained, "artificial insemination which is when the child the mother carries is genetically related to her..and in vitro fertilization which is when the child she carries has no genetic relationship to her."

"Exactly what steps should we take to pursue in vitro fertilization?" Roger asked.

"First, you should ascertain if you and your wife are capable of creating an embryo that could be transferred to a host surrogate mother," Robert said. "If you, Janet, can produce viable eggs and your husband can produce effective sperm, then you have crossed the first hurdle and are halfway home."

"Is that the only way it can be done?" Janet asked.

"By no means...An embryo can be created with the use of only one parent or with neither," Robert answered. "Many couples are considering surrogate parenting who are candidates for the comprehensive egg donor program."

"Then you don't think that...ah...we may be too old?" Janet asked.

"That's not as much a consideration as you may think," Robert said, smiling. "The important fact is that if you and your spouse can produce a healthy embryo...then you can seek out a compatible and young host mother who can carry the child for you."

"You mean Janet and I...we could have our own baby?" Roger asked, anx-

- 153 -

iously. "Our very own flesh and blood?"

"Providing you two, together, can produce a viable embryo," Robert continued. "If not...then you would have the option of either one of you being the natural parent...or you join the egg donor program...either way...you get your baby."

"Then...what do we do?" Janet asked quickly. "How do we get started?"

"First, you should contact an Infertility Specialist," Robert explained. "They will provide you with psychological counseling, medical screening, continuing psychological assessment, and legal consultation...You will both undergo a strict medical procedure."

"Wow!..You're saying...if Janet and I are found to be psychologically and physically sound...we could still have our own child?" Roger needed confirmation.

"You got it!" Robert confirmed. "But remember...you still have to find that host mother."

Roger stared hard at Janet who is now beaming with hope!..They both turn back to Robert, who is still grinning at them...

"Is there anything else?" Janet asked, cautiously.

"It'll take a few days to get the test results but I can arrange for you to be tested here and I happen to know of an Infertility Specialist who would be happy to talk to you...Shall I call her?"

"Yes, Bob...please do!" Janet answered quickly. "This is so exciting!"

"We're not leaving this office until you do!" Roger said as he reached over and squeezed his wife's hand!..

Chapter Sixteen

Grand Island was big, beautiful and bashful. The mystery of it's vast and unspoiled woodlands, it's miles of great lakes' shoreline and inviting interiors offered visitors a mystic place where dreams could come alive, linger for weeks and fade away in a storybook ending. In late summer, many forest trails are covered in an emerald canopy of maple, birch, poplar, cottonwood, cedar, spruce and pine. The forest floor is a rich carpet of velvety deep green mosses, brown, yellow and scarlet mushrooms, the green leaves and shiny red fruit of bunchberries, wild raspberries and blueberries which serve as dessert for black bears preparing for winter hibernation. Deer seem to be everywhere on the island. An entire afternoon of wandering through this wilderness, one might never see another human being. The island is so large that it also contains a half-dozen internal lakes that flow with clear, blue water. A hike through the forest reveals a beaver's paradise. Many trees, some of them towering giants with massive trunks, show signs of the beaver's industrial teeth, which intermittently adds a fresh beam to the wild tangle of mossy lumber on the forest floor. Much of the rocky shoreline, especially along the island's north side, is gently sloping and ideal for beachcombing and watching the huge shapes of great lakes freighters gliding majestically through the foggy waters...

As The Herald's helicopter skillfully maneuvered over the island, Adrian looked at Gene and smiled as the huge craft gently landed and settled in the clearing, blowing leaves swirling around them like a mini tornado. The pilot quickly assisted them out of the helicopter to a waiting station wagon. A man and a woman grabbed their bags and placed them in the back of the vehicle. As the station wagon bounced over the hilly and winding dirt roads, Gene squeezed Adrian to him and lightly kissed her on the cheek.

"Adrian...this is Mr. and Mrs. Jones," Gene said. "They live up here and maintain the grounds to our hunting lodge...Harry...Marie...This is Adrian Grant."

Marie turned and looked at Adrian with a big smile on her tanned face. "Nice meeting you, Ms. Grant...welcome to our island...I hope you enjoy your stay."

"I know you will," Harry shouted over his shoulder as he drove along the steep hills. "Me and Marie love it up here...and we live here year around."

"I'm sure I will too," Adrian answered, smiling at Gene. "If this island is as nice as it looks...it's gonna be paradise!"

Harry Jones drove the car into a spacious clearing where a massive lodge loomed up in front of them. The entire area looked like a giant stage surrounded by huge pine trees. The lodge was laid out like a horse shoe with the enormous lodge building in the center and ten smaller units, motel like log cabins, on one side of the lodge and the main house with an attached garage on the other side. All of the buildings were made up with a log exterior. Adrian gasped in surprise!..

"Oh, my GOD!" Adrian cried out. "This place is fantastic!..I thought you said it was just an old log cabin!"

"It is...they're all made out of logs," Gene laughed. "My father had this place built for his hunting club...It hasn't been used much in the last twenty years."

"This is so enchanting!" Adrian said as they climbed out of the station wagon. She pulled up the collar of her jacket as the cold winds swept in from the lake giving her a slight chill.

"Better button up, young lady," Harry Jones laughed as he carried their luggage towards the main house. "S'pose to come a storm in the mornin'!"

"A storm?..What kind of storm?" Adrian asked.

"Bout six inches of snow," Marie answered.

"Six inches!"

"Maybe more...We get snow earlier up here," Marie said. "Our winter starts in October."

Adrian turned to Gene as they walked towards the main house. "Is that true?" she asked. "It's cold enough to snow now?"

"It probably will snow anytime now," Gene answered, with a big grin on his face. "I love it...It's like a winter wonderland around here...Trees become covered with snow and their heavily laden branches sway with the slightest breeze. The lakes are frozen over and the animals become bolder as they forage for food."

The wind began to whistle as they hurriedly walked inside the large home and closed the door. Adrian smiled at Gene when the aroma of burning white birch logs drew their attention to the flashing lights from the dancing fire in the old, stonefaced fireplace. Adrian giggled like a little girl with a delightful surprise..."Hey!..Who started the fire?" she asked as she quickly ran over and stood with her back to the fireplace. She quickly turned around, trying to get warm all over.

Gene looked at her and laughed. Harry and Marie set the bags of groceries on the kitchen table and left the luggage in the dining room.

"Well, Mr. Stanton," Harry said, grinning. "I guess you're all set for awhile...Me and Marie will be goin...If there's anything you need, just give us a jingle."

"Thank you both," Gene said. "I really appreciate your help...and thanks for that fire, too...that was a real nice touch."

"No problem," Marie replied with a twinkle in her eyes. "I hope you enjoy your stay up here, Ms. Adrian."

"Not Ms. Adrian," Gene corrected. "It's Dr. Adrian."

"You a doctor?" Harry asked, surprised, "Well I'll be damned!"

"Yes...but you can call me Adrian," she said, smiling. "I would prefer that you do...please."

"Then that's it...Adrian...Have a good day."

Adrian watched through the large picture window in the living room when huge snowflakes began dancing out of the dark gray skies as Harry and Marie pulled away in the old station wagon. Gene walked up behind her and slipped his arms around her waist as he buried his face into her hair.

"You remind me of a little girl," he whispered in her ear. "A very cold little girl."

She turned around and looked up, directly into his eyes. "Tell me the truth...Have you brought many other women up here?"

"No...I knew you were thinking that," Gene answered. "But nobody comes up here anymore except me...alone...I use to bring the family up here but they all outgrew it...Seems nobody really likes to get this close to nature anymore."

"What about your wife?"

"She hasn't been up here in ten years."

"And what about...Harry and Marie?"

"What about them?"

"Can you trust them?..You know...are they discreet?"

Gene smiled as he released her and walked over to poke at the logs in the fireplace. "Harry and Marie are native American Indians who's tribe was forced to move because of new state highway construction," Gene answered, thoughtfully. "My father provided them with legal representation to get them relocated and a big financial settlement...That was nearly thirty years ago. He hired their families to maintain this lodge and they've been here ever since...They are fiercely loyal to me...we can trust them."

Adrian walked over to him with a stern expression on her face. "And there's one more thing I'd like to clear up."

"What's that?"

"I thought we were going to rough it...You call this roughing it?..This place looks like a luxurious ski resort! You are a liar, Gene Stanton!"

Gene stood up and moved closer to her, gazing down into those soft, hazel eyes. He quickly swept her up in his arms and gently pressed his lips to hers, tasting the warmth of her passion..."Guilty," he whispered.

Adrian leaned back in his arms, staring into his eyes and slightly smiling...He hungrily began kissing her all over her face and neck...

"It's snowing hard outside now," Adrian said, softly. "The fireplace is crackling...we're all alone on this entire island and we've got two whole days...Now...I'm going to make love to you like you've never been loved before!"

She stopped and stepped backward with a puzzled expression on her face.

"What's the matter?" Gene asked.

"Are...Are you sure you can handle this?" she asked, concerned. "It's not too soon?"

He answered her question by kissing her feverishly full on her mouth, his tongue joining hers...He hesitated, stopped and stared at her..."Be gentle with me," he whispered.

She returned his passion, unbuttoning his jacket and pulling off his scarf...As she pressed her body to his, her moist lips met his as her tongue again invaded his mouth, searching and exploring. She melted in his arms as she continued kissing him all over his face, neck and ears. Everything just seemed naturally to follow in progression. There was no urgency, no hurrying. Just a beautiful warmth and gentleness as they kissed and caressed each other in front of the crackling fireplace. Gene's hand deftly opened her jacket and his fingers lightly traced her nipples through her blouse and bra. She guided him to the huge sofa in the living room, staring deeply into his eyes. She started to undress herself but he stopped her and took over...With each article of her clothing he removed, he slowly continued kissing and caressing her. He slipped off her lacy bra from the back and cupped her erect breasts in each hand. His tongue skillfully teased her hard, swollen nipples. He worshipped her breasts, sucking and kissing them until she couldn't stand it any longer!..

"Hurry!..Please!" she urged. "I don't want to wait...I want you inside of me!"

She nuzzled her face into his neck as he completed undressing. Now, they lay in each other's arms, both completely naked as he continued kissing her body, her face, neck, down to her breasts, and her navel. Finally, he raised himself above her on his elbows and slid in between her long, shapely legs, and as though they were made for each other, he slowly found her moist opening almost automatically, moving slowly at first as they pressed their bodies together. The long awaited feeling was just too much for her and she moaned her approval and joy as she locked her arms around his neck and her legs wrapped around his back as he increased the tempo with each thrust into her body!..They moved in complete coordination, each stroke, each caress, each kiss, as their moist bodies rythmetically moved against each other like giant waves slapping against the shore!..

When Gene awoke the next morning, his arm automatically searched for Adrian even before he opened his eyes. When he failed to find her, he sat up in bed looking around the huge master bedroom..."Adrian...Adrian!..Where are you?"

"I'm over here...enjoying the view."

Gene saw her, wrapped up in a skimpy robe and sitting down on the floor with her arms around her knees, next to the large picture window in the bedroom. It was the crack of dawn and the drapes had been fully opened presenting a panoramic view of silently falling snowflakes covering the giant pine trees on the vast landscape with the dramatic lights of daybreak peeking over the horizon in the background.

Gene slowly got out of bed and slipped on his robe. He walked over and knelt down beside her, burying his face in her long, black hair and lightly kissing her cheek and neck as she laid back into his arms and sighed pleasantly.

"C'mon back to bed, baby," he whispered, "it's too early to get up."

"Oh, all of this snow, daybreak and these huge pine trees!" she exclaimed, happily. "This is so beautiful!..I couldn't pass up a view like this!"

"I could."

"And you know what?..I just saw a big black bear walk over that mountain!"

"What mountain?"

"Over there," she said, pointing out of the window.

"That's not a mountain...that's a hill...that's my hill."

"Your hill?" she asked. "Why is that your hill?"

"When they were building these cabins up here...all the members of the lodge would bring their children up here to watch the workers finish the construction. Me and a bunch of kids took the scrap lumber and made wooden swords. We fought with our swords to see who would be "King Of The Mountian" and I won...That's been my hill ever since."

"King of the mountain?" she asked, smiling.

"Yeah...don't laugh...And right now the King is hungry as hell!" Gene said, thoughtfully. "Why am I so hungry?"

"Because we forgot to eat anything last night," she laughed. "All we did was make love...and it was terrific!"

"Yeah...it was great...and you were marvelous!" Gene said, kissing her neck and sighing. "C'mon back to bed."

He put his arm around her slim waist and they slowly got up and moved back over to the bed, still kissing and caressing.

"You gonna close the drapes?" she asked.

"Naw...I think we can teach nature something."

He quickly pulled off his robe and slipped back into bed. He reached for her and her robe fell off. She stood there, completely naked with the light of dawn behind her. She stared at him and smiled.

"Damn, you're gorgeous!" Gene said. "Come here...let me make love to you...I might as well starve to death!"

Adrian laughed softly as she slipped back into bed and kissed him, plunging her tongue into his mouth..."You're a wonderful lover...You make me feel so brand new!"

"I love you, Adrian," Gene whispered as his arms embraced her. "I've known that for some time now."

"I know...You've never said it...but I knew," she said, kissing his chest and lightly pulling at his chest hair. "I love you, too...Of course I'm sure you knew it."

"We're very lucky people, Adrian."

"It's more than just luck...This love that we've found is very, very special...I feel like I've known you before."

"That's strange...I feel the same way...your touch...your taste...the smell of your hair...you're like a dream come true."

She slowly moved on top of him, her legs straddling his thighs. She placed both hands on his shoulders as she slowly positioned herself, joining their bodies together. She bent over and kissed him, deeply. As he kissed and mouthed her breasts, he could barely see her smile as the shadows and her long black hair partially covered her face as she began slowly moving up and down...

"I love you SO MUCH!" she whispered, softly. "I'll NEVER leave you, Gene!..We'll be together forever...You are my very true love!"

Patricia Parker Stanton stood behind the podium in the spacious White House conference room that was crowded with administration officials and representatives from all over the country. Several microphones set directly in front of her as a bespectacled Patricia continued her speech...

"...In the past, many good and honest politicians passed federal laws intended to prevent racial discrimination in employment while the extremist right wing politicians put forth no bright ideas about job opportunities," Patricia said, sternly, "other than to cry and whine about what a hardship it was for businesses if they couldn't discriminate against Black Americans the way they use to...They wanted their fictitious rights as racial bigots preserved as if these rights were guaranteed by the U.S. Constitution...Today, many of the African-Americans who weren't even born during the civil rights marches of the sixties, are not aware of the tremendous strides this country has made against racism...As a result of these bloody victories, the large majority of African-Americans are now middle-class or higher...This proves that the civil rights marches of the sixties were successful!..But there are still more than ten million Black Americans still under the poverty level...Many minorities...Hispanics, Asians, as well as Blacks and Whites, are suffering every day because of systematic racism in the media!..Included are many of our major daily newspapers across the country, who, even after actually being hit with a series of racial discrimination lawsuits, still reluctantly respond with positive actions in hiring and assignments...Television programs featuring Black actors center primarily on comedy instead of portraying Black families in dramatic or business environments...In the 1990s Hollywood welcomed new, young Black film-makers, provided they produced movies which were consistent in denigrating and maintaining the stereotype of Black urban ghetto dwellers as criminals, drug abusers, and prostitutes...Where are the middle-class Black Americans ever depicted?..In addition, television and newspapers and magazines are all guilty of treating African-Americans as invisible people...When a Black American looks into the warped mirror of advertising they see stereotypes or nothing...When an African-American examines their personal lives they see families, professionals, working people, scientists and teachers...But when they see advertising on TV or in the print media they see Blacks who are athletes, musicians...or they see a kid bouncing a basketball...or moving to the beat a boombox on his shoulder...or they see White men, White women and White children using the soap, eating the food, driving the car...and a Black person in the background...America has done a lot to fight racism in the past...but our government and all of the media...Must do more!"

Everyone began applauding, standing up and shouting, showing their approval!..Patricia quickly walked back to her seat at the long, conference table...

Patricia's speech electrified the audience and it was carried on every national TV newscast that evening. She received glowing accolades from women's and civil rights groups as well as a special invitation from the White House to extend her stay another week and attend various functions.

It was later in the afternoon the following day, during a winter snowstorm in Washington, D.C. as Patricia, engrossed in researching statistics at her temporary office, suddenly stopped working and threw her pen down on the desk. She got up and walked over to the window in obvious frustration. She watched the heavy snowfall for awhile until she felt the presence of someone else in the office. She quickly turned to find Bill Clark standing in the doorway, covered with snow. Surprised, she stood there and stared at him...

"I...I thought we agreed...to disagree," Patricia stammered. "I mean...you said you wouldn't push...and here you are!"

I'm sorry...I'm not really pushing," Bill said. "I...I just needed to see you...I was so proud of you yesterday!"

"Oh, Bill!..This is no good!"

"Just give me a few minutes...please!"

"Why?..What good will it do?"

"Let's talk about this thing," Bill said. "I honestly believe Gene is taking advantage of your loyalty. He knows what kind of person you are...responsible...your whole life centered around your family...You even put your law career on hold...just for him!"

"That's true...and I am...I'm also still in love with my husband."

"I think you're in love with being in love with your husband," Bill shot back. "You'd like for it to be so...but it really isn't and you know it!"

Patricia stared at Bill as he stood in the middle of the office all covered with snow and his face flushed from the cold weather. A smile flickered across her face and he relaxed. She motioned for him to take off his coat.

"I'm sorry...take off that coat...You're covered with snow!..Would you like some coffee?"

Bill quickly took off his coat and shook off the snow, stomping his feet. Patricia poured two cups of coffee and handed a cup to Bill.

"What a day!..It's so cold outside it's absolutely miserable!" Bill said, shaking off the chill. "The traffic is bogged down and the snow is getting heavier!"

"Yes it is...One would have to have a good reason to travel in weather like this."

"I did!..You're my reason."

"We've been all through this before and you promised."

"I've been thinking," Bill interrupted, "I might have a solution to our problem...will you listen to it?"

"There's nothing to discuss!"

"You're about to make a major decision that could effect both our lives," Bill said, concerned, "I'm only asking that you consider all of the facts...Gene has made his move. He turned down your request for him to retire and now he's got his daily newspaper that he's married to...Now it's up to you to realize you have a life of your own to live and react to...I'm just asking for a little more time for our side."

"Our side?"

"Yours and mine...Let's find out how deep our love for each other really is...I know how much I love you...I think you're afraid to find out how deep your feelings are for me!"

"I haven't denied my feelings for you."

"Then find out how strong it is...If it's only a flash-in-the-pan, stimulated by memories that have been embellished with the passage of time...you'll know what to do...but if it's something more...meaningful...something that is really true love...it'll come to the surface and the truth will guide you to me!"

Patricia turned and walked back over to the window with her back to Bill..."And if you're wrong...are you willing to let go?.. Would you be willing to step out of my life?"

"I'm not even worried about that."

She quickly turned around and faced him. Her eyes searched his, closely. "Then let's have it...let's hear your solution."

"While we're here in Washington...my family has this wonderful New England resort up in Maine...Now, when skiing is at it's peak, it becomes a picture of pure winter beauty with the towering pine trees and snow covered mountains glistening in the sunlight. At night the wind whispers through the icicles guarding the windows while the aroma of cappuchino tantalizes your senses and warms your heart and soul while you rest comfortably in the deep leather sofas and chairs that surround a massive fireplace."

"That's some kind of commercial!" Patricia chuckled.

"I only want a few days...You can always say you were asked to stay longer again by the White House."

"What are you asking me, Bill?"

"I'm asking you to go away with me...to my winter Shangri-La...Gene has had his time...He's in love with that newspaper...You know the feelings you have for him. They're all confused with the memories of raising your family and your commitment to being a good wife and that one-way loyalty!..I'm only asking for a few days to determine the rest of our lives!"

Patricia stared hard at Bill as he walked over to her and they slowly embraced...His lips gently met her's as her arms brought him closer to her...He held her tightly, kissing her face and her neck while she could barely catch her breath!..

The offices of The Forgotten Child Foundation were nearly empty when Adrian and Marcy became the first customers at the foundation early in the morning. Edna Chabot greeted them in the waiting room.

"Good morning," Edna said, smiling, "can I help you?"

"Yes...I'm Marcy Grant...I called you yesterday for an appointment," Marcy said, anxiously, "and this is my very close friend, Adrian Dugas."

"Oh, yes...You're right on time, Ms. Grant," Edna replied. "Did you bring..."

Before she could complete her sentence an obviously distraught couple barged into the office!.."Where's your husband, Edna?" the man shouted, angrily. "We've paid you over fifty thousand and we still don't have our baby!"

"Mr. Bannister...please!" Edna replied, nervously. "Can't you see that I'm busy?"

"Either we get our baby or I demand our money back!" the man screamed. "Every red cent!..Do you understand?"

Luther Chabot suddenly bolted into the waiting room!..He moved in front of the couple in an attempt to calm them down. "Hey!..Hey!..What's all the racket about?" Chabot asked Bannister.

"You know what it's all about, you crook!" Bannister's wife screamed at Luther. "Either we get our money back or we're going to the police!"

"I told you sometimes it might take a little longer to locate the right child," Luther explained, calmly, "but if you don't want to wait...you can pick up your check tomorrow afternoon."

"OK...You've got twenty-four hours," Bannister warned. "Twenty-four hours to refund our money...or else!"

The Bannisters angrily stormed out of the office!..Adrian and Marcy glanced at each other, knowingly, while they tried to continue their conversation with Edna...Chabot hesitated before he returned to his office. He looked at Adrian and Marcy and smiled broadly at both of them.

"Don't pay any attention to those people," he said, calmly, "they're just unhappy because we couldn't come up with their special kind of baby."

Chabot quickly went back to his office as Edna turned to Marcy and Adrian, smiling.

"Did you bring the medical report from your doctor?" Edna asked.

Marcy fumbled in her large briefcase and pulled out a large manilla envelope and handed it to Edna. "Yes, I did...Just like you told me to."

Edna opened the envelope and pulled out a file of papers. She looked them over quickly and slipped them back inside the envelope.

"Is anything wrong?" Adrian asked.

"Not that I could tell," Edna answered. "Our staff physician will look it over and we'll get back to you tonight or tomorrow...You understand our requirements...You will sign over your child to the foundation for you room and board as well as any medical needs you may require...including delivery."

"I just want to get this over with," Marcy said, anxiously.

"Fine...just wait here a few minutes...I believe the doctor may want to speak with you."

Edna quickly left the lobby. Marcy and Adrian looked at each other, wondering what was going to happen next. In a few minutes a tall, balding and bearded man came out, holding the medical papers..."I'm Dr. Morton," the man said, "which of you is...ah...Marcy Grant?"

"I am, doctor," Marcy answered.

"Alright, Ms. Grant...Follow me please."

Marcy got up and Adrian also stood up to go with her, but Luther Chabot walked into the lobby and blocked Adrian's path. He looked her up and down, hungrily. "Wow!" Luther Chabot exclaimed. "Who are you, young lady?"

Adrian tried to step around him but he grabbed her hand, grinning broadly.

"Please!" Adrian said, irritated by Luther's bold actions. "You're blocking my way!"

"I'm Luther Chabot...I'm the director here...Dr. Morton only wants to speak to the patient in private."

Adrian sat back down on the leather sofa as Chabot continued to leer at her, licking his lips.

"Is something wrong?" Adrian asked.

"Gosh, you're beautiful!" Chabot said. "Would you care to have coffee with me in my office while you wait for your friend?"

"Yes, thank you," Adrian replied, smiling back at him. "I think that would be nice...I would like to know you better."

Bolstered by Adrian's flirtatious response, Chabot smiled confidently and led Adrian back to his office. As soon as she stepped into the office he closed the door behind her, offered her a seat on a deep cushioned velvet sofa and sat down next to her, admiring her beauty. He placed an arm behind her shoulders and quickly kissed her, flush on her lips!..Adrian struggled to get loose as Edna walked into the office!..

"What's going on here?" Edna demanded, angrily. "Let go of my husband!"

Adrian broke out of Chabot's grasp and stood up, alarmed by his sudden attack on her! "Let go of him?" Adrian shouted, indignantly. "I wish you'd keep a leash on him!..What nerve!..I'll wait in the lobby!"

Upset, Adrian stormed out of the office, slamming the door, angrily!..She bumped into Marcy out in the hallway and hurriedly dragged her out of the building!..As they got inside Adrian's car, Marcy looked at her, puzzled.

"What's the matter?..You look upset about something!"

"That jerk in there!"

"Who?"

"Chabot...the director of the foundation!"

"What'd he do?"

"He invites me into his office for some coffee...I figured it was a good opportunity to gather some information about the foundation. As soon as I sit down on the sofa in his office...he grabs me and kisses me and his wife comes in and tells me to let go of him!"

Marcy threw her head back and began laughing loudly as the car screeched out of the parking lot!..

Roger and Janet Carlson sipped their coffee after finishing their dinner in a plush downtown restaurant. They were still anxious about the fertility tests they had just taken at City Hospital. Roger stared at his wife thoughtfully. "You're very disappointed about being turned down by the foundation aren't you." he asked.

"No...not really," Janet replied, sadly. "You told me they would probably reject our application because of your position with the Herald."

"We even provided them with a ready excuse."

"My hospitalization?"

"Yes...they had to find something that would legitimately get them off the proverbial hook without the fear of a lawsuit...But have no fear...all is not lost."

"You mean the fertility tests?"

"What do you think?" he asked quietly. "If we could pull this one off...we will be magicians."

"I think we passed our tests...at least I hope so...but remember, it's no big deal if we didn't...We'll just join the Egg Donor Program."

"Yeah, I know...Don't get me wrong," Roger said, "I'll be happy anyway we can get a baby...but if we're the biological parents to boot...you know...It'll make a big difference!"

"You mean it would carry on the blood line," Janet said. "It's only natural to feel that way."

"How very true that is," Roger agreed as he looked around the spacious restaurant. "You about ready to leave, honey?"

They both stood up and prepared to leave. While Roger was helping Janet with her coat, they were suddenly shoved into the next table as a man ran towards the exit!

"Hey!..WATCH IT!" Roger shouted, angrily. "You almost knocked us over!"

Janet began looking for her purse which had been laying on the table!.."My purse!" Janet screamed. "He stole my purse!"

A waiter who heard Janet's screams, took off after the purse snatcher!..Everyone in the restaurant was alarmed by the commotion when the waiter charged out of the door and down the street after the man!..Roger squeezed Janet's arm.

"You alright?" Roger asked. "He didn't hurt you?"

The manager of the restaurant hurried over to them, visibly concerned. "I'm so sorry this happened!" the manager said. "Are you alright?..We have never had anything like this happen before!..Are you really alright, ma'ma?"

"What kind of place is this?" Roger snarled, angrily. "Don't you watch out for this sorta thing?"

"I'm sorry, sir," the manager answered. "Sometimes they'll sneak by. It was so crowded in here today...he just wasn't spotted."

"Well, here they come," Janet said, happily. "It looks like your waiter has recovered my purse!"

"And he's got the purse snatcher, too!" Roger shouted.

The waiter had an arm lock on the purse snatcher as he forced the man in the direction towards Roger and Janet!..

"Here's your purse, ma'm," the waiter said, breathlessly. "We're sorry this happened."

"Good job, Williams!" the manager said, proudly. He turned to the purse snatcher, angrily. "And I'll call the police for you, fella!"

Roger extended his hand to the waiter and patted him on the back, proudly. "Hey!..You're alright...He didn't put up much of a fight did he?"

"Much of a fight?" the waiter asked, smiling. "Look at this!"

The waiter snatched the hat off of the purse snatcher's head and a thick wad of blond hair fell down to her shoulders!..A beautiful young girl glared at them with anger blazing in her eyes!..

"Well I'll be damned!" the manager exclaimed. "It's a girl!"

"Oh, my GOD!" Janet screamed.

"What the hell are you doin' stealin' purses?" Roger demanded, angrily.

"I gotta eat don't I?" the girl snapped, angrily. "What do you expect me to do...go out on the street and sell my body?"

"You poor child!" Janet said, turning to Roger. "Do something!"

"What can I do?"

"Don't worry about her!" the manager shot back. "She'll get plenty to eat in Wayne County Jail!"

"Hold it!" Roger interrupted. "You're gonna put this young girl in jail?..She won't stand a chance!"

"What else can I do?" the manager asked.

"I'll tell you what you can do," Roger said, turning to the girl. "You said you were hungry?..Tell this man what you want to eat."

"Don't do me any favors, mister!" the girl growled. "I'll get my own food!"

"Shuddup and sit down!" Roger commanded with anger. "While you're eating I'll decide whether you'll go to jail or not!"

Roger turned back to the startled waiter and manager who both stood there, speechless..."Alright...let her go!..She's not going anywhere!"

Everyone in the crowded restaurant stood up and began applauding as Roger, Janet and the girl all sat down at the table...

Chapter Seventeen

Gloria StantonTompson sat on the sofa in the library of the Stanton mansion drinking coffee with her mother, Hattie. She had just returned from a week long trip to Milwaukee to complete some unfinished business with her former home. She was frustrated in her attempts to arrange a breast cancer mobile diagnostic clinic to spend at least one month at The Detroit Herald Newspaper's offices. She felt that the central downtown location of The Herald and the exceptional publicity it would generate would encourage women working in the downtown area to come to the mobile clinic to learn self-examination exercises, and if a lump was detected in anyone's breast, they could immediately arrange to have a mammogram test performed at a hospital and follow through with future visits and information. Naturally, she had received permission from The Herald along with a suite of offices on the third floor, but the cooperation she was getting from City Hospital was non-existent...

"I cannot believe the indifferent attitudes I received from the hospital administrators, mother," Gloria said in disgust, "they acted like I was some candy striper collecting for flowers!"

"Did you speak to Bob about it?" Hattie asked.

"Yes...there's nothing he can do."

"What about Gene?"

"I shouldn't have to go to my big brother to run interference for me all the time...This is important!" Gloria exclaimed, passionately. "Breast cancer is expected to kill 46,000 American women this year!...Over two million and a half women in this country have been diagnosed with the disease or likely to have it!"

"If it was a man's disease I bet they'd listen to you."

"That's what's so sad about it," Gloria said. "If breast cancer is discovered early something can be done to stop it. It is not uncommon for women to wait and see what happens, even after her first mammogram uncovers a suspicious area. Some might call it denial...even after a cancer diagnosis."

"You mean after they've been told they have breast cancer they will still try to hide it?" Hattie asked, surprised.

"Exactly...It's part of their denial...they hide it to deny to themselves they have cancer. The less they know about it, the less others know about it...but those women are cheating themselves because they lack a support system."

"Support system?...How would that work?"

"It would be a follow-up to the original diagnosis," Gloria replied. "This mobile diagnosis clinic could act as the stimulus to start the support system...Breast cancer presents the kind of emotional pain that can affect an entire family. The support system can help prepare patients who find lumps or actually have a cancer diagnosed. They are a network of friends and neighbors and others who can help them through their breast cancer ordeals."

"How far would your...support system actually go?"

"Some may do laundry. Others will simply pray. Professionals with experience will explain biopsy reports word by word. Some will seek out specialists...Some will sit in waiting rooms for one another during lumpectomies or mastectomies. They will accompany patients on doctor appointments, select a prosthesis, or suggest reconstruction...In general, just be there for them."

Their talk was interrupted as Willard walked into the room, visibly upset...

"Willard...you're home kinda early," Gloria said, "has something happened to you since I've been gone?"

"I wanted to speak to you about it last night when you came home, " Willard answered, solemnly. "But you didn't seem to think I was that important since you got on this breast cancer thing."

"Your mother was tired, Willard, she had to get her rest," Hattie said. "I think what she's trying to do is a wonderful thing."

"Yeah...you're right, grandma."

"He's been actin' strange for the last few days," Hattie said.

"I have something very important to talk to you about, mother, "Willard said, firmly.

"Maybe I'd better leave," Hattie said as she stood up. "If this is private..."

Willard put his hand up to stop her from leaving. "No, grandma...I think you should stay here...This involves you in a way, also...You can confirm or deny."

"Confirm or deny what?" Gloria asked, resenting her son's attitude towards his grandmother. "Who have you been talking to?"

"I was contacted earlier last week by The Daily Press' personnel office," Willard replied. "They wanted me over there for a job interview."

"You just started at The Herald," Hattie said, "don't they know that's your uncle's newspaper?"

"Let him finish, mamma," Gloria said, quietly.

"I told them that...but they persisted...so I went over there," Willard explained. "During the interview, the publisher, F. Walton Dugas, sat in...I thought that was rather strange...They even offered to double by salary...They said they were trying to get their affirmative action program started."

"What happened?" Gloria asked, nervously.

"Mr. Dugas took me up to his office on the fifth floor," Willard continued, "he told me something...I still can't believe!"

Hattie and Gloria quickly glanced at each other.

"That bastard!" Gloria snapped, angrily.

"Let the boy talk," Hattie said, sadly.

"You know what he told me, don't you?" Willard asked, looking from his mother to his grandmother. "Is it true?..Is he my biological father?"

Hattie began quietly sobbing as Gloria walked over to her son, staring into his eyes, searching!.."You've got to understand how it happened," Gloria pleaded, "I was just a freshman at college!"

"Then it is true!" Willard screamed, angrily. "My father never died!..You!..All of you have been lying to me all my life!"

"No one knew except mamma and daddy," Gloria cried. "Gene didn't know until he bought The Herald!..Then, when Dugas began threatening him, claiming his father had loaned my father money to save The Journal...then I had to tell Gene the truth!"

"When were you going to tell me, mother?" Willard shouted. "On your death-bed or mine?"

"Willard!" Hattie cried. "Give your mother a chance to explain!"

"And what about me, grandma?..My own mother raised me under a lie!..She was willing to deny me my heritage....which could mean millions of dollars..simply to save her dignity!...Well that sounds rather self-serving to me!"

"You don't need his money!" Gloria snapped, angrily.

"I'll tell you what I don't need, mother!..I don't need you lying to me anymore about anything!"

"But your mother had no choice!" Hattie said. "She had been victimized by a reckless and rich White boy who was just out for a good time!"

"That may be true," Willard shot back. "But I shouldn't have to pay for it!...If that man is my father I should've been told!..Not lied to like it was just a bad dream that wouldn't go away!"

Willard turned and angrily marched out of the room, slamming the door behind him!..The two women stared at each other, stunned and crushed by his outburst of anger!"..

THE WINDS OF TOMORROW

Roger and Janet Carlson sat at the table in the plush downtown restaurant and watched the girl who had just tried to snatch Janet's purse, as she studied the menu. She quickly summoned the waiter and ordered. After she had placed her order she stared back at Roger and Janet, indignantly...

"Well?.." the girl smirked. "Haven't you ever seen one of the homeless up close before?"

"You don't have a home?" Janet asked. "What are you doing here?"

"I was a freshman at Bag Lady University," she replied, sarcastically, "until some jerk stole my shopping cart!"

"And you've got a smart mouth, too!" Roger shot back. "Don't you know when someone is trying to be nice to you?"

"Yeah...I know," the girl answered, ashamed. "I'm sorry about your purse, lady."

The waiter reluctantly brought the food to the table and the girl quickly began eating like a wild dog!..Roger and Janet watched in amazement!

"Slow down!" Roger said. "You'll choke on all that food!"

"Uh, huh," the girl mumbled with a mouth full of food.

"What's your name?" Janet asked.

"Mike."

"Mike?"

"Michelle..Around here...in the streets," she gulped. "It's a lot safer if they think I'm a dude."

"How long have you been in the streets?" Roger asked.

"About two weeks...I had a job but I was fired because the boss wanted more than I was willin' to give up," she said, staring at Roger. "He kept comin' on to me."

"Where are you from?" Janet asked.

"Minnesota..Duluth."

"Why don't you call your parents and go back home?" Roger asked.

"I can't do that!" Michelle answered, determined. "I'd never hear the end of it."

"Well, sometimes you have to be humble," Janet said.

"Not me!" Michelle shot back. " I ain't gonna be humble to anybody!"

"How old are you?" Roger asked.

"Why?..You expectin' somethin' for this?"

"Like what?"

"Listen, mister," Michelle answered, seriously, "I appreciate what you and your lady have done for me...buying me food and all...and not sending me to jail..but I don't do things these other girls do...That's why I don't have any money...I don't fool around with men or women...I may be poor and homeless...but I got my self-esteem!"

Roger smiled at Janet. "How old are you?"

- 171 -

"I'm twenty," the girl answered.

"You don't look twenty," Janet said.

"I got good genes."

"You interested in getting a job?" Janet asked.

Michelle became suspicious..."Doin' what?"

"Can you type, use a word processor or do any office work?"

"That's what I was doin' before...typing...but I can only type forty-five words a minute...no errors."

"That's good," Roger said, smiling. "Where are you staying tonight?"

"I'll find a shelter somewhere."

"Look...that's dangerous," Janet said, thoughtfully. "We've got a big house...nobody stays there but us and our cat, Bosco...You can stay with us tonight. If you really want a job, I'll get you one tomorrow at The Herald...It's all up to you."

"Yeah...you got a choice...either you go home with us, get a job and straighten you life out," Roger warned as he leaned closer to Michelle, "or you go to jail!..Do not pass "go"...do not collect two hundred dollars!..It's up to you..What will it be?"

Michelle looked from Roger to Janet. In the background she saw the restaurant manager talking to two police officers!

"O.K!..Alright!" Michelle said, meekly. "It looks like you got a house guest...and I got a job."

Patricia Parker-Stanton sat behind her desk in her Washington D.C. temporary office, across from Bill Clark, who was completely confident that Patricia was going on a short vacation with him. The seminar on racism in the media had been successful and they were ready to leave the capitol. Bill watched patiently as Patricia cleaned out her desk, preparing to vacate the office.

"When did you plan to tell your family about your...extended visit to Washington?" Bill asked.

She stopped and looked up at him before she continued. "I've mentioned it a few times." she said.

""What about Gene?..Have you mentioned it to him?"

"Yes...I told him I had to go away and sort things out."

"What was his reaction?"

"He was quite furious...and suspicious."

"Are you completely sure about this?" Bill asked. "I didn't intend to force you into anything."

"I'm sure...in fact...maybe this is something I should have done long before now," Pat answered, solemnly. "Our marriage has been falling apart for years."

"Do you think he still loves you?"

"I think he appreciates me."

"That's not what I asked."

"That's what I said."

"Appreciate?"

"Yes...We're not the same two young people who married each other way back then," she said, thoughtfully, "Hell...we're not even the same two people who raised our children together...No..I don't think he loves me anymore...but he does appreciate me for being the mother of his children and for being his wife all of these years...Like you would appreciate a long-time employee."

"There's nothing left?"

"No...nothing."

"Then let's look forward to an enjoyable vacation," Bill said as he reached over and lightly kissed her on the cheek.

"How enjoyable?" Pat asked, smiling. "You make it sound like it's gonna be the best thing since chocolate chip cookies."

"You'll love it out there!" Bill beamed. "The resort is managed by my favorite uncle. He's a nice old geezer who believes in live and let live...he'll treat you like a queen...and if you don't mind being botherd by me...I'm sure you'll enjoy the peace and rest."

"I'm looking forward to it." Patricia replied. "Should I bring a pair of skiis?..I could buy a pair right here in town."

"There'll be plenty of skiis and sports equipment at the lodge," Bill answered. "They have ice skating, tobogganing and excellent food!"

"What about the company?"

"The company will adore you!"

"Everyone suspects something...I can tell...They all believe I'm involved with another man."

"Does that bother you?"

"No...not really. I sorta like it...They know about the problems we've had all these years. Karen even seems to encourage this...and she should know. She almost lost her marriage a few months ago because of the indifference of her husband...which is probably why she feels the way that she does."

"My kind of girl," Bill said, smiling broadly.

"But from what Karen has said Kim told her...the rest of my family isn't too happy about you, Bill."

"Oh?..Why not?"

"The Stantons want you or any other man out of my life."

"They don't really know me."

"They know about you."

"Big deal."

"How do you feel about going up against the Stantons?" she asked, teasingly. "It could affect your political career."

"They're being loyal to Gene...I can understand that...but parental loyalty has to include you, too...it's a two way street."

"Are you still planning to leave tonight?"

"Our flight leaves at six P.M."

Patricia got up and walked around the desk, closer to Bill. She stared into his eyes as he stood up and embraced her.

"This means a lot to you, doesn't it?" she asked.

"You bet it does...and I think when this week is over...it'll mean as much to you, too!"

They kissed...long and sensual, as she pressed her soft body against his, holding him tightly...he lightly kissed her all over her face as the movement her body aroused him.

"Oh, Bill!" she whispered, huskily. "I don't know...I just don't know!"

Gene Stanton walked into the Fashion Director's office at The Detroit Herald Newspaper. He looked through the glass enclosed studio wall and saw his daughter, Liz, busy supervising a photograph session. Liz turned around and noticed him standing in her outer office. She quickly turned the project over to her assistant and walked towards the office. She greeted her father with a big kiss on his cheek. She stopped short when she saw that he was upset.

"What's the matter, daddy?" she asked. "You look like you just lost your best friend."

"I've been trying to reach your mother all day," Gene replied. "Where in the hell is she?"

"I guess she's still in D.C....Other than that...I have no idea."

"Is she still talking about some fool vacation?" he asked.

Liz quickly turned away from Gene's glare. "She mentioned something about a vacation...she wasn't too definite about it."

"You and I have always seen eye to eye," Gene said, calmly. "You know I would never hurt your mother...Is there something going on that I ought to know about?"

"Like what?"

"Well...when a man's away from his wife for awhile...his mind starts wandering...dreaming up all sorts of things."

"Are you asking me if she's seeing another man?"

"No...Not exactly...but if there is something going on...I should know about it."

Liz became thoughtful..."I don't know...I haven't noticed anything unusual."

"Would you tell me if you did?"

She pondered the question momentarily before she looked up at him, directly in the eyes. "No...no, dad...I don't think so."

Gene hesitated before responding. "Well...thanks...thanks for being honest with me."

"Dad?.."

"What?"

"That goes both ways," Liz said, somberly, "Listen, if it's bothering you that much...why don't you hop on a plane, fly out there and find out for yourself?"

"I thought about doing just that," Gene replied. "But I know your mother and she'd resent me for flying in without telling her I was coming!"

"Then tell her."

"I can't reach her."

"That's your call, dad."

"She knows I'm willing to compromise on any problems we have...why won't she respond to my calls?"

"Give her a little space...She said she wanted some time to straighten out her life...that's what that vacation is all about."

"You mean she needs time to decide when and if she's coming home or not?" Gene asked, angrily. "I'm her husband....She should be with me."

"She probably feels the same way." Liz answered, cooly. "She's always let you have your way about everything...She was dead set against buying this newspaper, but you did it. Maybe this time she wants to do something her way...and she's just a little unsure."

"Are you saying I oughta drop everything here and fly to Washington to help her make up her mind?"

"No...I'm not telling you that," Liz replied. "You should do what you think is best."

"It's best if she's with me," Gene said, angrily. "We've got things to talk about."

"Look, you've got what you've always wanted...You own The Detroit Herald Newspaper...All the women in town are after you!..And you're earning more money in a week then what you use to earn in a year!"

Gene stopped and stared at his daughter. "What in the world are you talking about?"

"By the way, dad...Did you have a nice weekend?"

Gene stared at her, thoughtfully. "OK...thanks, Liz...I know what to do now!"

"Meaning what?"

"I got a few loose ends to tie up here...but as soon as I do...I'm flying to Washington, D.C."

Patricia's temporary office in Washington, D.C. was ready to be closed down. She sat among stacks of boxes around her desk as she spoke on the telephone to Janet Carlson and explained her tentative vacation plans. She was obviously irritated by Janet's probing questions over the phone...

"Are you sure this is what you want to do?" Janet asked, cautiously. "I mean...don't let Gene's actions or Bill's persuasion force you into a worse situation."

"No...this is completely my decision and it's based upon what I want out of life, not what they want," Patricia answered, firmly. "Time is passing by...I've got to know where my heart really is."

"And you think Bill may be the answer?"

"I...I don't know...but at least I've got to give it a chance."

"But to risk your marriage!..Is it really worth it?"

"I don't know if I even have a marriage," Patricia replied. "Gene could care less about me!"

"Are you sure he feels that way?"

"We never touch each other anymore...He doesn't bother to return my calls to his office...He's too busy being the big time and dashing newspaper publisher to have any time for me...I'm sure the women are all over him."

"What would you do if he asked you not to go?"

"I'm not sure...the plans are all set...plane reservations have been made."

"When are you leaving?"

"This evening...our plane takes off at five-fifty. I'll just have time to pack."

"Oh, Pat!..Please think about this...for GOD's sake!"

Patricia paused, sensing the sound of despair in Janet's voice..."You sound so worried, Janet!..I'm sure everything will work out for the best."

"If anything should ever happen between you and Gene," Janet whispered over the phone, "it would tear Roger apart!..It would crush us both!"

"Oh, Janet!"

"We love you both so much!"

"I know...We love you and Roger, too."

"You're very close to me, Pat...Like a sister...and I care about you!..What you're doing toady...takes a monumental decision!"

Their conversation was momentarily interrupted as the buzzer on Janet's second phone started buzzing. "Pat, I'm going to put you on hold for a minute..don't go away."

"OK..take your call..I'll wait."

Janet quickly picked up the second phone. "Mrs. Carlson speaking."

"Mrs. Carlson...this is Mr. Garrison in personnel...that new employee..er...ah Michelle Mathews...She's completed her typing test...I'll send her right up to your office."

"How did she do?"

"She passed our minimum requirements...I think she'll work out alright."

"Fine...Send her right up."

Janet smiled broadly to herself as she put the second phone down and returned to Patricia. "I'm back...that was personnel. My new employee passed her typing test."

"Is that the lost sheep you and Roger met in the restaurant?"

"Yes...She's a beautiful child...I can't believe that she was homeless!"

"Doesn't she have any family?"

"Roger is checking that out...If everything is alright we'll send her back home...If not...at least she'll have a job...Then she can do what ever she wants."

"By the way...what were the results of your fertility tests at the hospital?"

"We may know something this afternoon...Roger is as anxious as a little boy!"

"I think the whole idea is simply fascinating!..I'm so happy for both of you!"

"I wish everybody felt like that."

"Some of your folks giving you a hard time?"

"They weren't too happy when we were trying do adopt," Janet said. "Now, they're more against it than ever."

"Don't they realize how important this is to both of you?" Patricia asked.

"They can't seem to understand what it means to us...Roger's parents resent our adopting someone else's child and my brother and sister think we're too old to consider raising a child...When it comes to their lives they want to be able to do as they please while we stay at home and become paunchy couch potatoes."

"Well, I wouldn't worry about anybody else but you and Roger," Patricia said. "A little age isn't what it use to be...this is why we have to reassess our lives and snatch any chance at happiness we can get."

"Is that what you're doing, Pat?"

"That's what we both should do."

"Then you've made your decision?"

"Yes."

"Call me..as soon as you get back."

"Alright."

"And Pat...remember...I love you."

"I love you, too...Goodby, my dear friend."

"Goodby, Pat."

Janet turned when she heard someone walk into her office. She hung up the phone and smiled at Michelle. "How'd you do on your tests?"

"I passed them all, " Michelle answered, proudly. "When do I start?"

Detroit's Metropolitan Airport was packed and crowded when Gene Stanton, carrying a small overnight bag, rushed up to the ticket counter. He waited impatiently as the clerk behind the counter talked over the telephone. In a few minutes the clerk hung up the phone and turned to Gene.

"May I help you, sir?" the clerk asked.

"I'd like to get booked on the next flight to Washington, D.C.," Gene replied.

The clerk checked his computer monitor for a few seconds before turning back to Gene. "The next flight is at one forty-five and it arrives in Washington at five-fifty, but it seems to be full...The next flight after that is at eight twenty-five...Would you like for me to schedule you for the eight twenty-five flight and put you on standby for the one forty-five?"

"The one forty-five flight is all full?" Gene asked, disappointed.

"Yessir, I'm sorry."

"OK...put me on standby for the one forty-five and if there's no cancellations...I'll take the later flight."

"That'll be fine, sir."

Gene looked up at the giant clock on the wall behind the clerk as the loudspeaker announced the arrival of another passenger plane.

Chapter Eighteen

Dr. Robert Whyte and his wife, Karen Stanton-Whyte, had been getting along comparatively good in their turbulent marriage. After they had agreed to put the control of their stock in The Herald newspaper in the hands of Robert and began to make a sincere effort at damage control after Karen's sexual tryst, their union had been surprisingly stabilized, which was attributed in part to Karen's new job at the Herald. Dr. Whyte had reduced his long hours at City Hospital considerably and Karen had been working diligently on her job. The positive effects of the new and better relationship could even be seen in the conduct of their three children, who now, under a more controlled home environment, began bringing home better grades in their school work. The entire atmosphere in the household was so positive that Dr. Whyte had began planning special afternoon dates with his wife like they had done so many times earlier in their marriage.

Today, Karen and Bob were enjoying one of their "dates" as they relaxed in their bed early in the afternoon, munching on pizza and drinking wine while watching their favorite television soap series. Bob sighed happily as he leaned over and kissed Karen on the cheek.

"Oh, boy...now this is the life!" Bob said. "The kids are away and we can play."

"You like my little surprise?" Karen asked, smiling. "Love in the afternoon."

"What a way to end the day!" Bob answered, grinning. "All that hustle and bustle at the hospital...I got to fight the doctors, the patients, the damn stingy administration...All I'm doin' all day is spending time and burning up energy!"

"Well you rested last weekend didn't you?...All that food and all those football games!"

"That part was alright...but everytime you look around it's over here for this meeting. back here for another...get this new equipment...buy this...buy that! Even your Aunt Gloria started buggin' me yesterday!...I need a break!"

"Gloria?...What's her problem?"

"She's tryin' to arrange to establish a breast cancer diagnosis clinic at The Herald to encourage female workers at the newspaper and in the downtown area to come in for a free self-examination seminar on early detection."

"I think that's wonderful, don't you?"

"Well, yeah...if we had the portable equipment to do it."

"And they're worried about the cost."

"Of course...but you know Gloria...that won't stop her."

"You don't think the hospital will go along with it?" Karen asked. "It sure would help save lives."

"Well they didn't turn her completely down," Bob replied. "They told your's truly to work on it...as if I didn't already have enough to do."

"Oh, stop being such a grouch!"

"But this...this is fantastic!..I can relax with you, eat pizza and completely enjoy ourselves."

"You're just spoiled...ever since we resolved our...our little problems...I've spoiled the hell out of you, doctor," Karen said, chuckling.

"Makes me feel guilty, too...Poor Gene...all alone by himself...his wife in Washington, D.C."

"Well, he made his bed."

"You know...your dad called me this morning."

"Dad called you?" Karen asked, surprised. "About what?"

"An investigation's the paper's got going on some baby selling clinic," Bob answered. "I could tell he was concerned about Pat."

"How do you know that?..He never seemed to miss her before...Certainly not last weekend."

"You resent your father going away by himself for one lousy weekend?" Bob asked, disgusted. "Oh, well...he's real uptight because Pat's not coming straight home from Washington."

"Yeah...I bet he is!" Karen said, sarcastically.

"No...He really is concerned about her!..You know what he told me?"

"What?"

"He said he was flying to Washington to get her."

Karen almost choked on her pizza and she quickly sat up in bed!.."Wh...What?"

"What's the matter with you?" Bob asked. "That bite go down the wrong pipe?"

"When is he going?" Karen asked, anxiously.

"Who?..Your dad?..He should be there sometimes this evening, why?"

"You big, stupid oaf!" Karen shouted, angrily, "Why didn't you tell me?"

Karen quickly picked up a pillow and slammed Bob in the face!..He sat there, stunned, with pizza all over his chest!..

Mel walked through the apartment door with a tired expression on his face. Soft music drifted from the stereo, filling the air as he noticed a bottle of champagne and a bottle of ginger ale sitting on the portable bar in the living room. An ice bucket filled with freshly made ice cubes, set in between the two bottles and two glasses. Mel glanced at his watch and looked towards the kitchen as the aroma of cooking lobster tail reached him. He set his briefcase down and followed his nose..."Kelly...Kel...what's goin' on, hon?" he asked, searching. "Did Duke call from the NBA?"

Mel walked into the kitchen, but still no Kelly...He turned around and found her standing in the doorway leading to the kitchen. She smiled at him, seductively. She was dressed in a sexy black teddy that revealed more than it covered. Her long, blond hair draped over her bare shoulders.

"Hi, honey," Kelly whispered, huskily. "I've been waiting for you."

Mel stared at her, unbelieving..."Kelly!..What the hell is goin'on?..Did Duke call from NBA headquarters?"

"The phone hasn't rang all day...I haven't heard from anyone," she purred.

Mel was suddenly deflated. "Then what's all this for?..I thought you heard from Duke Crocket at the NBA...C'mon Kel, what's goin' on?"

Before Kelly could answer the phone began ringing. Mel eyed Kelly suspiciously as he picked up the phone. Kelly slipped up behind and hugged him tightly.

"Hello," Mel answered, disgustedly.

"Hey, big fella...you ready to go back to work?" a deep voice asked, chuckling. "I just tried to get you at the newspaper...they said you went home."

"Duke?..Duke?" Mel asked, anxiously. "I was just talkin' about you...What's up?"

"You passed your physical with flying colors!" Duke replied, happily. "You're as clean as a whistle!"

Mel was greatly relieved. "So...what's the next step? Will the NBA waive the balance of my suspension?"

"They already have, Mel!" Duke answered, laughing. "The Memphis Mustangs are anxious to get you back to work, ol' buddy!..They said they would contact your agent today, so stay at home by the phone!"

Mel shoved a clinched fist up into the air in victory and shouted..."Alright!..It's finally over!..Thanks, Duke!..Thanks a helluva lot!..You've made my day...hell!..You've made my year!"

Mel reached around and pulled Kelly closer to him...

"Congratulations, Mel," Duke said. "You're one heck of a player!..You ought to have a fabulous career!..Just remember, from here on in...stay clean!"

Mel hung up the phone and hugged Kelly, happily, lifting her off her feet and twirling her around in circles!..She kissed him passionately as he continued to swing her around in joy!..

"Whoa, there!..Not so rough, honey!" Kelly said, smiling. "I'm afraid your good news day isn't half over...yet."

"Wh...What?..What else could there be?..It can't touch that!"

"Don't bet on it...You know I went to the doctor last week."

"And she said you were clean...You already told me, remember?"

"But that's not all...she had to perform several tests to confirm her suspicions and she didn't get the results until today...I didn't mention anything to you because you were so depressed, waiting to hear something from the NBA."

"Well...what is it?"

"After I found out...I had made up my mind to tell you today...come hell or high water!" Kelly said, determined.

"What, Kelly?..What is it?"

"She said I was pregnant, Mel...We're going to have a baby!"

Mel was stunned by the news...He stared at Kelly as tears welled up in his eyes...

"Oh, baby!" he whispered in awe, "that's the best news in the world!..My sweet Kelly!..GOD, I love you!"

They embraced and he kissed her all over her face and neck as tears streamed down both of their faces and they slowly slipped down on the sofa...

The sounds of desk drawers slamming came from the office of the director of The Forgotten Child Foundation as Luther Chabot hurriedly stuffed papers from his desk into his two briefcases. He was furiously mumbling to himself as his wife, Edna stood in the doorway with a disgusted look on her face.

"What are you doing?" Edna asked, angrily.

Luther continued pulling files out of his desk without bothering to look up at his wife. "What do you think I'm doing?..In case you haven't noticed, my dear, our little game is about up!..It is splitsville time!"

Luther quickly rushed over to two metal filing cabinets, unlocked them each, and began pulling out more files.

"Will you stop that and listen to me!" Edna demanded, slamming one of the file cabinet drawers closed. "If you had tried to control those hormones of your it wouldn't be!"

"What do my hormones have to do with that phony medical report those two women brought over here?..They were trying to set us up and I'll lay you ten to one that damn lawyer from the newspaper put them on to us!"

"Every time you looked at that Adrian girl you drooled!" Edna snapped. "I knew you were up to something!..If it hadn't been for Dr. Morton you never would've realized those medical records for Marcy were phony!..No, not you!..You were too busy staring into Adrian's eyes!"

Luther stopped packing and glared at Edna, angrily!.."I'll get even...with both of them!"

"If you would just stop and think for a minute you'd realize there still might be a way out," she said.

"The only way we can get out of this...is going to jail," Luther shot back.

"Listen...there have been no charges filed against us!" Edna said. "They haven't had time to gather any evidence. The only people who really know anything have no conclusive proof...that's why the police aren't knocking on our door right now."

"What do you expect me to do?" Luther asked, sarcastically, "sit and wait here until they do?..I am not going to jail again, Edna, no matter what you may say!"

"We have seven couples who are prepared to shell out fifty thousand in cash each to get a baby!..That's three hundred and fifty thousand we can pick up before we leave!"

"But we don't have that many babies ready to go!..The most we can get is only two!"

"Then we'll get the other five."

"How?..Go out and raid some hospital nursery?"

"Exactly!"

"Are you out of your friggin' mind?" Luther shouted. "How in the hell can we do that?..And even if we could...the feds would be after us for kidnapping!"

"Don't worry about that," Edna answered with confidence. "I figured we might have to leave in a hurry some day...so I made plans...all you have to do is take care of those two nosey broads from that newspaper...to make sure we have enough time to take care of business and get away!"

"Now wait a minute...what kind of plans have you made?"

"I've already discussed it with Dr. Morton," Edna said, "but first, why don't I call little Ms. Adrian and ask her to bring Ms. Marcy over here to sign the final papers?..Once they get here...you can take care of that business!"

Luther sat back down behind his desk, thoughtfully. He turned to Edna and smiled, broadly. "So you and Dr. Morton have made plans, eh?..That's interesting, Edna...very interesting...OK...alright...call Adrian and ask them to come over...but before you do...I wanna talk to you and Dr. Morton about this plan."

Edna smiled at Luther as he chuckled to himself, confidently. He stood up and walked over to the office window with his hands clasped behind his back.

Adrian and Marcy were surprised to hear from the Forgotten Child Foundation so soon. They both realized that Marcy's copy of her accepted application for admission into the foundation could be used to verify their story. They were excited when they walked into Luther Chabot's office just as Edna was walking out. She stopped when she saw Adrian and Marcy. She sneered at Adrian and smiled at Marcy.

"I understand that you're all set to sign the final papers," Edna said to Marcy.

"Good luck...you're making the right move."

Adrian pulled Marcy's arm. "She knows what she's doing," Adrian snapped, "and she doesn't need any cheerleading from you!"

"Has Dr. Morton reviewed all of my medical records?" Marcy asked.

"He's on his way over here...I'm sure he'll be able to answer all of your questions...Every one of them," Edna replied, smiling.

"Thank you," Adrian said, "and I'm sure The Forgotten Child Foundation will be happy with your latest recruit."

Edna quickly turned and walked down the hallway. When Adrian and Marcy walked into Luther's office he was busily writing. He stopped writing and stood up, greeting them warmly.

"My favorite two beautiful women," Luther said, smiling. "Something tells me this is going to be a red letter day!"

"Are her papers ready to be signed?" Adrian asked.

"What's the hurry?" Luther asked. "Have a seat and relax. Dr. Morton should be here shortly and we'll proceed. He still has a few questions he'd like to ask you."

"Questions?..Like what?" Marcy asked, nervously.

"Well...you know...family background and history."

The two women sat down in front of Luther's desk. He poured two cups of coffee and handed each a cup.

"That information is all in my medical records," Marcy said.

"Yes...and besides, Edna told me the papers were all in order," Adrian said. "What's going on, Luther?"

Luther slowly walked back behind the desk and sat down, eyeing the two women, suspiciously.

"Is there something you're not telling me?" Luther asked, smiling knowingly.

Puzzled, Adrian and Marcy glanced at each other and then back to Luther, who is now grinning broadly.

"I...I don't know what you could be referring to," Marcy stammered.

"No...I mean you, Adrian," Luther interrupted. "Is there something you're not telling me?"

"About what?..What are you talking about?" Adrian asked, still puzzled. "My friend understands everything that's going to happen...She trusts me."

"I'm glad somebody trusts you!" Luther snapped, angrily.

"Now what does that mean?" Adrian asked.

"And you, too, Marcy!" Luther shouted. "You're both in deep trouble!..One would think you'd be more careful about who you become involved with!"

"I do not appreciate that remark, sir!" Marcy said, indignantly.

"What's this all about?" Adrian asked, suspiciously.

"It's about liars!..I don't like liars!" Luther barked.

"I beg your pardon!" Adrian said, calmly.

"That medical report was a complete farce," Luther said. "And you, Marcy, are not pregnant!"

"What are you talkin' about?" Marcy pretended shock.

"We called Dr. Robert Whyte's office at City Hospital and his secretary denied that you had ever been examined by the good doctor and they had no records that you have ever been his patient!"

"She must've overlooked..." Adrian said.

"Shuddup, Adrian!" Luther shouted, angrily. "I'll deal with you in a few minutes!..Right now I'd like to know how Marcy is going to explain a fraudulent document to the authorities!"

"And how are you going to explain this...this crooked foundation to the federal government and the Better Business Bureau?" Marcy asked, angrily.

Adrian quickly stood up!.."We don't have to listen to this bunk!..If you're not prepared to go through with this, we're leaving!"

"Sit down!" Luther commanded. "I'll tell you when to leave!"

Marcy stood up next to Adrian. "Drop dead, you...you big phony!"

"We know that you two have been snooping around trying to dig up evidence against us!" Luther said. "You think we're total idiots!..We knew what you were up to and we intend to put a stop to it!"

"Like the way you handled that baby for the Bannisters?" Adrian asked. "That was a joke!"

"The LORD moves in strange ways," Luther said. "That baby was not meant to be with those people and we followed the LORD'S word!"

"You followed the words that meant more money!" Marcy said, angrily. "And don't hand us that regligious stuff!..The Forgotten Child Foundation!..Well, we're not buying it! C'mon, Adrian...we're outta here!"

"I don't think you're going anywhere!" Luther said menacingly. "We know you're both reporters for the Herald and we got plans for you...Big plans!"

The two women turned to leave and stopped dead in their tracks when they were confronted by Dr. Morton standing in the doorway pointing a gun at them!..They quickly turned back to Luther who was now standing behind his desk and angrily glaring at them as a broad smile creased his face!..

Chapter Nineteen

Most of the offices of The Forgotten Child Foundation were dark except for two offices at the rear of the suite. In one, Adrian and Marcy, both bound and gagged, sat back to back in two straight chairs. They struggled to loosen their ropes but soon realized it was useless. In a few minutes Luther Chabot and Dr. Morton walked into the room and glared at them. Luther walked closer to Adrian and stood in front of her, smiling. He reached down and gently cupped her face in his hand. She stared back at him with anger flaring in her eyes!

"How's my little buttercup doin?" Luther asked. "Would you like me to take off your gag?.. Maybe you've changed your mind about being nice to me now."

Luther reached behind Adrian's head and quickly untied and removed her mouth gag. He motioned to Dr. Morton to do the same for Marcy.

"Ow!..That hurt!" Adrian cried out, angrily. "What is wrong with you, Luther?.. You can't get away with this!.. When we're missed tonight someone's gonna come over here looking for us!"

"You'd better release us now," Marcy warned, "or there'll be much more severe charges you'll have to face!"

"They make a lot of noise for such small, little people don't they?" Dr. Morton said, chuckling.

"If you promise not to shout, we might keep the gags off," Luther explained, calmly, "but if you start hollering and screaming we'll put them back on."

"What do you intend to do with us?" Marcy asked.

THE WINDS OF TOMORROW

"Just shuddup and be quiet!" Dr. Morton snapped. "You will know in due time."

"You all will get stiff sentences," Adrian said, "because you'll never get away with this!"

"Listen...we have something to take care of this evening and as soon as we complete it...we'll set you two free and leave Detroit for good," Luther said, calmly. "Mean while, I want you to be patient and quiet and nothing will happen to you...but if we come back and find out you've made a ruckus of some kind...we might take you with us... Do you understand?"

"I could kill you!" Adrian snapped.

"OK...that's OK... We won't make any ruckus," Marcy assured them. "Just go about your business...we'll wait, but hurry back and let us out of here."

Luther looked at Marcy, surprised. "If you really intend to be cooperative...it would be wise... However, if you're planning some trick...you'll regret it!"

"Can't you loosen these ropes?" Marcy asked, patiently. "We're not going anywhere."

"Well...I guess they are pretty tight." Luther said, thoughtfully. "Let me make it a little more comfortable for you."

Luther bent down next to Adrian, his face close to hers. His lips lightly brushed across hers as she spit and turned her head away in disgust. He chuckled as he loosened both of their ropes.

"Hurry, Luther," Morton said, "we're losing precious time."

"Where are you goin?" Adrian asked.

"That's none of your business," Luther snapped. "Just be good girls and don't get into any trouble... There is someone here in the building who will be guarding you... If you holler or scream he'll come in here...and I will not be responsible for what he might do to you."

"Don't worry," Marcy said. "We'll still be here when you get back."

Adrian glanced at Marcy with a puzzled look on her face. She quickly turned back to Luther. "Yeah...don't worry about us," Adrian said, "we're not planning on going anywhere."

"Good...remember, The Forgotten Child is a child in need who deserves a good deed!" Luther said, grinning.

Marcy and Adrian stared at each other as Luther and Dr. Morton turned and quickly left the office.

The airport in Washington, D.C. was jammed with the rush crowd as people milled about in the spacious lobby. Bill Clark met Patricia at Gate C - 21 and embraced her with a long, sensual kiss. They happily got their seating assignments and waited to board their flight. Bill put his arms around her and kissed her again after they were sitting in the waiting area. People, thinking they were just wed, smiled at them knowingly.

"Are you excited?" Bill asked, smiling broadly.

"I'm looking forward to it," Patricia replied, nervously. "You promised me the world."

"You're worth the world...I...I wanted this chance for both of us. We are givers...we've given so much to our families...our work, to other people's lives. Now, it's time for us to give to each other and ourselves...I love you, Pat... If I had only ten minutes left to love...I'd give them all to you."

"You seem so sure of everything," Patricia said.

"I'm sure of us...I'm sure that if we allow ourselves this opportunity to love...we'll never be apart again!"

"Oh, Bill... I do love you," she sighed.

He pulled her into his arms and kissed her full on her lips. While they held the embrace, they could hear the public address announcer reporting the arrival of an incoming flight from Detroit and the boarding of Flight 702 to Maine. Patricia and Bill quickly got up, his arm still around her waist, and stood in the long line waiting to board their plane. The line slowly began to move as the tall doors to the passenger ramp opened.

In the next waiting area, in preparation for the incoming flight from Detroit, a flight attendant came out of the passenger ramp and opened both doors as passengers began emerging from the ramp.

With a look of desperation on his face, Gene Stanton was the third passenger to come through the doors. He rushed past the flight attendant to the long hallway that led out to the lobby. He was so intently engrossed in his thoughts, he completely ignored the extended line of passengers waiting to board the flight to Maine in the next waiting area, as he briskly walked down the long, wide hallway.

The hospital corridor in front of the nursery window displaying the newborn babies was crowded with people admiring the infants as Edna Chabot, dressed as a head nurse, came out of an office across the hall and began addressing the crowd of people.

"That's it folks...time to leave," Edna said, smiling, "babies have to be fed, changed and take their afternoon naps...sorry...it's time to leave."

Everyone in the crowd groaned as they slowly began backing away from the window of the nursery. As the crowd slowly dispersed, Edna walked into the nursery and immediately began selecting five babies and separating them from the rest. In a few minutes she was joined by three doctors and another nurse. Two of the doctors were Luther Chabot and Dr. Morton dressed in white smocks complete with stethoscopes. They pretended to examine the babies carefully.

"Are these the infants to be quarantined, nurse?" Luther asked in a business-like manner.

"Yes, doctor...these are the five," Edna replied. "We'll move them directly to room 504...are you ready?"

"Yes, nurse," Luther answered, looking around at the others, "Is everyone all set?.. Then let's go!"

The group quickly marched out of the nursery pushing the five baby carts in front of them. They waited patiently for the elevator to arrive and nodded at several doctors, nurses, and hospital personnel as they walked past them. When the elevator arrived they quickly stepped on and smiled confidently as the doors slid closed.

Adrian and Marcy continued to try frantically to get loose before Luther and Morton returned. Finally, Marcy spotted a pair of scissors on a bookcase on the other side of the room.

"There's a pair of scissors on top of that small bookcase over there against that wall!" Marcy whispered, anxiously as she poked at the bookcase with her foot. "If I can just..."

The two women tipped their chairs, leaning over until they fell down with a loud bang!.. They looked at each other, frightened and not making a sound. When nothing happened, Marcy worked her foot against the bookcase, tipping it over with another loud crash!.. Marcy quickly squirmed over and reached for the scissors that had fallen to the floor. In a few moments she had it clutched in her hands!

"I got it!.. I've got the scissors!" Marcy whispered. "Now be still while I cut your rope."

In a few minutes Adrian's hands were free!.. She quickly untied Marcy and they both breathed a deep sigh of relief! They stood in the center of the office, rubbing their arms and wrists.

"Now what?" Adrian asked. "There may really be somebody out there in the hall."

"The phone!.. Let's dial 911," Marcy said as she quickly grabbed the phone and listened for a dial tone. She suddenly had a disappointed look on her face!.. "It's dead...this damn phone is dead!"

"Let's check out the hall," Adrian snapped.

Adrian slowly opened the door to the office a slight crack. As she peeked out between the crack she saw a huge security guard sitting at the end of the hallway reading a comic book. She quietly closed the door. Adrian turned back to Marcy who stood staring at her, anxiously.

"Well...is anyone out there?"

"You bet there is!.. He looks like a sumo wrestler stuffed into a guard's uniform!.. We'd never get by him!"

Marcy rushed over to the window and tried to open it. The window easily slid up as snow flakes were blown into the room. Marcy stuck her head out of the window. They could hear the wind howling outside.

"Brrr...it's cold out there," Marcy groaned, "and not a soul in sight...but ...but."

"But what?"

"There's a wide ledge running along the side of the building," Marcy said. "We could walk that ledge around the corner of the building to the window facing the next corridor...climb back in through that window and leave without that guard over seeing us."

"C'mon, Marcy...get real!.. We're five stories up!"

"It's our only way out...unless you prefer waiting here until they return..as desperate as they are...there's no telling what they intend to do to us!"

Adrian looked back at the closed office door and then at Marcy, still undecided. Finally, she nervously nodded her head. "OK...let's go for it...but you go first...and I'll follow...but for GOD'S sake...be careful!"

Marcy bravely climbed out of the window and stood on the ledge with her back, flat up against the building and both arms extended and spread wide apart, braced against the cold bricks of the building. "C'mon...it's not so bad." Marcy whispered, frightened. "Just don't look down...don't look down."

Adrian climbed out on the ledge and tried not to look down but the sounds of the traffic and a gust of strong wind unnerved her, causing her to lose her concentration and give way to temptation... She looked down and froze!..

"Adrian... Adrian... C'mon...don't look down!"

Marcy stood further down on the ledge and tried to coax Adrian into moving. The howling wind blew snowflakes into their faces, hampering their vision and creating an additional hazzard...Adrian finally swallowed, took a deep breath and slowly began to inch her way towards Marcy. She thought about her ritual of jogging a mile, two, sometimes as much as three times a week to stay in condition and hoped that now was the time her endurance at physical exertion would pay off... She thought about being in Gene's arms and making love to him on the island...the warmth and comfort of his caresses and his vow to love her forever... Before she knew it, she was next to Marcy, clutching her cold hand against the building. They began moving again and the wind became stronger, the snow heavier, and the temperature colder as the afternoon sun began to go down.

Roger Carlson worked at the desk in his study at home until his concentration was interrupted by the ringing of the telephone. He quickly picked it up and answered. "Hello."

"Roger... Jack Green... You wanted a run-down on that Michelle Matthews broad?"

"Oh... Hi, Jack...yeah, that's right I did...and she's not a broad... What'd you find out?"

"Not a whole lot...typical spoiled little rich kid that runs out on her family."

"Rich?.. Are you sure?.. I got the impression they weren't too well off."

"Her old man's a big tycoon in Duluth."

"Really?.. What's he into?"

"He's at National steel... Seems this Michelle is his oldest daughter... Listen to this...the kid graduates magna cum laud from high school, gets a scholarship to college and flips for some jock. She gets knocked up, refuses an abortion and her parents throw her out."

"You got a number on her parents?.. I'd like to speak to them."

"Yeah...call the old man's office at National. They'll put you through. His name is Walter Matthews and he's vice president in charge of operations... Big time."

"Thanks, Jack," Roger said, "I appreciate the help."

"Anytime, ol' buddy."

Roger hung up the phone, picked it back up an dialed information. In a short time he was on the line with Walter Matthews, of National Steel.

"Mr. Matthews, I'm Attorney Roger Carlson of Detroit. I'd like to talk to you about your daughter."

"Which one?" Matthews asked. "I've got three daughters, you know."

"I'm calling about Michelle. Did you know she's been living in the streets here in Detroit?"

"Is... Is this some kinda blackmail?" Matthews asked, suspiciously.

"Blackmail?.. For GOD's sake, man!.. My wife and I ran across your daughter when she tried to snatch my wife's purse!" Roger replied, angrily. "We took her in, fed her and we're trying to help her."

"Good luck."

"Maybe you don't understand, Mr. Matthews... Your daughter has been living in the streets...she's one of the homeless!"

"That's too bad, Mr...did you say...Carlson?.. I'm sorry but Michelle is no longer my responsibility. My wife and I gave her a good home and a loving family...she threw all of that back in our faces when she left."

"Everybody makes a mistake...especially at that age," Roger snapped, angrily. "I just want to know...will you accept her back if we put her on a plane and send her to you?"

"No...we don't want her back."

"Why you big jerk!" Roger shouted into the phone. "How can you be so heartless?.. I.."

Roger suddenly heard the sound of a "click" when Matthews hung up his phone. He stared at the phone in his hand in complete disbelief.

Gene II sat behind the desk in his office at The Herald with a concerned look on his face. He anxiously talked to Max Jenkins, an assignment editor. Both men were frustrated and upset. Max had dated Marcy Dugas several times and he had encouraged her to investigate The Forgotten child Foundation. Now, it was almost dark and neither Marcy or Adrian had called in for hours.

"Did you see Marcy at work today?" Gene II asked. "It's not like her to fail to call in for her messages."

"Come to think of it...I'm not sure," Max answered, thoughtfully. "She's usually asking me something about that flaky foundation by now...you think something could've happened to them?"

"I...I don't know. I haven't heard anything from Adrian either... It may be nothing...maybe I'm over reacting." Gene II answered, concerned.

"You call her apartment?"

"I've talked to her recorder twice," Gene II replied. "Her apartment manager says the security guard saw her leave this morning at the regular time."

"Hey, wait a minute," Max said, "she was here for awhile this morning... They're probably still over there at that foundation... Have you called over there?"

"A half a dozen times... I get no answer.'

"No answer?.. That doesn't sound right."

"I think I'll run by there and see what's going on," Gene II said. "It may be nothing...but I don't wanna take any chances."

"Yeah, that sounds like the best thing to do... Call me when you find out something," Max said. "I'll stick around here in case they call in or show up."

Gene II stood up and put on his coat as Max waited for him. When they were walking out of Gene II's office they bumped into his secretary coming into the office.

"Oh, you're leaving?" the secretary asked. "We just got a call from City Hospital!"

"Well put it on hold until I get back... I got something to do that's pretty important."

"The secretary refused to move. "I...I think this may be more important," she shot back.

"Why, what's it about?"

THE WINDS OF TOMORROW

The secretary looked from Gene II to Max, anxiously.
"Five babies have just been kidnapped from the hospital nursery!"

Gene II stood in the hospital corridor just outside of the nursery and talked to several policemen, doctors and nurses. Reporters from both newspapers interviewed witnesses while a television crew filmed the entire scene and talked to several nurses and attendants who were crying and visibly upset. One detective talked to the head nurse as Gene II stood by and listened.

"You say that right after visiting hours you discovered the babies missing?" the first detective asked the head nurse.

"No...it wasn't immediately after," the head nurse replied. "We usually change and feed them just after visiting hours in order to let them sleep undisturbed."

"Is that when you discovered they were gone?" the detective asked.

"One of my nurse's aids realized after feeding, that she had more food than she had babies," the head nurse answered.

"And when you made your count," a second detective said, "you realized you were five infants short?"

"That's correct...I can't understand how something like this could ever happen!" the head nurse was upset.

"Is it possible that one of the visitors could have done this?" the first detective asked.

"They're all issued passes with identification cards," she replied, "and they turn them in when they leave... We have a daily record of each and every visitor who came on this floor."

A doctor walked up to the group and listened as the head nurse talked to the detectives.

"Besides, the visitors are all carefully screened and watched," the doctor intervened, "they don't have access to the babies. We guard the infants against any contract from visitors to prevent infection...No, the only way this could have been accomplished is by staff personnel...or people dressed up like staff personnel who knew our procedures."

Gene II motioned for one of the detectives to step off to the side with him while the questioning continued.

"You think some of the staff might be involved?" Gene II asked, "and that this could be an inside job?"

"I don't think so," the detective answered, "those people are so upset they're almost hysterical...some of 'em had to be sedated."

"Did they report seeing any new or strange staff people around here today?"

"This is a big hospital...half the people on the third floor don't even know the personnel on the fourth floor," the detective said, "but we'll get the ones who did this. We'll get a lead sooner or later. The F.B.I. is on the way over here now."

Janet and Roger Carlson sat in Dr. Robert Whyte's office waiting for Dr. Whyte to return with their test results. They figeted nervously as they grew more impatient...

"What the hell is taking him so long?" Roger asked.

"Relax...be patient," Janet answered. "We'll know soon enough."

"With all these modern techniques they're suppose to have you'd think they'd be able to tell us in a few hours instead of days."

Just as Roger completed his last sentence, Dr. Whyte walked briskly into the office with a big smile on his face and several sheets of paper in his hand. "Sorry it took so long but my old secretary was replaced by a new one yesterday and I have to help her find everything." Dr. Whyte said as he sat down behind his desk. In addition to that, they have big problems on the third floor...seems they've misplaced five babies...

"Five babies are missing?" Roger asked.

"They're not missing...they were kidnapped. The police are all over the place... But I know what you're waiting for and I'm happy to report that you two passed the tests with flying colors."

"You... You mean we can be the biological parents?" Roger asked, anxiously. "Thank the LORD!"

"I heard that," Bob laughed. "Our tests revealed that you both are capable...all you need now is a host mother."

"Oh, thank you, Bob," Janet sighed in relief, "this gives us a whole new lease on life!"

"How soon can we actually get started on this?" Roger asked, anxiously.

"As I said before, you'll have to work with an Infertility Specialist," Bob replied. "I've done everything I can do... Did you contact the name I gave you the other day?"

"Yes...we have an appointment set up for next week," Janet answered.

"Fine...I'll give you these test results and you pass them on to the specialist...she'll handle it from there...that is ... if it's alright with both of you."

"It works for me!" Roger beamed, happily.

"We really appreciate your help, Bob," Janet said, smiling broadly. "You've been just swell."

"Congratulations to you both," Bob said, grinning. "You're only half way home but I want you to know that you both are my very good friends and I am happy to be able to do anything I can for you... This is an important step you're about to take... What about your families, how do they feel about this?"

Janet glanced at Roger who shook his head thoughtfully as a frown crossed his face. "They don't seem to understand how strong we feel about this," Roger said, regretfully.

"They may...eventually," Janet said, "but most close relatives don't want to see any radical changes in their loved one's lives...they prefer that we remain on dimensional. They refuse to realize that, like themselves, we have dreams, hopes and aspirations, too."

"You're absolutely right to feel that way," Bob agreed. "And hang on to those dreams and live your lives to the fullest... We only come this way once in our lives."

Chapter Twenty

Adrian and Marcy slowly inched their way on the ledge of the building, five stories high. When they reached a window, Marcy tried to raise it up and it slid open. The two women quickly climbed inside to a completely darkened room. Exhausted from their spine tingling walk along the ledge, they sat down on the floor and leaned back against the wall of the room and tried to catch their breath.

"My GOD...we could have been killed!" Adrian groaned, breathlessly.

"We had no choice," Marcy sighed. "If we had stayed in that room...there's no telling what they would've done to us."

"Where are we?.. What is this room?" Adrian asked. "I hear water running."

Marcy stood up and located the light switch on the wall. She quickly flipped it on.

"The mens' room," Adrian whispered.

"At least we can get out of this damn building without being killed!.. C'mon, let's get out of here!"

Adrian got up and followed Marcy to the door. Just as she opened the door they could hear the voices of Luther and Dr. Morton coming down the hallway towards them!

"That was a smooth operation," Luther said, chuckling, "let's check out our two friends in a few minutes...I have to make a pit stop first."

"Me too," Dr. Morton said, "wait up."

The two women looked at each other in fear!.. They quickly disappeared back inside the mens' room, each to a different stall. In a few seconds Luther and Dr. Morton walked into the room. The men were only there for a few minutes when Luther, as he was washing his hands, looked into the mirror and saw Adrian's head bob up above the door on one of the stalls.

"Morton...don't say anything," Luther whispered, "but I think we've got company."

"In here?" Morton asked, surprised.

"Yeah...our two friends are in the last two stalls...I don't know how they managed it, but just relax...they're not going anywhere."

The two men finished washing their hands, turned around and faced the two stalls. "Alright, girls... we're BAACCKK!" Luther teased. "C'mon out...we know you're in there!"

There was a moment of silence before the two stall doors slowly opened almost simultaneously and Marcy and Adrian walked out, obediently, with their heads down in embarrassment.

"I don't know how you two managed this," Luther said, angrily, "but you're going right back in that room...and this time those ropes will be a lot tighter."

The men each grabbed one of the women and twisted their arms behind their backs roughly as they marched them out of the men's room...

"The police are going to get you," Adrian snapped, angrily. "They're going to get all of you!"

"Just keep quiet and you won't get hurt," Luther said.

"We've got a few transactions to take care of ...then we will all be leaving Detroit and you'll have a chance to meet Lonnie... He'll love you two."

Adrian and Marcy were again tied up tightly to two straight chairs, back to back. After Luther and Dr. Morton left the office, the two women listened closely when they heard faint conversation in the other offices and the sounds of people coming and going along with babies crying. In a few minutes Edna came into the office and glared at them.

"We're all finished now," Edna said, "are you two all ready to go?"

Edna removed the mouth gags and began loosening their ropes.

"We heard you in there!" Marcy said, angrily. "Where did you get those babies?.. You were selling babies like hamburgers in a fast food drive-in restaurant!"

"You'll pay for this, Edna!" Adrian shouted. "You all will pay...I'll see to it!"

Luther and Morton walked into the room and grinned at the two women. They stood in the middle of the office and chuckled.

"Where we're taking you will make this place look like a garden party," Luther said.

"Why are you doing this?" Marcy asked. "You can get away scott free...you don't need us!"

"We need more time...if we let you go too soon you'll go to the police and get them on our trail," Luther replied, calmly, "but if we detain you for a while we'll have more time to cover our tracks."

"You're lucky we don't kill you," Dr. Morton snarled.

"You don't scare me," Adrian shot back.

Edna quickly slapped Adrian across her mouth!.. Luther stepped in between the two women. Edna glared at Adrian.

"You better be more careful the next time you go after somebody's man," Edna warned Adrian.

Adrian and Marcy were hurriedly marched out of the office and down the hallway. The two women were shoved roughly if they hesitated or slowed down as the group vacated the building.

Gene Stanton, having just returned from Washington, D.C., stood in the family room of his daughter, Karen's home discussing his wife's sudden vacation with Karen and her husband, Bob. Karen kept her three children out of the room because she could see that her father was extremely upset at not having found his wife.

"What I can't understand is that when I got to her hotel they said she had just checked out," Gene said, puzzled. "She just suddenly jumps up and leaves...and nobody knows where in the hell she is."

"When did you speak to her last?" Karen asked.

"A few days ago...she was vague...wouldn't make up her mind."

"I thought you two were working things out," Bob said, "what happened?"

"I thought so too," Gene answered. "We had began to agree on a few things."

"That's not the impression I had," Karen said.

"Huh?.. What did she tell you?" Gene asked.

"She said you wanted her to spend more time with the Herald," Karen said, "and that you wanted her to quit that anti-racism committee."

"That's true...we both agreed that was the best thing to do."

"Are you sure she agreed to that?" Bob asked.

"Yes, I am...why?"

"Are you really sure, Gene?.. Or is that just what you wanted her to do," Bob asked.

Gene became perturbed by that question and stopped and stared at both Karen and Bob. "What are you two getting at?" Gene asked.

"She said she discussed you proposal," Karen replied, "but she never agreed to it."

"Listen...both of you... Ever since we switched to a daily newspaper she's been saying I was ignoring her...so I told her if she really wanted to be around me more to drop that committee and work with us at The Herald...I was trying to compromise with what she wanted...that's all...but the way it looks now...I'm the bad guy."

"Do you really want to get this resolved, dad?"

"That's why I went to Washington...to get this thing straightened out once and for all."

"Did you tell her you were coming?" Karen asked.

"What difference would it have made?" Gene asked, angrily. "She's my wife and I want her with me in Detroit where she belongs."

"She told me she's tried to reach you several times and you never returned her calls," Karen said. "She said she tried to reach you all last weekend while you were on Grand Island, but there was no answer."

" I had a lot of things on my mind," Gene replied, "and I didn't want to talk to anyone...I wanted complete solitude."

"Complete solitude?" Karen asked, sarcastically. "Is that what you call complete solitude?"

Gene angrily began pacing the room, glancing out of the window, thoughtfully. Suddenly, he stopped and turned to Karen, "Is there something you're not telling me?"

"C'mon, Gene!" Bob interrupted, "Karen doesn't know anything."

"Do you know where your mother is?" Gene asked Karen, almost in a whisper.

Karen became nervous, shifting her eyes from Gene to Bob..." Honestly, dad...I don't know where she is," Karen answered. "I only know she left this afternoon on a five fifty flight out of Washington."

Gene slammed his fist into the palm of his hand!.. "Well I'll be damned!" Gene snapped. "I probably passed her at the airport!"

Bob poured Gene a glass of wine and handed it to him.

"Here, relax," Bob said, calmly, "you think you've got problems...the hospital had five babies stolen from the nursery today."

"Five babies were kidnapped from the hospital?" Gene asked. "They have any idea who did it?"

"Not a clue."

"That's terrible...I'm sure Gene II has somebody on it," Gene said.

"Yeah, he was there when I left," Bob replied.

Gene looked at Karen who shifted her eyes away from his. He downed the drink quickly before he spoke. "Did she leave Washington by herself?"

"Gene!.. Stop bugging her!" Bob protested.

"I'm your father, Karen," Gene said, quietly, "tell me...was she by herself or not?"

Karen turned to Bob with her eyes pleading for help.

Gene II walked through the now empty offices of The Forgotten Child Foundation. Papers were scattered all across the floor, empty drawer hung out of desks, empty briefcases and waste paper baskets were strewn about. It was obvious the previous occupants had left in a hurry! Gene II tested several phones before he found one with a dial tone. He quickly made a phone call...

"Let me speak to Max Jenkins," Gene II said as he continued perusing the empty offices. "Max?".. Yeah...I'm over here now...we got problems, man.. this place has been cleaned out!.. Everyone is gone...I don't know, man...there's not a sign of either of them!"

Max joined Gene II in the offices of The Foundation about thirty minutes later. Both men were obviously worried and upset as they wandered through the maze of empty offices, opening closets, checking papers and carefully inspecting each desk drawer...

"Damn!.. We don't know if they've got 'em or not," Max grumbled.

"If they don't have them...where are they?" Gene II asked. "I've called everywhere. If they're not back at The Herald by this evening we're gonna have to bring in the law...they could be in real trouble!"

"If that bastard, Chabot, has them...they're in real trouble now!" Max snapped.

"Tell me about it!"

"You have any idea where he'd take 'em?"

"Who knows?.. That kind of nut might do anything."

"You think he could be involved with that baby-napping at the hospital?"

"I doubt it...he wouldn't have the nerve," Gene II said. "He's small time stuff."

"What do you think we oughta do?" Max asked.

"Can't file a missing person's report for twenty-four hours," Gene II said, "and we can't wait that long!"

"Then what's our next move?"

"We're gonna lie a little."

"Lie?"

"Let's contact the police and tell them we think they've been kidnapped and ask them to put out an All Points Bulletin," Gene II said, thoughtfully. "If they show up we'll look like dopes but at least they'll be safe."

"It certainly couldn't do any harm," Max said, "as long as they don't think we're runnin' some kind of scam on 'em."

"If they do think that...we'll have to use our ace in the hole."

"Ace in the hole?" Max asked. "What's that?"

'We'll tell them that we suspect that the sudden closing down of this foundation is tied in with another crime," Gene II said, grinning. "That'll get 'em

THE WINDS OF TOMORROW

off their asses."

"What's the other crime?"

The two men looked at each other and grinned, broadly as they gave each other a high-five handshake...

"The kidnapping of those five babies at the hospital!"

Both men shout in unison...

The two stretch limousines slipped and whined up the treacherous mountain road. The steady, heavy snowfall reduced the visibility considerably. Everyone was tense and silent inside the cars as the constant thumping of the windshield wipers supplied the beat to the harrowing scene.

Finally, the two vehicles turned into a driveway, fishtailing around the turn and almost skidding into a ravine. After straightening out back on the driveway, they slowly moved along, up the hill, towards a small group of log cabins. When the two vehicles slid to a stop in front of the cabins several people quickly climbed out and rushed into the cabins trying to get out of the blizzard like weather. Two men, dressed in ski clothes, pushed two women ahead of them. They all went inside the first cabin. Once inside, Luther had Adrian and Marcy tied up again and they were roughly shoved into a corner, sitting on the floor, while the others shook the heavy snow from their coats and jackets. Two of the men began making a fire in a pot belly stove and in the fireplace. In a few minutes the heat from the stove and the fireplace began warming the small cabin. Edna was still shivering as she stared at Luther and Dr. Morton.

"Whew!.. It's a mess out there!" Edna said, shivering. "You think they can fly in here in this kind of weather?.. And where is that animal at?.. I don't want him anywhere around me while I'm here!"

Luther glared at Edna with an angry expression on his face. "I told you...don't call him animal!..His name is Lonnie...and as far as that helicopter is concerned...your guess is as good as mine. He said he'd get here after dark."

What about our two friends, here," Dr. Morton asked, "they goin' with us?"

"I hadn't planned on it," Luther looked at Adrian and shook his head, regretfully. "If only she had been a little more cooperative...maybe... As it is I'll just leave them both here for Lonnie to play with." He reached under the table and pulled out a large box, grinning broadly.

"What's that?" Dr. Morton asked.

"I brought Lonnie another living doll, but as soon as he bursts this one...he'll go after our two guests here!" Luther said, still grinning.

"He goes through those dolls like that?"

'He loves them...one time he..."

"Don't tell me about it!" Edna screamed, interrupting. "I never want to see another one of those dolls again...It's disgusting!"

Luther laughed loudly. "Those living dolls are the only things Lonnie has to look forward to."

"He belongs in a mental institution...you know that," Dr. Morton said, disapprovingly. "If you leave them here with no heat...they could freeze to death...it's going down below zero tonight and all of this snow makes it impossible to travel the roads!.. They're stuck here!"

"What else can I do?" Luther asked. "They brought this on themselves...the original plan was to leave them at the foundation."

"I don't want any part of murder!" Dr. Morton snapped.

Luther turned to Marcy and Adrian who were staring back at him. Although they were gagged, he got the message their eyes were sending...they were furious!.. "I won't leave them here with no heat...we'll bank the fires so they'll last at least eight hours."

"Eight hours?" Edna asked. "What good will that do?"

"I don't intend to kill them," Luther answered. "Eight hours will give us plenty of time to get out of the country...and by that time a state policeman or sheriff's deputy will check on these cabins and find them...they check on these cabins about every other day...especially in weather like this."

"You mean you hope they will," Morton said.

"Get the food ready, the fire's going good now," Luther said, "Let's feed everybody and wait for that chopper."

"Shall I have them untied so they can eat?" Dr. Morton asked.

"Yeah, sure...they ain't goin' nowhere in weather like this," Luther chuckled, "unless they want to party with Lonnie."

Morton directed the two other men to untie Adrian and Marcy while Edna prepared the food. Everyone sat down at the long table and began eating while they watched a small portable television set in the cabin. Adrian nodded to Marcy as everyone ate. Suddenly the front door to the cabin was thrown open and a giant of a man with a long, scraggly beard and all covered with snow, stood in the doorway as snow was blown in behind him!.. The seven foot giant stood there with a crumpled, life-like doll under his arm!..

"Close that damn door, Lonnie!" Luther shouted, angrily. "You tryin' to freeze us to death?"

Lonnie kicked the door shut and walked over to Luther, haltingly. "You here?.. I didn't know you were comin' to see Lonnie!" the giant stammered. "You bring Lonnie another doll?.. My doll all broke!"

Luther smiled, knowingly and reached under the table for the large box. "Yeah, I brought you another doll... You gotta stop burstin' 'em, Lonnie!.. You squeeze 'em too hard!"

Lonnie grabbed the box happily like a small child!.. Lonnie go play with new doll!" He turned to leave and stopped suddenly, surprised to see Adrian and Marcy staring at him. "Luther got two live dolls!"

Luther quickly got up and escorted Lonnie towards the door while Lonnie continued staring at Adrian and Marcy back over his shoulder. "Alright, Lonnie...that's enough now," Luther said. "You go back to your cabin and play with your new doll."

After Lonnie left the cabin and Luther had sat back down at the table to continue eating, Adrian and Marcy stared at each other, shivering in fear!..

"Did you see that monster?" Adrian whispered to Marcy. "How are we gonna get out of here?"

"We gotta figure out something," Marcy answered, whispering softly. "That beast could kill us both!"

Edna glanced at the two women and smiled knowingly. "A little information you may be interested in, girls...we are about one hundred miles from Detroit...high up in the mountains. If you're thinking about walking back to the nearest town you better forget it."

"We don't believe anything you might have to say," Adrian shot back.

"If I were you," Edna chuckled, "I'd enjoy these few peaceful hours and hope I don't become Lonnie's next love doll."

Hours later it had stopped snowing and everyone in the cabin was becoming upset and jittery waiting for the helicopter. Luther paced back and forth, nervously, while Edna and Dr. Morton played gin rummy. Marcy and Adrian sat quietly, trying not to draw attention to themselves. Luther's other two men were stationed at separate windows, looking for the chopper. When the first sounds of the helicopter were heard off in the distance, Luther jumped up excitedly! "It's them!.. They're here!.. C'mon, let's get the hell outta here!"

"It's about time," Edna said. "I didn't think they'd make it!... Alright folks, let's load up!"

Everyone began carrying luggage and boxes out of the door as the huge helicopter settled in the swirling snow just in front of the cabin. When Luther's crew was finished loading up, two of the men walked back into the cabin and began tying up Adrian and Marcy. The women protested, angrily.

"You're making a clean getaway," Marcy complained, "is this really necessary?"

"C'mon...give us a break, "Adrian protested.

Luther rushed back into the cabin while the two women argued with their captors at being tied up again. He stared at them and laughed loudly. "Look...I'm giving you a break now... If you don't appreciate it we could leave you out in the cold... And don't worry about Lonnie either ...those dolls usually last him two or three days."

Adrian and Marcy suddenly became submissive while they are tied up securely. When they were left alone in the cabin they sat silently until they heard the sound of the helicopter taking off. Marcy hobbled over to the window and began shouting... "They're gone...now let's get out of this place...I don't intend on being dessert for Lonnie!.. We've got to get out of here right away!"

"Get out?.. We can't even get loose!" Adrian snapped.

"Oh, yes we can... I hid my dinner knife while we were eating that horrible food!" Marcy replied as she hobbled over to the bench they had been sitting on. She knelt down with her back to the bench as her tied hands searched the floor directly under where she had been sitting. Soon a big smile lit up her face. 'Here it is...my little ol' knifey!"

Marcy quickly hobbled back over to Adrian, and standing back to back, she quickly cut the ropes between Adrian's wrists. In a few minutes they both were free!.. Marcy examined her swollen and bruised wrists, rubbing them carefully. "I'm getting so good at this I oughta join a circus!"

Adrian sighed in relief. "You are resourceful...no doubt about it... We might be loose but what are be going to do now?.. We're one hundred miles from nowhere, in two feet of snow, temperatures plunging and...dear, sweet, oversexed Lonnie!"

Marcy looked out of the window. "Now it's snowing again...and...hey, they left the cars!"

Adrian ran over to the window and looked over Marcy's shoulder. Really?.. Then we can get out of here!"

"Forget it..it's no use, "Marcy said, disappointed, "we don't have any keys."

"We don't need any keys...this is a little something I learned on the side while I was earning my P.H.D."

"You know how to hot-wire a car?"

"You're damn right I do...I had to do a thesis on this entire process during a seminar at state prison," Adrian said, anxiously, "it was part of my doctorate requirements."

Adrian suddenly stopped in mid-sentence and began screaming, loudly! "AAAHHHeee!" She found herself staring face to face at Lonnie through the frosted window!.. Both women quickly ran towards the door to lock it before Lonnie could come in!.. But they were too late!.. The door was thrown opened and Lonnie stood in the doorway and glared at them!..

He looked from the deflated doll in his hand back to both of the frightened women!.. The giant stood, unmoving, silhouetted against the blizzard behind him. A grin slowly creased his hairy face as he stared at the women with saliva dripping from his mouth!.. Suddenly, he threw the deflated doll down on the floor and slowly began moving towards the two women, menacingly!.. "Lonnie wants live dolls!" He drooled as he staggered towards them!

Marcy quickly picked up a log and held it high above her head, poised to strike!.. "Go away, Lonnie!..go away!"

Lonnie stopped and kicked the door shut. He slowly began walking towards them again with his arms outstretched! Moving closer and closer!..

"Go away, Lonnie!" Marcy warned, backing up.

"Lonnie wants live dolls!" He shouted, staggering forward.

Just as he reached for Adrian, Marcy cracked him across the back of his head with the log!.. Stunned by the blow, he turned his attention to Marcy, growling angrily, deep within his chest!.. As he moved towards Marcy with blood streaming down the sides of his face, Adrian struck him again on the back of his head with another log!.. Lonnie stopped, wavered unsteadily and collapsed in a massive heap at Marcy's feet!

"Oh, my GOD!" Marcy screamed. "I think he's dead!"

"It was him or us!" Adrian said, breathlessly. "Let's get out of here before he comes to!"

They quickly ran out of the cabin towards the two limousines parked in the driveway. They tried the first car but it was locked. When they reached the second car they found the driver's door unlocked. Marcy stood outside the car with the log still in her hand while Adrian crouched down beneath the dash board on the driver's side and tried to cross the wires to start the motor.

"Can you do it?" Marcy asked, shouting, nervously.

"A piece of cake."

"Well?"

"Uuuhhgh... I'm... I'm not sure...dammit, I can't find the right wires!"

"Hurry, Adrian!" Marcy screamed anxiously. "We don't have much time...and...and it's cold out here!"

Adrian's legs were protruding from the car and they began to wiggle as she crawled further under the dash board..." I... I think I've got it now," she grunted, "here goes!"

Marcy stood shivering in the cold weather and waited for the sound of the ignition as the icy winds blew down from the mountains...suddenly she saw the door to the cabin flung opened!.. The silhouette of Lonnie stood in the doorway for a moment before he began slowly staggering out towards them!.. Marcy screamed in horror!.. "Adrian!.. Hurry!.. Lonnie is coming!"

In a few seconds Marcy heard the sound of the ignition starting the big motor as the limousine came to life!..

"I did it!" Adrian shouted, happily. "I did it!"

"Then let's go!" Marcy screamed, climbing into the stretch limousine.

"We're outta here!"

The stretch limo began to creep, slip and slide down towards the road... Suddenly they heard a loud banging on the windows of the car!.. They both turned and looked back in time to see Lonnie climb on top of the car trunk and began beating on the rear car window!.. As the long, limousine careened and fishtailed around the turn to the mountain road, Lonnie slid off the car trunk and disappeared into the deep drifts of snow on the roadside!..

Adrian drove the car slowly in the heavily falling snow and tried to follow the steep, narrow trail through the twists and turns back down the dangerous mountain road. Both women strained their eyes to see the road, in stark terror and listened to the humming sound of the windshield wipers as they worked furiously!.. Suddenly, they both began to scream as the car went out of control and slid sideways off the road, crashed through a wooden fence and plunged down the side of the steep cliff!..

Chapter Twenty-One

Willow Creek General Hospital is located approximately ninety miles north of the City of Detroit. Extra police were put on highway patrol during heavy snowstorms because of the treacherous roads that run through the mountains near the small town of Willow Creek. The police cruise and patrol the most dangerous areas constantly because they realize a car could have an accident, go over the side of the mountain and disappear under huge drifts of snow completely unnoticed by anyone. Willow Creek General Hospital carried extra staff during these periods in case of an accident emergency.

When a sheriff's patrol car spotted blinking lights down in the valley next to the mountain, they knew what had happened and they expected the worse. They immediately put in a call for an ambulance and went down to the car to save the occupants.

The total amount of time that lapsed was no more than fifteen minutes when the two large doors leading into the emergency room of Willow Creek Hospital were suddenly thrown open as ambulance attendants wheeled Adrian and Marcy threw the doors on two separate gurneys. An emergency room doctor rushed over to them with several hospital attendants as they quickly began examining the two women. Another doctor began questioning the ambulance drivers.

"Are these the two women from that limo that went off the mountain?" the doctor asked.

"You got it, doc...they were pretty well banged up, too," the ambulance driver said. "When they went over that cliff it would've been fatal, but their car snagged on a tree on the way down and it triggered the two air bags in the limo...it actually saved their lives...just a few cuts and bruises...they're still unconscious but we couldn't find too much wrong with 'em...they're your problems, now."

"Fine...we'll take if from here," the doctor replied, impatiently.

The slight moaning that came from Adrian attracted the doctor's attention. He leaned down, closer to her face.

"Hello...miss...can you hear me?"

"Yes...yes...," Adrian responded, weakly, "where am I?"

"You're in Willow Creek General Hospital's emergency unit...You've been in a terrible automobile accident."

She tried to sit up but groaned in pain. "Marcy...where's Marcy?..Is she alright?"

"Marcy?..Is that the name of the woman who was with you?"

"Yes...where is she?"

Adrian looked around the wide room as a policeman walked over to the doctor. "Are these the two accident victims?"

"Yes...this one is conscious," the doctor answered.

The policeman stared at Adrian and shook his head. "What's yer name, miss?"

"Adrian Grant...How's Marcy doing?"

"Your friend's doing just fine," the doctor said, "but don't you worry about her...just answer the officer's questions."

"Adrian Grant?" the policeman asked, surprised. "Is your friend's name Dugas...Marcy Dugas?"

"Yes."

The policeman turned to the doctor, anxiously. "We just got and APB on these two women...they're reporters for the Detroit Herald Newspaper...They were reported kidnapped earlier this evening by the same people who stole those five babies from City Hospital!..."

The Detroit Metropolitan Airport was dark and quiet as the helicopter appeared out of the black skies and descended on a designated landing pad near the airport. The snow had finally stopped and most of the jetliners had been grounded. Many ground crews were working to get the giant aircrafts back up in the air to meet their schedules. When Luther and his crew climbed out of the helicopter they were met by several airport maintenance workers who quickly relieved them of their luggage and placed it on a mobile carrier. As Luther and his associates followed the carrier they were joined by a smiling crew supervisor.

"Welcome to Metro Airport, Mr. Chabot," the crew supervisor said, "I hope you find everything satisfactory."

Luther was surprised by the politeness of the supervisor and he smiled at Edna and Dr. Morton, knowingly..."Thank you very much," Luther replied as they walked briskly towards the airport.

"What flight are you taking, sir?" the supervisor asked.

"Northwest 502 to Toronto," Edna answered, smiling.

"Going out of the country, sir?"

"Yeah...what's it to ya?" Luther snapped, irritated.

"I don't think so."

"What?"

"You're not going out of the country."

"Why not?"

"Wayne County Sheriff's Office," the supervisor said, flashing a badge. "You're under arrest for kidnapping five babies form City Hospital in Detroit!"

"Hey, wait a minute!" Luther protested.

Before Luther's crew could react they were surrounded by uniformed Wayne County Sheriffs with drawn guns!..The sheriffs quickly began reading them their rights and handcuffing them as Edna glared at Luther!

"How...how'd you find out where we were?" a perplexed Luther asked. "There was no one looking for us!"

"Those damn women!" Edna snarled.

"Your helicopter pilot filed a flight plan for the Forgotten Child Foundation," the sheriff answered.

"Well...what's wrong with that?"

"There's been an All Points Bulletin issued on your organization since six this evening...When the flight plan was filed and registered in your company's name the computer picked it up," The sheriff explained. "Now...we want to know where are the two women reporters from The Detroit Herald?..What have you done with them?"

Willard Thompson sat across from his cousin, Karen as she completed administrative details and prepared to leave her office at The Herald. She stopped writing and looked up at Willard, carefully studying his face. "You alright?..You look unhappy. Don't you like your job on the advertising staff?"

"It's not that," Willard answered, "I just found out something that's really blowing my mind...I gotta talk to somebody."

"What about your mother?..You two have always seemed so close."

"She's the one who blew my mind," he answered.

"What happened?" Karen asked. "You can tell me...if it's not too personal maybe I can be your sounding board." "It's personal..very personal, but I gotta figure this thing out," Willard said, thoughtfully. "I got a call from the Daily Press' personnel department...they offered me a job on their advertising staff."

"Didn't you tell them you were working here?"

"They already knew about that...in fact...they knew more about me than I did."

"What are you talking about?"

"I went over there for the appointment to be interviewed...While I was there...the publisher sat in on the interview."

Karen was surprised and suddenly more interested. "F. Walton Dugas, publisher of The Daily Press sat in on your interview?..Why?"

"That's what I wanted to know!..After I went up to his office with him...he started to explain."

"What's going on, Willard?" Karen asked, suspiciously. "You look like you've just seen a ghost."

"Yeah...it was a ghost alright...a ghost of things from the past."

"What do you mean?"

"It seems that when your dad was shot...mom thought that Dugas may have had something to do with it."

"He had called and threatened dad."

"I know about that...Anyhow, the next day after the shooting, mom went out to Dugas' home and dropped this bomb on him."

"What bomb?" Karen asked.

"Dugas had been upset with the Stantons because of some money Dugas' father had lend granddad in the seventies. He didn't think that the Stanton's buying the Herald and becoming his main competition, was the right way to show gratitude for that loan," Willard said, calmly.

"Yeah... we know all about that," Karen said, sarcastically.

Willard lowered his voice as he continued. "What you don't know... is that it wasn't a loan that Dugas' father made to granddad... it was a pay-off."

"A pay-off?" Karen asked, surprised. "A pay-off for what?"

"For his son raping my mother."

Karen dropped her pen on the desk and leaned back in her chair, stunned. "Now wait a minute!... How could she prove something like that after all these years?"

Willard got up and walked across the office to a large bay window, overlooking downtown Detroit. He hesitated before he answered her... "She's got the proof, alright."

"What kind of proof?" Karen asked.

"Me... she says I'm his son!"

Karen was shocked. They both remained silent and waited for a response from the other. Karen spoke up first, "What about your... other father?"

"You mean the man who was suppose to be my biological father?" Willard said softly. "You ever met him?"

"Well.. no."

"I didn't think so... I asked her about him today... I use to wonder why there were no pictures or anything... You know what she told me?"

"I've got a sneaking suspicion," Karen whispered.

"She said he never existed... She confirmed that Dugas is my father."

"I'm... I'm so sorry, Willard... I don't know what to say."

"I know... but you can still help me."

"What can I do?"

"I've been thinking about this all day," he replied, sadly, "and it may not be such a bad spot to be in... The Daily Press is one of the most successful newspapers in the country... It's ten times richer then The Herald... no offense but it is."

"You'll own a part of both newspapers, Willard... The man with the golden press card... but how can I help you?"

"I've been lied to since the day I was born... I just wanna make sure that what they're telling me now is the truth. Once I can verify that it is, then I'll know what to do... Your husband is a doctor and a big wheel at City Hospital... You can help me."

Willard turned away from the window and stared at Karen, waiting for her reply.

"How?"

"I want a DNA test performed to verify that either Dugas is or is not my father... but I want this to be strictly confidential... If he isn't, no sweat... If he is... then I want what's due me... my full heritage... every single dime!... I understand that he has a son and a daughter... I want what they have... it's my right!"

"I agree... you should have what they have... His daughter works here. She's Marcy Dugas in editorial."

"I know.. I've met her and I like her."

"We better get this cleared up."

"Then you'll help me?" Willard asked. "You'll get Robert to set up the tests?"

"We've got to be careful... we don't want anyone to know what we're doing," Karen said, thoughtfully. "We'd better camouflage our actions."

"How can we do that?"

"We'll both have the tests performed... like we're searching for a family trait for potential organ transplants... What about your... parents... are they agreeable to this?"

"It was Dugas' idea... he wants to know for sure before we go any further... He's an amazing and powerful guy who seems to be willing to include me in his life even though I'm Black."

"And your mom... how does she feel about taking the tests?" Karen asked.

"She feels guilty as hell for not telling me the truth about my father... She's agreed to do whatever I ask her to do."

"Then I'll speak to Robert tonight. As soon as it's set up... I'll call you... In fact, I even go with you."

"Are you serious about having the test performed on you, too?" Willard asked. "It would enable us to disguise what were really doing."

"Absolutely... I'll have a DNA test performed also. My parents both have blood specimens stored at City Hospital," Karen said, determined. "This thing may turn out to be beneficial for both of us."

Willard looked at her and smiled. He quickly embraced her. "I won't forget this, Karen... I really appreciate your help."

Adrian and Marcy sat up in their hospital beds across from each other and read "get well" cards from their co-workers at The Herald. Gene II and Max Jenkins walked into the room carrying huge bouquets of flowers. Both women smiled warmly.

"More flowers?... Fantastic," Adrian squealed, "I love 'em!"

"Isn't this great?" Marcy said, stretching, leisurely.

"You two were lucky you weren't killed," Gene II said. "Are you guys feeling alright?"

"Yeah, how you doin?" Max asked, sitting down next to Marcy's bed. "Those were some dangerous people you were with!"

"Have you heard any more about them?" Marcy asked.

"Yes, it's all over... they were picked up last night at Metro Airport with over five hundred thousand in cash!" Gene II answered, proudly. "Wayne County Sheriff's department turned them over to the F.B.I... All of the kidnapped babies have been recovered and retuned to their rightful parents... Luther Chabot and his gang will be put away for a long time."

"Thank GOD for that!" Adrian exclaimed, relieved.

"No... thanks to you and Marcy... If there hadn't been an APB out for you and that phony foundation they would've gotten out of the country!"

"Did anyone locate a mentally disturbed man named Lonnie?" Marcy asked, concerned. "He's wandering around the mountains up there and he's dangerous."

"They picked up some guy nearly frozen to death just down from the cabin they had you guys in," Max replied. "He was found under an avalanche... a giant of a man... I don't know if that's him or not... he could barely make any sense."

Everyone's attention was suddenly drawn to the doorway as Gene Stanton stood there, holding several newspapers and smiling, proudly... "I thought this was suppose to be a sick room!... You two don't look like you belong here!"

Everyone laughed as Gene gave them each a copy of the first edition of the day's Detroit Herald Newspaper. Adrian and Marcy's pictures were under bold headlines which read:

"TWO HERALD REPORTERS EXPOSE BABY SELLING RING!"

Max grinned at Marcy, proudly. "We thought you two might like this headline."

"This is fabulous!" Marcy screamed in delight. "Can we run this headline all week, Mr. Stanton?"

They all laughed again as Adrian and Marcy read the article?"

"This is good, "Adrian said. "Are we gonna do a follow up article?"

"You bet you are." Gene II answered. "Your public wants to hear all of the graphic details from you two directly."

"I just spoke with your doctors," Gene said, chuckling. "You're being evicted...they need this bed space for sick people."

Gene walked over to Marcy and squeezed her hand. "You said you were going to make me proud of you...well you certainly have...I"m very proud of you Marcy...both of you."

THE WINDS OF TOMORROW

"Thanks, Mr. Stanton," Marcy said, grinning and blushing at the praise, "but this is only the beginning."

Gene turned to Adrian who looked up at him and smiled, slightly, not wanting to show too much reaction. Gene walked over and sat down next to her bed. Their hands automatically clasped, not letting go...

Gene II and Max quickly glanced at Marcy as a nurse walked into the room. The nurse looked at Gene and Adrian as they stared into each other's eyes. She quickly began drawing the curtain around Adrian's bed.

"Let's give these folks some privacy," the nurse said, winking her eye knowingly at the others in the room.

"Thank you," Adrian whispered, softly.

Gene II and Max became uncomfortable as Marcy's eyes widened in surprise.

"I guess we better get back to the office," Gene II said to Max. "Marcy, you comin' in tomorrow?"

"I sure am," Marcy replied.

"Good...I'll take you to dinner tomorrow," Max said.

"It's a date."

Gene II and Max quickly left the room. Marcy stared at the curtain drawn around Adrian's bed and tried to continue reading the newspaper. She could barely hear Gene and Adrian's conversation.

Gene sat in the chair and stared at Adrian, shaking his head slowly. "GOD!...I almost lost you!"

"I want you to kiss me," she replied, softly. "I've been dreaming about you all night."

He leaned over and kissed her lightly. She quickly reached up and placed her arms around his neck, pulling him down to her and plunging her tongue into his mouth. Gene savored the kiss for a long moment and sat back down.

"Orange juice," he said, smiling. "Are you really alright?"

"I am now...I've missed you so much," she whispered.

It's been almost three days since...since I last saw you."

"That's three days too long," she said as she wiped the lipstick from his mouth. "You've got tears in your eyes."

"I could've lost you, baby," he whispered, "you mean the whole world to me."

"I love you, Gene... I'll never leave you."

"Would you like to visit the island this week?"

"I'd love it... you know that."

"OK... I'll arrange it... Call me at the office as soon as you get home this afternoon and I'll come right over."

"You'd better."

"And no more adventures... it's too risky... from now on you'll just be assigned to the City-County building. At least those crazy politicians won't hold you at gunpoint."

Gene stood up to leave. She stared up at him, waiting. He sat back down on the bed and embraced her tightly, kissing her all over her face, stopping at her mouth, as his tongue lightly touched hers. "I love you, Adrian...I love you so Damn much!"

When Gene left he said goodby to Adrian, Marcy and the two nurses who had been so accommodating. All of the women stared at him admiringly. As one of the nurses pulled open Adrian's curtain from around her bed, Marcy looked at Adrian with a twinkle in her eyes...

"Ah, hah!" Marcy said.

"What?" Adrian blushed.

"I always knew you had a different agenda from everyone else, Dr. Grant," Marcy teased. "Now I know what it is...the publisher...big time!"

Adrian stared at Marcy with an innocent and puzzled expression on her face, pleading ignorance. The nurses softly snickered as they smiled at each other.

"Now that's a goodlooking man!" the first nurse said.

"He could sure make my day...and that ain't all!" the second nurse laughed.

Roger, Janet and Michelle all sat in Roger's office at The Detroit Herald as Roger finished talking on the phone. He turned to Michelle with a big grin on his face. He felt she would be pleased to know he had spoken to her father in Duluth. "Michelle...Janet and I asked you up here because I've spoken with your father and..."

"You talked to my dad?" Michelle interrupted, angrily. "How'd you find out who he was?"

"That's not the point," Roger replied, calmly.

"You had no right to do that!" she screamed. "Sneakin' behind my back!"

"Calm down, Michelle," Janet said, "he was only trying to help."

"He shoulda asked me first!"

"Now just a minute, young lady," Roger said, angrily, "mind you manners!..I brought you up here today to let you know that since your parents did not want you to come back home and you were doing so well on your job...that you were welcome to remain at our house as long as you want."

Michelle was surprised and her anger quickly subsided. "You...you mean that?"

"Absolutely...only before you make up your mind," Janet said, calmly. "I want you to be aware that we plan to have a few changes in our household soon."

"What kind of changes?"

"Are you familiar with a birthing process called in vitro fertilization?" Roger asked.

"Is that the program with the surrogate mothers involved?"

"Why, yes...it is," Janet answered.

"I thought you were plannin' to adopt."

"We were...but we ran into a few problems," Roger said. "That's why we're considering in vitro fertilization."

"But aren't they havin' a lot of trouble with those mothers changin' their minds?" Michelle asked.

"That's why we plan to carefully screen any potential host mothers we might choose," Janet replied.

"Wouldn't an infant be too much work for you two?"

"We were trying to adopt an infant," Roger said. "So...either way...what difference would it make?"

"Well to tell you the truth," Michelle said, "I figured that's why you've been turned down...Don't you realize how old you'll be when your baby reaches the age of eighteen?..You certainly won't be able to provide much companionship or guidance."

"Hell!..You ever try to be a companion or a guide to an eighteen year old?" Roger chuckled. "C'mon, get real...besides, we can afford to get a whole household of nurses or nannies...whatever it takes."

"OK...how do you know how healthy it would be?" Michelle asked. "you could get a baby whose parents were on drugs...or worse yet...one with an incurable disease."

"I'm afraid you don't understand, dear," Janet said, "the biological parents...well, we could be the biological parents...our tests have indicated that we can produce a viable embryo."

"But at your age...is that possible?" Michelle asked, disbelieving. "Have you two actually thought this thing completely out?"

Janet smiled confidently. "Of course we have...we've scheduled an appointment with an Infertility Specialist tomorrow."

"If you're acceptable...then you're going to use a surrogate mother," Michelle said. "Have you given any thought as to who it will be?"

"Are you volunteering?" Roger asked.

"No way!" Michelle snapped. "But I think you should carefully select who it's going to be."

"We plan to," Janet said, smiling. "You seem to be pretty knowledgeable about this whole process."

"We had a debate on this in school," Michelle said.

"There's just one thing," Janet said, "in this case she'll be considered a host mother."

"How much will you pay her?"

"Whatever is required," Roger answered. "Let me impress you with one thing, Michelle...this baby...whether we're it's biological parents or not...This baby could be a jump start on the rest of our lives...and we're in a better position than most people to raise a healthy, happy child."

Michelle became very quiet suddenly. Roger and Janet looked at each other, puzzled at Michelle's lack of response.

"Michelle...is something wrong?" Janet asked.

"No...it's just that...you both have been so nice to me...better than my own parents," she said, thoughtfully. "You take me in, get me a job...and today you tell me I can stay in your home as long as I'd like...I don't know how I can ever repay your kindness."

"Don't worry about it," Roger said, "we like having you there."

Janet reached over, placed an arm around Michelle's shoulders and squeezed her, affectionately. "You can repay us by living a good, clean and loving life...maybe, someday you can go back to your parents and tell them that you love them...then we'll be repaid."

Michelle stared down at her hands, thoughtfully. She looked up at Janet and Roger with a concerned look in her eyes..."Can I...can I be your...your host mother?" she asked, her eyes searching theirs, "I'd be honored."

Roger was surprised. "But I thought you just said you wouldn't..."

"I know...I've changed my mind, "Michelle whispered.

"You don't have to do this just because you feel you have to repay us for anything," Janet said. "There are plenty of women who would be happy to do it for the right price."

"That's right," Roger agreed. "You don't have to feel beholding to us."

"No...I really want to do this...please," Michelle said. "It would make me feel like I'm part of this family."

Janet and Roger were speechless. They stared at each other, then back at Michelle...surprised at her sincerity...

Gene II unlocked the front door and walked into his home slowly. He glanced at the mail laying on the desk in the front library. He was momentarily distracted by the sound of a suitcase being snapped closed. He looked across the hall and into the living room where he saw Susan nervously packing several suitcases. She looked up at him and acknowledged his presence without saying a word. He slowly walked into the living room, resigned to his wife leaving.

"So you're finally going to leave," Gene II said.

"Isn't it about time?" she asked. "The way this marriage has been going downhill...it's something that should have happened years ago."

"I'll ask you...one last time," Gene II spoke, softly. "Please, Susan...don't go...give us one more chance."

"Gene, please...let's not go through that again...it's over...all over." she replied, gently.

"But why?..What have I done?"

"It's nothing you've done," Susan replied. "You know that...the love has just gone out of our relationship like air goes out of a leaking tire."

"You mean you've found someone else."

"I didn't say that."

"You don't have to," Gene II said. "Why won't you tell me who it is?"

"Because there is no "who" that's why!" she snapped. "You've been trying to fabricate another man for the last year or so...ever since we stopped having sex."

"That's why I know there is somebody else," Gene II said, angrily. "You like sex too much to do without it...So if it's not with me I know you're screwing somebody else."

"Oh, for crying out loud!" Susan shot back, angrily. "What do you think I am...a bitch in heat!..This is why our marriage has failed...because you think in one dimensional segments...your brain is just like the rest of you...a limited capacity with atrophied components!"

She slammed the suitcases shut and stacked them up neatly in the hallway. She stared at Gene II with her eyes blazing in anger!.."We're leaving for New York the first thing in the morning...The children know we're separating so you can speak to them truthfully...Make sure you say your goodbyes tonight."

"Susan...wait, please!"

She turned and angrily marched out of the room!..Gene II stared after her with tears in his eyes...

Chapter Twenty-Two

Gene Stanton sat in his office at The Herald and studied several reports on his desk. The Herald's circulation was growing at a phenomenal rate. The latest Audit Bureau of Circulation's report showed The Herald with an increase in circulation to 350,000 subscribers...Gene's goal was 500,000 in three years and they were at a pace to surpass it...

Gene looked up when his secretary, Lois, walked into the office, anxiously. "Lois...what is it?" Gene asked.

"There's some strange old man out there waiting to see you," she whispered. "Shall I call security?"

"You're becoming paranoid," Gene answered, smiling. "Does he have an appointment?..I don't have anything on my calender."

"He says his name is Wedemeyer..Dr. Wedemeyer...He's from Israel and he said it's extremely important."

Gene quickly stacked the reports on his desk together in a folder and slipped the folder in a drawer. "Did he say what it was about?"

Lois continued to whisper, secretively. "That's what's really strange...he said...he said you had a Nazi war criminal working for you!"

Gene welcomed Dr. Wedemeyer into his office. He was a small, rumpled old man in his late seventies. He carried and old leather briefcase that had several, dog-eared pieces of paper sticking out of the sides. His face was ruddy with piercing eyes behind thick, bifocal glasses. His sparse gray hair reminded Gene of Einstein with a close cropped haircut. He wore a wrinkled pin striped, charcoal gray suit with a vest, tie and blue shirt that all revealed what he had for lunch recently.

THE WINDS OF TOMORROW

The old man sat down and Gene waited patiently as he fumbled inside the thick, cluttered briefcase. He finally, sighed and raised his head. he smiled at Gene and revealed stained and crooked teeth. He handed Gene a tattered manilla folder. Gene spread it open on his desk. Several wrinkled photographs, almost completely yellow from aging, were among the documents. The old man leaned over the desk and pointed to the documents with a shaking finger...

"I have been tracking down this man, Albert Herman Miller, for over forty years, Mr. Stanton... He was a Nazi guard at a concentration camp in Bad Tolz, Germany during the second world war... He was tried as a war criminal at the Nuremburg War Trials and found guilty and sentenced to be hanged. When the soldiers went to get him to be executed, they found the soldier who had been guarding his cell... hanging in the cell and Miller was gone!... He escaped the day of his execution... that's when I picked up his trail."

Gene stared at Dr. Wedemeyer, thoughtfully. "That's an interesting story, Doctor... but what makes you think he's working here at the Herald?" Gene asked as he perused the photographs. "We don't have anyone like this employed here... at least I've never seen him."

"I traced him to South America... Argentina... where he lived until 1972," Wedemeyer explained as he slowly sat back down in the chair, catching his breath.

"Why didn't you arrest him then?" Gene asked.

"I couldn't produce conclusive proof that he was... who he is... and the governments in South America have a way of ignoring ex-Nazis."

"Can you prove that this man works for The Herald?"

"Absolutely... He left Argentina and surfaced as a Cuban exile in Miami. He got a job as a newspaper typesetter at The Miami Examiner. He worked there for ten years until he became employed in a similar job here at The Detroit Herald."

Gene smiled respectfully at Dr. Wedemeyer. "But his man... why he'd have to be too old to work here... He's gotta be between seventy-five and eighty!"

"I assure you, Mr. Stanton... he is exactly seventy-three years old," Dr. Wedemeyer said confidently. "He was in his early twenties during the war when he committed all those crimes fifty years ago."

"What is his identity now?"

"Our contact agent... A Mr. Irving Steinberger, was just about to identify him... He had worked diligently on this case for the last thirty years. He reported to me that he knew that Albert Miller was working here.. He expected to know his new identity at any moment."

"That's encouraging... what happened?"

"First let me explain the character of this... this animal I've been after all these years," Dr. Wedemeyer said, thoughtfully. "When he was a nazi officer he was known for his cruelty and his insidious mental games he would play with his prisoners."

"Insidious mental games?" Gene asked.

"Yes... extremely evil games he would play with the prisoners. You see the Nazi high command were limited to the amount of prisoners they were allowed to maintain at each concentration camp. When they went over these limits, they would leave it up to the chief guards as to who would be exterminated to get down to their allowable quotas. It became Albert Miller's responsibility to determine who would live and who would die. Those... favorable to him would live and those who were expendable to him would die... He wouldn't walk up to them to inform they were going to be executed... He would merely leave his calling card on their bunk in the evening when they returned from working in the yard."

"His calling card?"

"Yes... a stick drawing of a man hanging from the gallows... He took a particular delight in hangings and that was his method of execution."

"That's horrible... but how does this relate to Steinberger?" Gene asked.

"Somehow Miller discovered that someone was closing in on him... A few days ago authorities found Steinberger's body in a burned out warehouse in southwest Detroit."

Gene was surprised. "They found his body?"

"That's why we know that Steinberger was on the right track and that Miller is working at The Herald... Steinberger, in his excitement, became careless and it cost him his life. They found him hanging from a steel beam after the warehouse had burned down around him."

"But how do you know it was Miller who killed him?" Gene asked. "That could've been done by anyone."

"True... but they found this card on the body," Dr. Wedemeyer said as he handed Gene a business card.

Gene looked at the stick figure drawing of a man hanging from the gallows. "He left his calling card!" Gene said.

"Exactly!" the old man snarled.

Gene looked up at Dr. Wedemeyer as he stared back at Gene with hate and fury in his eyes!.. At that moment, Gene's intercom buzzed on his desk... "Yes, Lois," Gene answered.

"Dr. Grant on line two."

Gene immediately switched to the next line without taking his eyes off Dr. Wedemeyer. "Good afternoon, Dr. Grant."

"You have company?" Adrian asked.

"Yes, that's right."

"I just got home... I was expecting you."

"I'll take care of that right away."

"Will I see you within the hour?" she asked.

"Yes... I can do that... Should I bring anything to the meeting?"

"You're damn right... You!"

"That'll be fine."

"I love you... I can barely wait."

"That's my feeling, too."

"Goodbye, love."

"Goodbye," Gene said.

He looked up at Dr. Wedemeyer and motioned to the file Wedemeyer had laid on his desk. "I'm very interested in this project, doctor... If this joker is working here at The Herald I'd like to smoke him out... Can you leave this file here so I can study it further?... I'll discuss it with my associates and get back to you tomorrow afternoon."

Dr. Wedemeyer nodded his head affirmatively as he stood up to leave. "I prepared that file for your records. If you should need any additional information, Mr. Stanton, please call me. My number is on the cover of the folder."

"Good," Gene said as he shook Dr. Wedemeyer's hand. "If he's here... you'll get your man."

Gene couldn't believe how anxious he was to have Adrian in his arms again... He felt like a teenager looking forward to his first date with the high school beauty... GOD, he thought, she's changing all my priorities. He thought about her soft, yielding body and the sexual urges within him began to stir. When he drove into her townhouse complex he quickly parked his car and walked towards her unit. He saw the curtains in her front window slightly move as he walked closer. By the time he reached her door it was opened and Adrian quickly pulled him inside. As he stepped in, she closed the door and turned to look at him as he stood in the small vestibule smiling at her. Before he could say anything she threw her arms around his neck and began kissing him, pressing her body against his and grinding her hips into his pelvis. They were deeply engulfed in their powerful feelings of love for each other. They continued kissing, undressing and trying to talk, all at the same time...

"Oh, baby," she pleaded, "I've missed you so much!"

"You've been in my thoughts every minute we've been apart," he replied, breathing heavily. "These few days without you have been very difficult... I don't know.. but something's has to be done."

"Do you still love me?" she asked.

"More than ever before."

"Then don't talk... make love to me."

He stopped her from talking by crushing her full, luscious, red lips with him mouth. He held her tightly as he whispered rapidly in her ear. "I want you so damn badly that my throat goes brick dry and I can feel this throbbing sensation deep down in my chest... it's not pain... just a feeling that won't go away until I've got you in my arms like I'm holding you now... and I feel the softness of your body pressing against mine...every nerve I have aches to be inside of you...to feel your warmth, tightness, moisture and the contours of your body as I feel you maneuver it in a sexy position to gratify my lust...to taste your mouth, your hair, breast and your skin...to place my tongue deep inside of you and smell, feel and taste the flow of your juices that are like a sweet nectar of love and desire... When I explode within your body it's like the sun rising above the horizon, gently giving life and light to my entire being!... When you love somebody the way I love you... you care about their thoughts and their safety... the thought that I almost lost you racks my brain like a tight-rope walker fighting to keep his balance... I makes me realize that we've got each other now and that alone diminishes the importance of everything else and I don't care if the rest of the world disintegrates and disappears... I've got my Adrian and that's all that matters!... That's what my love for you is, baby... and that's why I'll love you for the rest of my life."

"Then make love to me now... right where we stand," she begged as she slowly backed away, pulling him towards her.

They were both naked in a matter of seconds with their clothes scattered all over the living room floor. Her head tilted up to meet his as she slightly opened her mouth. His mouth went down to her wet, trembling lips. Their kisses were hot and spurred on by the gentle stabbing of her tongue. Gene's brain was whirling as he felt her teeth lightly bite his lip and her hand slowly began stroking his erect member. Her eyes were wet and soft tears were coming down her cheeks. He picked her up and laid her gently on the sofa. Her body became a vibrating machine as it responded to his slightest caress. Each kiss, each stroke was perfectly placed. He gently kissed and mouthed each breast, sucking and nibbling her nipples like worshipping a goddess. She trembled as he ran his tongue across her stomach, stopping at her navel and punching the tip of his tongue deep into her navel cavity. She slowly laid back and sighed deeply as his head moved in between her thighs and nestled gently, pressing against her as she spread her legs wider apart, placing one leg on his shoulder as his head hungrily moved back and forth and his darting tongue joined them together. She continued to tremble and shutter in great pleasure until she signaled to him to move up on top of her. He plunged his soaking wet tongue deep into her mouth, allowing her to taste her own juices. In seconds his stiff member was deep inside her as they slowly positioned themselves and began moving in complete coordination and synchronization as each movement created a reaction that heightened their pleasure until their passion overcame them both and they began a furious pace... their moans and groans became louder as he increased his movements continuously until their bodies suddenly froze and convulsed in a series of severe spasms as they clung together and slowly relaxed, locked in each other's arms and still joined together as the world stopped spinning and was at peace once again...

Later that evening, Gene relaxed in his recliner chair in the family room of his home and carefully went over the thick folder Dr. Wedemeyer had left with him. He found it difficult to concentrate as the smell of Adrian seemed to be all over his body.

He sniffed at the back of his hand and the aroma of her cologne conjured up her smiling image, distracting him. He glanced over the personnel files spread out in front of him and compared them with Wedemeyer's files. Gene shook his head, thoughtfully. He looked up when Patricia entered the room...

"Hi... what's the big mystery about?" she asked.

Gene closely eyed Patricia before he spoke. "Mystery?..The only mystery I'm aware of is where you went on your extended vacation when you left Washington, D.C."

"I told you...that is no mystery," she said, disgusted. "I just had to get away for awhile...will you please drop it!"

"Thou dost protest too much," Gene chuckled. "Then what mystery are you referring to?"

"Mel and Kelly...I wonder what's going on with them?"

Gene shrugged his shoulders and glanced at the clock just as they heard the door chimes. In a few minutes Mel and Kelly walked into the room with big smiles on their faces. Patricia and Gene looked from one to the other...

"Well, c'mon...what's going on with you two?" Patricia asked, anxiously.

Kelly turned to Mel. "You go first...tell them your news." Kelly said.

"OK...here goes...mom...dad...I got a call from the NBA yesterday," Mel said, trying not to smile, "they said the last physical I took showed no signs of any foreign substance...so they lifted my suspension and I'm officially back on the active playing roster of the Memphis Mustangs!"

Patricia threw her arms around Mel and hugged him. Gene smiled, stood up and shook his hand proudly. "We're all proud of you, son," Gene said, grinning broadly. "We knew you could do it."

"Give most of the credit to Kelly," Mel said. "She's worked her butt off to keep both of us clean as a whistle. And that's not all!"

"Wh...what else?..Is there something you have to tell us, Kelly?" Patricia asked, concerned.

"Well...I mean," Kelly stammered, "there is something else that has happened to me...I mean...us."

"Go on...tell us," Patricia urged.

"I...I hope you like the news," Kelly said in a small voice as she glanced at Mel who was grinning from ear to ear.

"What is it?" Gene asked.

"It's me...I'm pregnant...We're going to have a baby."

Patricia was stunned. "Oh, Kelly!..I'm so pleased!"

Patricia quickly embraced Kelly, smothering her with kisses. Gene looked at Mel, beaming with happiness. "Well I'll be damned!..That is great news! Now maybe you two will settle down and get married."

"You just said the magic word, dad," Mel said. "We plan on getting married as soon as possible."

"No...wait!..I'll have to make plans for the wedding and arrange a guest list," Patricia said, thoughtfully. "Kelly have you called your parents?..We have so much to do!..Is your pregnancy alright?"

"Hold it, mom," Mel interrupted, "maybe she doesn't want a big wedding."

"Shuddup, Mel," Kelly snapped, "your mother knows what she's doing."

"Well...pardon me!" Mel said, surprised.

Kelly turned to Patricia with enthusiasm. "Where do we start?"

"Number one...the wedding will be held here, if you have no objections," Patricia said. "We'll have more room to invite all those friends of yours who are professional basketball players and their families...I can just see you now, coming down that wide staircase in your wedding gown!..Kelly, you're going to be so lovely!..And the baby!..You want a boy or a girl?"

Kelly and Patricia continued to chatter excitedly as Patricia led her towards the front of the house, describing in detail how each room will be decorated for the wedding.

Gene looked at Mel and grinned. "Damn!..I haven't seen your mother that happy in years!..Have you told anyone else?..You better tell your grandma...I know she'll be happy about it...She's always loved Kelly."

Karen and Willard anxiously sat in a small waiting room just outside the lab department of City Hospital. They nervously glanced at the wall clock as they waited for the results of their DNA tests. Several hospital attendants rushed back and forth, ignoring them. Karen disgutedly threw down a magazine she had been trying to read and sighed. Willard stared at her, puzzled...

"Do you think they're having any problems?" Willard asked. "We've been here almost an hour...that seems kinda long."

"Just be a little patient," Karen answered. "Bob said it normally takes a week or two and they're processing our tests especially fast. He said they promised him we'd know this morning...on both tests."

Willard still had a confused look on his face as he stared into Karen's eyes. "There's one thing I don't quite understand...Why did you have your tests performed?"

"We had to set it up...to mislead anybody who became suspicious...and I was also curious. I wanna make sure I am who I think I am...Why?..Does that bother you? I would think that if anyone would understand it would certainly be you."

"But...do you have any reason to question your parentage?" Willard asked.

Karen started to answered, but hesitated, looking at Willard, thoughtfully. "Look...my husband is Chief of Surgery at this hospital...I don't think it's improper for me to take advantage of any of it's resources...they're doing it for you...there's no reason why they can't do it for me."

A lab supervisor walked out of an office nearby and motioned for Karen and

Willard to follow her into a consultation room. After they had sat down at a small conference table the lab supervisor handed them both a large brown envelope.

"Since this is a family consultation I'm assuming neither of you mind sharing this information with the other," the supervisor said. "This priviledged information, you know."

"No...it was Karen's suggestion that we come here together," Willard said, "it's no problem with me."

"Fine...Your tests, Mr. Thompson, has been determined to be almost one hundred percent positive...The DNA proves that Mr. Dugas is your father at a rate of 99.8 percent," the lab supervisor said, "which means that it is less than one percent out of a hundred that he is not your father."

"That is pretty conclusive," Karen smiled at Willard.

The lab supervisor turned to Karen, biting her lip nervously before she continued. "On the other hand, Mrs. Whyte...we've had to perform your DNA test several times and it still comes out negative."

"Negative?" Karen asked.

"Yes...since Mr. Stanton was recently hospitalized here we had adequate blood samples and specimens...but each test performed indicated that Gene Stanton could not possibly be your father."

Willard stared at Karen completely dumfounded!..Karen remained motionless in her chair, stunned!..The lab supervisor reached over and patted Karen's hand, gently..."Would you like a glass of water, Mrs. Whyte?"

"No...that's alright," Karen replied, hoarsly, still in shock. "Are you certain there were no errors or mistakes?"

"Absolutely...as I said earlier...we conducted several separate tests to make sure."

Willard slowly put an arm around Karen's shoulders as he tried to comfort her. "You suspected something didn't you...I'm...I'm sorry, Karen...are you alright?"

Karen quickly removed his arm and tried to compose herself, but the involuntary shaking of her body betrayed her.

"You mentioned that this is privileged information...I don't want anyone to ever know...not even my husband!"

"Certainly, Mrs. Whyte...I understand," the lab supervisor answered, nervously.

"I'm not sure you do!" Karen shot back, angrily. "This could involve millions of dollars!..If any word of this ever gets out...I'll sue you and this hospital for every penny it's ever earned!"

With her eyes flaring in anger, Karen snatched the envelope from the table, stood up and angrily stomped out of the room, slamming the door behind her!..

Gene II stood behind his desk in his office and closely studied several folders spread out in front of him as Max Jenkens bounced through the door.

"Hey, good buddy," Max said, jovially, "I got your message...what's going on?"

Gene II looked at Max's smiling face. "Boy, that relationship between you and Marcy must be moving by leaps and bounds."

"Oh, man...she is absolutely the greatest!"

"Do I hear wedding bells?"

"I'm working on it...if she'll have me."

"It's a good feeling isn't it?..Having that certain someone in your corner."

"How are you and Susan doing?" Max asked.

"Well, it's happened," Gene II said, dejectedly. "I'm a bachelor...at least for a while."

"She left you?"

"Lock, stock and barrel."

"You said for a while...do I detect some light at the end of the tunnel?"

"Yeah, maybe...I don't know how much of a chance I have," Gene II said, thoughtfully. "She promised not to file for a divorce right away. Maybe...if we let things cool off, it might give us the time we need to reconcile."

"Aw, Gene...I really hate to hear that...I know how much you love her...I'm sure she loves you, too...I thought you two could beat this thing."

Gene II motioned to the folders that laid on his desk. "Then today...my old man is leaving town and he lays this on me...Can you believe that we might have an old ex-Nazi working here?"

"You're kiddin!..Is that what your message has all about?..Who is it?"

"That's what we've got to find out...Some senior citizen Nazi hunter has been on this jerk's trail for the last forty years and he has evidence that the guy is working here.

"But...shouldn't the F.B.I. or some federal authority be doin' this?" Max asked.

"Not enough evidence to support Dr. Wedemeyer's suspicions. He does have credibility, though. He and his Nazi hunters have nailed and uncovered thirteen ex-Nazis since the end of the World War II...Most of his family were victims of the holocaust and he has a debt to collect...He knows what he's doing. He's persistent, smart and determined...As soon as we can substantiate his suspicions we are suppose to contact the Justice Department's Office of Special Investigations in Washington...It's their job to identify, denaturalize and deport alleged war criminals living in the United States...but if it's hot...they told us to call the F.B.I."

"What evidence do we have that he's here?"

"Wedemeyer was working with a contact agent named Irving Steinberger who was about to identify the Nazi."

"So what happened?"

"His body was found hanging from a steel girder in a warehouse in southwest Detroit that had just been burned down...They found this Nazi's calling card on the body."

THE WINDS OF TOMORROW

"Calling card?"

"Yeah...a drawing of a stick figure hanging from the gallows. This was his trademark when he was running a concentration camp...It's his way of laughing at his pursuers...It was significant because it indicated that Steinberger was getting too close."

Max picked up one of the folders and sat down across from Gene II's desk. He studied the contents of the folder and rubbed his chin, thoughtfully. "Wow...It looks like we may be on to something here...Why would anyone want to kill Wedemeyer's contact if he wasn't getting too close?"

"Exactly...my dad figured that if this guy is working at The Herald, he's involved in the craft unions and his records would indicate that he's worked at The Miami Examiner in the seventies or early eighties."

"But wouldn't he be too old to work here?"

"Union rules call for thirty and out. He could be in his early seventies...and there's something else I want you to take a look at...We've narrowed it down to five possible candidates that fit that profile. Personnel pulled their files, complete with photographs, work history and families."

Gene II handed Max another folder. He began to read it immediately. "This is interesting."

"These other three guys check out pretty good...The other two are kinda confusing..," Gene II said.

"Confusing?..How?"

Gene II tossed several photographs on the desk in front of Max. "These are the photographs of Ralph Rhineholt when he was an apprentice typesetter in New York in the early seventies...check 'em out, see what you think."

Max studied the photographs for a minute, going from one to the other..."So?..What am I suppose to be looking for?" Max asked.

Gene II placed another group of photographs on the desk in front of Max. "Rhineholt is third from the left in the family photograph. He must've been about nine or ten years old...In the teenage pictures I'd say he was about thirteen or fourteen. Compare those pictures with these recent ones for his I.D. card."

Gene II laid two additional photographs next to the first ones. Max studied each photograph carefully, comparing the features in each picture.

"It's difficult to tell if they're one and the same isn't it?" Gene II asked.

"Hey!..Something's wrong here!" Max said anxiously. "These aren't the same guy...what're you tryin' to pull?"

"I'm not trying to pull anything!..That's what I thought, too!..Here we have a child with dark features and an adult who's totally the opposite!"

"Of course...it's not that unusual. It does happen sometimes...but...I can't find any matching features...are you sure these are the correct photos?"

"Absolutely!..I checked them out twice," Gene II replied. "Look on the back of each picture and you'll find the same name...Ralph Rhineholt!..Too bad we don't have any pictures of him in his late teens or early twenties."

"And this I.D. picture...I've seen this guy around here a lot," Max said, firmly, "In the composing room, press room, cafeteria...even in the parking lot...and I gotta tell ya...this guy ain't even sixty-five!..Somethin's not adding up...If he's the ex-Nazi...he'd have been a twelve year old prison guard in the second world war!"

Gene II looked at Max thoughtfully. "Yeah, I thought about that."

"It says here that Ralph Rhineholt also had a brother that was a printer and they were both born in Little Rock, Arkansas...Where's that brother at now?..He could help clear this whole thing up in a flash!"

"That's another strange coincident."

"Why...what happened?"

"The brother had been working here at The Daily Press about ten years before Ralph Rhineholt showed up here from Miami."

"Whats so strange about that?" Max asked.

"Ralph Rhineholt didn't show up here until AFTER his brother died in the early eighties."

"Died?..His brother is dead?..How'd it happen?"

Gene searched through the personnel files until he found the correct file. He thumbed through it and suddenly stopped!.."I got it!..Listen to this...it says here that his brother's body was found...hanging from the rafters of a burned down warehouse!"

When Gene reached the executive garage of The Herald the security guard waved at him and smiled. Gene waved back and quickly got on the elevator and rode it to the top floor. He was anxious to began this weekend with Adrian and he smiled to himself as he climbed into his car.

When he parked his car and walked into the inner area of the luxurious townhouses he saw the security guard at the gate who was waving his arm and motioning further back in the huge complex where Adrian stood smiling with several suitcases. Gene hurriedly walked over to her they embraced as he kissed her tenderly. He stopped and motioned to the suitcases, chuckling.

"Don't you ever plan to come back?" he asked.

"Who knows?" she answered, kissing him on the cheek. "You know how I feel about pine trees, wild berries and black bears."

That weekend at Grand Island accelerated the love between Adrian and Gene. Their love for each other seemed to dominate their every waking moments. After nearly losing her when she was held captive by The Forgotton Child Foundation, Their love grew from minute to minute. At first, they would only be together on Grand Island two or three times a month. This was soon increased to every weekend, then twice and sometimes three times each week. They couldn't seem to get enough of each other. Their love making had no boundaries in sexual pleasure or locations. As the tempo increased, they found themselves making love in such diverse places as Gene's office at The Herald, Adrian's townhouse apartment, in Gene's car in the executive garage, and even in the helicopter on the way to Grand Island. Gene kept the helicopter pilot on twenty-four hour standby. The many hours they were together on Grand Island were spent making love all night long and was followed by long, early morning walks in the forest where many times more love making would occur.

Gene marveled at her exceptional beauty and he would suddenly stop kissing and caressing her. He would just hold her in his arms, admiring her looks and whisper in her ear, "Damn, honey...how come you're so pretty?" to which she would always reply, "I had to be...because I was custom made just for you."

Adrian staunchly maintained that they had been lovers in another life and she was constantly amazed at the development of her suddenly larger breasts, hips and butt as Gene's lovemaking was obviously causing a change in her physical stature although her weight remained the same. Gene would stare at her lovely naked form and worship her firm, full, pointed breasts, narrow waist, widening hips and long, shapely legs. Her long dark hair framed her beautiful face like an artist's portrait.

Their relationship blossomed to the stage of constantly preying on their minds each minute of each day. Gene would be addressing the entire editorial staff and his eyes would fasten on Adrian who stood out like a sparkling jewel in the back of the giant editorial offices. She would smile at him seductively, causing him to lose his train of thought...

Employees, friends and relatives all knew what was going on but they also realized how much the relationship meant to both Gene and Adrian...It was a threshold no one would dare cross...Gene realized that ultimately they would be together forever and Adrian, in her infinite sophistication, made no demands except to be constantly loved by Gene. She knew that Gene's sexual relations with Patricia had ceased as long as twenty years earlier and that, by her coming into Gene's life now, it would permanently sever any remaining vestiges of a friendly and respectful relationship that was merely the remnants from a long and tired marriage...

Chapter Twenty-Three

United States Congressman Charles Ghetts sat in front of Gene Stanton's desk in the publisher's office of The Detroit Herald Newspaper, obviously nervous. He remembered the last time he had seen Gene and how he had angrily warned him not to switch to a daily newspaper. Today, he was hoping their long time friendship would overcome any hard feelings Gene may harbor. He was startled momentarily when Gene walked briskly into the office and stood behind his desk, staring at him. Ghetts became more uneasy when Gene offered no handshake or smiles.

"I was surprised to get your call," Gene said in a business like manner. "After our last meeting I didn't think I'd hear from you for a while."

Ghetts motioned to the office with a sweep of his arm. "I don't mind admitting that I was wrong...this building looks great since you brought it back to life...Your newspaper is more successful than anyone could've imagined and you've restored more than 1500 jobs to the community!...The city owes you a debt of gratitude, Gene."

"Thank you," Gene said, smiling. "I was confident I could bring it back."

"I know...and I was wrong...I hope you'll accept my apology and forgive my impertinence."

"Consider it accepted...and don't worry about it, Charlie," Gene replied as he reached across his desk and shook Ghetts' hand. "We all make mistakes...it's water under the bridge now. What can I do for you?"

"I was selected by a group of city business people and local politicians to speak to you about an urgent matter. They felt that since we once had a close relationship, I would be the person most likely to get a favorable response form you."

"Favorable response...to what?"

THE WINDS OF TOMORROW

"As you know I've enjoyed the support of a diverse group of constituents all of these years I've been in congress...white, black...rich and poor, business people, the clergy and plain working folks."

"I know all of that...that's why I've supported you in the past." Gene said. "What's your point?"

"This group first met with me about two weeks ago...They were upset because they were afraid the mayor was going to run for re-election."

"I thought he was too ill to run."

"They did too...In fact some of them were getting ready to back other candidates...the mayor got wind of it and blew his stack!"

"That's typical of Mayor Powell," Gene said, thoughtfully. "Anytime he feels thing's aren't going his way, he's subject to losing his cool."

"That's why he ought to retire!" Ghetts said, firmly. "If he doesn't retire the city of Detroit will be the big loser!...The man is over seventy-five, he's sick and the city is going straight to hell in a handbag if he runs again!"

"It's a pretty depressing situation," Gene agreed.

"And that's not all...Our industrial jobs have steadily dwindled and as a result retailers have gone to the suburbs which has reduced the city's tax base considerably and consequently other jobs have disappeared....Our unemployment rate is growing and crime is skyrocketing despite a lot of B. S. statistics...and worst of all...nothing is being done to correct this situation!"

"So this group...they asked you to run for mayor?"

Ghetts ignored Gene's question. "This group isn't too happy with the candidates who are running...none of them have any economic program...they're all talking about handouts from the federal government...We got a woman ex-judge who has never ran for any office before...and an assistant prosecuting attorney who's lost more cases than he's won and is already catering to the suburbs...and a maverick politician who couldn't beat a rabbit in a race for dog-catcher!...If any of these clowns run against the mayor...he'll win again just because of his popularity and the city will be flushed down the toilet again for another four years with no agenda for bringing the city back from economic chaos!"

Gene studied Congressman Ghetts thoughtfully. "So they're asking you to run?...That may not be such a bad idea. I'd support you against the others...including Mayor Powell. What kind of economic program would you institute?"

"No..I couldn't run...I'm too deeply involved in Washington fighting those conservatives who are blocking any help going to the cities...We could lose important programs if I left congress now," Ghetts replied.

Gene was surprised. "You tuned 'em down?"

"I wasn't asked...they wanted a businessman who had shown that he could bring a major business back from death with new ideas, new innovations...They wanted a native Detroiter with a record of civic involvement who could create employment and stimulate retail business in the city...A man with impeccable credentials."

"Who do you have in mind?" Gene asked, concerned.

"Your father started and maintained a voice for minorities when it wasn't popular...he fought tooth and nail to keep The State Journal above water...When you took over you increased it's circulation and built up that Black weekly newspaper until it couldn't go any higher...Then, despite so many people being against you...including yours truly...you switched from a Black weekly to an integrated daily...A daily newspaper that had been floundering in debt...You took it over and with new, revolutionary newspaper innovations, you brought it up to being one of the most exciting newspapers in the country!"

Gene smiled, "Sounds good...don't stop now."

"No...the group I met with didn't want me to run for mayor, Gene," Congressman Ghetts said, sternly, "they wanted you!"

"Wh...what?" Gene asked, still in shock. "They want me to run for mayor?"

"We don't expect an answer now...take your time and think this thing over...Make sure you make the right decision."

The congressman stood up in front of Gene's desk, reached over and shook Gene's hand, still grinning broadly.

"I wasn't prepared for this, Charlie," Gene said, looking directly into his eyes. "How do you feel about this?"

"You were my first choice," Ghetts replied. "Too many of our Black politicians seem to turn against their Black constituents as soon as they get in office in order to gain approval from the White establishment. They act like the words "civil rights" aren't even in their vocabulary, anymore. These Black politicians benefited from the civil rights movement when they were getting their educations and jobs but as soon as they get in a position to help other Blacks make those same gains, they go on TV and proudly announce that they will not use their newly elected positions and offices to advance civil rights!...I don't believe you would ever do that, Gene!...You've been preparing for this job all your life."

"I could never do that...That kind of political backstabbing is the main reason many people mistrust politicians," Gene answered.

"And by the way...I'll see you at Mel's wedding. My wife and I appreciate being invited."

"I couldn't have one of my kids getting married without you being there...you know that."

Congressman Ghetts turned to leave and stopped, turning to look at Gene. "You'll make one helluva mayor, Gene. If you can bring this newspaper back from death's doorstep...you can bring Detroit back, too!...See ya at the wedding, Mayor Stanton!"

All of the employees working in the Detroit Herald's personnel office were

THE WINDS OF TOMORROW

excited when the managing editor Gene II, and his assistant, Max Jenkins, walked into the Personnel Director's Office. They both smiled and sat down, waiting patiently for Mrs. Vasquez, the deputy director of the personnel department, as she thumbed though various records. She handed Gene II the hospitalization records for Ralph Rhineholt and gave Max his work records. she continued searching for other documents.

"I see that Rhineholt has been utilizing his hospitalization benefits quite a bit," Gene II said, thoughtfully, "What's that all about?"

"I noticed that, too, but I didn't get into any details," Mrs. Vasquez answered.

Max studied a single sheet of paper. "Wow!..Listen to this..He's been hospitalized each year for at least a week, for the last seven years!"

"Does it give any reason or explanation?" Gene II asked.

"It's not clear," Max answered, "these computerized hospital invoices are so confusing."

"There should be some kind of notation," Gene II said.

"Let me see that," Mrs. Vasquez said, taking the invoice from Max. "The hospital issued a card with the legends on it that explained what each hospitalization bill is for."

She also took the single sheet of paper from Max and began matching it up with the letter from the hospital...She suddenly became puzzled. "That's strange!"

"What's that?" Gene II asked.

"It seems he's been having the same identical surgical procedure each time." she said.

"Maybe it's a recurring problem," Max said.

"Naw...I doubt that," Gene II said, reaching for the documents. "Let me see...there should be some identification of the particular procedure that was performed...maybe if we withheld some of these payments they would be more specific in describing what was actually done."

"I wish we could," Mrs. Vasquez said, disgustedly.

Gene II closely studied the sheet form the hospital and the invoices. "It's confusing as hell!"

"Let's take it over to the hospital," Max said. "They ought to be able to tell us."

"That don't work...it's not a local hospital," Mrs. Vasquez said. "It's up in Ann Arbor...I could call and find out what their records reveal."

"That's a good idea," Gene II said. "We'll wait."

Mrs. Vasquez quickly got on the phone as Gene II and Max talked softly.

"What do you think?" Max asked. "There's gotta be a good reason for all these operations."

"Something's wrong about this guy," Gene II answered, "But we'll need more evidence before we can turn this over to the feds."

"Well...I still say he's not old enough to be the guy they're looking for...This man isn't a day over fifty-five."

Mrs. Vasquez got off of the phone and tuned to Gene II and Max with a perplexed expression on her face...

"What'd you find out?" Gene II asked.

"This is weird," Mrs. Vasquez replied, shaking her head, thoughtfully. "I knew you men were more vain and self-conscious...but this is ridiculous!"

"What are you talking about?" Max asked.

"The surgical procedures that Mr. Rhineholt had were not any chronic physical condition or illness," Mrs. Vasquez answered.

"Then what were they for?" Gene II asked confused.

Mrs. Vasquez eyed them closely before she spoke.

"Mr. Rhineholt must be a very vain man...it seems he's been having a series of annual face lifts!"

Willard followed Karen into her office at the Herald. She slammed her briefcase on top of her desk and plopped down in her executive chair behind the desk. She grimaced as she rubbed her forehead in deep frustration. Willard sat down across from her.

"You alright?" Willard asked, timidly.

"I guess...I'm OK now," Karen answered, " I just needed a little time to think this thing completely out...What about you...you tell Dugas it's been confirmed?"

"Yeah...he seems to be happy about it."

"Happy?...You'd better be careful and watch your back."

"He acts like he wants me over there."

"At The Press?"

"Yeah...I believe he does...Maybe he's proud to have a Black son. He said he could see himself in me...That's why I think he wants me over there."

"Wishful thinking," Karen smirked as she slowly stood up and walked around to the front of her desk, sitting down next to Willard. She studied his face thoughtfully. "I don't think that's a good idea...not right now."

"Why not?...I probably have more of a stake over there than I have here."

"That's exactly my point," Karen said, excitedly. "Don't you see?...We're both in a position now where we can join forces and make sure the operations of both newspapers could be under our control, yours and mine!..And no one would ever know!"

"Under our control...how?"

"We'll be able to manipulate business from one newspaper to the other...without anyone knowing what's going on."

"But why do that?" Willard asked, innocently. "What good would that do us?"

"Listen...we're in this position through no fault of our own...both of us are," Karen answered. "I say we take advantage of our situation and use it for all it's worth...and that could be plenty!"

"How can we do that?"

"Major daily newspapers are going out of business and dropping like flies all across the country," Karen said. "The costs for operating newspapers and dealing with labor unions are eating up their profits...I predict that only one of these two newspapers here in Detroit will survive...and you and I are in a position to wind up in control of determining the surviving newspaper...I'm talkin' millions of dollars, Willard...possible billions!"

"But...but that could mean going against your own family...sabotaging your father!"

Karen got up and walked back behind her desk. She picked up a copy of her medical tests and waved it in Willard's face, tauntingly..."This allows me to do what I damn well please!" Karen snapped. "I'm not committed to anyone's father!"

"But you couldn't turn against your own father!"

"Wrong again!...Gene Stanton is not my father!"

Willard was silent as he watched Karen. "Are you sure you want to try something like this?"

"Relax...think about it for a few days. There's no rush...We'll discuss it in detail after the wedding. Just remember that the decision you make can change the rest of your life."

Gene Stanton sat on the sofa in his office at The Herald across from Gene II and Max as they explained the information they had gathered after going over all of the documents from the personnel office including the hospital invoices. Gene listened closely, thoughtfully rubbing his chin...

"From all of the information we have uncovered it looks like this guy, Rhineholt, could be our man," Gene II said, "even the photographs he had as a child don't match up with his appearance of today...by all accounts...I think he's a fraud."

"I'm not to sure about that, Mr. Stanton," Max said. "I think we could be making a big mistake...and if we're wrong, we could wind up being sued by Rhineholt and the union."

"What else do we have?" Gene asked.

"Just this...he fits the profile in that he worked at The Miami Examiner during the time Wedemeyer said he did," Gene II continued, anxiously. "His brother conveniently died just before Ralph Rhineholt showed up here which could indicate two things."

"What?"

"If this guy is a fraud...no one knows what happened to the real Rhineholt and he was trying to cover up his tracks," Gene II answered, "and he was holding back nothing to make sure no one would know who he really is...His first act was..."

"That he murdered his so-called brother," Max interrupted, "so the fact that he wasn't really his brother would not be revealed."

"And the second?" Gene asked.

"His brother's murder was almost identical to the murder of Wedemeyer's contact, Steinberger!" Gene II answered. "Both victim's bodies were found hanging form steel rafters in a torched warehouse with Miller's calling card on them!"

"Sounds like he's sending Wedemeyer a message," Gene said, thoughtfully. "You think he wants to get caught?"

"Not this guy," Gene II replied. "I think he was just sending a message to Wedemeyer...Catch me if you can!"

Gene turned and looked at Max, puzzled. "Then I don't get it...with all this incriminating evidence against him, what's your hang up, Max?...You seem hesitant about something."

"I am...this guy simply does not look old enough to be the right man," Max answered. "According to the information we're gotten from Wedemeyer's records, he'd have to be between seventy and eighty years old...Believe me, the guy I know as Rhineholt is not that old!"

"That's explainable," Gene II shot back. "Hospital records indicate that he's been having face-lift surgery every year for the last seven years...beginning in Miami, New York and now Detroit."

"You're kiddin!" Gene said, surprised. "Face-lifts?"

"Yeah...that and a good body conditioning program with some hair weaving and hair dye can easily knock off ten to fifteen years," Gene II answered, "especially if it means life or death...or deportation back to Germany or Israel."

Max remained doubtful. "That may be true...I just can't go out on a limb like that."

"I can appreciate that attitude, Max," Gene said, smiling. "I'd rather be safe than sorry...but I'll decide...Get him up here so I can see him."

Max had shed any responsibility. "That might be best...another opinion will give us the assurance we'll need before contacting federal authorities," Max said, relieved.

"How are we supposed to get him up here?" Gene II asked. "If the unions find out we're planning some kind of entrapment of one of their members...they could file charges against us and shut us down!"

"I seriously doubt that they would do anything to protect an ex-Nazi," Gene replied, firmly. "Listen, I'll tell you what...you tell the union I'm considering the creation of an assistant production manager's position in the near future and I want four candidates from their union...Select three guys plus this Rhineholt...Tell 'em I believe in promoting from within the ranks and I want to personally interview all candidates as soon as possible."

"Now that could work," Max said.

"I'll have Wedemeyer sit in on Rhineholt's interview and both of you will also be present...If our suspicions are confirmed, we'll turn this information over to the feds."

"According to the union contract any promotion like this has to be posted," Max said, thoughtfully.

"So?...Get it done...Check with Roger first," Gene said. "I don't want to violate any union contract, but have his office take care of posting the notice."

"When do you want the interviews held?" Gene II asked.

"As soon as possible...we got a wedding we gotta get ready for, remember?...I'd like to have this all cleared up before then."

"OK, dad...I'll take care of it," Gene II said.

"What about you, Max...am I gonna see you at the wedding?" Gene asked, smiling.

Max grinned back. "I wouldn't miss it for the world. I think Mel's got himself a gorgeous bride."

"You bringing anyone?" Gene asked.

"The love of my life."

"Who's that?"

Max beamed with pride. "Marcy...Marcy Dugas."

"You got great taste...She's a winner, a beautiful woman and an excellent reporter," Gene said, smiling broadly. He turned to Gene II. "What about Susan and the kids...they gonna be there?"

"She said they'd be there," Gene II whispered, hoarsely. "I hope they will...I'd better get this set up with Roger."

Gene II, having cut short the conversation about his family, quickly stood up and left the office followed closely by Max.

Gene sat back down in his chair, leaned back, picked up the phone and began dialing. He placed both feet on the corner of the desk and crossed his legs. In a few moments he smiled when he heard Adrian's voice on the line.

"Hello," Adrian answered.

"If you're not coming to work soon...I'm coming over there...I miss you, baby...I really miss you!"

Gene II and Max had skillfully arranged the interviews through Roger's office for the new position of Assistant Production Manager. Much to their surprise the response from the union was excellent since it had been stressed that the publisher wanted to promote from within the ranks of the union rather than bringing in some company oriented outsider. The first three interviews all had been very smooth and Gene felt he could eventually select a good candidate for the executive position.

As they prepared for the last interview, Gene's thoughts were centered on Rhineholt who was scheduled to appear at any moment. Dr. Wedemeyer had just arrived, still wearing the same old, baggy suit, but today his eyes sparkled with anticipation behind his thick bifocal glasses. Gene II and Max sat nervously, unsure of the outcome. A chair in the middle of the office remained vacant. Gene checked his watch and buzzed his secretary.

"Yes, Mr. Stanton?" she asked.

"Is the last candidate out there?"

"You mean Mr. Rhineholt?...Yes, he is."

"Fine...send him in, please."

Dr. Wedemeyer leaned back in his chair and slowly stroked his goatee, thoughtfully. "The man has nerve...this should prove to be very interesting...I am sure it is him."

Everyone in the office but Wedemeyer looked up as Rhineholt slowly came into the room. He was a tall, clean cut man, neatly dressed in slacks, sport coat and an open neck white shirt. He had the appearance of a man in his early fifties. His dyed dark hair on his head, eyebrows and mustache contrasted sharply with his bleached white skin. He smiled politely as he shook everyone's hand, firmly. He hesitated momentarily before he slowly shook Dr. Wedemeyer's hand. If he was surprised by Dr. Wedemeyer's presence he did not show it. He sat down in the vacant chair and crossed his long, lanky legs as he leaned back with confidence, staring at Gene. Gene studied his personnel file briefly and then looked up at Rhineholt.

"Mr. Rhineholt...have you ever had any experience as a production manager?" Gene asked. "I mean...if only for a few days or weeks at a time...like a vacation replacement."

"Just what you see in my file," Rhineholt answered stiffly. "I've never had any extensive experience in that capacity."

"Do you think you can handle an executive position like this?"

"I can handle any job you might have, Mr. Stanton."

Dr. Wedemeyer leaned forward in his chair and smiled as he studied Rhineholt carefully. Rhineholt became nervous as he sensed Wedemeyer's eyes penetrating him. He glanced at Dr. Wedemeyer momentarily and then turned back to Gene. Wedemeyer began to play his hand.

"What about security, Mr. Rhineholt?" Dr. Wedemeyer softly asked. "Have you ever handled security personnel at an executive level?"

Rhineholt slowly turned slightly in his chair, glaring angrily at Dr. Wedemeyer. "I know everyone here, sir...Who are you?"

"I'm sorry...I should've introduced you," Gene said. "Mr. Wedemeyer is a corporate associate...do you object to his presence?"

"Would it make any difference if I did?" Rhineholt shot back, angrily.

"Not one bit!" Gene snapped. "Go on...answer his question."

Rhineholt slowly turned his head towards Dr. Wedemeyer and then, back to Gene. "Look, Mr. Stanton...let me be perfectly frank with you...I didn't come here begging for any job. I was told that you wanted to see me for some kind of interview

THE WINDS OF TOMORROW

for Assistant Production Manager...I certainly did not come up here for some inquisition from..from just anyone off the street."

"Now just a minute!" Gene II interrupted, angrily.

"Be careful, Rhineholt," Max warned.

"No...let him go on," Gene said, calmly. Let's hear what he has to say."

Rhineholt now had the floor. "I don't know if you're aware of this, Mr. Stanton...but many of us are not too happy to be working for you...In fact, many are taking about quitting...and going back to The Daily Press."

"Why are they thinking about quitting?" Gene II asked.

"No offense," Rhineholt smirked, "but they resent working for a...a Black man."

Max became furious!..."Then why did you come up here?.." Max demanded angrily. "And...and why in the hell don't you quit?"

"Me?...I was perfectly satisfied and content," Rhineholt answered, calmly, "until you started playing this...this...childish little game of yours."

"Game?...You think this is a game?" Gene asked, angrily.

"I'm not a complete idiot," Rhineholt replied. "I know you've been investigating me."

"That's normal procedure when we're considering a promotion of this stature," Gene II said, firmly.

Rhineholt slowly turned towards Dr. Wedemeyer and smiled. Wedemeyer smiled back, knowingly.

"Is it also normal procedure to bring in this...this Nazi hunter?...I don't think so!"

"Do you have anything to hide?" Dr. Wedemeyer asked.

Rhineholt turned away from Dr. Wedemeyer and glared at Gene..."I 'd rather not speak to this man!"

Rhineholt could not surpress his growing anger any longer. He took a deep breath as he slowly looked from man to man with an expression of complete disdain and contempt on his face.

"Polish...Nigras...and a Jew!...No..I don't want your stinkin' job!" Rhineholt sneered, angrily as he quickly stood up, proud and erect. He turned to face Gene directly. He backed up a few steps, clicked his heels and slightly bowed. "Good day, gentlemen...I believe this interview is concluded."

With that last statement Rhineholt quickly turned, marched out of the office and slammed the door!..Everyone in the office looked at each other in total amazement!...

"That pompous sonofabitch!" Max said in anger. "Did...did you see that?...He actually clicked his heels!"

"It's a wonder he didn't give the Nazi salute!" Gene II said.

Dr. Wedemeyer smiled, stroking his goatee thoughtfully. "He is a proud Nazi...and he is calling our bluff...he feels that if you had enough evidence against him you would have had him arrested...Since you didn't...he doesn't think you can."

"Well, he may have just over-played his hand," Gene said, thoughtfully.

"What do you mean?" Gene II asked, puzzled.

"Did you take a look at his hair and his skin?" Gene asked. "That guy's a helluva lot older than any fifty-five. More like seventy."

"Did you examine his hands?" Dr. Wedemeyer asked, anxiously. "They were old man's hands..like mine."

"And he was wearing pancake make-up," Max conceded, "to hide those surgical scars from the face lifts."

"Why didn't he try to hide his true identity more?" Gene II asked.

"I figure there was two reasons he didn't," Gene answered. "Like Dr. Wedemeyer just said...he doesn't think we have the evidence to prove who he is...And the second reason is...well, maybe he's just plain, old tired of running...but we can help him out there."

"What do you mean, dad?"

"Call the F.B.I...Let's throw that bastard in jail!"

Walking briskly, Gene Stanton led an entourage of people through the composing room of the Detroit Herald Newspaper and out to the press room. As the large group hurried by the busy employees, the workers all stopped and stared at them, puzzled. Gene led the group into the glass enclosed offices of the general superintendent, who looked up at them in surprise...

"Mr. Stanton...is...is something wrong?" the superintendent asked, looking all around him. "Who are all these people?"

Gene motioned to the group of neatly dressed men and women standing in the office behind him. "Mr. Spaulding, this is Mr. McAndrew and several members of his staff...They're all with The Federal Bureau of Investigations and they're here to arrest Ralph Rhineholt...Get him in here, now!"

Without any hesitation, Spaulding quickly picked up the telephone and made a call. In a few moments Ralph Rhineholt calmly walked into the office. He looked around at the large group of people and stopped when he saw Gene, Gene II, Max and Dr. Wedemeyer. Rhineholt smiled broadly as FBI Special Agent McAndrew flashed his identification and began speaking in a stern voice.

"Albert Herman Miller...I am arresting you for the commission of war crimes, illegal entry into the United States of America and murder...It is my duty to inform you that you have the right to remain silent for anything you say can and may be used in court against you...You have the right to an attorney. If you do not have an attorney..."

As McAndrew continued to read Miller his rights, Miller looked at Gene and a slow smile creased his face. He placed his hands above his head as he was instructed to do and he was thoroughly searched by the F.B.I. agents. When they were ready to leave, Miller turned back towards Gene and smiled. He motioned to his hands that were handcuffed behind his back.

"I would like to shake your hand, Mr. Stanton...but as you can see...I am not able to."

"You know what you can do with your hand, Mr. Miller?" Gene replied, sarcastically. "You can shove it where the sun doesn't shine!"

"I merely wanted to give you credit for having the nerve to do what had to be done," Miller said respectfully. "I am a sick old man and I am tired of running...Thank You."

Gene stood in the office and watched as the agents swiftly completed their job. Gene II and Max patted Dr. Wedemeyer on his back as the old man smiled broadly. The F.B.I. agents quickly escorted their prisoner back out of the press room and through the composing room as employees watched the entourage march by. One of the workers pulled off his cap and wiped his brow, revealing the grinning face of Damien!...

Chapter Twenty-Four

Gloria Stanton Thompson slowly walked through the freshly painted suite of offices Gene had assigned to her at The Detroit Herald Newspaper building. She couldn't stop herself from smiling. That Gene...tell him about your dream and he'll make it come to life. This was perfect, she thought...By setting up a breast cancer detection and education center right in the newspaper's offices she was not only confident she could get most of the women employed at The Herald to participate, but also women working down the street at The Daily Press as well as many of the women working in the downtown area

Gloria was so engrossed in her thoughts she didn't notice Gene standing in the doorway to the suite, smiling at her. "Well?..Do you like it?" Gene asked. "They just finished installing the carpet this morning."

Gloria was surprised to see Gene..."This is just perfect!..Are you sure you could spare this much space?"

"Oh, yeah...this was going to be the computer room when the Times was here," Gene answered. "Our computer room is next to our editorial department on the second floor."

"This is simply marvelous!" Gloria exclaimed, bringing both hands up to the sides of her face. "I can't get over it!..And all of this furniture you've put in here...desks, chairs, sofas, examining tables, mirrors!..Oh, Gene...you're such a wonderful brother!"

"I got a wonderful sister," Gene said, grinning. "I think what you're doing is one of the nicest things a person could do!.If you just save one life by providing this early detection...it's worth it!"

"Early detection is the best protection," Gloria said, looking around each spacious room. "If we could get these women to learn how to perform a breast self-examination each month...it could save their lives...I think we're on the right track, Gene...Thanks to you."

"Are you getting any help from City Hospital?" Gene asked.

"Yes...those stuff shirts over there finally relented when I told them we planned to do a series on breast cancer, featuring various hospitals and how they're serving the community."

"Are they sending over any equipment?"

Yes...it's due in this afternoon," Gloria replied, smiling. "In fact they're assigning two technicians and a radiologist on a part time basis to help with the classes. We'll teach the women monthly breast self-examination and counseling. If they find anything during a breast self-examination we'll send them over to the hospital for a mammography and further screening...The main thing our little office here will do is stimulate interest, provide instructions on breast self-examination to encourage early detection, education and provide a "buddy" support system."

"All of that at no cost?..It's gonna be completely free?" Gene asked.

"You betcha...that way no one will have an excuse not to come," Gloria answered. "I'm hoping for maximum participation."

"We're assigning you a receptionist also," Gene said, "she'll work from 9 to 5 right in this office."

"What about your different departments?" Gloria asked. "Are they urging their employees to participate?"

"So far...it looks like they will. We have to be careful...we can't force them."

"One of the problems with this disease is ignorance...There are mainly two things we don't know about breast cancer . We don't know the cause, and we don't know the cure. Until women make a commitment to learn about themselves...they're dancing in the dark."

"What is this "buddy" support system?" Gene asked.

"If breast cancer is discovered our group is prepared to have someone accompany the patient from the self-examination and mammography stages to surgery...to breast reconstruction or a prosthesis...whichever they may choose. This could be a devastating period in a woman's life and many of them will need someone standing by, sitting in the doctor's office or waiting room and for comforting home visits."

"Knowing you...I'm sure you'll become involved in providing close, personal care to any woman who discovers she has the disease."

"You bet I will," Gloria answered. "Nearly half a million American women will die of breast cancer this decade...It will be diagnosed in about two million women and 460 thousand women will die!"

"I...I didn't realize it was that bad." Gene said.

"Since 1950, the incidence of breast cancer has increased 53 percent, making it one of the fastest-growing killer diseases in the nation."

"Then maybe I should do more," Gene said, thoughtfully. "When do you plan to get your operation started?"

"As soon as all the equipment, literature and personnel are in place, why?"

"I'm going to arrange a series of P.S.A. advertisements to run daily for the next couple of months through our promotion department. We'll place 'em R.O.P. each day."

"Hey, wait a minute...what in the world is P.S.A.?"

"Public Service Announcement,," Gene answered, smiling. "I'll call advertising and get one of our best account executives to coordinate it with you and the promotion department. We'll run quarter page ads until you get the response you want."

"What's this R.O.P. mentioned?"

"Gloria...I thought you were the daughter of a newspaper publisher," Gene laughed. "R.O.P. stands for "run of the paper"...referring to the total circulation a newspaper has rather then a partial circulation or zoned circulation."

"Yeah...right," Gloria answered. "Will someone contact me from advertising?"

"Yes...one of our best ad copywriters."

"What's his name?"

"Willard...Willard Thompson."

"Oh, Gene!"

Patricia Parker-Stanton knocked softly on the apartment door and nervously looked up and down the long corridor. She could hear the faint strings of music coming from the apartment. She knocked again, slightly harder. She heard muffled footsteps coming towards the door. In a few moments the door opened and Bill Clark was smiling at her. She quickly stepped inside the apartment and hurriedly closed the door. Before she could say anything he embraced her and kissed her hungrily. She responded to his kiss in spite of herself. She stepped back and stared into his eyes.

"Whose apartment is this? she asked, looking around the stylish apartment.

"It's mine," Bill replied, grinning. "I did it...I left my wife."

"Oh, Bill!"

"Isn't that what you wanted?"

"No!..I didn't want you to leave your wife now!" Patricia protested. "We agreed to wait...I'm not ready to leave Gene!"

"I thought you said you loved me."

I do...I'm just not ready to make that kind of commitment."

Bill embraced her again, lightly kissing her all over her face. "But I love you, baby...and you love me!..It's time we began living our lives together...you know that."

"I know...you're right...it's just so difficult to break the bond."

"If you don't do it now...it may become more difficult in the future," Bill warned, studying her face carefully.

"I doubt that...I know he's seeing someone else and knowing Gene...he won't continue leading a double life too much longer...he is an honorable man."

"That's not what I was referring to."

Patricia leaned back in his arms and stared at him. "What are you talking about?"

Bill took her hand and slipped off her coat. He quickly hung her coat up in the closet and led her into the dining room where he had laid out a complete dinner with champagne and candles. The soft music playing on the stereo seemed to float through the air. Bill poured them both a drink and looked deeply into her eyes.

"I do love you, honey...more than you could ever know. I had no idea that someone like you would ever come into my life...especially now," Bill whispered into her ear.

"I know...I thought this feeling of passionate love was finished in my life, too." Patricia said. "I have grown children...a long time marriage...I thought my opportunity for love was all over."

"That's why it's so special don't you see?" Bill said, anxiously. "We both have another chance at a beautiful love and I'm not about to lose it!"

He placed his arms around her slim waist and pressed his straining body against hers. He smelled her hair and inhaled deeply as her firm body yielded to his hardness...He kissed her passionately, his tongue meeting hers in a warm, searching kiss. She suddenly stopped and stepped backwards, moving away from him. He looked at her, confused...

"What's wrong?" he asked, softly.

"It's something that you said...about Gene...You said it may become more difficult for me to leave him in the future."

Bill slowly sipped his drink, eyeing Patricia over the rim of his glass, "Yes, there is something you should know." he said, softly.

"Well...I'm waiting."

"Last week I met with a group of local politicians," Bill said. "They were all upset because of the candidates who are running for mayor...this group feels that any of them would be easily defeated by Mayor Powell if he decides to run."

"I thought he was too sick to run," Patricia said.

"We all did...If he runs in the primary against this weak field of candidates he'll win again and we'd have to put up with his terrible administration for another four years!"

"How does all of that affect me?" Patricia asked.

"We decided we needed a stronger candidate who would either discourage Mayor Powell from running...or one who could beat him one on one if Mayor Powell did run," Bill answered, calmly. "This meant he would have to be someone who has proven he is the man that could bring businesses back to Detroit to begin to rebuild our city...Your husband brought that newspaper back to life and created more than 1500 jobs..."

Patricia quickly covered her mouth with her hands.

"Oh, no!..They didn't!"

"Oh, yes we did!" Bill replied. "We selected Gene to run for mayor of Detroit."

"Did he agree to do it?"

"He said he would think about it."

"It wasn't you who asked him!"

"No...Congressman Ghetts asked him."

"So that's why you think my leaving him could become more difficult in the future," Patricia said, thoughtfully. "You mean if he runs for mayor."

"That's right."

"How did you vote?"

"The vote was overwhelmingly in his favor."

"That's not what I asked...How did you vote?"

"I nominated him."

"Me thinks I smell a rat!"

"What?"

"So that's why you left your wife," Patricia said, "you were putting the old squeeze play on me...You knew that if you got this apartment and told me about Gene running for mayor...I'd have to make up my mind before he accepted."

"Sure...I love you...is anything wrong with that?"

"You could have told me."

"I just did."

She walked closer to him, smiling. She put her arms around his neck and kissed him long and hard.

"It feels so good to hold you in my arms," he whispered. "Damn!..You excite me, lady!"

She leaned back in his arms pressing her body against his protruding member. Her eyes followed his closely...to the table full of food and back to each others eyes.

"Can you stay with me tonight?" he asked in a whisper. "All of these days...I've missed you so much."

"Just for a few hours," she answered. "Since you went to so much trouble to manipulate this arrangement...I guess I can stay awhile."

"I need you, Patricia...I've wanted to make love to you so bad...it's painful...I want to stay deep inside you and feel your warmth...your moisture. I want to feel your body shiver with pleasure from each stroke, each kiss and each caress."

Patricia closed her eyes and smiled. "I think dinner's gonna get cold," she whispered.

"To hell with dinner...I want you!"

They kissed again. His tongue explored her open mouth as his hands gently roamed over her body, slipping off the shoulder straps of her dress, partially revealing her firm, pointed breasts. In a few moments they had descended to the floor, rolling on the thick carpet and tearing at each other's clothes. When they were both completely naked he began lightly kissing her neck and breasts. His tongue skillfully teased her hard, swollen nipples while her small hand gently stroked his stiff member. He slowly moved down her body, lightly nibbling at her navel. He moved further down, licking the insides of her thighs. When she felt his hot breath on her skin, she spread her legs wider for him as he moved his body in position between her long, shapely legs and his tongue stabbed at her insides like the touch of a darting feather. She sighed deeply as his head moved into her even closer...and closer, until her head began to spin in the rapture of his gentle lovemaking...

F. Walton Dugas sat in the deep leather armchair in the family room of his mansion and quietly sipped a drink as he thoughtfully studied the crackling fire in the massive fireplace. He looked up as his wife, Julia, walked into the room and quickly poured herself a drink. She sat down across from her husband with a worried expression on her face as she rubbed her brow, nervously. Dugas glared at her and frowned.

"OK...let's have it," he asked, "what's the problem now?"

"It's...It's Douglas...he's sick again," she answered.

"You want me to have him commited?..You know what the problem is...If he keeps using that junk it's gonna fry what little of his brains he has left."

"I told you...he's not using that stuff anymore!"

"You'd believe anything he told you," Dugas said, angrily. "I cannot understand for the life of me how a kid can be born into a good family like ours...and fall completely apart before he's even thirty!"

Julia became pensive. "I...I don't know what happened, but it's not drugs...I guarantee you."

"His sister turns out to be an intellectual dynamo," Dugas said in disgust. "I may not agree with her politics, but she's smarter 'n hell!..She broke up that baby selling ring and made Gene Stanton look like a hero...And just look at her brother...not worth a damn!..He can't even piss without wettin' his legs!"

"You're his father...why don't you do something to help him?" Julie shouted. "Make him feel like he's worth something instead of ridiculing him every chance you get!"

"Do something?..Like what?" Dugas asked. "He's as useless as the tits on a bore hog!"

"Just give him a chance...maybe he needs a little more help than Marcy," Julia pleaded. "He's your only son!..You did it for Marcy and you can do it for him!"

"She did that on her own...I wanted her with me at The Press but she wouldn't budge."

"Now she's making headlines for Gene Stanton," Julia sneered.

Dugas took a sip of his drink and smiled confidently. "I won't have to worry about Gene Stanton too much longer."

"Why not?..What are you planning to do?"

Dugas reared back in his chair and chuckled, softly. "Me?..I'm not going to do anything. The word is out that Gene Stanton may run for mayor of Detroit...If he does, The Herald will fall apart because that oldest son of his isn't much better than Douglas."

"But at least he gave his son a chance," Julia shot back, angrily.

Suddenly a sound in the hallway attracted their attention. Douglas Dugas stood in the doorway, slightly swaying drunkenly. "Did somebody mention my name?"

"Dougie...I thought you were in bed," Julia said. "Do you feel any better?"

Douglas staggered into the room over to the portable bar and shakingly poured himself a drink. He stared at his father over the rim of the shaking glass.

"Yes, mother...I'll feel better...a lot better...in about a minute," Douglas mumbled.

Dugas was disgusted with his son. "Why in the hell don't you grow up?" Dugas snarled.

"Grow up into what?" Douglas slurred, "Another you?..No thanks...The world doesn't deserve another F. Walton..."Puke us"..."

"Dougie!..Don't say that!" Julia shouted. "That's being disrespectful!"

"No...let 'em rave on," Dugas said, angrily, "this way he doesn't have to face the truth of being a flat-out failure."

"Failure?..Failure at what?" Douglas asked. "Meeting your lousy standards?..Marcy's a success and she hates your guts!..You call me a failure...and I hate your rotten guts too!..No...no!..I think you're the failure, dearest daddy...not me!"

"Oh, go to hell!" Dugas shouted. "You're just a waste of time!"

"I hear your daughter's gonna go to the Stantons for a big wedding...Well...I guess that'll frost your balls, Mr. "Puke-us" !.." Douglas said, grinning in his father's face, tauntingly.

Dugas suddenly stopped and glared at his son. He was surprised by the news and Douglas achieved the effect he was seeking.

"What wedding?" Dugas asked.

"She's been invited to Mel Stanton's wedding by one of the editors at The Herald," Julia said, calmly.

"A Black man?" Dugas asked, anxiously.

"He's White," Julia answered.

"Then you knew about this and didn't tell me?" Dugas asked, angrily as he got up and poured another drink.

"You'd know about it if you read The Herald instead of that excuse for a newspaper you call The Daily Press!" Douglas teased.

Dugas quickly lost control and backhanded his son with a slap across his face!..Douglas fell over backwards across the coffee table, striking his head against an end table!..Julia screamed as she knelt over her son who was sprawled on the floor, groggy!..

"Stop it!" Julia screamed. "Don't hit him again!..He's hurt!"

Douglas slowly sat up as blood trickled down his chin. He glared at his father with hate in his eyes!.."You're gonna regret that!..If it's the last thing I do...I'll make you regret that!" Douglas muttered in anger. "Too bad I'm not the son you've always wanted...but I got news for you...you ain't the father I've always wanted either!"

Dugas stood over his son with clenched fists!.."You can't even get up and fight like a man!..No, you're not the son I've always wanted...but this game's not over yet...not by a long shot!"

Julia helped Douglas get to his feet and stagger out of the room. Dugas sat back down in his chair and calmly sipped his drink. In a few minutes Marcy walked into the room. Dugas stared at her with a frown on his face.

"Let me be the first to congratulate you," Dugas said, sarcastically.

"Congratulate me...for what?" Marcy asked.

"Well...first for winning that journalism award about that baby selling ring."

"That's old news."

"And second...I understand you're attending a wedding at the Stanton home."

Marcy stared at her father suspiciously before responding. "What's this leading to, dad?"

Before he could answer they suddenly heard Julia screaming horribly!..Dugas and Marcy ran up the stairs to Douglas' bedroom where the screams seem to be coming from. They saw the light from the bathroom and charged inside to find Douglas laying on the floor in his mother's arms and covered with blood!..They were shocked at the grotesque scene!..

"Wh...what the hell's happened?" Dugas shouted.

"You drove him to this!" Julia screamed. "I told you to leave him alone and help him!"

"What did he do?" Dugas demanded, anxiously.

"He slashed his wrists!" Julia cried, rocking back and forth. "He's slashed both of them!"

Marcy slowly backed out of the bathroom with her hands covering her mouth in horror!..She ran over to the phone next to the bed and dialed 911. Dugas and Julia began wrapping towels around Douglas' wrists as he slowly closed his eyes!..

Later that evening Patricia Parker-Stanton sat in her kitchen in the Stanton home sipping a cup of coffee, thoughtfully. Her daughter, Karen, walked in and lightly tapped her on the shoulder. Patricia turned and smiled.

"Hi, Karen...I thought you were still at the newspaper."

"I just dropped by on the way home to see how you were doing," Karen answered. "I've been thinking about you and this wedding...Is there anything I can do?"

"No, not really...Kelly's parents have been wonderful and they'll be staying here for a few days," Patricia replied. "The house is going to be crowded with professional and college athletes and coaches...that means some press, too...I hope Connie doesn't go into one of her famous fits and crash...You look kinda upset about something...are you alright?"

"No...I'm just fine, why?"

"I'm your mother...I can tell when something's bothering you...what is it?"

Karen walked over and poured herself a cup of coffee. She refilled Patricia's cup and smiled at her. She sat down across from her mother and slowly began stirring her cup, thoughtfully. Patricia placed a hand on top of Karen's.

"Oh, honey...tell me what's bothering you," Patricia urged in a soft, reassuring voice.

"The other day...Willard told me about Aunt Gloria and F. Walton Dugas."

Patricia relaxed and sat back in her chair. "That happened years ago," she said, "they'll work it out."

"But don't you think a parent owes it to her child to tell the child the truth about it's parentage?" Karen asked.

"Not necessarily."

"Willard was crushed," Karen said. "She should have told him."

"Sometimes it's not practical, Karen," Patricia said in a firm manner and avoiding eye contact. "It depends on the circumstances."

"Sometimes?..Oh, c'mon, mother...you're a lawyer."

"No...I mean it...in Gloria's case it was more prudent not to say anything until she was forced to."

Karen remained silent.....She just stared at her mother and sipped her coffee. Suddenly the kitchen became so quiet you could hear a pin drop. Karen cleared her throat before she began speaking in a calm, soft voice...

"What about our case...yours and mine, mother?"

Patricia was stunned!..She slowly looked up into Karen's eyes as they welled up in tears..."Wh...what did you say?"

"You heard me, mother," Karen answered, tearfully. "Was it also more prudent for you not to tell me the truth?"

"What are you talking about?"

Karen couldn't hold back any longer and the tears began to flow down her cheeks...

"I...I went with Willard when he had his DNA tests performed...Since I was there and...and for some reason I have always been curious...I had the tests performed also...It proved that dad couldn't possibly be my father," Karen said, searching her mother's eyes for any response. "Of course, I'm sure you already knew that...I want to know, mom...if dad isn't my father...who is?..Who is my father?..Tell me, mother, please...who is my father?"

Chapter Twenty-Five

The entire Stanton Estate was in an uproar on Mel and Kelly's wedding day. The huge mansion was teeming with electric excitement as the magic hour drew near. The weather had cooperated with a bright, sunny spring day with temperatures at a crisp sixty degrees. With over two hundred guests expected, the stately home was bursting with people as newly hired maids, butlers, and security guards rushed from one place to the next, inside and outside of the home. With so many people going in and out...bridesmaids, florists, photographers, guests, friends and relatives...the home looked more like a busy airport at the peak of the holiday season.

Inside of the main guest suite on the second floor, Kelly was surrounded by most of the women from both families as Karen, Liz and Patricia, together with a hair stylist, a make-up artist and a special security woman, all caught up in the joyous atmosphere, crowded into the large suite. Kelly sat nervously in front of a gigantic mirror, wearing a beautiful breathtaking low-cut, off-the-shoulder, silk and satin, white wedding gown with a lavishly hand beaded bodice with French lace.

The twelve foot long cathedral train and the matching cathedral tulle veil was edged in Belgian embroidery and decorated with iridescent Austrian crystals and pearls. Kelly's thick blond hair was in an elegant upsweep with large curls and strands of dangling curls down one side of her face.

Suddenly, everyone in the suite was distracted by the sounds of women and girls screaming and squealing in delight somewhere downstairs!..Kelly turned around at the sound just in time to see Kim Stanton rush into the bedroom towards her with both arms outstretched!..Kim and Kelly began to scream and embraced each other warmly as tears streamed down their cheeks!..

"Kim!..You made it!" Kelly cried out in happiness. "I'm so happy you're here!"

"Oh, Kelly, girl!..This is simply fantastic!" Kim screamed. "And you!..You look gorgeous!.. You know I wouldn't miss you and Mel getting married!"

"Be careful, Kelly...your make-up!" Liz warned as she turned to Kim. "When did you get in and why didn't you call?"

Kim squeezed Liz's hand as she kissed her, Karen and Patricia. She purposely waved her left hand under their noses.

"We got in late last night," she replied, smiling.

"What's that on your finger?" Kelly asked, anxiously.

"Well if you got in last night, why didn't you come home?" Patricia asked, puzzled.

"Look at her hand!" Kelly screamed.

Liz quickly grabbed Kim's hand and began shouting!..

"Mom!..Look, she's engaged!" Liz shouted.

"I don't believe it!" Karen exclaimed, stunned, as she stared at Kim's finger.

"Believe it, girlfriend!" Kim said, grinning. "That's why I didn't come home last night, mom...I was being proposed to!"

Kim, Kelly, Liz and Karen began jumping up and down and squealing as everyone else in the suite began laughing at them.

"Is it Steve?" Liz asked.

"Not in this lifetime!" Kim snapped. "I hope I never see that jerk again!"

"I understand his career has gone down like a rock since his accident," Karen said.

"Accident?" Patricia asked. "What happened?"

"Word is he was mugged at a Los Angeles hotel a few months back," Karen answered, "and he was thrown down an elevator shaft...six broken ribs, punctured lungs, and a broken jaw...He hasn't worked in months."

"Well who is it, then...that movie star?" Kelly asked.

Kim nodded her head affirmative, too excited to speak!

"So THAT'S what all that screaming was about downstairs," Patricia said, "you brought that movie star with you!..Well where is he... am I ever going to meet him?"

"He's downstairs being molested by some of Kelly's oversexed bridesmaids," Kim laughed. "We tried to sneak in through the back door but we almost got shot by one of those security guards!..It's like trying to get through the iron curtain!"

"And what do you think of our Kelly?" Patricia asked, waving her hand towards Kelly. "Isn't she just beautiful!"

"GOD!..You're sexy and wild!" Kim squealed.

"You mean...for a pregnant lady?" Kelly Laughed.

Kim grabbed Kelly and hugged and kissed her again. Patricia pulled them apart, patting Kelly's hair back in place.

"Kelly...get your family so Kim can meet them," Patricia said.

"This is really going to be a great day." Kin said, sighing happily. "I'm just so happy for you and my brother, Kelly...He loves you and don't you ever forget it!"

Kelly grabbed Kim's hand and quickly led her over to her family who had been laughing as they watched the entire scene..

Mel Stanton was cool...With a little more than an hour left before the big moment, he was upstairs in a third floor butler's suite he use to live in before he went off to college. He stood in front of a long mirror putting on the final touches. Mel wore a dark tuxedo complete with white embroidered shirt, bow tie and matching cumber bun. He was the perfect picture of being calm. No nervousness, beads of perspiration or any frantic last-minute preparations. His two brothers, Joe and Gene II, followed Mel from room to room, gently taunting and teasing him, trying their best to unnerve him...Roger Carlson and Max Jenkins watched the proceedings with big grins on their faces...

"You sure you wanna go through with this?" Gene II asked, confidentially. "You can still back out, you know."

"Cut it out!!" Mel answered, smiling. "I'm on to you two jokers...I know what you're tryin to do and it ain't gonna work...you know that...That's the same trick North Carolina tried in the NCAA finals and you see what it got them...whupped!"

"What're you talkin' about?" Joe asked, innocently. "We're only trying to help out our little brother who's too stupid to get out of something he can't handle."

"Yeah, right." Mel answered, sarcastically.

"Listen to your brothers, Mel," Roger said, seriously. "You better think this over before it's too late...I still might be able to get you out of it."

"Now it's a full court press...I thought I could depend on you, Rog," Mel said, shaking his head.

"Maybe we ought to tell him about Ed Boatwright," Gene II said, sadly. "He had a best man that was seven feet tall, too."

"Naw...don't tell him that," Joe said.

"Who's Ed Boatwright?" Mel asked.

"Mel, my man...you are in deep do-do!" Max said.

"Who the hell is Ed Boatwright?" Mel asked again.

"Don't say anymore about Boatwright," Joe muttered.

"I wanna know...who the hell is this Ed Boatwight?" Mel demanded.

"Ok...tell him if you want to," Joe said to Gene II. "I'm washing my hands of the whole thing."

"You sure you wanna know?" Gene II asked Mel.

"Yeah...those seven footers are dangerous," Max chuckled. "And they're faster than Speedy Gonzales."

"What's his height got to do with it?" Mel asked. "Earl's been my homeboy since high school...he'll make a good best man...You guys are just jealous because I didn't pick either of you."

"What?" Joe asked, indignantly. "Ok...I'll tell him about Ed Boatwright!"

"Get outta here" Mel answered, sarcastically. "Who in hell is this Ed Boatwright?"

"Ed Boatwright was a good friend of mine and Gene's" Joe began, solemnly. "When he got married...he had a best man who was seven foot tall. Just like you and Earl Goodwin."

"I think you guys are jerkin' me around," Mel said, suspiciously.

"No...No...just listen," Gene II said. :"Boatwright wasn't married a week when he came home early one day and caught his new wife in bed with his best man!"

"The poor guy was shocked!" Joe continued. "He didn't know what to do...so he stood in the doorway of the bedroom and told his wife..."I've given you everything...diamonds, furs, a new car...anything you ever wanted and you do this to me!"

"What'd he say to his best man?' Mel asked, interested.

"He turns to his best man...that seven footer...just like you got...He turns to his best man and he says..."And you, my best friend...I've always fought for you, given you my last dime...been like a brother to you...the least you can do is stop while I'm talking!"

Everyone roared with laughter as Mel's two howling brothers ducked a towel he threw that them!

Gene Stanton stood at the far end of the great room talking to several people while other wedding guests milled around in small groups throughout the mansion, sipping drinks and tasting samples from snack food trays as they waited fro the big event. Gene saw Adrian when she first walked in and attracted everyone's attention. She joined a group of women on the opposite side of the spacious room. Gene tried to be nonchalant and continue his conversation but everytime he would look up, she would stare at him and smile...He felt a surge of warmth in his chest whenever she looked at him. Adrian was stunning in a light blue mini-suit that was expensively tailored. Her thick black hair was swept up on top of her head complimenting the smooth contour of her neck and her beautiful and delicate facial features. She held herself straight and erect as the short mini-skirt accentuated her long, shapely legs. She wouldn't move her eyes away from Gene's as he stared back at her, almost hypnotized by her seductive smile. Gene felt a slight tug at his arm. He turned and faced one of his business associates who was staring at Adrian in awe!..

."Wow!..Who in the world is that?" the man asked. "Now she is absolutely drop dead georgeous!"

"What?..Er...ah...Will you excuse me?" Gene said to the group of people surrounding him. "I've got some urgent business to attend to."

Gene slowly made his way across the crowded and spacious great room as the laughter and endless chattering seemed to grow louder. Adrian watched him take each step towards her and smiled broadly as he came closer. Gene wanted to get away from this noise and hold Adrian in his arms. He walked over to her and without saying a word, he grabbed her hand and quickly led her down the hallway into his library. Once inside, he smiled at her, backed up and snapped the lock on the door. He stood there admiring her. She was beautiful. She was impeccably dressed for the occasion and Gene had been infatuated with her appearance ever since she had arrived. She looked Gene up and down and smiled with satisfaction. Gene wore a complete tuxedo, bow tie, cumber bun and the works. Adrian stepped closer to him and pressed her soft body against his as he embraced and kissed her passionately. She pressed harder against his body, slowly grinding her hips until she could feel his hardness bulging against her. Breathing heavily, her tongue flickered across his lips. His hand slowly moved up under her mini-skirt, exploring her smooth, soft inner thighs as she sighed deeply in response. He felt her hand massaging his stiff member as she quickly unzipped his fly and moved her hand inside the opening. Suddenly, there was a soft knock at the door! Adrian stepped back quickly, straightening out her skirt and staring at Gene with a questioning look. Gene hurriedly zipped up his trousers!..

"Your wife?" Adrian asked in a whisper.

"No...they're all upstairs with Kelly."

They heard a muffled voice on the other side of the door as Adrian dabbed at the lipstick on Gene's mouth. She quickly sat down in the chair across from the desk, sipping her drink and crossing her long, shapely legs, casually...

"Damn!..I can't get enough of you," Gene whispered.

"You never will, " she said, softly.

"Gene?..Gene Stanton...you in there?" a man's voice asked.

"Yes...yes I am," Gene answered, calmly. "Just a second...I'll get the door.

Gene opened the door and several men and women walked into the room. The large group was headed by Congressman Ghetts and City Councilman Bill Clark. Several ministers and business people along with representatives of the United Auto Workers Union and the Teacher's union were among those present. Adrian looked nervously at Gene as the group crowded into the library. Gene stood behind his desk, looking uncomfortable. He quickly broke into a smile as he welcomed the large group, who were all obviously very concerned about this impromptu meeting just before Mel's wedding.

"I'd like you all to meet one of The Herald's star reporters," Gene said. "I know some of you have probably seen her around the City-County Building...She helped expose that baby selling ring last fall...I present to you...Dr. Adrian Grant."

Everyone greeted Adrian with handshakes and smiles, congratulating her for a job well done. When they were all settle down and most of them seated, Councilman Bill Clark began speaking.

"Gene...I'm sure you're figured out why we're here," Bill Clark said.

"I have a sneaking suspicion," Gene answered, smiling.

"Congressman Ghetts told us you needed more time," Bill said, "But several things have happened since he spoke to you."

"You see, Gene...there are a few other people who want to toss their hat into the ring," Ghetts said, "but they won't do it if we can count on you."

Surprised, Adrian looked from Gene to the anxious faces of all of the people in the room. A wide smiled flashed across her pretty face.

"I figured something like that might happen,": Gene said, "I do understand your concern...and I appreciate your support."

"You're not gonna turn us down, are you?" a minister asked. "We need you, Gene Stanton...Detroit's in trouble!"

"That's right!..We need someone who would make a dynamite mayor!" a priest shouted. "Somebody who can turn this city around...and you're that man!"

"I think it's a great idea!" Adrian said, smiling.

Gene quickly glanced at Adrian and smiled. "No...I'm not turning you down." Gene replied. "In fact I'm honored that such a distinguished group of civic activists like yourselves would ask me to run...The only thing I'm concerned with is...do you REALLY know what kind of mayor I would be?"

"What do you mean?" Bill Clark asked.

"Today...most politicians run for office to gain power, money, prestige," Gene said, "or to lay the groundwork for higher aspirations. Most of them offer no cogent platform. Just themselves with no definite plans to improve the city. These candidates believe it is chic to promise the people everything before the election...and then it's business as usual after."

"I admit in many instances that's been true, Gene," Ghetts agreed, "what's your point?"

"I don't need that...I've already got power, prestige and a multi-million dollar corporation that's on the way up," Gene replied, studying the reaction of the group, carefully. "If I run...I'm determined to run to bring this city back...to make the City of Detroit the most economically successful major urban area in the country!"

"That's exactly what we want," a woman said.

"Today, we can no longer depend on government handouts or the auto industry...Our tax base has dwindled each year as auto plants have closed down and retail stores have moved out of Detroit to the suburbs...As a result, more than ninety percent of the people who live in Detroit...shop outside of Detroit!..The only way we can become financially independent is for the City of Detroit to create it's own industry...an industry that will provide jobs and economic stability for the entire metropolitan Detroit area...Once our suburban neighbors see that Detroit is becoming the anchor of southeastern Michigan again by creating economic stability, they will be anxious to join with us to insure their survival and prosperity," Gene said, confidently. "We must initiate a business climate in the city that will guarantee success...and I am not talking about gambling!"

"What's your plan, Gene?" Bill Clark asked.

"Before I can accept your nomination for Mayor of Detroit...I've got to know that a grass roots group like yourselves would support me," Gene answered, "and that you are willing to place the economic success of our city as your top priority...for with economic success I intend to double the size of our police force to reduce crime, drugs and to stop this insane violence!..I will create jobs, bring retailers back into the city and rebuild our neighborhoods and our schools to increase the value of our homes. I'm talking about an industry that could pump over one billion additional dollars into our city's treasury each year!!...But before I commit...I've got to know that I'll have your unqualified support and backing!"

"I don't wanna seem redundant," Congressman Ghetts said, smiling. "but we can't commit to giving you our unqualified support until we know what your plan is...so again we're asking...what's your plan?"

Everyone in the room glanced nervously at each other as they anxiously waited for Gene's response.

"This decline in our country's urban areas is a direct result of the indifference of former conservative administrations who ignored the plight of our major cities with large black populations and black leadership," Gene explained, "consequently, a city like Detroit that also had to suffer the downsizing of the automobile industry and the flight of citizens and businesses to the suburbs...was hit with a double "whammy" at the same time of loses in federal revenue, businesses and people...The only more effective way I know of crippling a city more than this is to drop an atom bomb on it!"

"But how do you plan to fight a massive movement like that?" Bill Clark asked. "We certainly can't tax businesses and people who are no longer here in the city."

"I believe it is time for cities to become self-sufficient as much as possible and not have to rely solely on federal subsidies and taxing their citizens to death," Gene replied. "It is time for the City of Detroit to utilize all of it's natural resources to survive."

"What natural resources do we have that we would possibly utilize?" a second woman asked.

Gene smiled, walked over to the wall and pulled down a large wall map of the greater Detroit area. He used a pointer as he began indicating certain points and landmarks...

"Detroit is in the unique position of having this lovely island just off of it's coast...Belle Isle," Gene answered pausing briefly for effect. "For many years Belle Isle has remained untouched and unproductive."

"You can thank that group, The Friends of Belle Isle, for that" the second woman said. "They've fought like mad to save the island and most citizens appreciate their efforts to save Belle Isle."

"That's true...and I appreciate their efforts, too," Gene replied, quickly, "but now things have reached a drastic economic stage in Detroit...I'm not just talking about saving Belle Isle...I'm talking about saving Detroit!..My plan is to work with the giants of industry in metropolitan Detroit to develop Belle Isle into a Disney World type of fun island...a science fiction theme park that will feature a space world complete with a Solar System, and animal kingdom, an actual castle imported from Scotland, a state-of-the-art Sea World, a wax museum and all of the new mega-thrill rides with a revolutionary Flying Saucer-roller coaster and the cork-screw roller coaster that will go all around the perimeter of the island...and also several yacht excursions that will cruise the Detroit River."

"You said something about the giants of industry," Coungressman Ghetts said. "What role would they play?

"The first Corporation might donate or sponsor The Space World Project which would include a complete galaxy with all of the planets and stars in the Solar System, a giant Redstone Missile, an actual Space Shuttle and a real Flying Saucer craft that people would get into and ride on the new high tech roller coasters."

"What about the other corporations?" Bill Clark asked.

"A second could donate the Sea World Project which would be much more elaborate than the other Sea Worlds all across the country," Gene answered. "And a third Corporation could donate The Wax Museum which would feature movie stars, inventors, historical figures, sports legends, and various fiction writer's impressions of Space Aliens...The castle from Scotland or England could be imported here by school children of metro Detroit each buying a brick for a quarter. This would allow participation by the suburbs and children which is sure to boost it's popularity...The island would expand and enlarge it's zoo and have many other fun projects and rides such as motorized dinosaurs...There would be enough individual projects on the island to allow the participation of most of the giants of industry to sponsor as many as they may want while the island still maintains over fifty percent of the aesthetics now offered...The luxurious yacht rides would provide citizens and tourists with a delightful excursion for the entire family."

"What about parking?" the first minister asked.

"No cars would be allowed on the island. Cars would be parked in the lots immediately adjacent to the McArthur Bridge...People would flock to the greatest tourist attraction in the mid-west and pay entrance fees comparable to Disney World."

"How would they be transported to and from the island?" the second woman asked.

"The tourists would board a ground traversing Space Shuttle at the entrance to the bridge and be takened to the island where they would sight-see, buy rides, toys, souvenirs, attend different theatres and restaurants. They would be allowed to get on any mini-train, free, to get from project to project," Gene answered.

"What about picnics?" the first woman asked.

"Everyone will be encouraged to picnic at all times," Gene replied. "Some of the island's employees will be dressed in large and small space alien and animal costumes to greet visitors."

"Do you plan to shut down during the winter months?" Bill Clark asked. "We can't be year-around like Disney World."

"Shut down?..No way," Gene answered, "In the winter the island will be designed with small ski slopes, ice skating rinks, tobogganing and be totally converted to a Winter Wonderland with horse drawn sleigh rides and ski rides," Gene said, smiling broadly. "Of course the castle will be redecorated to correlate with the current holiday season...In October it would become a Witches' Castle and in November and December...what else but Santa's Castle!..Every child in the country would want to visit there before the Christmas holidays!"

"Now that is creativity!" Ghetts said, smiling. "And we can tell you've given this a lot of thought...It sounds wonderful!..It may require an amendment to the State Charter but I think we could pull it off!..Damn!..It'll mean more revenue for the state and federal government too!"

"Something tells me this isn't some new idea either," the first woman said, "how many jobs are we lookin' at?"

"This entire venture could create over ten thousand year around jobs." Gene answered. "It would also give Detroit and the State of Michigan one of the most popular tourist attractions in the world!"

"What kind of gross receipts are you expecting?" Adrian asked, enthused.

"Based upon gross receipts from other theme parks across the country...I'd say the yearly gross should exceed one billion dollars the first full year!" Gene replied. :"And it should constantly grow each year thereafter."

"How long would it take to have it constructed?" Ghetts asked.

"My contractors estimated that the entire conversion could take place within two years of it's start date," Gene answered. "or possibly sooner...I planned to have a table model mock-up of the island with each project in place before I start campaigning."

"Wow!..That is very impressive!" the second woman said.

"But it's only the beginning,": Gene said, determined. "With that kind of additional revenue coming into our city treasury we'll be able to double the size of our police department to reduce crime, drugs and violence!..The high visibility of police will make all of Detroit, including our neighborhoods...safer than the suburbs!"

"Well...what about the neighborhoods?" the second minister asked.

"Our neighborhoods have been seriously ignored for many years," Gene replied, angrily, "with this new influx of wealth from the Belle Isle Theme Park we can rebuild our neighborhoods and update them with mini-parks, cul-de-sacs, strip shopping malls, and new home building starts at a minimum of five thousand new homes each year...We will institute stiff city ordinances that will require continuing maintenance on all homes and property or be ticketed after a thirty day warning...All old, deteriorating housing will be demolished, removed and replaced."

"What about downtown?" Bill Clark asked. "How do you propose to get our downtown back?..Over thirty-five percent of our downtown buildings office space is vacant."

"With the addition of the Belle Isle revenue I will propose that the downtown shopping area on Woodward Avenue between Kennedy Square and Grand Circus Park, be made into a massive shopping mall, encircled by rows of free parking," Gene replied as he indicated the area on the map. "The center of the mall will be covered by a retracting translucent plastic dome...A five to ten story municipal free parking garage will be constructed and buttressed up against the J.L. Hudson's building so the shoppers can come downtown, park their cars free, and walk right into the mall through the Hudson's building, without being exposed to the weather. The more than ten thousand free parking units in the garage combined with the more than ten thousand outside free parking spaces will provide our downtown shopping mall with more than twenty thousand free parking units...twice the parking spaces available in most suburban malls."

"What about attracting major retailers?" Bill Clark asked. "The smaller retailers are not going to come back downtown until the shopping mall is anchored by a major retailer."

Gene smiled confidently. "With the new Belle Isle tourist attraction only a few miles down the road bringing in people from all over the world, the Windsor gambling casinos just across the Detroit River, and with over twenty thousand free parking spaces...I don't think we'll have any problem attracting a major retailer back downtown...But if we do..I am prepared to form a business consortium of city and suburban business people and re-open the J.L. Hudson's store as the major retailer to anchor the downtown shopping mall...The overflow of tourists from the Belle Islle Theme Park and the Windsor gambling casinos will enable downtown merchants to have as much as triple the amount of customer floor traffic normally found at suburban shopping malls...I also plan to have all of the major arteries leading into downtown which now have many boarded up stores and buildings...remodeled and subsidized to create an International Village of specialty shops, sidewalk cafes, restaurants, clothing stores and gift shops from countries all over the world!..This will really enhance the area as a tourist attraction, especially with all of the downtown hotels and theatres re-opening and a new Tiger Stadium being constructed in the heart of downtown, just next to the new shopping mall!"

"You're right there," the first woman said, "it'll create more jobs and stimulate additional growth!..This sounds great!..We have heard everything except how you plan to get the people to move back into Detroit...our population has shrunk to less than one million."

Gene smiled and slid the large map back up the wall. He glanced at Adrian who was sitting on the edge of her seat, beaming proudly...

"I'm glad you asked...this is the coup-de-gras!" Gene said, grinning broadly.

"We can stimulate attendance to Detroit's schools by enhancing the future of Detroit's school children over other communities by committing a portion of the revenue derived from the Belle Isle Theme Park and the increase revenue from business taxes to provide two years of free college or higher education for every Detroit student who's family has lived continuously in the City of Detroit for three consecutive years preceding their college application."

"That is enough to motivate both Blacks and Whites to move back into the city," Congressman Ghetts said, anxiously.

"It will also increase the value of our homes and our property," the first woman said, smiling." It's about time!

"More businesses will also move back into the city to pick up the increased customer traffic," the second woman said, thoughtfully.

"I...I think this could really bring the city back to life!" Adrian remarked, somberly. "It seemed so hopeless before...but now...this could work!"

Gene smiled and closely eyed the expressions on everyones faces as he continued..."Now, do you understand why I must have your total support?..My plan is to recommend that a referendum be put before the people for them to vote on this project. Everyone recognizes that the cities must look to new sources to survive...it'll be the voter's choice...If I can't have your backing on these projects...I will not run!..Ladies and gentlemen...the ball is in your court...I would like your answer as soon as possible...but right now, I think we're all expected at a wedding!"

Everyone got up and shook Gene's hand and encouraged him. They were all impressed with his plans. When they finally left the room, Adrian quickly kissed Gene on the cheek.

"No wonder I love you so damn much!" she said.

Chapter Twenty-Six

The wide spacious great room was crowded with more than two hundred guests, all waiting patiently for the ceremony to began. Mel had already made his dramatic appearance and he waited at the altar with his seven foot tall best man and the minister. In a few moments everyone turned their heads to the rear of the long room and looked down the aisle when they heard the first strings of the wedding march. The huge crowd was moved into spontaneous awe as the little flower girls came down the stairway and tossed rose petals on the stairs and into the aisle as Kelly, carrying a bouquet of white orchids and baby breath flowers, followed the flower girls down the winding, wide staircase and into the long aisle on the arm of her father until she reached the altar for the beginning of the double-ring, non-denominational ceremony. For many of those in attendance it became one of the most elegant, glamorous and romantic wedding ceremonies they had ever witnessed...

The reverend slowly began to speak..."Dearly beloved...we are gathered here today to join this man and this woman in Holy Matrimony under the eyes of GOD...and as authorized under the laws of the State of Michigan...Do you, Melvin Terry Stanton...take thee, Kelly Yvonne Millard...to be your lawfully wedded wife?"

"Yes...I do."

"And do you, Kelly Yvonne Millard...take thee, Melvin Terry Stanton...to be your lawfully wedded husband?"

"I do."

"Please state your vows to each other as you place the rings on each other's finger...Melvin?"

Mel turned to face Kelly as the best man nervously handed him the ring. Mel stared into Kelly's blue eyes lovingly as he spoke..."Kelly, dearest...please accept my vows of everlasting love for the rest of our lives...no matter what may happen...in sickness and in health, richer or poorer...my love for you shall endure through victories and defeats, good times and bad times...and you shall always be the only one in my heart...til death do us part."

Mel placed the ring on Kelly's finger. She looked deep into his eyes and spoke in a slight whisper..."Mel, my love...my vow of love for you is forever and a day...it comes from the depth of my heart and soul and it's strength shall overcome all obstacles in sickness or in health, richer or poorer...I shall always love you and remain yours until death do us part."

Kelly placed the ring on Mel's finger. They both turned and faced the reverend

"Does anyone know of any reason why these two should not be married?.." the reverend asked, pausing. "Who gives this woman away?"

"I do." Kelly's father said, proudly.

"Then under the powers vested in me by the State of Michigan...I now pronounce you...husband and wife...You may kiss your bride."

Mel turned and embraced Kelly, planting a series of deep kisses on her mouth and holding her tightly. The crowd sighed in relief as everyone rose from their seats and friends and family gathered around the happy couple to congratulate them. The couple slowly moved back down the crowded aisle to join their guests at an elegant sit-down dinner. After the dinner the newlyweds danced the first dance in the mansion's gigantic ballroom. They cut the first slice from a four foot tall, three hundred pound, three tier, nine layer cake

Later, they entertained their wedding guests with a reception in the ballroom attended by a number of big-name celebrities and professional and college basketball, football and baseball players and coaches. Just before they left for their honeymoon in the Caribbean, Kelly threw the bouquet of flowers in a strike...directly to Kim...

That evening, after hundreds of guests had dispersed and left in small groups, Patricia sat at the table in the stylishly modern kitchen and sighed as Connie set a cup of steaming hot coffee in front of her.

"Sit down, Connie...I know you're tired, too." Patricia said.

"I been tired ever since they said they was gettin' married," Connie said as she sat down across from Patricia, "but wasn't that the best little ol' weddin' you ever saw!"

"Yes...it was really something," Patricia agreed. "I wanna thank you, Connie...everything went so smooth."

"And that little Kim wearin' that big ol' rock...they set a date yet?"

Before Patricia could answer, Karen walked into the kitchen and poured herself a cup of coffee. She silently joined them at the table. Patricia looked at her and smiled..."You certainly caught the mens' eyes in that sexy gown...you look beautiful, dear," Patricia said.

"What a fabulous wedding!" Karen said. "I bet you two are proud."

"Connie ran the show...you can thank her."

"Thanks, Connie...you always come through," Karen said, turning back to her mother. "What do you think of Kim's fiancee?"

"MMMmmm!..That's the prettiest man I ever saw," Connie said.

"I don't know...he seems to be nice," Patricia said, thoughtfully. "We'll see how it goes."

Karen stirred her coffee, quietly..."Mom...I want to talk to you about something."

Connie quickly stood up to leave. "I'll leave you two to yourselves."

After Connie had left the kitchen, Karen turned back to Patricia with a serious expression on her face. "You feel like answering a few questions?"

"Not now...I know what you're going to ask," Patricia replied, annoyed, "and...and this isn't the right time. We still have a few guests left."

"No...it's not that...I just want to know if he was here tonight."

"Why...what difference would it make?" Patricia snapped. "Let's discuss this tomorrow."

"OK...I'll drop it for now," Karen relented. "But what's this I hear about dad running for mayor?"

"That's true...I think he will if those people are willing to support him all the way."

"I thought that's why they asked him to run."

"Well you know your father," Patricia replied. "If he runs he wants to run on his terms, not theirs."

"How did they respond to that?"

"According to your dad...they cornered him today before the wedding and he laid it all out for them...The ball's in their court now...he's waiting for them. He outlined his program...it's up to them to give him their unqualified support...or he won't run."

Karen bit her lower lip, thoughtfully. "Has he given any thought to who's going to run the newspaper if he runs for mayor?"

"If he runs...I think he'll probably rely more on Gene II, Roger...you and Liz," Patricia answered.

"Oh?..We're going to rule by committee?"

"Why...you have something else mind?"

"No...only, don't you think it's time he gave his children more authority in the business?" Karen asked

"I suppose you want to be named General Manager," Patricia replied, sarcastically, "that would go over with your brother like a lead brick in a swimming pool!"

"I just thought...since Gene II is all involved with his divorce, maybe he wouldn't mind being relieved of some of that responsibility."

"He and Susan aren't divorced yet...they're just separated. They may still get back together."

"I doubt that," Karen snapped. "They certainly didn't look like it today."

"Besides, even if your father does run for mayor he won't become involved in campaigning for at least a couple of months. The election isn't until next year, we've got plenty of time to make that decision."

"I just wanted you to know, mother, that I would like to be considered for the position of General Manager," Karen said, I know I could do the job...with no hang-ups"

"You implying that Gene II or Liz may have hang-ups?"

"Well...no, only Gene II may become involved in a nasty divorce...and...and Liz is involved with Ze-Ze."

"You call that a hang-up?" Patricia asked, plainly irritated. "I don't think so...I'd say if anybody had a hang-up its you."

"Why, because I want to know my true parentage?..You can resolve that one in a hot second."

"If I remember correctly, you were almost divorced a few months ago."

"That's all in the past, mother," Karen said. "Robert and I are getting along just fine, thank you."

Karen suddenly stopped talking, got up and walked across the kitchen, closing the door. She walked back over to Patricia and stared down at her.

"He was here today wasn't he?" she asked, firmly. "In this house...and he knows who I am doesn't he?"

"I told you we'd discuss this later."

"Who is it, mom?" Karen demanded, angrily. "Is it Bill Clark...or Dan Jordan?..Both of these men have known me all of my life!"

Before Patricia could respond, Kim suddenly bounded through the kitchen door, laughing loudly as Vic Martin charged in after her. Karen angrily glared at them both!.. Kim stopped, thinking she may have intruded on a serious conversation.

"Oops!..I'm sorry...I didn't know anyone was in here!...Are we intruding or something?" Kim asked.

Patricia was relieved and smiled at the two lovers graciously. "No, dear...you and Vic are welcome to sit down and join us...Would you like some coffee...and talk?"

"That sounds great, Mrs. Stanton," Vic said, grinning. "Maybe you and Karen can explain why your youngest daughter was dancing with all those basketball players at the reception...I felt like I was lost in a forest of giant trees!"

"Yeah, sure...why don't you two sit down," Karen said, obviously disappointed, "I'll get you some coffee."

Karen slowly got up and poured the coffee, rolling her eyes at her mother. Kim and Vic continued giggling and laughing as he reached around her shoulders and tickled her ribs. Patricia smiled at them. Karen suddenly looked up at her mother seriously as if she suddenly remembered something.

"Where's dad?" Karen asked. "Mr. Jordan is still sitting in the library waiting to talk to him."

"He is?..I thought he had left," Patricia replied, surprised. "I better go out there."

Karen quickly placed two cups of coffee on the kitchen table and stepped right in front of Patricia as she stood up to leave...

"No, mother...I'll go," Karen said, sternly, "you stay here and calm these two down before their hormones get out of control."

Just as Karen turned to leave, Gene and Robert walked into the kitchen. They stopped Karen from leaving as Gene spread out his arms..."See...I told you they'd all be in the kitchen...running their mouths and drinking coffee."

"Dad...did you know Mr. Jordan has been sitting in the library waiting to speak to you?" Karen asked as Robert kissed her on the cheek.

Gene hurriedly walked into the library and held out his hand to Dan Jordan who stood up and shook Gene's hand firmly. Gene was very apologetic..."Dan...I'm sorry...I wasn't aware that you were here waiting to see me."

"No problem...I understand...it was a hectic day...Let me congratulate you on a beautiful ceremony and thanks for inviting me. They looked like a couple really in love."

"Yeah, they are," Gene said, smiling, "they've been going together since they were both freshman at Michigan. Love at first sight I guess...What can I do for you, Dan?"

Before Dan could reply, Roger and Janet Carlson walked into the library followed by Michelle. Roger noticed Dan and stopped.

Oh, I'm sorry...I did'nt know you had company, Gene."

"No problem, Mr. Carlson," Dan said, smiling, "it can wait."

"Thank you, Mr. Jordan," Roger said, turning to Gene. "We're about to leave and Janet and I just wanted to let you know that we think it would be great if you ran for mayor!"

"Thanks, but it's not certain, yet," Gene said, grinning, "I may or may not, but thanks for your vote of confidence."

"You gonna run for mayor, Gene?" Dan asked, alarmed. "Damn!..That's the best news I've heard all year!..I'll support you one hundred percent!"

"What do you mean it's not certain?" Janet asked, disappointed.

"I'll only run under certain conditions," Gene answered. "I don't wanna stick my neck out there and not have any grass root support."

"Did you tell that group of people today how you felt?" Janet asked.

"You bet I did...I'm just waiting for their response."

"That's the right way to start off," Roger said. "You know you can count on us, don't you?..Anyway we can help...we will!"

"How have you been, Michelle?" Gene asked. "I saw you dancing with all of those sports jocks today...did you enjoy youself?"

"I sure did, Mr. Stanton," Michelle answered, "it was beautiful,"

"Have you heard about our good luck?" Roger asked.

"Good luck...what's happened?" Gene asked.

"Roger and I passed our tests for in vitro fertilization," Janet replied, proudly.

"Yeah, Patricia told me about that...It couldn't happen to better people...Congratulations," Gene said.

"And that's not all," Janet said, anxiously. "Michelle has agreed to be our host mother...she's going to carry our baby!"

Gene grinned broadly and walked around his desk to Janet and Roger. He hugged Janet warmly and shook Roger's hand. Roger beamed, proudly. Gene turned to Michelle and smiled at her. "Thank you, Michelle, for making my dear, dear friends so happy...I love these two people very much and I'll never forget what you're doing for them...Thank you."

Roger, Janet and Michelle said their goodnights and quickly left. Gene closed the door to the library and turned back to Dan Jordan. "Can I get you a drink, Dan?" Gene asked.

"Yes...I need a drink...scotch and water on the rocks," Dan said as he rubbed his brow with a worried expression on his face.

Gene poured two drinks, handed one to Dan and sat down behind his desk, studying Dan thoughtfully.

"What's the problem?..You look troubled."

Dan took a sip of his drink and paused before he began.

"I'm in a deep mess...You've known me for almost thirty years and I've always played it straight."

"Is it your funeral homes?" Gene asked, concerned. "I thought they were doing great...I understand you've got about four or five branch offices now."

"Yeah...the business is going great...too great!"

"What's happened?"

"The Drug Enforcement Agency...They're about to arrest me!"

Gene became visibly upset and leaned across his desk towards Dan. "Why in the hell would the D.E.A. want to arrest you?"

"To be honest with you, Gene...I should've known better when the branches kept showing these big profits every month."

"What was really going on?"

"Each branch was showing sizeable profits so I didn't supervise them too closely...I thought they were doing that much business, but whenever I went by there...they were just doing the normal amount of business...nothing else was going on."

"What did the books show?"

"That they were doing good business...I had no complaints so I let it ride...hell, I was turning a pretty good profit."

"When did you become suspicious?"

"My branch managers began ordering these real expensive caskets from some Miami manufacturer...the costs were reasonable but we could've beat it by ordering the same units from Ohio with a twenty percent discount."

"Why didn't they?"

"I thought they were...but then I found out they were still ordering the same units from Miami but at Ohio prices with the twenty percent discount...I didn't complain because I was still showing big profits...I couldn't understand why all these poor people in those run-down neighborhoods wanted these high priced units...until one day I get a visit from a D.E.A. inspector...he takes me over to one of my branches. They had just received a shipment of caskets from Miami and he and I went down into the basement and opened up the crates."

"What'd you find?"

Dan rubbed his forehead nervously and downed his drink. "It was amazing!..I still can't believe it...but the entire unit...beneath the satin lining...was stuffed with packages of cocaine!"

"They were smuggling cocaine in the lining of the caskets?" Gene asked

"Not all of them...I'd say about every other one. The D.E.A. had been watching all of my branches for some time."

"Wait a minute...I don't understand, Dan...Why would the D.E.A. want to arrest you?"

"Because I refused to set up a sting for them."

"Well...why didn't you agree to work with them?" Gene asked. "It seems to me that would be the way to get you off the proverbial hook."

"Because the guys pushing these drugs are international terrorists!" Dan replied, nervously. "I was warned that if I tried to work with the D.E.A...I was a dead man!"

"How'd they know about the D.E.A.?"

"I...I was careless...I made a big mistake," Dan answered, avoiding Gene's eyes in shame. "You know...I've tried to be an equal opportunity employer and many of my funeral homes are located in poor, Hispanic neighborhoods,...So, naturally, I tried to hire more Hispanics to run the homes. One of my most profitable homes was in southwest Detroit...It was doing more business than all the others put together. I had hired this Hispanic woman to manage it...I thought I could trust her...She was beautiful and smart...did everything the way I wanted it done...and I fell in love with her."

"And you told her about the D.E.A.?"

"That was the biggest mistake I ever made!"

Gene got up and began pacing the room, thoughtfully. He stopped walking and stared at Dan..."What's this woman's name?" Gene asked.

"Theresa...Theresa Gonzalez."

"How does she really feel about you?"

"Gosh, Gene...I...I don't know...The other night she began to act cold towards me."

"What do you mean?"

"It wasn't really Theresa...it was her brother who threatened me," Dan said, nervously.

"What'd he say?"

"He said he'd blow my brains out...and wipe out my entire family if I tried to work with the Drug Enforcement Agency!"

DONALD WILSON

Chapter Twenty-Seven

The woman was so attractive as she strutted down the long sidewalk in front of The Detroit Herald Newspaper building that she actually stopped traffic. Car horns blew and wolf whistles shrieked down the street, following her as she headed towards the big revolving doors leading into the lobby of The Herald. The woman wore a low cut , pink tank top, a short, tight red mini skirt and red high heel pumps. Her long, blond pony tail bounced jauntily as she accentuated the movements of her well developed hips with each step. She carried a large purse, almost the size of an overnight bag, slung over her shoulder. Every passerby looked at the woman admiringly as she walked into the lobby with the loud clicking of her high heels striking the asphalt floor signaling her approach.

In side the lobby, everyone turned their heads and stared at her as she quickly marched up the two steps towards the security guard's desk, pulled out her wallet and flashed her identification. She waited impatiently as the guard glanced at her identification and then looked back up at the woman with a startled expression on his face. She snatched the I.D. and put it back inside her purse as she quickly stepped on to the elevator behind the guard.

When the elevator door slid open on the third floor, the woman stepped out and continued strutting down the hallway with breasts bouncing and her hips swaying suggestively. Other employees walking by stared in awe as she entered the woman's rest room. In a few minutes, the restroom door slowly cracked opened and Michelle Matthews, timidly walked out with a confused expression on her face. She paused long enough to straighten out her long skirt and heavy turtle neck sweater. She wore flat heels and carried a large handbag as she slowly walked down the hall to Janet Carlson's office.

Michelle sat across from Janet's desk with a passive expression on her face as Janet finished speaking on the phone and glared at Michelle, Disapprovingly. Michelle stared back at her, puzzled...

"Is...is something wrong?" Michelle asked.

"I was just speaking to Joyce Cambell, your supervisor," Janet said, sternly, "she said you were late again this morning."

"I'm...I'm sorry."

"You seem to be having a lot of problems lately...is there something I can do to help you?"

"Help me what?"

Janet got up and walked around her desk, thoughtfully. She sat down in a chair next to Michelle and placed a hand on top of her's. Janet was concerned..."Are you feeling alright?...Is this too much for you to handle?"

"No...I'm OK...The reason why I was late...I saw the doctor this morning."

"Is that where you were?..Why didn't you tell me?"

Michelle shrugged her shoulders shoulders, nonchalantly..."Nothing to tell...she said I was doin' just fine...and that the implant took."

"It took?" Janet was surprised.

"That's what the doctor said," Michelle answered. "So I guess I'm pregnant."

"You're pregnant?" Janet cried out, happily. Why didn't you say so!..Oh, Michelle, I'm so happy!"

Janet hugged Michelle tightly. Michelle looked at her and smiled. "Isn't this what you and Roger wanted?" she asked, calmly." I'm happy for the both of you...you've been so nice to me."

"What about your overall health?..Is everything OK?"

"She said I was as healthy as a horse...No problems."

"Should you be working?"

"I guess...she didn't say one way or another."

"Roger's gonna be thrilled!" Janet said, anxiously.

"I'm gonna call him right now...we'll have lunch today...all three of us."

Michelle smiled coyly as Janet reached for the phone.

Gene Stanton smiled as Congressman Ghetts and City Councilman Bill Clark strolled into his office at The Herald. Both men had big grins on their faces. Gene stood up and shook their hands..."I can tell from the looks of you two...I'm gonna be busy for a while," Gene laughed.

"You got that right," Bill Clark said, chuckling. "We've all discussed your economic platform...I've been getting calls late at night and early in the morning...Gene Stanton...you're costing a good man a lot of sleep."

"I like it...We all like it!" Congressman Ghetts said. "The only question I've been getting from everybody is why haven't we ever done anything like this in the past?"

"Because most politicians are not creative people," Gene answered. "No offense and present company is excepted, but this is generally a fact of life...Politicans are almost compelled to be ultra-conservative in order to insure their re-election. They're too afraid to rock the boat with new innovations such as this because they might fail. Especially here in Detroit...we've always had the auto industry and auto related businesses to rely on...If it wasn't that it was fat federal handouts...As a result, anybody could run for office and they usually did."

"That's why our city's been going down hill ever since the conservative administrations cut off aid to the cities," Bill Clark said. "Crimes, been going up and businesses have been moving out."

"That's precisely why I had to have your grass root group's support," Gene said, "I'm proposing that we take a giant economical commitment to turn this city around and I can't do it without your strong support."

"What about the other cities across the country, Gene?" Ghetts asked, thoughtfully, "I wonder where they'll turn?"

"All they can do is hope that the administration will increase urban handouts," Bill Clark said, "if they don't they're in deep trouble."

"It's not a good situation...if these urban areas have no where to turn to raise revenue..it could signal the demise of a way of life that was once the nucleus of this country's strength," Gene said, sadly. "Third world countries are siphoning off our jobs...retailers are moving to the suburbs and the cities are being left high and dry...That's why Detroit is fortunate to have this unique and beautiful little island just off our coast...we can take a natural resource and make it the hub of our cities' rebirth."

"What's the answer for the other cities, Gene?" Ghetts asked, "this cancer is spreading all across the country and it's creating a modern American apartheid with the cities becoming almost ninety percent Black and Hispanic, surrounded by suburban areas that are over eighty percent White...this is terrible."

"There's only one answer and that answer is a Federal Full Employment Bill," Gene said. "Eleanor Roosevelt first presented a Full Employment proposal to the Democratic National Convention in 1924...they ignored her and five years later we had the great depression in 1929...Employment should be a given right of every American citizen. The only problem is that the people who pass these laws are employed and they simply cannot empathize with people who are out of work...consequently, if you check your vital statistics you'll find that unemployment is the specter lurking behind high crime rates, violence and perpetuating racism. Just examine the areas of high crime stats such as violence and drugs and you'll find that those statistics are synonymous with high unemployment rates...everyone knows this is true...they just don't give a damn!..Many of the conservative politicians in Washington DC were raised on farms, educated in small towns and attended colleges located in small towns. The only times they've ever even visited a city is when they were passing through or for political rallies. They know nothing about city life except from exaggerated tales in movies and books...and in truth, they could care less what happens in the cities...Until this problem is resolved, it's gonna get worse. As an example, over seventy-five percent of criminals who are arrested for committing a crime are unemployed when they commit the crime!..Americans want a better quality of life and they want to work to earn it, but if they're deprived of employment because some big, rich company sends their jobs overseas for cheaper labor...lookout!..The crime rate is gonna escalate!..I believe it is up to the federal government to work with private industry and the labor unions to enact a strong, cogent Federal Full Employment Bill that will put Americans to work, control inflation, reduce crime, violence and drugs plus stabilize our national economy...Just think there are presently ten million Americans who are considered unemployed at a 6.5 percent unemployment rate . There are another eight million Americans whose unemployment benefits have expired and they are no longer counted. If these 18 million Americans were given jobs this would amount to over $50 billion dollars going into our federal treasury in the form of income tax each year!...What a unique way to pay off the deficit!..Our welfare rolls would decrease substantially, our prison populations would diminish and every American would have a better quality of life!"

"That's incredible!" Bill Clark said, anxiously. "Why hasn't anyone picked up this "Full Employment "banner and presented to the people?"

"That's something we never hear about anymore," Ghetts said, thoughtfully, "I'm gonna look into that."

"The country better do something soon or it's in deep trouble...if the major cities fail, the suburbs will be right behind them," Gene said. "Do you realize if all of those people, 18 million, were put to work...Every business would make more money and our nation would become much stronger morally and economically!..The answer isn't in building more prisons...it's in building better people!"

"How do you plan to initiate the Belle Isle project, Gene?" Bill Clark asked.

"After I'm elected I'll submit a proposal for a referendum on this Belle Isle Theme park," Gene answered. "We'll let the people vote on it."

"When do you plan to contact these businesses to see if they're interested?" Bill Clark asked.

"I have to make it official that I am running for Mayor. After that I'll talk to them about my program," Gene answered. "Once one of the major players come aboard I think the rest of them will fall into place."

"I know you, Gene," Ghetts chuckled, "and I'm sure you've already tested the waters."

"That's true...and it looks encouraging."

"How do you think the state and federal government will respond to the Belle Isle Theme Park?" Ghetts asked.

"Very favorable...In fact I expect to get some subsistence from each of them to have this project successfully launched...I think they both will have key representatives at the ground breaking," Gene said, confidently, "you see anytime a city like Detroit can turn around from being a liability to becoming an asset...they'll get behind us because it not only gives them a project they can share the credit on...it also provides them with an answer to fiscal problems many other cities are having without putting them in the untenable position of raising taxes...As it is, both the state and federal government stand to earn huge taxes from the success of this venture...In addition, it enhances their own personal reasons to be re-elected."

"How can we help?" Bill asked. "I'd like to be a part of this."

"Get me elected and you will be," Gene replied, quickly. "I believe we should get maximum support for this program and business expertise is mandatory prerequisite if we are to be successful...All of you politicians can make sure you solicit your constituents to support this project...It means the life or death of our city!"

"What about the average Detroiter?" Ghetts asked. "What can each citizen do to give this project legs?"

"Each school student can become involved by paying twenty-five cents per brick to have the castle imported from Scotland or England," Gene answered, smiling. "Families that are interested in applying for the two years of free college education can put in their application through a coupon we'll run in The Herald...This would not only give us a viable list to began working from after the project is complete, but it will also provide us with an unlimited list of voters who support the Belle Isle Theme Park...as well as my candidacy!...This will put additional pressure on the state and federal governments to lend their support and amend the charter to allow this city to become involved in this kind of enterprise."

"This is an excellent plan," Bill said," have you given any thought to gaining the support of the Detroit Police Officer's Association?"

"I plan on increasing the strength of the police department from it's present thirty-eight hundred officers to ten thousand police officers within a three year period," Gene replied. "Do you think they'll support me?..Of course they will."

"I think you're right," Bill said, thoughtfully, "and that would also include the support of the fire department and the city employees...You're giving them job security and that's something they haven't had in twenty years."

"Have you thought about a campaign manager?" Ghetts asked.

"No, not really...it wasn't one of my priorities at that particular time," Gene answered.

"How does your family feel about it?" Bill asked.

"You mean my wife?" Gene asked. "Pat...my daughters and my sons...they're all for it...of course many of them expect to work on my campaign, but it may be too difficult since their responsibilities at the newspaper will be expanded when I began campaigning. Pat's still involved with the Anti-Racism Committee which I believe is extremely important, especially with me running for mayor...I haven't given too much thought about a campaign manager...If either of you have any recommendations...I'll be glad to consider them."

"What about that reporter we met at the wedding?" Ghetts asked. "You know...Dr. Grant...She's familiar with most of the local politicians from working at the City-County Building...I was very impressed with her."

Gene looked at Congressman Ghetts and slightly smiled as he considered the idea...

"Yeah, ...she's a good looking woman and smarter 'n hell!" Bill Clark said. "It works for me."

"Yes...she is very impressive," Gene agreed. "I'll take it under consideration."

Joe Stanton sat across from his father's desk in the publisher's office at The Detroit Herald. He shook his head and smiled at Gene. "I just can't get over it...Mel's a married man...I gotta give you credit, dad...you and mom really know how to throw a party."

"It's good to get those two squared away," Gene chuckled. "I think it's a great move for both of them."

Joe became serious as he leaned closer to Gene's desk. "What's this trouble Dan Jordan's got himself involved in?"

Gene got up, walked over and closed the office door. He slowly walked back behind his desk, thoughtfully. "How long you gonna be here before you return to Washington?"

"Why...you got something you want me to do?"

"Maybe...Can you stretch out your visit here for awhile?"

"For a few days, dad...What's up?"

"I might need your help on this Dan Jordan situation," Gene answered. "Not only is he an old friend of the family, he use to be my best buddy...now he's gotten himself into some trouble. The D.E.A. is threatening to arrest him if he doesn't cooperate with them."

"The Drug Enforcement Agency?..What's he done?"

"He got tied up with one of his branch managers and fell in love...then somebody starts smuggling cocaine up from Miami to Detroit by hiding it in the lining of the caskets...The D.E.A. found out about it and they're blaming Dan because he's the owner of the funeral homes. They told him the only way he can avoid being arrested is by working out a sting operation with the D.E.A. to bust the whole ring wide open."

"So?...What's his problem?" Joe asked. "This happens everyday."

"When this smuggling first surfaced, Dan didn't know who was running it...so when the D.E.A. made him this offer, he told the woman about it."

"And she was the one behind it in the first place!" Joe said, disgustedly. "How dumb is this guy?"

"It's deeper than that...it seems the woman's brother is one of the main forces running this drug organization...he cornered Dan in his office and told him that if he tried to run a sting with the D.E.A...he was a dead man!"

"Sounds pretty tough!"

"That's why I called you...Dan got himself between a rock and a hard place...it's either jail or a slab in the morgue!"

Joe suddenly became angry..."What'd he come to you for?...Damn!...You're gettin' ready to run for mayor and this jerk shows up!..You can't get involved in this mess!"

"He's an old friend...we've known each other since high school...went to college together," Gene replied, solemnly. "He thought I might have some connections with the feds...do I, Joe?"

"What the hell can I do?" Joe snapped, angrily. "Isn't Dan Jordan still married?..What's he doin' messing around with his branch manager in the first place?"

"That's not the point...we're not here to judge his morals...I'm trying to help an old friend out of a mess."

"OK!..OK!..I'll make a call to Carlos Cortez at the D.E.A...I'm sure he probably knows all about this...but don't be surprised if this long-time family friend has been tellin' you a pack of lies!"

Joe got up and walked angrily towards the door. He turned back to Gene, thoughtfully...Gene looked up at him.

"Is there something else, Joe?"

"You know what, dad?" Joe said, smiling. "You're a pretty nice guy."

"Thanks, son."

Yeah...I'll see what I can do and I'll get back to you this afternoon...If Dan calls just tell' em you're workin' on it...no details, please."

"I knew I could depend on you," Gene said, grinning.

Karen and Willard were deeply engrossed in an advertising tabloid layout spread out on top of her desk in her office at The Herald. Karen looked up at Willard with a sparkle in her eyes. "You said this is the first time United Department Stores has ran a series of advertising tabloids this size?"

"I checked their ledger with their accountant for the last five years," Willard said, eagerly, "they've averaged a one million line contract each year...but now they've got new owners and they're increasing their advertising linage to two and a half million lines for each daily newspaper."

"Each newspaper?..The Herald and the Press?" Karen asked, surprised. "Then they're talkin' five million lines!"

"And at an average of seven dollars per line...that's thirty-five million dollars!" Willard exclaimed.

Karen leaned back in her her chair, thoughtfully. She looked up at Willard and smiled. "When did you pick this up?" Karen asked.

"I had an appointment with their ad department this morning...I just got back and I thought you should see it first...this is big time, Karen."

"Does anyone else in the advertising department know about this?"

"They knew I had the appointment, but they don't know any of the details."

"When is this campaign scheduled to begin?"

"More then two months from now...they're waiting for the final itemized prices on the merchandise," Willard said. "We're all sworn to secrecy so nobody can undercut their anniversary sale prices."

"Good...don't tell anyone here at The Herald....not just yet," Karen said, thoughtfully.

"You look like you're plotting something."

"You're new here...how'd you get such a big account so fast?"

Willard thought about it for awhile..."I dunno...I guess it's because I'm the publisher's nephew."

Karen got up and began pacing towards Willard and snapped her finger..."This is it!"

"What?"

"Don't you see?..This is our chance to start squaring accounts...and with dad running for mayor...it offers us a perfect opportunity."

"How?..I can't see how we can use this...United has already decided to use both newspapers...and Uncle Gene hasn't even made it official that he's running."

"Think, Willard...Think!...We may not be able to use this particular ad campaign, but when dad does make it official we'll know exactly how to initiate our plans."

"I still don't follow you."

"Just pass all of these kinds of advertising campaigns by me before you show it to anyone else...I'll hold on to this until someone asks for it...When are you planning to meet with Dugas again?"

"All I have to do is call him...he wants me to meet my half brother, Douglas...who's recovering in the hospital from some accident he had...I already know Marcy...she seems really nice."

"Do they know who you really are?"

"Do chickens have lips?"

"Good...let's keep it like that," Karen said, "and when you meet with Dugas I want to make him an offer he can't refuse."

Karen slowly sat back down behind her desk with a sly smile on her face as Willard stared at her, confused.

Michelle and the Carlsons finished their dinner in the plush downtown restaurant and all three of them were beaming. Roger wore a big grin on his face, ear to ear.

"Michelle...I don't think we can ever thank you enough," Roger said, "you've made us both very happy."

"This is one of the best days of our lives and we owe it all to you,' Janet said.

"I'm glad I can have the baby for you," Michelle said. "I understand this is becoming quite normal...all across the country."

"That's true," Roger said, "have you been reading up on this subject?"

"A little," Michelle answered.

"We'd like to do something meaningful for you, dear," Janet said. "I know you said we didn't have to, but we'd like to pay your college tuition or something...Some of these host mothers are charging as much as ten thousand dollars...have you thought about that?"

"I'm glad you brought that up," Michelle answered, "I've been thinking about it all day."

Roger was surprised. "You have?"

"What did you decide, dear?" Janet asked.

"I know you've been very nice to me...letting me live in your house, getting me a job and everthing."

"That's no problem, " Roger said, "that's why we offered to pay you when you first volunteered to be our host mother."

"But that was before we knew I could become pregnant, Roger," Michelle said, nonchalantly, "it's all changed now...I am pregnant with your child."

Roger stared at Michelle as he felt her hand squeezing his knee. He quickly moved his knee away.

"What do you think we should do, Michelle?" Janet asked.

Michelle slowly sipped her lemonade, eyeing Roger over the rim of her glass in a seductive manner. "They said I shouldn't drink or smoke while I'm carrying the baby...did you know that?...There's so many rules and regulations it could really put a strain on my entire life...I can't do this and I shouldn't do that...a girl could really get confused and do something that might harm the baby, you know what I mean?"

"What would you like for us to do ?" Roger asked.

"Well...I think I should be paid for doing this for you. I am risking my body and my mind," Michelle replied, looking down at her glass.

"That sounds reasonable," Roger said, "I can go along with that.'

"What amount are you thinking about?" Janet asked. "Ten thousand dollars?...Fifteen?"

"Delivering a baby can be extremely painful," Michelle answered, "it could change my figure for life."

"What amount have you decided upon?" Janet asked.

"I was thinking...fifty thousand dollars," Michelle replied, cooly, "twenty-five thousand now and twenty-five thousand upon delivery!"

Chapter Twenty-Eight

Douglas Dugas had been released from the hospital with a clean bill of health. The hospital psychiatrist and Julia Dugas had convinced F. Walton Dugas to give Douglas a viable position at The Daily Press Newspaper to bolster his self-esteem. F. Walton was reluctant at first because he had arranged for Douglas to be accepted at one of the most prestigious law firms in the state shortly after he graduated from law school, but that relationship was destroyed when Douglas was caught having sex with the firm's receptionist in the law library. Dugas relinquished his vowed decision to never allow Douglas into The Daily Press Building when he almost lost him to the suicide attempt.

Today, F. Walton Dugas, followed by his son, son walked briskly into the Daily Press' general manager's office. The receptionist quickly got up and opened a door to her boss' inner office. Dugas and his son marched right into the office as a bespectacled, heavy set man sitting behind a wide, executive desk, slowly stood up...

"Harvey...this is my son, Douglas," Dugas said, curtly. "He's going to be your assistant."

Harvey was stunned..."What?"

"You got a problem with that?" Dugas challenged.

Harvey answered, barely able to control his anger. "Does he have any experience?"

"Yeah, me...I'm his experience," Dugas snapped back. "I want you to take him under your wing and teach him the ropes...he just got out the hospital so take it easy...Every place you go...every meeting...every decision...I want you to have him sit in on it...you understand?"

Douglas took off his glasses and cleaned them with a napkin from Harvey's desk as Harvey glared at him over Dugas' shoulder.

"I think we'll work together very well, Harvey," Douglas said, smiling, "I don't think we'll have any trouble at all."

"Wh..when does he plan to start?" Harvey asked, nervously.

"He'll be with me the rest of the day," Dugas answered. "I want to personally introduce him to the staff and department heads...he may wind up being the publisher one day...so work with him."

"I understand, Mr. Dugas...I'll have his office set up down the hall."

"Hell no!..I want his office next to yours so he'll be in close contact with you!" Dugas ordered, angrily.

"But I got Steve Simmons next to me," Harvey protested. "He's been my assistant for two years!"

"So now you got two assistants...just move Simmons out of his office to another one...move him down the hall. He'll understand...if he doesn't have him see me!"

"I'd appreciate it, Harvey, " Douglas said, calmly. "This way I'd have a better opportunity to learn from you."

"This may not be the best time to do this, Mr. Dugas,' Harvey said, thoughtfully.

"Why not?" Dugas asked.

"Union negotiations are coming up in a few weeks," Harvey replied, "we're gonna be busy as hell!"

"Good!..That's what I want!" Douglas said, anxiously. "I wanna learn all about those unions!"

"Baptism under fire!..That'll be great!" Dugas agreed. "I couldn't have selected a better time to do this...Here's what I want you to do for me Harv...get Douglas one of the best secretaries you got...someone who will help him learn this business from the ground up."

"Yeah...OK, Mr. Dugas...I"ll do my best."

Dugas stared at Harvey without saying anything. Harvey could feel his shirt collar becoming tighter.

"Something wrong with you, Harv?" Dugas asked. "You look like hell!"

"No...I'll...I'll be alright," Harvey replied, hoarsely. "Just been workin' hard the last few days."

"That's why I'm giving you my son to work with you...He'll take some of the load off your back and help you get ready to battle those unions," Dugas said with confidence. "Then we're all set now...Douglas will be here at nine in the morning tomorrow...ready to go to work."

"Yeah, great...I'll be waiting." Harvey mumbled, unhappily.

"Thank you, Harv," Douglas said, politely. "It'll be good working with you."

Dugas and his son quickly left the office. A few moments after the office door had closed and Harvey was sure Dugas was out of earshot, he stood up, picked up a waste paper basket and hurled it across the office, striking the closed door with a resounding bang!..

Gene Stanton sat on the front of his desk and embraced Adrian tightly, kissing her passionately as she squirmed excitedly in his arms. She broke the kiss, sighing deeply and leaning back in his arms. She stared at him and smiled..."I haven't seen you in two whole days...what's gonna happen when you run for mayor?" she asked, huskily.

"I could have you working on my campaign...would you like that?"

"Really...as what?"

"You think you could manage my campaign?"

Adrian tighten her grip around his neck, pushing her body against his. She brought his head down closer to her and kissed him long and sensual, her tongue lingering his mouth eagerly. She stopped and stepped backwards.

"I've never managed a campaign before.'

"So?..I've never ran for mayor before...if you're willing, then I'm willing."

She kissed him again, letting her tongue trace his lips, lightly. "Won't somebody become suspicious about our relationship...being more that just a candidate and a campaign manager?"

"Hey....it wasn't my idea," Gene replied, innocently. "Congressman Ghetts already nominated you for the position. I happen to think he's got great taste."

"But...what about your family?"

"They're all too busy managing their own little lives instead of managing my campaign...Besides, you're better qualified...You've been dealing with all those political types at the City-County Building...You know 'em all and who's doin' what to whom...and you have a P.H.D...I'd say you're damn better qualified than most...and that's without mentioning your best asset!"

Adrian kissed him lightly on the nose, chuckling softly. "You dirty old man."

Gene glanced at his watch and quickly stood up straight. "Hey...it's getting late...Joe will be her any minute."

Adrian picked up her briefcase and prepared to leave. "Shall I put the brandy and benedictine on ice?" she asked.

"You're my brandy and benedictine."

"What time shall I expect you?"

"As soon as I get through here," Gene answered, holding her hand as she slowly walked towards the door. "That will be around eight...and I'll probably be there for a while...since we're gonna work on the campaign."

"Yes, right," she replied, laughing. "Shall I get some food?"

"Yeah surprise me...I intend to do a lot of hard work."

Adrian smiled..."Now that sounds absolutely delicious."

Gene slipped his arms around her small waist and pulled her to him. He kissed her several times, long and passionately.

"GOD, you're beautiful!" he whispered in her ear. "I love you, Adrian...I've missed you so much these last two days!"

"I know...I can tell...but I'd better leave now or it will be too damn late to stop!"

Gene reluctantly released her and she turned slowly, still looking at him as she formed her lips in a kiss and sexily walked out of the office...

Gene stood behind his desk as Joe and Carlos Cortez, an agent from the Federal Drug Enforcement Agency and and an old friend of Joe's, arrived to discuss Dan Jordan's situation. Gene shook Carlos' hand warmly.

"It's good meeting you, Carlos," Gene said, "Joe's told me a lot about you...and thanks for coming over tonight."

"I've been hearing a lot more about you, Mr. Stanton," Carlos said, chuckling, "on radio, newspapers, TV...you gonna run?"

""It's a good possibility."

"Carlos is one of the supervising agents at the Detroit headquarters of the D.E.A," Joe said. " I filled him in on most of the details surrounding Dan Jordan's funeral homes."

"Yes, Mr. Stanton...we had been wise to the drug trafficking at the Jordan's funeral homes for quite sometime," Carlos said in a matter-of-fact manner. "Dan Jordan lied to you about not knowing what Theresa Gonzalez had been doing with those caskets...don't you think a man would know if his funeral homes were making money or not...and how?"

"That's what I suspected," Gene replied, sadly.

"They weren't having any funerals or buryin' any bodies," Carlos continued. "He had to know what was going on. I think he was enjoying the woman and all that extra cash too much to think straight...the longer he put it off, the deeper he dug the hole."

"I see...Is there anything that can be done?"

"You say Theresa's brother threatened Jordan if he cooperated with us?" Carlos asked, thoughtfully.

"He said Jordan would be a dead man!" Gene replied.

"Listen...we're not interested in Dan Jordan or Theresa Gonzalez," Carlos said, "they're just small fry...they don't bring that poison into the country, they just distribute it!"..However, Theresa's brother has a direct connection to Alvarez Columbo's drug cartel."

"What kind of connection?" Joe asked.

"Alvarez Columbo is the drug lord of one of the largest drug cartels in South America...We've been trying to get to that family for years," Carlos said, exasperated. "Ricardo Montoya is Theresa's brother's close friend and also one of Columbo's lieutenants...If we can get to Montoya...we'll have a vital connection to the Columbo cartel."

"How can you get to this Montoya?" Gene asked.

"Through Theresa's brother," Carlos replied.

"What's the connection?" Joe asked.

"We know Montoya is in this area somewhere," Carlos explained, "if we can smoke him out...we'll nab him an put the squeeze on him for a line on Columbo."

"You lost me," Gene said, 'am I missing something?..How is grabbing Montoya gonna give you a connection to the drug cartel in South America?"

Carlos smiled, knowingly. "Alvarez Columbo has been with Montoya for many, many years...they are more than just friends..Once Montoya is in custody, Columbo will be willing to deal to try and get his release."

"How much is that worth to the D.E.A?" Joe asked.

"The Columbo cartel is holding two of Interpol's top agents," Carlos answered. "I've got authority to completely absolve Dan Jordan and Theresa Gonzalez of any complicity in this conspiracy...if we can get Montoya...they're both off the hook!"

"What do they have to do?" Joe asked.

"Lead us to Montoya," Carlos snapped.

"I don't think Dan Jordan is aware that some guy named Montoya even exists," Gene said.

"That's just fine...we know he exists," Carlos shot back. If Dan knew who we really wanted..."

"He'd tell Theresa and blow the whole deal!" Gene said.

"You got that right," Carlos agreed, "This is a case where what Dan doesn't know...is gonna help him...because they won't become suspicious of Dan."

"How do we smoke this...Montoya out into the open?" Joe asked.

"The key is Theresa's brother, Ramon Gonzalez," Carlos explained. "We've got to put enough pressure on him to make Montoya surface."

"How do you plan to do that?" Gene asked.

"Through you, Dan Jordan and Theresa," Carlos replied.

"They've got to let Ramon know that we've got a guy with a half ton of packaged cocaine he wants to dump."

"How's that gonna get Montoya to surface?" Gene asked.

Carlos chuckled softly..."Because that's exactly how much that was ripped off from the Columbo cartel in Miami over a month ago ...they've been lookin' for it ever since it happened...they'll think this load is theirs and they'll try to take it back...Montoya could verify that it is their shipment."

"If this doesn't work...what?" Joe asked.

"Then your dad's buddy goes to jail," Carlos answered, turning to Gene, "he, his squeeze and her brother."

"But if it's successful they're off the hook?" Gene asked.

"Not the brother...he's a bad dude and I want him off the streets," Carlos answered, "but don't give 'em any details...just tell him about it...mention that one of your crime beat reporters found out about this half ton of cocaine through the grapevine...they'll take it from there and probably contact you."

"I don't want that scum calling my dad!" Joe protested.

"Cool it, Joe...I'm a big boy," Gene said.

"Have no fear...they know who your dad is," Carlos said with confidence, "hell, everybody knows who Gene Stanton is...they'll contact him through Dan Jordan."

"When do you want this to go down?" Gene asked.

"As soon as possible...We've been after Montoya for years!" Carlos said, anxiously. "He's been a terror in Miami...if we don't nab him before he gets back to South America the deal's off...That jerk has killed more people than the bubonic plague!"

Joe turned to his father and studied his face carefully..."You sure you wanna get involved with these people, dad?" Joe asked, cautiously. "They're all killers."

"What do you mean?" Gene asked, "I'm only delivering a message...that's all."

"When do you plan to talk to Dan Jordan again?" Carlos asked.

"He's expecting me to call him tonight."

"Fine...just tell him you're working on something," Carlos said, quietly, "then casually drop the line about the half ton of smack...I'll bet he takes the bait...but make sure he understands that if you get him out of this mess this time, he'd better stop shipping those drugs and close down all of those phony funeral homes...or we'll shut all of his places down and throw his ass in the joint!"

Joe chuckled at Carlos' threat..."Let's go over this thing to make sure we understand how it's gonna work...If dad gets a response from Dan about the half-ton, you will set up the exchange, right?..How much are you asking for it?"

"Just two hundred thousand," Carlos replied, " when you steal from the dope man, you sell it back at reasonable prices or you can get dead!..Tell Jordan your reporter will arrange for somebody to call him if he's interested...and I'll set up a time and a place for the closing."

"What if Montoya doesn't show up?" Gene asked.

"We'll follow Ramon from the meet," Carlos replied.

"If Montoya is still in the Detroit area...Ramon will lead us directly to him with a half-ton of packaged cocaine!"

"Who's gonna deliver the stuff?" Joe asked.

"Me"

When Joe Stanton got home that evening he casually walked into the Stanton mansion slightly perturbed about his father having anything to do with Dan Jordan's situation...He noticed a light on in the library and out of curiosity he went into the room and found his sister, Liz, sitting at Gene's desk and sipping a cup of coffee. Liz looked up at him with a stern expression on her face...

"I've been waiting for you, Joe," she said, somberly.

"Oh, yeah...what's up?"

"Why are you still here?" Liz asked. "I thought you had to get back to Washington."

"I had a little meeting with dad in his office, why?"

"I'm concerned about your brother, Gene."

"What's wrong with Gene?"

"Don't play innocent with me!" Liz replied, angrily. "You know damn well what I'm talking about!"

"If you've got something on your mind....spit it out!"

"I'm the one who introduced you to Susan, remember?" Liz shouted. "I saw the way you two were staring at each other during the wedding!..You've been seeing her haven't you!"

"You're imagining things, Liz" Joe lied, "I have not been seeing Susan...she's my brother's wife!"

"I know who's wife she is!..I also remember how you two were clinging together before you joined the C.I.A!"

"That was then ...it all ended when she married Gene!"

"Well they're getting a divorce and it's driving him crazy!"

"Don't blame me...it's not my fault," Joe said, softly.

"Don't you even care?..You know Gene can't handle anything like that," Liz said, "I thought you would have some feelings for your own brother."

"Of course I do."

"Then don't see her anymore!" Liz pleaded. "Leave her alone and they might have a chance!"

"Listen...I told you once and I'm telling you again...I have not been seeing Susan!"

Liz calmed down and stared Joe directly in the eyes. "I spoke to Susan last night."

"And..."

"She denied she was seeing anyone."

"Then why in hell are you giving me the tenth degree?"

"Because I know better ....I think you're both liars!" Liz screamed. "I noticed how you were going out of your way to avoid each other at the wedding...you wouldn't even acknowledge one another...it was pretty obvious that something's been going on."

"You're wrong, Liz."

"The hell I am!" Liz persisted. "I know you're fucking your own brother's wife and I'm warning you...if you don't want to tear this family apart...leave her alone!"

Liz quickly got up, grabbed her purse and angrily marched towards the doorway!..She stopped and turned back to her brother, whispering in determined furor!.."I mean it, Joe...stay away from her...or else!"

Liz stormed out of the room and slammed the door behind her!..

Gene laid in the bed in Adrian's townhouse apartment and spoke to Dan Jordan over the phone while Adrian snuggled next to him, resting her head on his naked chest.

"I don't have anything concrete to tell you, Dan...my people are still working on it."

"Did they say they could do anything?" Dan asked.

"No comment...all we can do is wait, but I think we'll know something by tomorrow...By the way, one of my reporters ran across something today that'll blow your mind."

"What's that?"

"He ran across a junkie who claimed he knew where we could find a guy trying to peddle a half a ton of coke!"

"Whew!..That's a lot of dreams!"

"Yeah, that's why we figured he was just blowin' smoke up his ass," Gene said in disgust.

"What'd he say the guy was askin' for it?"

"Two hundred thousand...which only proved that he was bullshitting."

"How come you think he was just talkin' a lot of bull?..When they got hot drugs they'll drop it for just about nothin."

"Really?"

"Two hundred grand ain't a lot of money...so it must be hot," Dan replied, "that's why he's tryin' to dump it."

"Yeah, you're probably right," Gene said, quickly changing the subject. "Listen, Dan, you just relax...I'll contact you tomorrow...maybe I'll have some good news."

"Damn...I sure hope so," Dan said. "I'm depending on you, ol' buddy."

"If anything else comes up, feel free to call me," Gene said. "I wanna stay on top of this thing."

"Thanks, Gene."

"You're an old friend of the family, Dan, and I want to clear this up for you as soon as possible."

"I really appreciate everything that you're doing, Gene...and I won't forget it."

As soon as Gene hung up the phone, Adrian rolled over on top of him, smothering his face with wet kisses. He looked at her and smiled as he pulled her back down into his arms and kissed her deeply with his tongue quickly moving into her mouth.

"Hey, honey...how come you're so damn beautiful?"

"I had to be...I was custom made just for you."

Chapter Twenty-Nine

Michelle Matthews, wearing only her panties and bra, sat in front of her dresser mirror slowly arranging her long, blond hair into a conservative bun style in her bedroom at Roger and Janet Carlson' home. Suddenly, she stopped and bent her head down, dropping the comb to the floor. She rested her head on the dresser for a few moments and then quickly looked up, staring at herself in the mirror as if for the first time. She smiled at her reflection, broadly. She ran her fingers through her hair with a disapproving expression on her face. She loosened her hair, allowing it to fall down, cascading over her shoulders. Satisfied with the new hair style, she smiled as she moved a few strands of hair back in place. She turned and walked over to the bed. She frowned as she quickly picked the clothing up and hung them back inside the closet. She brought out a see through, deep cleavage blouse, a short blue mini-skirted suit and matching high heels. She happily began dressing, bouncing jovially around the room and humming a popular tune...

In the master bedroom, Roger slept lightly after a late evening at The Herald. His arm moved over to a vacant spot on the bed that Janet had occupied. He rolled over on his back and sighed deeply. He opened his eyes and glanced at the clock-radio on the nightstand. He frowned and turned over on his side, trying to go back to sleep. In a few moments he opened his eyes again and he was startled to see Michelle standing in the doorway of the bedroom, staring at him and smiling seductively!..

"Michelle...what's the matter?" he asked. "Is there something I can get you?"

"Where's Janet?..I'm ready to go to work."

Roger looked at her long, slim legs in the short mini-skirt, about six inches above her knees and grimaced in disapproval..."Like that?..You think you should wear those clothes to the office?" he asked.

She walked further into the room, turned around and strutted back and forth, modeling her outfit for him...

"Don't you like it?..I know you men," she purred. "You'll say it's not right and start licking your chops...the higher the skirt, the better...don't you think I have a nice figure?"

Roger was aghast..."What are you trying to do?" he asked. "I think you're out of line, young lady."

"Oh, c'mon...I know you men."

"That's not the point...I don't think it's appropriate, besides Janet's already left. She had an early morning meeting to attend in the Circulation Department...She said she told you about it last night."

"Oh, that's right...I forgot about that meeting."

"You seem to be forgetting a lot lately," Roger said, concerned, "but don't worry about it...I'll get up and take you to work."

Roger started to get out of bed but hesitated when he realized that Michelle wasn't moving.

"You don't have to...I can drive myself and either Janet or I can pick you up this afternoon...that way you can stay home and get your rest."

Roger relaxed and smiled. "That's very considerate of you...I appreciate it...you amaze me sometimes."

"No problem...I understand," Michelle said, smiling.

Roger handed her his car keys from the nightstand. Her hand lightly touched his when she took the keys. She stopped and hesitated, staring into his eyes and smiling.

Michelle quickly went back to her room and began to undress...She slipped on a sexy teddy and sprayed cologne all over her body. She turned, checked her appearance in the dresser mirror, winked at her image and sexily strutted out of her bedroom. She slowly sauntered down the hallway to the master bedroom where the door was now partially closed. She slowly opened the door and quietly walked inside the room.

Roger laid on his side, asleep. She silently walked over to the bed and slowly inched back the covers. She gently slid in between to sheets, putting her arm around Roger's shoulder and pressing her body against his back as she began kissing the back of his neck...

Roger smiled in his sleep when he felt the small hand began to massage his stiffening member. He rolled over on his back, enjoying the feeling. His hand automatically encircled her back as she moved her thigh over his body and slowly straddled him as she continued to rapidly massage his fully erect member. Roger suddenly opened his eyes as Michelle was about to position herself over him!..He roughly shoved her off of the bed and propped himself up on his elbows, shocked!..Michelle looked up at him, licking her red lips and smiling...

"Wh...what the hell do you think you're doing?" Roger shouted, angrily. "Get out of here!"

"It's alright...I'm having your baby," Michelle said, softly. "It won't make any difference now...and your wife will never have to know...We might as well reap all of the benefits...C'mon, please...I'll make you feel like it's the end of the world!"

"Are you out of your mind?" Roger shouted, "After all Janet's done for you...you'd try a stunt like this!"

Roger quickly got out of bed and angrily put on his robe. Michelle stood there staring at him...

"You...you're gonna turn me down?" she asked, angrily.

"Get the hell outta here!"

"You're gonna regret this, dammit!" she yelled as she backed out of the room. "I'll make you pay, you...you bastard!"

Michelle quickly marched out of the bedroom and slammed the door in anger!..Roger stood in the middle of the bedroom, shaking in rage!..

Willard Thompson sat in The Daily Press' publisher's office nervously. He stared at all of the boxes and crates stacked up in the office. He glanced at his watch impatiently as F. Walton Dugas strided into the office. Dugas shook Willard's hand firmly before he walked behind his desk and sat down. He studied Willard's face closely...

"You've changed your mind about coming over here?" Dugas asked.

"Not exactly...What's with all the boxes and crates?" Willard asked. "You moving somewhere?"

"Damn right we are...we're gettin' ready to move to our new plant in Troy...a suburb about twenty miles from here."

"Is it ready to operate?"

"The new computerized presses are being installed this week," Dugas beamed, proudly. "All high-tech equipment...We expect most of the business offices to be moved out within the next two weeks."

"Wow!..I didn't know you were gonna move this soon."

"It'll save us money," Dugas replied, "with all of that state-of-the-art equipment we'll be able to out produce The Herald by ten to one."

"That's interesting...it's what I wanted to talk to you about," Willard said, anxiously. "I'd like to help you put the Herald out of business."

"Wh..what?"

"Listen...you said I had a vested interest over here because I'm your bastard son...you willing to put that in writing?"

"I didn't say "bastard"...those are your words," Dugas said as he reached inside his middle desk drawer and pulled out a business card.

"I call 'em like they are," Willard answered. "A spade is a spade."

"Oh, stop with the inuendos...it doesn't become you," Dugas said in disgust as he handed him the business card. "Here...I already have put that into writing...That's my attorney. Ask him to draw up verification that you're in my will and have an equity in this newspaper...I think you'll discover that we Dugases take care of our own."

"That's good...I will contact him," Willard said, "mean-while, I have a proposition for you...As long as I stay at the Herald you'll have direct line to their upcoming advertising plans and promotions...with your new facilities and production equipment and with me feeding you information...you should be able to low-ball the Herald's advertising rates and take up most of their advertising accounts' budgets. You'll be offering them a larger circulation at a lower cost...and if any of them still want to use the Herald's home delivery customers, you can have flyers of their ads and special sections printed seperately and hand delivered to The Herald's customers at no extra cost...At that rate, The herald will lose more and more advertisers while The Daily Press gains...eventually, with shrinking advertising revenue and increasing production costs...The Herald will be driven out of business."

Dugas stared at Willard, slightly stunned. He couldn't believe what he was hearing!.."That's a brilliant idea and it took a cunning mind to come up with it...but...why would you do something like that?" Dugas asked, thoughtfully. "You don't have to destroy them...you could have the best of both newspapers."

"I got my reasons...good ones!" Willard shot back. "We got a deal?"

"What's your reasons, Wil?" Dugas asked, suspiciously. "The real reasons."

"Listen...you know better than me that newspapers all across the country are folding up because of escalating production costs...Joint Operating Agreements are being reached in major urban areas in order for many newspapers to survive...the handwriting is on the wall...in a few years there'll only be one newspaper in this city...and I'd like it to be the one I'll have an interest in."

Dugas smiled and drummed his fingers on his desk, thoughtfully. "That's good planning...you think you can manage something like that by yourself?...I admire the Dugas courage and spirit but this might be too much for you to handle."

Willard smiled and reared back in his chair with a confident smirk on his face..."I won't be by myself...one of the Stantons will be working with me on every project...in fact it was her idea...we've formed a pack to succeed."

"Who is it?"

"Karen."

"Why would she turn against her father?"

"You should be familiar with that," Willard replied. "I talked with Marcy at Mel's wedding...she's a fabulous woman...She has no idea who I really am and that's just fine with me."

"Good point...what's Karen's gripe with her father?"

"He's not her father...but he doesn't know it," Willard answered. "Karen just found out a few weeks ago and she's upset because she's been lied to all of her life."

"I'm sure you know how that feels," Dugas said.

"Karen believes that if the Stantons ever learn the truth...she might be cut out of her ownership in The Herald," Willard said. "That's why we've joined forces...we both realize there's only gonna be one newspaper left in this town and we intend to be a part of it!"

"I understand, Wil," Dugas said. "I'm proud of you."

"I picked up an advertising tabloid layout from United Department stores the other day," Willard said. "They're under new ownership now and they're increasing their advertising lineage contract from one million lines to two and a half million lines in both newspapers."

"I was aware that they planned to increase their advertising...but not that much," Dugas said, thoughtfully.

"Their newspaper advertising budget is increasing from approximately twelve million per year to thirty million," Willard said.

"So?..We'll be getting fifty percent of whatever it is," Dugas shot back.

"Wouldn't you rather have one hundred percent?"

"Why hell yes!" Dugas answered. "But how?"

"Listen...with your new high-tech computerized presses your newspaper is capable of producing tabloid sections better, faster and cheaper...if you passed some of that savings back to United they would give you a bigger slice of their advertising budget...instead of it being fifty-fifty...it would be more like seventy-five for The Daily Press and twenty-five for The Herald."

"Are you sure The Herald doesn't have the latest in computerized presses?" Dugas asked.

"That's right...they don't."

"I thought they ordered the latest equipment when they first opened up."

"The orders haven't been filled yet. They're still working with the old presses that were in the building when they bought it...those presses require more people, more supplies and more equipment to run it and the overall costs are much higher...I'm sure you're aware of those facts."

Dugas got up and walked around his desk, sitting down across from Willard, thoughtfully..."How would you go about getting this...ah...program...started?"

"We'll have to be very careful...Karen came up with a plan of me trying to get more of United's budget for The Herald by showing how much our circulation has been growing compared to The Press' circulation."

"That's true...your uncle and all those special sections he's been running have been giving us headaches...The Herald's circulation has been steadily creeping up."

"But not to the degree that would warrant a fifty-fifty split of United's advertising budget," Willard snapped. "That's how your account executive should approach United...He should say that based upon circulation and the actual per line rate, United is paying almost twice as much to advertise in The Herald, just to reach fifty percent less of the circulation they'll get at The Daily Press!"

Dugas smiled..."You're good...you're very good!"

"Then we agree?" Willard asked. "You'll have the papers drawn up to reflect at least five percent ownership for both Karen and I?"

"It may not be five percent...probably a little less," Dugas answered. "But it will be contingent upon what happens within the next three months...A performance contract."

"Performance?"

"Yes...let's see how you both perform within the next ninety days," Dugas replied. "As I told you...you've already been taken care of..we'll see how this goes before we include her...tell her...tell her that...I'm sure she expects it and she'll understand...but there is one other thing we haven't considered...even if we do get more of United's budget...how can we account for the Herald's home delivered customers who will not see United's tabloid sections because they won't be advertising as much with The Herald?"

"Have your man explain to United that if you can get one hundred percent of their advertising budget you will double the amount of advertising they have planned for the year and guarantee that their tabloid will be printed by The Press and hand delivered to each and every home delivery customer of The Daily Press and The Herald at no additional costs!..This way, United will be getting twice as much advertising for the same cost they have already allocated for newspaper advertising...without having to pay The herald one red cent!"

Dugas sat back in his chair and smiled broadly...

Janet Carlson was busy working in her office. She had several folders stacked on top of her desk as she searched through a filling cabinet. She was so involved in her work she didn't notice when Michelle walked timidly into the office. Janet looked up and smiled at her until she saw how upset she was.

"Michelle...I didn't see you standing there," Janet said, surprised. "Is anything wrong?"

Michelle began softly sobbing..."You...you're gonna just hate me...but there was nothing I could do...he was too strong!"

"Who was too strong?"..What's happened?"

"Your...your husband, Roger!" Michelle cried. "As soon as you left the house this morning...he...he...he tried to rape me!" Michelle cried, sobbing loudly.

"What?"

"You heard me!" Michelle screamed as tears flowed down her cheeks. "He tried to rape me!"

"You must be mistaken...Roger would never do anything like that!"

"Are you calling me a liar?" Michelle shouted, backing up.

"Relax...just calm down," Janet replied calmly, trying to control her. "Just tell me what happened so we can straighten this out."

"There nothing to straighten out!" Michelle continued to cry. "Your husband tried to rape me and I stopped him!..Now you're calling me a liar!"

Janet walked around her desk as Michelle quickly turned to leave.

"Michelle!..Wait...Please!" Janet shouted after her.

Michelle, crying loudly, charged out of the office and ran down the hallway, bumping into several surprised co-workers!..Janet watched her from her office doorway and then went back into her office and called her home. In a few moments, Roger answered the phone...

"Hello."

"Honey, it's me...we got big problems!"

"You mean Michelle?..I think she lost it this morning!"

"I know...she just told me you tried to rape her!"

"Why that little bitch!" Roger said, angrily. "Can you come right home?..We gotta figure out what we're gonna do!"

"She just left my office...screaming and crying!" Janet said. "I've never seen such a radical change in someone like that before!"

"Come right home and bring Michelle with you!"

"If she's still in the building I will," Janet replied, as a security guard rushed into her office..."Hold on...a security guard just came into my office...something's happened!"

Janet turned her attention to the excited security guard who was waiting to talk to her. "Is something wrong, Harry?"

"I was just walking through the exec garage when I almost got run over by your husband's car!" the guard said, distraught. "I went over to check your two parking spaces and I found your car...all the tires were slashed!"

Patricia Parker-Stanton conducted a small press conference in her office at the Community Committee's downtown headquarters. Several men and women crowded into her office with notebooks and pens in their hands. Some were visibly upset with Patricia's latest proposal to form a national coalition across racial lines to pursue a federal Full Employment bill. One man was fuming at the idea...

"Mrs. Stanton...your proposals have been pretty much on target except for this idea of Full Employment," the man said, "many of us feel it's a "pie-in-the-sky" wish that will never happen...at least not in out lifetime!"

"Mr. MacNamara...I appreciate your honest critique but it's that attitude that has held this country back from wiping out racism in the first place," Patricia replied, sternly.

"What the hell has Full Employment got to do with fighting racism?" another man asked, indignantly, "I thought you were involved with fighting racism in the media."

"Mr. Farber, the concept of Full Employment was first introduced at the 1924 Democratic National Convention by Eleanor Roosevelt...It is a concept whereby our national unemployment rate never exceeds one percent," Patricia answered, calmly. "It provides each individual citizen with economic security as a right that will guarantee basic minimums in health, education, housing and employment ...This is precisely what this country needs to begin to eliminate racism, crime, drugs and violence and to stabilize our national economy...As an example, if the rioters in the Los Angeles' riot of 1992 had been employed...they wouldn't have been available to riot."

"What kind of jobs are you talkin' about?" Farber asked, "And how will they be paid for?"

"We have to refocus our priorities in this country and concentrate more on creating employment rather than building missiles, rockets and prisons," Patricia said. "Since the collapse of the Soviet Union it is no longer necessary to have a defense budget of $300 billion dollars! We have a rate of unemployment in this country hovering between six and seven percent, which equals in human beings a total of approximately ten million Americans... with another eight million citizens unemployed who are no longer counted in the unemployment statistics because their unemployment benefits have expired."

"How much would it take to put ten million people back to work?" MacNamara asked, disbelieving.

"Off hand I would estimate that $100 billion dollars could put the ten million back to work over a short period of time... a matter of months," Patricia replied, "If we could reduce our defense budget by one-third we could do it, and keep in mind that once those ten million got back to work and begin buying cars, appliances and homes... the economy would snow-ball, putting the other eight million Americans back to work."

"In what kinds of jobs?" Farber asked.

"Many jobs would emerge in doubling the amount of police right across the country," Patricia answered. "Major cities with high crime rates like Los Angeles would have sixteen thousand police officers instead of only eight thousand... as a result, crime would be reduced considerably just from the high visibility of the additional police... We could also create work forces to rebuild our cities, bridges, highways, schools, homes, apartments, build dam barriers, shore up construction in earth quake prone areas, plant trees and construct new high speed transportation all across the nation. Many depression area construction projects that are still standing today were the result of the Works Progress Administration, known as the WPA, which provided a means of thousands of jobless people getting employment by President Roosevelt. The WPA gave people jobs and a sense of contributing to their community instead of being alienated. It employed 8.5 million Americans over eight years. It built 651,000 miles of roads, 78,000 bridges, 8,000 parks and 5,900 schools. All over America, you can still find it's legacy..."

"But...if we put that many people back to work wouldn't that cause some kind of inflation?" MacNamara asked.

"Not necessarily...by careful coordination of policies and by negotiated agreements between major organizations such as the labor unions, private industry and the federal government," Patricia said, anxiously, "inflation can be controlled and unemployment can be maintained at minimum levels."

"If this all true...why aren't we doin' something like that now?" MacNamara asked.

"Because those making our laws are working with steady incomes, hospitalization and food on their tables...They don't seem to have the mind-set to realize that all of these current social problems such as racism, crime, drugs, violence, nationwide hospitalization, rebuilding our nation's infra-structure, the economy and the downsizing of welfare recipients...can all be made 75 percent easier to resolve with a federal Full Employment Act. With such an act, Americans will quickly realize that we don't have to increase taxes to achieve these goals because we'll simply have more Americans, approximately 18 million more, paying taxes!"

"What about the national debt?" a woman asked. "It's almost four trillion with a yearly deficit over three hundred billion."

"That's what's so good about a Federal Full Employment Act," Patricia answered, smiling, "with the average worker paying three thousand dollars a year in federal income tax, when you multiply that by the 18 million Americans going back to work, you'll see that our government could receive as much as $54 billion dollars yearly from those workers alone...which could be applied to reducing our yearly deficit...of course that doesn't include the huge additional tax during a flourishing economy!"

"In the past...what has been the conservative view towards a Full Employment Act?" a second woman asked.

"Previous conservative administrations have felt that unemployment is both necessary and acceptable to control inflation," Patricia answered, "they felt unemployment should be treated as an analytical tool of economic policy, to be increased whenever inflation threatens to rise."

"But is this a realistic goal?" the woman asked.

"There is no inevitable trade-off that prevents Full Employment," Patricia replied, "the necessary reforms can be achieved in the context of our country's economic institutions...The crucial elements of a Full Employment policy are supported by the majority of American people."

"Are you positive unemployment plays such an important role in sustaining racism?" MacNamara asked.

"The drastic effects of unemployment has demonstrated a clear relationship between economic downturns and increases in admissions to mental hospitals, cardiovascular disease, infant mortality, child abuse, spouse abuse, suicides and the increase in hate groups and racial conflicts," Patricia answered. "Over seventy-five percent of all criminals arrested are unemployed at the time the crime was commited...The government must initiate an effective economic program to reduce the national debt, control the yearly deficit, reduce the welfare rolls, stabilize our economy, provide a national hospitalization plan that covers every American and to give each and every citizen a better quality of life in these United States...This and only this will finally sever the head of that deadly snake that feeds racism...and that is the poverty that has grown from massive unemployment!..There is only one program that can do all of that and that program is Full Employment!"

The first woman sighed deeply and smiled, proudly at Patricia..."Well, I think Full Employment isn't the only thing we should reconsider," the woman said.

"What else should we reconsider?" Patricia asked.

"Which Stanton is going to run for mayor!" the woman chuckled.

Joe Stanton walked through the luxurious hotel lobby and into the waiting elevator. He was determined to get this issue settled once and for all. When the elevator stopped he quickly stepped out and walked down the long corridor, looking at the room numbers. Finally, he stopped and knocked softly on the door of one of the suites. In a few moments, Susan Stanton opened the door and smiled broadly. She reached out to embrace him but he quickly walked past her outstretched arms. He sat down on the sofa and stared at her as he rubbed his brow in frustration.

"What's the matter?" Susan asked, concerned. "I can tell something's wrong."

"It's liz," Joe mumbled, "she's figured it out."

"I know...she called me."

"She told me she did," Joe said, dejectedly, "and she's furious with both of us...and...the worse thing is...she's right."

"Oh, Joe...let's not go through that guilt trip again," Susan protested, angrily. "We belong together...we always have. If anybody should understand that it's your sister, Liz!"

"It just can't be...it'll tear my family apart!"

"And what about me?..Where am I gonna go, what am I gonna do?"

"Go back to your husband and put your family back together!" Joe snapped. "Forget about me...it just won't work!"

"Damn that Liz!" Susan shouted, angrily. "She threatened to tell the family didn't she!"

"Don't blame Liz!..it's nobody's fault but mine," Joe said, sadly, "I should've stayed away from you!"

"Your sister's got a lot of nerve!" Susan shot back. "Ridiculing us...I didn't see her staying away from Ze-Ze!"

"She 's not breaking up a family."

Susan angrily turned away and walked over to the huge window. She looked down at the heavy traffic on the street below..."Does your family know I didn't go back to New York?"

"No...they all think you and the kids went right back after the wedding," Joe answered.

"I'm not going back to Gene...if I can't have you...I'm still going to get a divorce."

"That's too bad...but I won't be a part of it."

Susan turned back to Joe, steaming with anger..." A part of it?..No matter what you may do now...you were then and you are now...the only reason why I'm divorcing my husband! And you can tell your dear sister, Liz, to go straight to hell!"

"I'm sorry, Susan...I'm sorry about this whole mess!"

"Get out!" she cried as tears streamed down her face." "Just get the hell out of my life once and for all!"

"But, Susan...I..."

"Get out!"

Joe slowly stood up and walked over to the door. He opened it and turned back towards Susan. She angrily rushed towards him with fury in her eyes!..Before he could say anything she shoved him backwards, out of the doorway and slammed the door closed!..

Chapter Thirty

Gene Stanton sat behind his desk at The Herald as everyone settled into their seats, waiting for the meeting to begin. In attendance were Gene II, Liz, Adrian, Karen and Max. Gene looked from one to the other..."Has anyone seen Roger or Janet?" Gene asked.

"I haven't seen Roger all day," Karen answered, "Janet left at noon...she was rather upset about something."

"Well...I wanted them to be here," Gene said, thoughtfully. "I can always bring them up to date later...I'm sure the rest of you all know what this meeting is about...I've decided to run for mayor."

They all began to applaud and some shook Gene's hand in congratulations. Karen and Liz kissed their father, proudly. Adrian remained seated and smiled as Gene continued.

"I'll be meeting with the business staff and all of the department heads later on, but I wanted you to hear these two announcements directly from me," Gene said. "First, Gene II will become our interim publisher effective sixty days from today...his direct assistants will be Roger and my two daughters, Karen and Liz...Second, I'd like to announce my campaign manager. I needed someone who was familiar with politics and with a political background...A person who could get behind the doors of those smoke filled rooms, but still had their hands on the pulse of the city.".

"Sounds interesting," Max said, "who'd you choose?"

"I selected someone from your staff, Max," Gene replied. "I selected Dr. Adrian Grant."

Surprised, everyone at the meeting congratulated Adrian on the appointment. She graciously accepted their congratulations, smiled modestly and continued jotting

THE WINDS OF TOMORROW

down notes. Gene II turned to Max and grinned. "Looks like you're gonna have to get another political reporter, Max."

"Whoever I get...won't be as good as Adrian," he said.

"Well, if I don't make the primary next spring we'll both be back," Gene said, smiling.

"Don't talk like that," Karen chided, "you'll probably win it hands down."

"OK, dad," Liz said, "What about the production schedule for next year...is it changing?"

"Not a thing...it just depends on how soon we'll be getting all of that new equipment," Gene answered. "Remember, I'll still be available most of the time so don't expect too many changes."

"You still planning to convert to those new computerized presses?" Karen asked.

Gene chuckled..."I'd like to...but according to Roger, the union will pitch a fit!..When The Daily Press converted the unions lost forty jobs. The only way we can do that is to have both the old and the new presses operating and cut back on union personnel through normal attrition. Which means we don't replace any workers when they retire, quit or die...When we get down to just the personnel we'll need to operate the new equipment, then we'll switch over completely and get rid of the old units."

"That could take a while," Karen said, "have you ordered all of the new equipment?"

"The first computerized presses should start arriving by next spring," Gene answered. "We anticipate the complete transition by September."

"You mentioned that you wanted the promotion department to get started on that table-size mock-up of Belle Isle," Adrian said. "do you want me to handle that?"

"I've already ordered it," Max said, "they told me it would be ready in a week...they're all anxious to work on your campaign...What about that, Mr. Stanton?..Can some of us still work on your campaign on our own time?"

"You're welcome to...Most of my family will be working on the campaign," Gene said, smiling. "We're gonna need as much help as we can get...Just check with my campaign manager."

Max turned to Adrian with a big smile on his face..."Hey, campaign manager...Marcy and I both want to work on the campaign...sign us up."

"I already have," Adrian laughed.

The meeting slowly broke up in the midst of jokes and loud laughter. Adrian glanced at Gene and flashed a smile. Suddenly, everyone's attention was drawn to the outer office when Roger charged by Gene's secretary, looking wild and upset!..

"Roger...you alright?" Gene asked, alarmed.

"Has anyone seen Janet?" Roger asked, anxiously.

"Not since noon," Karen replied. "She was going home early...there was some trouble she wanted to take care of."

"Well...she never made it!" Roger exclaimed.

Janet Carlson cursed the auto mechanic who had been dispatched to repair the four flat tires on her car. The man's slow work had caused her to lose almost two hours!..When she pulled up into her driveway, the tranquil neighborhood atmosphere seemed to calm her down. She quickly parked her car in the rear, in front of the garage. She cautiously walked into the home through the back door...She was shocked to find her kitchen in so much disarray!..Dishes and glasses lay broken on the floor, curtains and shades were partially ripped down!..As she walked, stunned, through the rest of the house, she saw bookshelves knocked over, tables overturned and food thrown up against the walls!..In the living room she discovered huge, wide rips in the upholstery of her expensive sofa and chairs!..The entire home had been thoroughtly trashed!..

Janet was in total shock when she slowly walked up the stairs, bewildered by so much destruction!..When she reached the top of the stairs she saw streaks of dried blood smeared all over the walls! Unnerved by the sight, she immediately began calling for her cat, Bosco, as she cried hysterically!

"Bosco!..Bosco!..Come to mamma, baby...Bosco!..Bosco!"

Getting no response, Janet slowly walked towards the master bedroom where she saw more streaks of blood on the walls!..Inside the bedroom the drapes were drawn and the complete room was cast in the late afternoon shadows...The covers on the wide king-size bed were pulled up to the headboard...She noticed a hump under the bedspread and she slowly began to pull back the covers!..She uncovered her large, Angora cat, Bosco, laying on the bloody sheets, completely decapitated!..

At that instant the door to the bedroom slammed closed and an ear-splitting scream filled the room!..Janet turned just in time to see Michelle rushing towards her with a large butcher knife held high in her hand above her head!..Janet quickly dodged the first plunge of the blade when Michelle blindly wielded the knife while she continued to scream, horribly!..Janet managed to avoid the deadly weapon and reached the bedroom door which she quickly opened and ran out of the room, slamming the door shut in Michelle's face!..Janet stood there in anguish, holding the door closed as Michelle pulled at the door frantically!..Finally, Michelle stopped pulling and Janet wondered what was happening until the long blade of the knife was plunged through the door, barely missing Janet's face!..

Janet screamed and ran down the stairs as Michelle pulled the bedroom door opened and ran, screaming, after her!..As Janet reached the bottom of the stairs a screaming Michelle bounded over the bannister and landed on her feet just behind Janet and tried to plunge the knife into her back!..Janet dodged again and quickly ran into the first floor powder room!..She quickly slammed and locked the bathroom door, backing up to the sink as Michelle shrieked in anger outside of the door, plunging the blade of the knife into the door several times!..Janet slowly sunk down to the floor, still shaking in fright and totally exhausted as Michelle continued her guttural screaming outside of the door!..

"Bitch!..Come out, you bitch!" Michelle screamed at the top of her lungs. "C'mon out and get whatcha got comin' to ya, bitch!"

Janet remained sitting on the floor, sobbing hysterically, until the screaming stopped!..Everything suddenly became silent. Janet thought she could hear other voice but she was unsure. In a few minutes she heard Roger's voice outside of the bathroom door.

"Janet!..Janet!..It's alright...the police are here!" Roger shouted, "they've got Michelle...it's all over, honey."

Janet began crying loudly and she became violently ill. She lifted the lid on the toilet as her stomach began to heave, uncontrollably...When she looked down into the commode she saw the head of her cat floating in the bloody water with it's eyes staring up at her!..Janet began screaming and convulsing as Roger broke into the bathroom!..

Janet and Roger, both still visibly shakened by the frightening ordeal, sat in a family counseling room at a long conference table. In a few moments, Dr. Wolford, the chief staff psychiatrist at the hospital, walked into the room and sat down just as a practical nurse carrying a tray holding several cups of coffee, walked in behind him. The nurse place the tray on the table near them and quickly left the room. Dr. Wolfort calmly sipped his coffee and eyed Janet and Roger carefully.

"Mr. and Mrs. Carlson...I'm Dr. Wolfort. I am the Chief of Psychiatry here at City Hospital. I know you have many questions to ask me...so let's get on with it."

Roger looked at Janet and rubbed his brow in exasperation as a worried expression clouded his face..."This is just terrible!..What happened to her, doctor?"

"I understand you've both been through a terrible experience," Dr. Wolfort said, sympathetically.

"It was awful," Roger said. "Like she was a totally different person!'

"What made her snap like that?" Janet asked.

"It's a very complicated condition," the doctor answered, "I've been examining her all evening."

"What's wrong with her?" Janet asked. "Sometimes she's so sweet and nice."

"Then she'll do something weird," Roger added, anxiously, "like coming on to me."

"Do you remember...lately...has she been very forgetful?" Dr. Wolfort asked.

"Yes...as a matter of fact...she has beem extremely forgetful," Roger answered, thoughtfully, "that's how the day started out...she forgot that Janet was going to work earlier today...and I distinctly heard Janet tell her that she was going to work early."

"I just thought it was her youthful indifference," Janet said, "this has been happening more frequently but I thought it was normal until the evening she stayed out late. The next morning when I asked her about it...she didn't remember a thing."

"Has she suddenly been placed under some stressful situation?" Dr. Wolfort asked. "Like...an unusual responsibility?"

Roger and Janet glanced at each other, nervously...

"Roger and I have just entered the in vitro ferilization program," Janet replied, "Michelle volunteered to be our host mother and carry the baby for us."

"We were reluctant to ask her," Roger said, "but it was her idea...I think she wanted to pay us back for taking her into our home."

"Now...I just feel so guilty!" Janet lamented.

"Tell me, doctor," Roger said, "do you think that's what set this off?..Is it too much of a strain on her?"

"Where are her parents?" Dr. Wolfort asked.

"Duluth, Minnesota," Roger answered. "I spoke to her father a few weeks ago...they don't want her back."

"That fits the pattern," Dr. Wolfort snapped.

"What pattern?" Janet asked.

"First, let me put you both at some ease," Dr. Wolfort spoke calmly. "Her situation as your host mother is not the major problem...her problem is much more serious than that and that responsibility can most likely be found with her family...Are you familiar with M.P.D.?"

"M.P.D.?" Janet asked, looking at Roger quickly.

"Multiple personality disorder," Dr. Wolfort said.

Roger's hand quickly held Janet's as she trembled in fear. Dr. Wolfort pulled out a thick pocket notebook and began to thumb slowly through the pages..."From what I can tell...the patient has several personalities. I know that one is a docile little girl...one is a combative grown woman...and one is a boy called Mike...this switch is often instantaneous and inexplicable."

"But why would she do what she did today?" Janet asked.

"Several alter personalities dwell within her," Dr. Wolfort explained. "I've only been able to uncover three so far...something has been happening that caused this furious personality to surface today...and so for...it hasn't come back out."

"What causes this...multiple personality disorder?" Roger asked.

"Many things...the most common being child abuse and or incest," Dr. Wolfort replied. "How much do you know about her family?"

"She's the oldest of three sisters," Roger answered. "According to her father, Michelle became pregnant and left home."

"Did the father act like he wanted her back?" Dr. Wolfort asked.

"On the contrary...he was very explicit," Roger replied. "He did not want her back at all."

"Didn't you think that's was a strange way for a father to react?" Dr. Wolfort asked. "Unless...her was the one who impregnated the child."

"Oh, my GOD!" Janet said, shocked.

"We have no proof that' what happened," Dr. Wolfort said, "I'm just theorizing what could have happened to create this disorder...this is usually what happens to children who are frequently, severely and repeatedly sexually abused...It is these children who usually develop this malady. It is spontaneous dissociation...a coping mechanism."

"But why are these children predisposed to this multiple personality disorder?" Janet asked.

"Just imagine, if you will, how this abuse starts," Dr. Wolfort explained. "The child is in a dark room, petrified and shivering. Her daddy or some close relative is giving her orders she doesn't want to follow...his voice is stern, unyielding...he tells her to take off her clothes...the child is small and overpowered...she wants to be another person...somewhere else...in another room, in another family...but there's nowhere to go, nowhere to run and nowhere to hide...So the way she runs and hides is by going inside her head and becoming someone else...someone who doesn't feel the pain and humiliation the first little girl feels."

"That's terrible!" Roger exclaimed, angrily. "Can...can this ever be cured?"

"It can be treated through hypnosis therapy," the doctor explained. "Since the prevalence of child abuse is believed to be the root of the disorder, hypnotism therapy allows the repressed memories to be released...uncovered and eventually dealt with."

"How deep does this go doctor?" Janet asked.

"Each recurring personality takes full control of a person's behavior...Each usually has little or no knowledge of the other's activities," Dr. Wolfort said. "In cases where symptoms are more severe, the switch may involve abrupt changes in mannerism and speech...In some patients, one personality may require glasses while another will have 20-20 vision...So to answer your question, Mrs. Carlson...yes..., it can go...very deep...it depends on the severity of the abuse."

Janet nervously glanced at Roger and then back to the doctor. "Is she now considered...in police custody?" Janet asked.

"That's up to you and your husband, Mrs. Carlson...I understand that she assaulted you, destroyed your cat, tore up your home and slashed the tires on one of your automobiles," Dr. Wolfort said in a clam voice. "Other than the cat, I'm sure your home owner's insurance will cover most of your losses...You could probably press charges on any of those points...but it would not accomplish anything...She needs treatment and therapy not a jail cell...that child's been abused enough...she needs help."

"She's pregnant you know," Roger said, sadly. "She's carrying our child...will this affect her condition?"

"I understand your concern, Mr. Carlson," Dr. Wolfort replied, "but if she receives the proper care, she should be able to live a good and normal life. Many people have this disorder and manage to keep it under control...I would just like to know what set her off this morning...has she recently suffered and kind of rejection?"

Roger and Janet look at each other, briefly.

"What do you mean?" Janet asked.

"A child harbors many emotions that can be released at any time," Dr. Wolfort said. "If Michelle has suffered a rejection similar to another rejection she may have had in the past...this could have triggered the explosion she had today...May I suggest that during the balance of her pregnancy that you see to it that she receives the best psychiatric care available."

"Will her mental condition...hurt the baby?" Roger asked, cautiously.

"Only if her health is allowed to deteriorate or if she harms herself by taking drugs, drinking or smoking," Dr. Wolfort answered. "Get her into a nice, calm enviroment...show her love...this commitment she's made to you and this baby could be the best thing that's happened to her in a long time...It could be the change in her life to help her overcome and control this illness."

"I certainly hope it is," Janet said, somberly.

"Would you like to see her?" Dr. Wolfort asked.

Janet and Roger stared at each other, undecided. Roger slowly began to smile. "Of course we would, doctor...I think we now understand this situation a lot better."

Dr. Wolfort escorted Janet and Roger into the next room where they could view Michelle through a one-way mirror. Michelle was sitting in the corner of the room, holding a doll and singing a nursery rhyme in a little girl's tiny voice as she rocked back and forth!..

The suite of offices at The Breast Cancer Detection and Education Center at The Detroit Herald Newspaper's building was crowded with women concerned and anxious to attend the afternoon class. The instructors continued explaining the procedures for monthly breast self-examination when Gloria noticed Adrian standing just outside of the classroom in the receptionist's office. She excused herself and made her way through the throng of students to welcome Adrian to the center.

"Adrian...I'm so glad you could make it," Gloria said, smiling broadly.

"Well...I know what you're trying to do and I think it's just wonderful," Adrian said, "I felt if you could arrange to do all of this...the least I could do is to find the time to look after my own health."

"That's true," Gloria said, "I just wish other women realized that...The best protection is early detection."

"I fully agree," Adrian said, "I may be some what of a health freak...I jog a mile two...sometimes three times a week."

"I can look at you and tell it's been paying off...you look great," Gloria said.

"Thank you."

"Can you come into my office for a minute?" Gloria asked. I've been wanting to speak to you."

Adrian quickly followed Gloria back to her office at the rear of the suite. Gloria motioned for Adrian to have a seat as she walked behind her desk. Adrian was slightly puzzled by Gloria's sudden attention to her.

"What can I do for you, Gloria?"

"I...I just wanted you to know that I...well...I love my brother very much," Gloria said, hesitatingly. "He's a wonderful person and as you can see...he allowed me to set all of this up."

"I know," Adrian said, still slightly confused. "Why are you telling me this?"

Gloria sat down behind her desk, clasped her hands and sighed deeply. "Because...I'm not trying to be a nosey sister or anything, " Gloria answered, "it's just that...I am aware of his feelings for you."

"Maybe I should leave..."

"No...please don't go...let me finish what I have to say," Gloria said, calmly. "Gene loves you very much...and...I couldn't be happier."

Adrian relaxed back in the chair as Gloria smiled at her. "Wow!..I didn't know what was coming next!" Adrian said, relieved.

"And I suspect that the love is mutual," Gloria continued.

"I love your brother more than life itself," Adrian confirmed.

"You know, Adrian...life can be very perplexing at times," Gloria said. "When couples first marry they are totally different people from who they are after thirty years of marriage. They've raised a family, worked or maintained a business...and then one day they'll look around and discover they are no longer the same two individuals who has married each other thirty years earlier...The love is gone but most of us refuse to admit it."

"In some cases that happens," Adrian said, "but not all of the time."

"You're right...it doesn't happen in all marriages...but it did with Gene's marriage...in fact, I'd say their marriage has been one without love for many, many years."

"I didn't realize that."

"I know...he'd never admit it. Gene is a very loyal and responsible person. He wouldn't want to hurt Patricia."

"That's true."

"I understand you're going to be his campaign manager."

"That's right...I hope to make him mayor."

"Is that all?"

"Isn't that enough?" Adrian asked.

"That depends."

"On what?"

"On what you want, Adrian."

"I just want him to be happy."

"He'll only be happy...with you."

"Then that's what I want...I want all of him...all of the time."

Gloria stood up and smiled broadly. "That's what I wanted to hear...he needs your love to be truly happy...the minute you walk into a room that he's in...he lights up like a Christmas tree!"

"So do I."

"Then love him as much as you can," Gloria urged. "Make him happy...and always...give him all of your love."

"I will...and thank you, Gloria...you're very kind."

Gloria slowly walked around her desk and took Adrian's hands in hers as she stood up. She quickly embraced Adrian. "I'm glad we had this little talk," Gloria whispered.

"So am I...and I can see that this wonderful trait of love and understanding runs in your family," Adrian said, smiling.

The two women walked out of Gloria's office with big smiles on their faces. They both stopped short, surprised to find Patricia standing in the receptionist's office, waiting to join the class in session. Gloria nervously glanced at Adrian before she began to speak to Patricia.

"I didn't know you were out here," Gloria said to Patricia, "Why didn't you call?"

"I just thought I'd sit in on one of your classes," Patricia replied as she noticed Adrian standing behind Gloria. "Oh, hello, Adrian...how are you?"

"Just fine, Mrs. Stanton...and you?"

"Are you here for the class, too?"

"Yes I am...as Gloria tells everyone...the best protection is early detection."

"I thought you were assigned to the City-County building," Patricia said, "where all the single men are...Have you managed to hook one yet?"

"Not completely...but I'm working on it," Adrian replied, quickly glancing at Gloria.

"Well...for your sake I hope he's not someone else's husband," Patricia snapped, smartly. "I think it would be better if you limited yourself to just the single men in the City-County building."

Gloria moved in between the two women. "Adrian, you should join the class now," Gloria intervened, "they're about to begin an exercise in breast examination. The nurse and the technician will take you through it...Patricia, can you step into my office for a minute?"

"Oh...before I go, Mrs. Stanton...I'd like to inform you that I'm no longer assigned to the City-County building," Adrian said.

"Really?" Patricia asked, "Where are you working now?"

"I was just appointed your husband's campaign manager," Adrian said, as she smiled broadly, turned and strutted into the class in session.

Adrian listened attentively as the nurse explained the proper procedure for monthly breast examination. Each woman stood in front of her chair in the class and followed the movements of the instructors as they performed the self examination, step by step...

"In the shower, raise one arm...with fingers flat, touch every part of each breast," the main instructor said as the students performed each step, "gently feeling for a lump or thickening. Use your right hand to examine your left breast, your left hand for your right breast."

All of the students repeated the procedure in a quiet and serious manner. When they were finished, the instructor pointed to mirrors hanging on the back of each chair and continued..."When standing before a mirror...with arms at your side, then raised above your head, look carefully for changes in the size, shape, and contour of each breast. Looking for puckering, dimpling or changes in skin texture...Gently squeeze both nipples and look for discharge."

The technician walked down the ailes of the classroom watching each woman examine themselves. The instructor contunued..."Now will you each lay down on the padded pallet next to your chair. Just remove the tissue paper wrapper. Each plastic pallet and pillow is sanitized and has never been used before...You can take it with you when you leave with the compliments of The Herald," she said as everyone slightly laughed..."When lying down, place a towel or pillow under your right shoulder and your right hand behind your head...examine your right breast with your left hand...with your fingers flat, press gently in small circles, starting at the outermost top edge of your breast and spiraling in toward the nipple. Examine every part of the breast...repeat this procedure with the left breast."

The students repeated the procedure as the technician assisted them in positioning their arms and hands. The instructor continued..."Now back to standing...with your arm resting on a firm surface, use the same circular motion to examine the underarm area...this is breast tissue, too."

Finally, after all of the women has completed the breast self-examinations, the nurse and the technician moved back to the front of the classroom.

"In conclusion...this self exam is not a substitute for periodic examinations by a qualified physician," the nurse warned. "Today, you all conducted an examination on your breasts and many of you have found something you didn't know was there...from experience, I know this is true...My advice is for you to arrange an appointment with your physician as soon as possible...Your doctor will arrange for you to have a mammogram immediately...Remember, the best protection is early detection."

After Adrian had dressed and turned in her application, she saw Gloria motioning to her from her office door. She walked into the office and Gloria closed the door behind her.

"Well...how did it go?" Gloria asked.

"I'm not sure," Adrian replied, thoughtfully. "I think I found a small lump or something...the technician said I should see my doctor right away...Please, don't mention this to Gene...he'll just get upset."

"Of course I won't...and the technician was right...Do you want me to go to your doctor with you?" Gloria asked.

"You don't have to."

"No problem...that's what I'm here for," Gloria said, smiling. "We lend support from discovery, surgery and through reconstruction...if necessary."

Adrian looked around Gloria's office, smiling. "Where's your sister-in-law?..I didn't see her in the classroom."

"After you told her about you new assignment she lit out of here like a rocket!" Gloria answered, smiling. "I'm afraid she suspects something's going on!"

Adrian smiled and turned to leave. "I've got tons of work to do...thanks for everything, Gloria...especially that little talk...you're sweet."

"What about that doctor's appointment...you gonna let me know?"

I'll call you as soon as it's set up...By-by."

The one-ton truck lumbed down the dark, lonely country road. When it reached the end of the road it stopped and two men climbed out, carefully studying the area. The driver got back inside the cab of the truck and blinked the headlights twice. As soon as he did, a pair of headlights blinked back from a road on the right and another pair of headlights blinked back from a road about a quarter of a mile away on the left. The driver climbed back down from the truck and lit a cigarette which revealed the rugged face of Carlos Cortez of The Federal Drug Enforcement Agency. Cortez slowly walked around to the front of the truck to his partner, Dave Phillips, who looked at Carlos and smiled...

"You think they're gonna show?"

"They will...the cartel was furious when we stole that shipment from 'em in Miami," Carlos answered, chuckling. "They want it back...they just don't know who has the nerve to steal from them in the first place."

"What if Montoya doesn't show up?"

"No deal...if they try anything we'll just let 'em know how much fire power we got...all I gotta do is take off my hat and it'll sound like a war's broken out!"

"There's a headlight...they're right on time!" Dave said, anxiously. "Here they come!"

"Two sets of headlights appeared out of the black night bouncing over the dirt road towards them. As the lights grew closer, the outlines of two stretch limousines slowly crept down the road. The cars stopped about twenty yards away. They set in the middle of the road for a while, sizing up the entire area. Finally, the driver of the first car got out and walked towards them. Carlos responded by walking towards the heavy-set man. The two men stopped about ten feet apart. Dave climbed back inside the truck while the two men stood in the middle of the road and stared at each other before speaking.

"You got the merchandise?" the fat man asked.

THE WINDS OF TOMORROW

"I got the mail," Cortez replied, "you got the postage?"

"Two hundred thousand."

"No damn deal!" Cortez snapped, angrily. "I said three!"

Startled, the man stared at Cortez, swearing under his breath. "You bastard!" the man shouted, angrily. "I oughta take you out!"

Cortez slowly walked up closer to the man, so close he could tell what he had for dinner. "If you feelin' froggish," Cortez snarled, "jump motherfucka!"

The man started to move but stopped. He stared back at the truck and tried to figure out what Cortez had behind him that would make him so brave!..He finally turned and walked back to the first limousine. He bent down at the rear window and talk to the passengers inside. In a few moments he stood up straight, turned around and began walking back towards Cortez. When he reached him, he wouldn't look him in the eyes.

"Lemme see the merchandise," the fat man grumbled.

Cortez smiled and turned towards the truck, walking confidently as the man followed him Cortez pulled back the tarpaulin showing the stacks of boxes. The fat man agily climbed up into the truck, breathing heavily. He ripped open one of the boxes and examined the contents. He methodically tasted a sample and closed the box back up. He examined a few more boxes and then, satisfied, he climbed back down from the truck, dusting his hands.

"The chief says you got to follow us back to get the rest of the bread," the fat man said.

"You think I just fell off the truck?" Cortez growled, angrily. "You tell your chief to come on out here and deal and cut out the bullshit!..I don't work through no damn messenger...What's his name?"

"You takin' a census?" the fat man shot back. "You don't need no friggin' names!"

Cortez turned and marched to the front of the truck. He stopped suddenly and turned back to the fat man standing in the road in front of the truck, confused. "You better get your lard ass off the road, my man, or you're gonna be pickin' your teeth up out of the dust!"

Cortez climbed into the truck and started it up, moving onto the middle of the road. Suddenly the doors to the two limos all opened up at the same time as several men stood in the middle of the road, blocking the truck!..

"OK!..OK!..Hold it!" the fat man shouted. "We'll deal!"

"Who am I dealin' with?" Cortez shouted back.

One man who was tall and lanky, stepped forward. "I am Ramon Gonzalez...I'll have to get you the rest of the money. Will you follow us, please?"

"OK, Mr. Gonzalez," Cortez replied. "I know who you are...as long as you're dealin' from the top of the deck...but if you try anything...you can kiss this load...adios!"

The men all climbed back into their vehicles. Cortez watched as the two limos made a wide u-turn and barreled back down the dirt road in a cloud of dust and gravel. Cortez grinned to Dave as he spoke into his radio..."OK, baybee!...Lift-off!..We're on our way to Oz!" he shouted as the truck roared down the road!..

The two stretch limousines pulled up in front of a large, luxurious ranch home located deep in the country. As they moved down the wide driveway the garage doors slid up. The two limos crept inside the garage and the doors quickly slid back down. Dave and Carlos remained inside the truck, parked on the apron of the driveway and waited. Dave looked at Carlos..."We all set?" He asked.

Cortez glanced into his rear view mirror and saw several shadowy figures creeping down the road towards the home.

"Yeah...the gang's all here," Carlos whispered, "tell 'em code red!..Move in!"

In a few moments the dark, shadowy figures moved in towards the house, running from tree to tree!..The letters stenciled on the backs of their jackets in iridescent paint read: "DEA"...The agents were all armed with rifles and automatic weapons as they surrounded the home, remaining in the shadows of the trees and bushes. In a few minutes Ramon Gonzalez and several of his men walked out towards the truck. Ramon walked up to the driver's door.

"OK...this is the end of the line," Ramon ordered. "Get the hell out of there!"

"You got my money?" Cortez asked.

"Naw...we decided not to pay you," Ramon snarled, angrily. "We're gonna shoot you instead, you bastard!"

Cortez turned to look directly into Ramon's face as he switched on the truck's headlights..."I don't think so," Cortez said, laughing.

Ramon chuckled at Cortez's response. He glanced back at his men who were all standing behind him and surrounding the truck, laughing softly.

"Why not?" Ramon asked, still laughing.

"Because you're under arrest, Ramon!" Cortez said, flashing his identification. "All of you are under arrest!"

Just as Carlos spoke those words, DEA agents came out from behind trees and bushes!..Floodlights were suddenly trained on the front of the home as the entire area was illuminated! Ramon and his men were quickly disarmed and handcuffed. Carlos Cortez went inside the home with fifteen armed agents when they knocked down the front door and began searching the rooms, bringing out women and children...Finally, one of the agents called Cortez down into the basement where he found himself face to face with Ceasar Montoya who was standing in the middle of the basement bedroom in his long underwear and fuming in anger!..

Chapter Thirty-One

The fashion department at The Detroit Herald Newspaper was filled with photographers and models who all crowded into the studio to participate in the initial shooting of the upcoming holiday season fashion section. Everyone in attendance was anxious and excited while several models were being photographed. It was a vintage scene of smartly dressed women, all professionally made up and adorned in the most lavish styles and posing in vogue fashion. The scenes were all centered around the major model, Ze-Ze Lablanc. Liz watched carefully as cameras rolled and photographers snapped a series of scenes. The chatter of excitement, the photographer's commands and loud, rhythmetic music all filled the background sounds as each model strutted and smiled seductively. When the session was finally over, the exhausted models all quickly retired to their dressing rooms to change back into their street clothes.

Liz went back into her office and checked the future shooting schedules with different photographers. One of her main photographers, Mac Johnson, went over the schedule with Liz.

"Mac... I think that completes all of the interior shots," Liz said.

"Then the only thing I got left are the harbor shots," Mac said, grinning. "That's a piece of cake."

"I think this is going to be one heckuva holiday fashion section," Liz said, proudly. "The girls were wonderful!"

"OK... I'll meet you and the crew at the Belle Isle Harbor tomorrow morning at eleven... right?" Mac asked.

"You got it, big guy," Liz confirmed, 'we should be completely set up by then... and Mac... you're doing a swell job!"

Mac grinned broadly as Ze-Ze walked into the office, smiling at everyone. She stopped Mac as he was about to leave. "Mac!... Sweet Mac!.. It's so nice to work with a professional like you!"

"Thanks, but you're the star, babe," Mac said, blushing, "All eyes are gonna be on you!.. I gotta go.. see ya tomorrow."

Ze-Ze turned to Liz who was sitting behind her desk wearing a pair of glasses and re-checking the shooting schedule, thoughtfully. She looked up at Ze-Ze and smiled.

"You all ready to go?... That was fast," Liz said.

"I've got to get home if you still want that special dinner you were craving for," Ze-Ze chuckled, "maybe you're pregnant."

Liz looked at Ze-Ze with an exasperated expression on her face... "I don't think so... you go on... I'll be there later."

"Oh, Liz!"

"I'm not nearly finished... I've got to re-do the shooting schedule to bring it up to date," Liz said, thoughtfully."That Mac moves fast... no wonder every agency wants to work with him."

"You want me to come back and get you?" Ze-Ze asked. "It's no problem."

"No... I just talked to my dad... he's working late, too... he said he'd drop me off."

"Fine... you be careful and call me when you get ready to leave," Ze-Ze said. "Don't work too late."

Ze-Ze quickly bent over and kissed Liz on her cheek. Liz looked up at her in surprise... Ze-Ze began laughing.

"Oh, don't get upset... everyone's gone," Ze-Ze chided. "There's no one here but you and I... I'll see you in what?... About and hour?"

Liz nodded her head with a slight smile paying at the corners of her mouth... "Yeah, that's about right... and you be careful too... it's dark outside."

Ze-Ze squinched her face at Liz and quickly turned and sauntered out of the office. The sounds of her high heels striking on the asphalt floor of the hallway echoed throughout the empty corridors of the building as she walked over to the elevator and pressed the button. When the elevator arrived she quickly stepped on. A security guard on the elevator smiled at her and Ze-Ze smiled back, flirtatiously.

"Workin' late tonight, eh?" the guard asked.

"Yes... we're closing out the holiday fashion section," she replied, "and we had a big shoot tonight."

"Oh, so that's where all those people were coming from! I thought it was kinda late for a business meeting... You plan on goin' through the loading docks to the garage?"

"Yes, why?"

"Just be careful... most of the trucks are out deliverin' the last edition," the guard said, "it's spooky in that big truck garage when it's empty at night."

"Well, if they're all out," Ze-Ze chuckled, "I don't think I'll have anything to worry about."

The guard threw his head back and laughed as the elevator stopped and the doors slid open. They both got off and the guard sat down behind the security desk in the lobby as Ze-Ze continued down the hallway leading to the truck garage and newspaper docks...

Ze-Ze walked briskly out to the loading docks and suddenly stopped... That guard was right. It was spooky!.. Most of the lights in the cavernous garage were off. The few lights that remained on cast dim shadows throughout the garage. She quickly went down the short flight of stairs and walked across the concrete floor, past the glass enclosed circulation offices which were all closed with the lights off. Her high heels beat a rhythmetic tune one the concrete. Just as she was half-way across the spacious garage floor, two shadows suddenly appeared before her!... She stopped in her tracks, trying to make out the two silhouettes... One of the two huge shadows stepped forward.

"Well, lookee here!" a gruff voice boomed. "A piece of prime meat struttin' around here in the dark as pretty as a picture and without a care in the world!"

"Get out of my way!" Ze-Ze demanded, angrily.

"A Frenchy, too!" a second voice bellowed. "My prayers have been answered!.. I bet you really know how to give a man a good time!... Damn, she's a beauty!"

Ze-Ze quickly reached into her purse and brought out a can of mace!... She pointed the spray can towards the two men as she nervously backed up!... "Stop!... Get the hell out of my way of I'll use this!...I mean it!"

The first man continued to move towards her, menacingly! "I don't think so, bitch!... You're gonna get fucked tonight!... You'll really enjoy this!" the man muttered as he walked closer. "You're gonna have three hard dicks shoved into you all at one time!"

Ze-Ze, now shaking in fear, looked around just in time to see the shadow of a third man behind her!.. Before she could scream the man behind her clasped a hand over her mouth and jerked her backwards, knocking the can of mace out of her hand!... The three men dragged her, kicking and trying to scream, towards one of the closed offices. She fought furiously but their strength overcame her! One man held her hands behind her back while another man wrapped a gag around her mouth!... The third man swept everything off the tops of two desks that were joined together. The other two men picked her up and forced her on the desks on her back!.. Two of the men held her down while one man quickly ripped off all of her clothes until she was laying there, completely naked!... The first man stared at her hungrily!... He slowly began smiling, showing a bunch of crooked teeth as he began unbuckling his belt!..

"Now, bitch... the fun begins!"

Patricia was furious as she sat in her husband's office, impatiently waiting for him to finish his work. Gene completed writing out a report and looked up at his wife, puzzled... "My secretary said you were up here earlier today to see me about something terribly important... couldn't this wait until tonight at home?"

"I have no idea what time you intend to come home anymore," she snapped, angrily, "besides... we need the privacy!"

"You're referring to Hattie and Connie?"

"Yes.. we need to talk... frankly."

"How frankly?... That goes both ways you know," Gene said calmly. "What's this all about?"

"It's about this... this Dr. Adrian Grant... who seems to be involved in everything you do lately."

"What are you talking about?... You're upset because I made her my campaign manager?"

"That and everything else," Patricia replied. "Why was she the only one of Kim's friends to visit you while you were recuperating?"

"I don't know... she shows more interest in Kim's family, that's all."

"And at the wedding... she couldn't keep her eyes or her hands off of you," Patricia said, "and I didn't see her with any date...as beautiful as she is... I've never seen her with a date!"

"Oh, c'mon, Patricia!.. You're imagining things."

"Then you suddenly have to select her as your campaign manager... it doesn't look right."

"Listen... she's more qualified to be my campaign manager than most people and she's familiar with a lot of political support groups," Gene said. "I'd be a fool not to utilize her ability."

"You even visited her in the hospital when that baby selling ring was broken."

"Let's get it completely straight, Pat," Gene shot back, angrily, "I visited both Adrian and Marcy Dugas... both of them!... And I was with Gene II and Max Jenkins!.. Stop trying to make it what it's not, counselor!"

"You better stick to your priorities!"

"Meaning what?"

"You're getting ready to run for mayor of this city... you better clean up your act or you won't be elected dog-catcher!" Patricia warned. "This is not the time for a family scandal!.. I am not going to have some young, glamorous, career driven bitch ruin my marriage!"

"I wouldn't worry about that... I think you're doing a pretty good job dismantling this marriage on your own," Gene said, calmly. "I hope you do a good job on the Anti-Racism Committee!... I'm not completely deaf, dumb and blind!"

Before Patricia could reply, Gene's direct phone line began to ring. He tried to ignore it.. "You were saying?" he asked.

She motioned towards the phone... "What's the matter?... You afraid to answer it?... You think it might be her?"

Gene quickly snatched up the phone, angrily. "Hello!" he growled.

"Dad!... Dad!... Something's happened!" Liz cried, frantically. "You've got to get down here!"

Gene covered the mouthpiece quickly and turned to Patricia!.. "It's Liz!... Something's wrong!" he said as he flipped on the speaker phone. "Liz... what's happened?"

Liz began sobbing hysterically!.. "It's Ze-Ze!... They just found her out on the loading docks downstairs!.. She's been raped, daddy!... She's been raped!"

The emergency room at City Hospital brought back frightening memories for the Stantons. Gene, Patricia and Liz stood in the hallway just outside of the emergency room. Liz cried loudly as her parents tried to comfort her. Police Sergeant Harris walked out of the emergency room towards them with a grim look on his face...

"Were you able to question her?" Gene asked.

"No.. not yet... Sgt. Driscoll is still in there," Sgt. Harris said. "It seems that a policewoman can probably accomplish a lot more in these cases."

"Didn't she say anything about who did this to her?" Liz asked, sobbing.

"Just three men... they were all drunk," Sgt. Harris said thoughtfully. "Two Black and one White... it was like they were waiting for her... they beat her up pretty bad."

Sgt. Harris looked up as a woman doctor joined the group. "How's she doin' Dr. Nixon?" he asked.

"Is she going to be alright, Doctor?" Gene asked.

"She's coming along...no serious injuries," Dr. Nixon answered, "just psychological...those animals ought to be castrated!"

"Can I see her?" Liz asked.

"Are you Liz?..She's been asking for you," Dr. Nixon said, "You can see her, but only for a few minutes...Sgt. Driscoll is still talking to her...and the Rape Counselor is on the way over here."

Ze-Ze laid in the hospital bed and barely answered Sgt. Driscoll's questions. Both of her eyes were blackened and her bottom lip was split and swollen. When Liz walked into the room, Ze-Ze seemed to brace herself. Puzzled at Ze-Ze's sudden tenseness, Sgt. Driscoll looked at Ze-Ze and then back to Liz...

"Are you Liz?" Sgt. Driscoll asked. "She's been asking for you."

Liz sat down on the bed and kissed Ze-Ze's forehead. Her eyes stared into Liz's eyes as they filled with tears. Liz lovingly embraced her, tenderly, as she whispered in a soft, purring voice..."Poor baby!..The doctor said you're going to be alright,"

Liz whispered, "how do you feel?"

"I...I think she'll be alright," Sgt. Driscoll said, quietly.

"Three...three men...two black and one white," Ze-Ze murmured, weakly, "they were all drunk and smelly...the bastards!"

We think they came from The Trojan Horse Bar just behind The Detroit Herald Newspaper building," Sgt. Driscoll said. "She gave us an excellent description. I think we'll get 'em...Dr. Nixon has done everything she could."

Dr. Nixon walked back into the room and joined the three women, deeply concerned. "The rape counselor will be here in a few minutes...The main thing we should be concerned with now is venereal disease...and...and Aids...She'll have to be tested every thirty days for next six months. We should be out of the woods by then"

"Aids?..Oh, my GOD!" Liz exclaimed.

Ze-Ze turned to Liz and squeezed her hand. Sgt. Driscoll and Dr. Nixon glanced at each other as they watched the two women, closely.

"I want her to stay in the hospital for the next twenty-four hours," Dr. Nixon said, "the x-rays were all negative but I want to make sure."

I'll contact you as soon as we arrest them, Ze-Ze," Sgt. Driscoll promised, "you just get well...soon."

"Will she have to go down there?" Liz asked.

"She'll have to identify them," Sgt. Driscoll answered, tuning back to Ze-Ze, "will that be a problem?"

"No problem," Ze-Ze answered in a weak voice, "My pleasure!"

Liz kissed Ze-Ze's forehead again and squeezed her hand. "We'll face this thing together, honey...and beat it!"

Sgt. Driscoll and Dr. Nixon smiled knowingly as they watched Liz put her arms around Ze-Ze and hold her...

Gene II sat in the family room of his big, empty home sipping a drink. He got up and slowly walked into the kitchen and looked around. He was lonely...no wife, no noisy children...no nothing. He automatically opened the refrigerator door. Although he wasn't hungry, he looked inside hoping for any reminder of his long, gone family. A half eaten candy bar...a neatly packed lunch...leftovers from their last dinner together...nothing...the cupboard was bare...just like his soul...It was bare without Susan and the kids, he mused. He walked over and picked up the phone and dialed Max's number...In a matter of seconds, Max was on the line...

"Hello."

"Hey, good buddy," Gene II said, "you wanna run with me tonight?..I'm buyin."

"No...not really," Max quickly answered, "I'm having a late dinner with Marcy tonight."

"Man!..You two are gettin' pretty close...this serious stuff?"

"Damn right it is...I'm, gonna ask her to marry me."

"Oh, wow...that is serious!"

"I told you, man...I love her and I'm gonna marry her if she'll have me."

"Don't worry...she's a smart girl...she won't turn you down," Gene II said. "Call me tomorrow and let me know what happened."

"Have you heard anything from Susan and the kids?"

"Naw...I guess she's still making up her mind."

"You'll get back together."

"I don't know about that...but good luck to you and Marcy...remember...let me know how it turns out."

"Sure will, partner," Max said. "Sorry I couldn't run with you tonight."

"No you're not."

"You're right."

"That's OK...with my ol' man runnin' for mayor I guess I better stay home and hit the books...You guys have a good time," Gene II said.

He hung up the phone, smiling and sipped his drink, thoughtfully. He reached for the phone again, stopped and shook his head negatively. He leaned back in his chair and gently shook his glass, listening to the ice cubes rattle. Suddenly, the sound of the door chimes interrupted his thoughts. He got up and quickly walked down the long hall leading to the front door. He flipped on the porch light and looked through the small glass window. He was surprised to see Susan and his three children, staring back at him, all smiling broadly. He quickly threw open the door!..

"Susan!..Hey, what are you guys doin' out here?"

"We're coming home, Gene," Susan said as tears filled her eyes. "We're coming home to stay!"

The children began screaming and hollering, happily as they hugged their father and quickly ran into the house, carrying their luggage. Gene stared at Susan and smiled.

"Welcome home, baby!..You've made me so happy!"

They embraced standing there on the front porch as the kids ran back and forth through the house. Gene II held Susan in a long, sensual embrace as his mouth found hers and their tongues met in a passionate kiss.

"Oh, Gene!" Susan cried, "I've been such a fool...can you ever forgive me?"

"Forgive you?..I love you!" Gene II said as he kissed the tears flowing down her cheeks. "Do you still love me?"

Gene II quickly picked up Susan's luggage and followed her as she slowly walked back into their home...

Max Jenkins busily prepared for Marcy's arrival by fluffing up the pillows on the living room sofa, turning the lights down, lighting the fire in the fireplace and playing soft music on the stereo. A bottle of champagne set in the middle of the cocktail table as the aroma of food cooking drifted in from the kitchen...When he was finished, Max stood in the center of his apartment stroking his chin thoughtfully. A soft knock at the front door made him turn around, anxiously. He glanced at his watch and quickly stepped in front of the mirror in the hallway and checked his appearance, pushing a few strands of hair back in place. He carefully checked the living room one more time, making sure everything was in it's proper place. Satisfied, he took a deep breath and opened the door...

Marcy stood in the doorway with a big smile on her face. Max was startled by her glamorous appearance...

"Wow!..You look marvelous!" Max stammered.

Marcy was elegantly dressed in a two-piece, neatly tailored, midnight blue, wool crepe dinner suit embellished with decorative jeweled sequins. Her skirt stopped about eight inches above her knees revealing her long, smooth legs in matching pumps. Her long, blond hair was neatly coiffured in a sophisticated upsweep with strands of hair dangling on both sides of her beautiful face and enhanced by sparkling earrings. She smiled modestly as she glanced into the apartment...

"You said it was gonna be a special evening...And you look great, too," Marcy said, calmly. "But there's just one more thing."

"What's that?"

"You gonna let me in?" Marcy asked, smiling.

Max quickly stepped aside as Marcy swaggered into the spacious apartment. She handed Max a bottle of wine which he promptly and nervously dropped. Marcy laughed as he quickly retrieved the rolling bottle.

"What's wrong with you tonight?" Marcy asked. "You're acting very strange...what's going on?"

Max set the bottle of wine on the cocktail table and took Marcy's coat she was carrying on her arm. She stood there, staring at him and waiting for an answer. He quickly left the room with her coat and soon returned, breathless. She sat down on the sofa, still smiling at him. He stared at her sitting on the sofa with her long legs crossed and exposing a lot of her upper thighs. Max swallowed hard as he sat down next to her. She reached over and kissed him, flush on his mouth. Her tongue played with his as her hand felt him slowly becoming aroused...He slightly pulled back...trying to compose himself...

"I...I've got something serious to speak to you about," Max stammered, nervously.

"OK...fine...just be still a minute," Marcy said as she put her arms around his neck and placed her leg over his lap, "let's get this business over first...I've missed you, baby."

She tried to kiss him again but Max quickly moved out of her reach..."You wanna drink?" he asked.

"Yes...that would be nice," she answered, staring at him, suspiciously.

Max poured the champagne, spilling most of it on the table. When he tried to wipe it up with a napkin, he knocked the bottle off the table, splashing champagne on Marcy's legs...

"Max!..Be careful!" Marcy screamed. "My goodness...what is your problem?"

Max finished wiping up the champagne. He stopped and stared at Marcy with a serious expression on his face..."How long have we been seeing each other?" Max asked.

"A few months now, why?" she asked, suspiciously. "Is this leading to something?"

"I think we should re-assess our relationship and find out exactly where it's going."

"You're not happy with the way it is?"

"No...I mean...I think we could do better."

"How?..We see each other two...sometimes maybe three times a week," she said, "I haven't missed seeing you one weekend...You want me to move in?"

"Uh,uh...I want more than that, baby," Max replied, smiling. "Look...I think we better get a few things straight first."

"Like what?"

"I enjoy working at The Herald," Max answered. "Gene II and I have become very close friends...in fact...he is my best friend."

"Pardon me?"

"Present company excluded."

"Thank you, sir."

"It's just...I intend to work at The Herald as long as they let me...it's a great newspaper," Max said.

"So?..I feel the same way," Marcy said, confused.

"But you own part of The Daily Press...Some day...it may all be yours and your brother's."

"What's that got to do with us?" she asked, impatiently.

Max stared into her eyes as he took her hand in his...

"I love you, Marcy," Max said, softly. "But what happens if you suddenly become a major owner of The Daily Press?"

"I'd want you with me, of course," she whispered.

"But I'm committed to The Herald."

"I thought you just said you loved me."

"I did."

"Then you're more committed to me, aren't you."

"More than you'll ever know, " Max answered.

"Then I don't see any problem," she said, smiling. "I love you...you love me...we'll always be together...Besides, I think "I'm pregnant."

"Are you serious?" he asked, stunned.

"It looks like you're gonna be a daddy, Max."

"Then that makes it perfect!" he said, happily.

"Wh...what?"

He reached over and embraced her, kissing her all over her face...He tried to speak but she began kissing him back. He held her away, staring into her eyes...

"Marcy, honey...I...I want you to marry me."

Marcy was surprised!.."Is that what this was all about?" she asked, her eyes widening. "Oh, Max...I had no idea you were gonna ask me to marry you!..I was gonna tell you about me being pregnant!"

Max handed her a small black velvet covered box. She slowly took it, her eyes remaining fixed on his. She snapped it opened and gasped!..

"Max..it's...it's just beautiful!..You...you sweet, sweet man, you!"

After he slipped the ring on her finger, they embraced with a long, deep kiss as her tongue touched his and explored his mouth with great passion. Marcy laid back on the sofa as he continued the deep, soul searching kiss while one of his hands unbuttoned her suit and blouse as the other slid under her skirt. She deftly unzipped his trousers as her hand began to massage his stiff member. Before he realized it, they were both naked from the waist down as she spread her long legs allowing him to insert himself deep into her trembling body...They moved in perfect synchronization, each touch, each warm caress. He hungrily mouthed her stiff breasts as his body increased the tempo until they both froze in a thundering orgasm, knocking the open bottle of champagne to the floor!..

Karen Stanton-Whyte walked into the general offices of Jordan Funeral Homes, Inc. She went up to the receptionist and gave her a business card. The receptionist studied the card for a moment and looked up at Karen...

"Do you have an appointment with Mr. Jordan, Mrs. Whyte?" she asked.

"He's expecting me," Karen replied.

"Please have a seat."

Karen sat down and looked the offices over, casually. In a few minutes Dan Jordan came out to greet Karen. He was followed by a strikingly beautiful Hispanic woman. Dan looked at Karen and smiled broadly. "Hi, Karen...I'd like for you to meet my executive vice president, Ms. Theresa Gonzales."

Karen shook the woman's outstretched hand.

"I'm very glad to meet you, Mrs. Whyte," Theresa said, smiling. "I intend to be one of your father's biggest supporters...If you'll excuse me...I have to attend to some pressing business."

As Theresa left, Dan escorted Karen into his office, still grinning broadly. Karen sat down as Dan closed the door and walked behind his desk and sat down. She eyed him closely before speaking. Dan began to feel uncomfortable.

"What can I do for you, Karen?" Dan asked. "I meant to compliment you and your entire family on that superb wedding. It was fabulous...and that gown you were wearing was simply stunning!"

"Thank you...we all put a lot of effort into that wedding and the reception," Karen said, " I'm glad you enjoyed it."

"What can I do for you?" Dan asked again, casually.

"You can answer a few questions for me...fill in a few blank spots," Karen said.

"If this is about some business I just transacted with you father, I..."

Karen quickly interrupted. "No...this is not about anything that's happened recently...I understand you've been a friend of my parents for more than thirty years."

"That's correct...I use to work for The State Journal right after they were married," Dan said.

"Whose friend were you...mother's or father's?"

"I don't follow you...I was a friend to both of them, Karen," Dan answered, concerned. "What're you getting at?"

"A few months after my brother Gene was born...my parents split up...like most newlyweds with a new born baby and little income...they were having problems."

"I remember that," Dan volunteered, "it was a difficult time for both of them...they took it very hard."

"Did you ever date my mother during that time?"

"Let's see," Dan said, thoughtfully, "I took her out a couple of times...to the show...maybe a picnic or two."

"Some friend."

"What?"

"That doesn't sound like anything a true friend of my father's would do," Karen answered in disgust. "How did he react to your dating his wife?"

"I don't believe he ever knew."

"You're damn right he never knew!"

"You're not gonna mention anything to him about this are you?" Dan asked, anxiously. "I was just trying to comfort Patricia...I didn't mean anything by it...Why are you asking me all of these questions now?"

"I got the results of my D.N.A. test a few months ago," Karen answered, watching for his reactions, closely. "It proved conclusively that Gene Stanton is not my father!"...I think you're my father, Mr. Jordan...and you know it!"

Dan Jordan became flustered as he quickly got up and walked around his desk towards Karen. He sat down next to her and loosened his shirt collar...

"Have you spoken to your mother about this?"

"Yes...Yes, I have."

"And what did she say?"

"It's not so much what she said," Karen snapped. "It's what she didn't day...she didn't deny it."

"Listen...your dad's done me a lot of favors," Dan whispered, hoarsely. "He just saved me from losing this business and going to jail!..If this gets out. Gene Stanton will crucify me!"

"Stop sniveling!" Karen shot back, angrily. "You could have acknowledged a daughter you had twenty-six years ago!"

"What good would that have done?..You're in good shape...you own part of the Stanton fortune...part of the Detroit Herald...Now, he's gonna become our next mayor!..Hell, you oughta thank me for keeping quiet!"

"You owe me!" Karen shouted angrily.

"Damn, woman!" he snapped. "I don't have anything...except...except this damn business!"

"And by rights...part of it should be mine!"

"What the hell do you want with a business like this?" Dan asked, surprised. "You're probably worth a hundred times what I have!"

Karen quickly stood up over Dan's chair, angrily!. "I want what's mine!..You don't have any other children and I want what should've been mine years ago!"

"I...I don't know what I can do," Dan said, meekly.

"You've got one week to have your attorney draw up the papers giving me twenty-five percent of this corporation!"..No...make that twenty-six percent...one percent for each year I've been born!..If you don't... your dear, dear friend, Gene Stanton, will fry your balls in boiling oil!"

With that last sentence, Karen quickly turned and stormed out of the office, slamming the door!..Dan Jordan put both hands over his face, shakened!..

Chapter Thirty-Two

Damien, dressed up as an auto mechanic and carrying a mechanic's tool box, jauntily walked up to the security guard on duty at the guard's station in The Herald Newspaper's executive garage. He pulled out a crumpled work order slip from Morgan's Mechanics and handed it to the security guard.

"I'm Ben Scott...auto mechanic from Morgan's. That's a work order to replace a muffler on executive cars number sixteen...and...er...a twenty-one."

The guard quickly checked the auto board on the wall carefully and turned back to the mechanic..."They're both out...come back around four in the afternoon and you can fix'em."

"No can do...that would take me into overtime," Damien said, disgusted, "I gotta be finished by five."

"That's OK...I'll leave the afternoon guard a note and he'll let you in here without nobody knowin,'" the guard said, smiling. "We do that all the time...we wage earners got to work together. That way you can report that you did the work this afternoon and go some place and goof off."

"That works fer me," Damien replied, "You got my name?"

The guard looked at the name tag on Damien's shirt..."Yeah...I wrote it down...Scott...Ben Scott from Morgans."

"You got it," Damien said, grinning as he turned to leave.

The private room at City Hospital was full of flowers as Liz sat next to Ze-Ze's bed. Ze-Ze was busy dressing and packing her clothes, preparing to check out. She stepped in front of the dresser mirror and studied her appearance with a frown on her face. She put on a pair of dark glasses and began a series of poses. Liz watched her and smiled.

"I put off the exterior shoot until next week," Liz said, "We'll still be able to make the deadline...those shiners of yours ought to be gone by then...you think you'll be ready?"

Ze-Ze slowly turned around and stared at Liz in a haughty manner..."My deah...Madam Ze-Ze is always ready to be shot...shiners or no shiners...but I feel like total hell right now!"

Liz laughed at Ze-Ze's imitation of a grand madam..."You look pretty sexy in those dark glasses," Liz said.

"Stop lying...My face all swollen up with two black eyes...I look like a pregnant raccoon!"

Liz chuckled as the phone began ringing. She picked it up as Ze-Ze continued posing with the dark glasses...

"Hello."

"Ze-Ze...Sgt. Driscoll...I got some news!"

"This is Liz Stanton, sergeant...just a minute," she handed the phone to Ze-Ze.

"Yes,, sergeant?" Ze-Ze asked.

"I've got some news for you, Ze-Ze." Sgt Driscoll said, cheerfully, "how are you feeling?"

"Like I just fought the heavyweight champion and lost," Ze-Ze answered. "What have you got?"

"We got those three vermin!" Sgt. Driscoll replied, triumphantly. "We need you to come down and identify 'em in a line-up ...Can you make it right now?"

"You're damn right I can!" Ze-Ze answered anxiously, "Where are you?"

Sgt. Driscoll liked her rapid response and chuckled. "Thirteen hundred Beaubien...Police Headquarters, downtown on the fifth floor...just ask for me."

"Check your front door, Sergeant," Ze-Ze said excitedly. "We're coming through it right now!"

Liz stared at Ze-Ze with a big smile on her face as Ze-Ze spun around, jerked one clenched fist backwards and quickly shoved the other clenched fist forward as she shouted, happily!..."got'em!"

The line-up room at the Detroit Police Headquarters was crowded with suspects as they marched out on a small stage and quickly turned to their left facing a darkened audience. In the room adjoining, Sgt. Driscoll and Ze-Ze stood in front of a two-way mirror as the line-up was formed. Liz waited in the background, watching the proceedings intently. Ten men stood on the stage under the glare of bright lights. Sgt. Driscoll gave the men commands over a microphone...

"Turn left, gentlemen...hold it...thank you...Now turn to the right...hold it."

Sgt. Driscoll covered up the microphone with her hand as she turned to Ze-Ze..."You see any of the three men who raped you?"

"I see all three," Ze-Ze snapped, angrily. "The one on the right end and the two on the left end...those are the three bastards who raped me!..I"ll NEVER forget their faces!"

"Are you absolutely sure?" Sgt Driscoll asked.

"Absolutely!..No doubt about it!" Ze-Ze said, bitterly. "I'd like to pull the switch!"

"You just did," Sgt Driscoll said, smiling. "Go girl!..We'll sock it to 'em."

Liz stepped forward and hugged Ze-Ze, proudly. She leaned back and stared into Ze-Ze eyes...

"You know what?" Liz whispered. "I think you got balls, lady!..You got balls!"

The Carlson household was full of workmen trying to repair the damage to the home and furnishings. The sounds of shouting and hammering could be heard from room to room as various workers roamed throughout the house. Janet and Roger sat in the family room, out of the workers' way. Janet thoughtfully sipped a cup of coffee as Roger went through the mail. He looked up at his wife, sadly...

"Damn!..I wish this had never happened!" Roger groaned. "I thought we were out of the woods!"

"Don't worry, honey," Janet said, "our insurance will cover most of the damage."

"It's not just that...poor Michelle...if her father did molest her...he should be made to pay...and I'll see to it that he does!"

"Are you having second thoughts about the baby?" Janet asked. "It's not genetic."

"I know...that may be true," Roger replied, "but after Michelle's been through all of this...has it occurred to you that we may be taking advantage of her if she carries full term?"

"I've thought about it."

"It could push her over the edge," Roger said.

"But an abortion might even create more problems for her," Janet said, thoughtfully. "We had no way of knowing about her multiple personality disorder."

"She's still first trimester," Roger said. "I don't think it would be right to go through with this...she's not responsible in her condition."

"You know how I feel about abortions."

"In this case...that might be self-serving," Roger said. "We're not talking about how we feel...we're talking about what's best for Michelle."

Roger got up, walked over and sat down next to his wife on the sofa. He put his arms around her and hugged her tenderly as he stared into her eyes. "You poor dear...all you wanted was to become a mother."

"We have to make a decision soon...we don't have too much time left," Janet said, sadly.

"It's not our decision to make, Janet...we're not even her parents."

"Her parents won't even talk to her," Janet said, concerned. "Somebody has to help her decide."

"Well, I think we're just stuck with the status quo...She'll be moved to Ann Arbor Trail Convalescent today. At least we can provide her with the best of care and let nature takes it's course."

"If her prognosis continues to be good...maybe she'll successfully deliver the baby," Janet said. "Remember that's what Dr. Wolfort said would probably help her the most."

"Michelle's illness can't be cured," Roger said, "it can only be treated...Let's see what her psychiatrist at Ann Arbor Trail advices us to do."

Janet reached over and squeezed Roger's hand. She looked up into his eyes, searching for an answer...

Gene Stanton worked at his desk in the publisher's office at The Herald. He looked up when Gene II and Max hurried into his office. He eyed them closely since it was obvious they were excited about something.

"Dad...I understand we had a little excitement around here the other night," Gene II said. "Why did't you tell me?"

"The guards say one of our models was attacked," Max said.

"That guard has a big mouth...it's all been handled," Gene said, firmly. "The men who did it are under arrest. I don't want this thing to snowball...out of consideration for the woman...So let's put a period behind it right now!"

"OK..OK!..I understand," Gene II said, calmly. "Ol' Max here has some news of his own."

"Oh?..What's your news, Max?" Gene asked.

"I asked Marcy to marry me...she said yes...we're engaged!" Max beamed.

Gene stood up behind his desk, reached over and smiling broadly, shook Max's hand. "Congratulations, Max!..She's a wonderful person!"

"I know...thank you," Max grinned, "and that's not the only good news we've got...your son has something to tell you."

"What's happened?" Gene asked.

Gene II smiled. "Susan and the kids...they came home last night."

Gene smiled at his son, knowingly. "How are they all doing?"

"Everybody's just fine," Gene II answered, "but Max and I have to get out of here...we have an early appointment this evening."

"Where are you going?" Gene asked.

"We have a meeting with the Lt. Governor at the state capitol," Gene II answered. "I called the garage and some mechanic is replacing the muffler on my car...I've got to get another one."

"Take mine. I won't be going anywhere until later," Gene said, "I'm holding a news conference this evening to announce my candidacy."

THE WINDS OF TOMORROW

"No good...I already tried that...he's replacing the muffler on your car, too."

Suddenly, Gene became gravely concerned. "They just replaced the muffler on my car...What the hell is going on?...Hold on a minute...I better check this out."

Gene quickly called the garage and spoke to the security guard on duty who confirmed that the muffler on his car was being replace. He then dialed the mechanic's number. In a few seconds the phone was answered.

"Morgans Mechanics...can I help you?"

"This is Gene Stanton at The Herald...Is HarryMorgan there?"

"Oh, hi, Mr. Stanton...this is Harry...is everything alright with your fleet?"

"Did you send a mechanic over to my garage today?" Gene asked, "To fix a muffler on two of my cars...namely mine?"

"No...we just put a muffler on your car two weeks ago."

"That's what I thought, Harry...it must be some mistake," Gene said, cooly. "Don't worry about it...I'll take care of it."

Gene slammed the phone down and stared at Gene II and Max!.."If you guys got an appointment...you better arrange to get somebody else's car...not any of ours."

"Why?..What's going on?" Gene II asked, puzzled.

"I think we just had a visit from my would-be assassin and he's still over in the garage working on our cars now!"

The two trouser covered legs of the auto mechanic extended out from under Gene Stanton's assigned newspaper automobile, as the mechanic worked on the car inside The Herald's executive parking garage. The mechanic worked methodically as two other cars came up the ramp and parked nearby. Other cars drove by going up to the upper ramps and the warning sounds of their horns blasted loudly before the vehicles turned at each corner of the ramps as members of the editorial and advertising staffs returned to their newspaper offices. In a few minutes, Damien, posing as the auto mechanic, slid out from under the car on a mechanic's board. He stood up and stretched before he calmly lowered the car with a rear bumper jack. He noticed two men carrying briefcases standing on the other side of the aisle-way, talking. He nodded to them and smiled as he wiped the oil and grease from his hands. He cooly began whistling as he put his tools back inside the metal tool box. The two men continued to talk and watched Damien preparing to leave...Damien turned to the two men, grinning broadly...

"You guys all through for the day?" Damien asked, casually.

"Yeah, we're just going over some advertising promos," the first man said, friendly. "You a mechanic?"

Damien laughed heartily. "Why?..You think I was laying under that car playing with myself?"

"Isn't that Gene Stanton's car?" the second man asked. "He's our publisher...what's wrong with it?"

"Needed a muffler...I just put one on."

"Oh, yeah?" the first man asked. "Where's the old one?"

Damien suddenly became nervous, looking all around the floor they were on. "Wh...why? he stammered.

"If you took the old one off," the second man said, "where is it?"

"Who the hell are you?" Damien asked, angrily.

"I'll ask you the same question," the first man replied, louder. "Who the hell are you?"

Damien began slowly backing up as the two men walked towards him, unbuttoning their coats. One man quickly opened his wallet, flashing a police badge..."Now...you gonna answer our questions?" the man asked as they walked closer...

"Look...I don't know what's goin' on around here but I'm just an auto mechanic from Morgans Mechanics," Damien lied, nervously. "We got a contract with The Herald to keep these units rolling."

"Morgans Mechanics said they didn't send anybody over here," the second man said, angrily. "I think you're a damn liar!"

"You said you put a muffler on this car?" the first man asked.

"Yeah, honest...maybe I went to the wrong garage."

"Well, Mr. Stanton is in the lobby waitin' for his car," the first man said. "Why don't you drive it over to the front of the newspaper building...he's waitin' for it."

Damien smiled confidently. "I don't have the keys."

"I knew you were gonna say that," the first man said, tossing Damien a set of keys. "Try these."

Damien caught the keys in an automatic response and tossed them up and down in his hand slowly as he turned to the car.

"Yeah...get in and start it up," the second man said, calmly.

Damien began to sweat as the two men walked closer. He looked at the car and then back to the two oncoming men, who suddenly stopped and stood in front of the car, glaring at him!..

"I ain't no friggin' porter!" Damien suddenly protested. "That ain't my job...We got a union....I'm not gonna drive that car!"

"OK...Alright," the first man said, softly. "Just start it up...see if the muffler is leakin' or somethin."

Damien began to stammer..."No...no...it's brand new...I know it's not leakin...but if you insist."

"We insist!" the second man interrupted, angrily. "Start it up!"

Damien smiled and slowly opened the driver's door to the car as the two policemen backed away, cautiously. He slid in behind the wheel and reached down towards the ignition. Damien looked up and smiled at the two policemen as he lifted up a gun and stuck the barrel of the weapon in his mouth!..The policemen quickly began shouting as they both crouched and reached for their weapons!

"Gun!..Gun!..Gun!" they both shouted as they dove for cover!

The resounding blast of Damien's gun and the sight of his body slumping backwards in the car as blood oozed from his head, signaled that the policemen's shouts were too late!..

The large lobby of The Detroit Herald Newspaper building was crowded with reporters, business people, politicians, Herald employees and interested citizens. Several television crews stood by, waiting for the news conference to begin. Adrian Grant had many people passing out press kits and brochures. In the rear of the lobby coffee and donuts were served. The electrifying excitement permeated the spacious lobby as everyone expected the announcement of a major mayoral candidate. Adrian moved behind the large podium that was loaded with microphones and tape recorders. She began to pound the gavel, trying to attract everyone's attention...

"Thank you all for responding so promptly to our invitation, ladies and gentlemen," Adrian said, "this will be marked as a prominent date in Detroit's history as Mr. Gene Stanton, publisher of The Detroit Herald Newspaper and one of the few native Detroiters running in the primary next spring, announces his candidacy for Mayor of the City of Detroit...It is my proud pleasure to present to you...the next mayor of our city...Mr.Gene Stanton!"

A long and loud burst of applause began as Gene casually moved to the podium and Adrian stepped down. Gene carried several sheets of papers with him as he began to speak...

"Ladies and gentlemen, members of the press, friends and citizens...thank you all for coming here today..before I could accept any nomination for mayor of Detroit, I had to know that I could obtain the support of grass roots groups and private industry to insure that the economic success of our great city would be a top priority of my administration...for with this economic success I intend to greatly increase the size of our public services...namely, I will more than double the size of our police department from thirty-eight hundred to at least ten thousand police officers!..This will insure a reduction in crime, drugs and violence. The City of Detroit will be safer than most suburban communities and have the lowest crime rate for many of the major urban areas in the country!..I believe that a high visibility of police officers is a mandatory pre-requisite for a safe city...Furthermore, with this economic success I plan to bring retailers back into our city by re-opening the downtown shopping mall with 20,000 free parking units...rebuild our neighborhoods with at least 5,000 new home starts each year until those despicable vacant lots and burned out shells of homes disappear...rebuild our schools to increase the value of our property and homes...I'm talking about an economic stimulation that could bring as much as two billion additional dollars into the Detroit economy every year...and I am not talking about any form of gambling!"

Everyone in the huge lobby became excited as they all realize the vastness of Gene's program!..Gene stopped speaking, allowing this realization to sink in...

"It is no coincident that the decline of America's cities is happening after almost 20 years of conservative administrations in the White House who ignored the plight of our urban areas and was completely indifferent to our major cities with large black populations and black leadership!..As a result...we are now looking at modern American apartheid...our cities are almost 85 percent Black and Hispanic surrounded by suburbs that are almost ninety percent White!..In the case of Detroit our problem was further compounded by the downsizing of the auto industry and the flight of Whites, middle-class Blacks and retail businesses to the suburbs!..I believe it is time for the Cityof Detroit to utilize it's natural resources to chart it's own destiny to survive!..After an extensive study we discovered that Detroit is in the unique position of having this beautiful little island just off of our coast...Belle Isle..For many years Belle Isle has remained untouched and unproductive...I believe we can thank the organization, The Friends of Belle Isle, for that...but now, our city's economy has reached a drastic stage!..I'm not just talking about saving Belle Isle...I'm talking about saving Detroit!"

Gene paused as voices were raised showing a great deal of interest and concern...After a few moments he continued.

"After conferring with some of my consultants from various grass roots organizations as well as some of the giants of industry...researching the yearly income of similar ventures all across the country...we've reached the conclusion that we could increase the Cityof Detroit's annual income by as much as two billion dollars by developing Belle Isle into a state-of-the-art science fiction theme park and fun island, similar to Disney World and Disney Land...with the potential for maximum gross income!"

As Gene spoke those words a table sized miniature of Belle Isle was slowly rolled in front of the podium. The mock island was surrounded by water, with MacArthur Bridge in place and several buildings and potential projects in place. Many cameras began clicking as everyone's attention was directed to the dining room size table. The sounds of "ooohhh!" and "aaahhh!" filled the crowded room as people crowded around the project, staring like they were hypnotized!..Gene used a pointer as he continued...

"All of the visitors to the island will be greeted by space aliens, giant animals and cartoon characters when they first arrive...We plan to have an entire space world, a wax museum, a sea world, a real and complete castle imported from Scotland or England, three separate motion picture production companies that could represent Detroit's answer to Hollywood...we will also feature unlimited mega-rides which will be led by a Flying Saucer Roller Coaster all around the perimeter of the island...The giants of industry would participate by donating the space world which would house a complete galaxy with all of the planets in the Solar System, a giant

Redstone Missile, and a Space Shuttle along with a real life-size Flying Saucer craft that people could inspect and ride in...Another corporation could donate The Sea World project which would far exceed the other sea worlds across the country and have shows and unique displays. A third industrial giant might donate The Wax Museum which would feature movie stars, inventors, historical figures, sports stars and special events...The castle would be imported here by each school student in the metro Detroit area paying a quarter per brick, which would give them an active role in helping bring back Detroit...The island would also have several theatres, restaurants and many forms of family entertainment such as swimming pools, high tech-mega rides and an enlarge family zoo while it still maintains over fifty percent of the aesthetics now offered for family fun and picnics. We will even have boat rides for an excursion around the Detroit river."

One of the reporters who was quickly jotting down notes looked up at Gene, puzzled..."Do you plan to shut the island down during the winter months?' he asked

"I'm glad you asked that question," Gene replied, smiling knowingly. "In the winter Belle Isle will be designed with small ski slopes, ice skating rinks, tobogganing trails...It will be totally converted to a Winter Wonderland with horse drawn sleigh rides, ski rides...of course the castle will be transformed into a Witches' Castle in October for Halloween...and converted to Santa Claus' Castle in November and December, which should attract children from all over the country...This entire project could become the biggest theme park and tourist attraction in the midwest!..Most of the other major cities would not be able to do this because they lack a separate island like Belle Isle...Our contractors estimate the total conversion could take place within two years of it's start date...This project will generate the kind of revenue that within three years we will be able to offer two years of free college education to every Detroit child who has lived at least three consecutive years in the city prior to applying to college...We will complete the downtown shopping mall with 20 thousand free parking units, rebuild our neighborhoods with bright, new, affordable single family homes, duplexes and arrange business loans to help establish an International Village of restaurants and specialty shops from all over the world...This International Village's businesses would be located primarily along all of the main arteries leading into downtown Detroit such as Woodward, Michigan, Fort, Gratiot, Jefferson and Lafayette...With the sizeable increase in our police force up to almost ten thousand police officers, this will not only create more jobs for Detroiters, but the entire metropolitan area!..And it is certain to bring people and businesses back to the city...With the influx of shoppers from the additional tourist traffic visiting the Windsor gambling casinos and Belle Isle, the new downtown mall will more than double the normal traffic at suburban malls because of it's close location to Windsor and Belle Isle. We also expect to lure a major retailer back downtown to anchor the mall...And this way, we can bring the City of Detroit back to Detroiters!..Everyone in the world will clearly see that Detroit is not dying and that our city is finally beginning to grow again!..I thank you!"

The applause was tremendous as everyone stood, yelled, shouted and whistled!..Throngs of people crowded around the podium congratulating Gene, while others made their way over to closely examine the detailed mock-up of the Belle Isle Science-Fiction Theme Park...

Chapter Thirty-Three

The publisher's office at The Detroit Herald Newspaper had been a flourish of business ever since Gene announced that he was running for mayor. Gene had had visitors from all walks of life and from all over the entire country...Today, Gene secretary showed a priest into his office. Gene stoop up and firmly shook the man's hand. The priest quickly sat down in front of Gene's desk and sighed, nervously. Gene stared at him before he spoke.

"Father McCarthy...I understand that you're the drama teacher at St. Anthony's Academy," Gene said. "What can I do for you, sir?"

"Mr. Stanton...I saw your news conference on TV," Father McCarthy said. "You're a good, honest man and you can help this city...After I heard your plans...I knew that you were the kind of man who could handle...a delicate and sensitive situation without expecting any personal inducement."

"A delicate situation?" Gene asked.

"Yes...very much so...You see every year at this time we select actors from our students for our Christmas Pageant," Father McCarthy said, "it creates somewhat of a problem because many of our students' parents are from wealthy and powerful families. Some are well connected to New York and Hollywood...In fact, one of our alumni is the casting director at a major Hollywood studio and he wants first shot at our stars when they graduate from high school, so it's like an automatic screen test for whoever I happen to select."

Gene became confused..."Did I miss something, father?" Gene asked. "I don't understand...what's that got to do with your...delicate problem?"

"For the past five years of our Christmas Pageant, the two leading actors, one boy and one girl...have found their way into major motion pictures...because of this casting director."

"I see...So I can assume you must be getting pressure from some of the parents...and the students."

"That's correct...in fact, I've had sexual propositions, death threats, sugar dumped in my gasoline tank...and I was actually assaulted by an irate parent because I didn't select her daughter for a starring role last year."

"It...it actually got that bad?"

"Worse...the school director has jumped on my back because they're pressuring him, too."

"But I can't see how I can help you father...what can I do?"

"This year...it really snowballed," the priest said with a worried expression on his face, "and I need someone or somebody to run interference for me before this thing gets out of hand."

"I'm sorry...I'd like to help you, but I think you need a lawyer not a newspaper publisher."

"What about a well known civic figure with a lot of clout?" the priest asked. "Everybody's talking about you and your plans for the City of Detroit...If you were to intervene on my behalf...they'd back off."

"I doubt that," Gene said, thoughtfully.

"You don't understand all of the ramifications involved, Mr. Stanton...This one set of parents is threatening to go to both newspapers and local television if I don't yield to their demands."

"With what?..We wouldn't be interested in printing anything like that and I'm sure the other media would feel the same way."

Father McCarthy rubbed his brow in a sign of frustration. "They've even gone so far as to recruit other students and their parents to support them."

"Support them in doing what?" Gene asked.

"Well...I hate to bring this up, but I'm sure you're aware of the problems many priests have been having lately. This particular mother and father carry a lot of weight in the community...He's an auto executive and she's a precinct delegate...They told me in no uncertain terms, that if I didn't choose their daughter for the starring role in this year's pageant...they'd arrange for five of my female students to file a complaint against me!..It could cost me my job and my reputation...it could destroy me, Mr.Stanton!"

"What kind of complaint?"

"Sexual molestation...they said these five girls would claim that I've been molesting them...if I didn't give in to their demands!"

Gene stared at the priest, sternly..."Have you been molesting them?" Gene asked, whispering.

"Of course not!..I'ver never touched a single one of them and I'm completely innocent of such charges!" Father McCarthy protested. "But you see how you just reacted?..With so much negative publicity all across the country, I wouldn't stand a chance in defending myself against such ridiculous charges!"

"OK!..OK!..I believe you, father, " Gene said, calmly. "Then you have nothing to worry about...if you're really innocent."

"But don't you understand?..With the problems the church has been having, a charge like that could make me lose my assignment and it would stick with me for life...I'd have that stigma following me around no matter where I went!..I'm just a drama teacher...all I want to do is my job."

"Have you chosen the two actors for this year's pageant?" Gene asked.

"I'm making the announcement in a few days...As soon as I do, all hell is gonna break loose!" Father McCarthy said, sadly. "I can't go to the police...so far they haven't done anything and I can't prove that they will."

"Then you're jumping the gun on them by telling me so we won't print anything?"

"No...I'm asking you to help me get the truth out...I am not a pedophile and I abhor the thought of anyone molesting children!..But unless someone can expose this conspiracy and stop it before I make the two actors I select known...I could be ruined!"

Gene got up and walked around his desk, thoughtfully. He pulled a chair up in front of Father McCarthy and sat down, looking him directly in the eyes..."I believe you, father...please write down the names of all of the principals and we'll look into this matter."

Gene handed Father McCarthy a pen and a notebook. The priest looked up at Gene and hesitated..."You're not gonna put anything in the paper are you?"

"I promise you...nothing will be put in the paper and none of the people involved will ever know that they are being investigated," Gene answered.

"Thank you, Mr. Stanton...I have faith in you."

"I'll put someone on this and get back to you...meanwhile, you continue your work as you normally would and call before you tell anyone who you've selected," Gene said. "I promise you...we'll get to the bottom of this."

Gene II and Max worked busily in Gene II's office in the editorial department. They were engrossed in making arrangements for Max to take over the editorial department when Gene II became interim publisher. They were soon interrupted by Gene II's secretary when she excitedly barged into the office. Gene II looked up at her, surprised.

"What's up, Sheila?" he asked.

"Your wife's on the line," Sheila replied, anxiously. "She said the furnace went out again and it's suppose to go down near zero tonight!"

"Relax...that happens all the time," Gene II said, smiling at Max as he picked up the phone. "Watch this...Susan, Sheila said the furnace went out again."

"It sure has and it's going down near zero tonight!" Susan replied, angrily. "What are we going to do?"

"You call the furnace people?"

"No answer...I think they're closed 'til after the holidays."

Gene II took command of the situation. "OK...now just relax...there's a reset button next to the pilot light at the front of the furnace...just press that little red button and hold it down for twenty seconds...it should start up again...call me back and let me know what happened."

Gene II hung up the phone with a confident smile on his face as Sheila marched out of the office. Gene II chuckled softly as he and Max went back to work.

"See that?" Gene II asked Max. "She needs me, man...she needs me."

"She needs a furnace!" Max chuckled. "That furnace has been giving you trouble for a while now hasn't it?..You ought to replace it, man."

"See...that's what you'll learn after you and Marcy get married...You've got to be economical and figure out ways to fix these small things yourself...If it can't be repaired I will replace it...it's not that old, but it never has acted right...if it wasn't for my mechanical ability it wouldn't have lasted..."

Sheila suddenly marched back into the office with a worried look on her face. She quickly interrupted Gene II in mid-sentence..."Your wife's on line one!"

Gene II smiled at Sheila who glared back at him with a disapproving smirk on her face. When Gene II picked up the phone Sheila stood over him with her arms folded and patting her foot, impatiently...

"Yes, honey...what happened?"

"Well that did it!"

"That did what?"

"It blew up!"

"What?"

Susan snapped back, angrily. "That damn furnace blew up, Gene!..Now what the hell are we gonna do? Here it is almost Christmas and we don't have any heat!"

Gene II looked up at Sheila who stared back at him in disgust...

"The house will stay warm at least for a couple of hours...I'll call you right back, honey," Gene II said as he turned to Sheila. She was waiting for him...

"I've already called four furnace repair services," she growled. "They're all closed until the first of next year!..You better get your family some heat!"

Max became seriously concerned..."Yeah, it's going down to..."

"Zero tonight!" Gene II interrupted, angrily. "Yeah, I know...I know!.."

Gene II got up and began pacing the floor while Max and Sheila stared at him, impatiently.

"Well...what are you going to do?" Max asked, anxiously. "Susan's waiting for an answer!"

"You should've been prepared for this, Gene," Sheila shot back at him, "that furnace has been coughing and wheezing ever since you had it turned on this fall!..Those furanace repair people all know me by voice!"

Gene II suddenly stopped pacing and pounded one fist into the palm of his hand..."I got it!"

"You got what?" Max asked.

"I'll just take my family over to the mansion for the holidays," Gene replied, smiling.

"But you got your tree up and your home's all decorated," Sheila protested, "and you and Susan have just got back together and everything!"

"She's got a point," Max said, concerned.

"So what am I suppose to do?" Gene II asked as he stood in the middle of the office with his arms spread, helplessly. "Just let my family freeze while mom and dad's got that great big, empty mansion?..No way!"

He quickly reached for the phone and began dialing. Max looked at Sheila and smiled...

Gene II and Max put the stacks of files and folders back into the metal filing cabinets next to Gene II's desk as they prepared to break for lunch. Max looked at Gene II and chuckled. "How'd your folks react to your little holiday surprise?"

"They love it...the more the merrier," Gene II said. "It's Susan who's upset...she wasn't too happy about leavin' her home over the holidays...but the kids are lookin' forward to it...besides, they're gonna have a houseful with Kim and Joe coming in...they won't notice us too much."

Both men turned to the door of the office as Marcy rushed into the office with an anxious expression on her face!.."Those Nazis and Skinheads out at Stonebrook are at it again!"

"What's happened this time?" Gene II asked, disgustedly.

"Not again!" Max groaned.

"Remember that half-page feature I did on that pediatrician who married the psychologist and adopted ten children from all different races?..It ran about three months ago." Marcy said, excitedly.

"Yeah...what about it?" Max asked.

"We just picked it up on the wire," Marcy said, "the Skinheads and Nazis just set their home on fire!"

"Aw, damn!" Gene II shouted, angrily. "Right at the holidays!..How bad was it?"

"The fire department's still out there, but they can't do very much!" Marcy answered, sadly. "The home is completely destroyed!"

"What about the children?" Gene II asked, concerned. "Was anybody hurt?"

"No, thank GOD!" Marcy sighed. "But I'm going out there with a photographer to cover it."

Max quickly reached for his coat. "Hold it, honey!..I'll go with you...that family's gonna need some help!"

"Hell!" Gene II shouted, grabbing his coat. "We'll all go out there!"

Sheila walked into the office as Gene II put on his coat to leave. She stopped and stared at him, surprised. "Where are you going, Gene?..Your wife is waiting for you to come home and help her and the kids get everything together to move!"

"Something important has come up," Gene II said, anxiously. "Call Susan and tell her to contact dad...better yet...you call dad and ask him to get somebody over there to help her!..We're heading out to Stonebrook...the Nazis and the Skinheads just burned down an inter-racial family's home!"

Sheila stood in the office as all three of them rushed out!..She watched them leave, completely speechless!..

The northern suburban neighborhood just outside of Detroit was tree line with winding streets and long, rambling front lawns that were all covered with snow. The bedroom community was made up of mostly brick ranch styled homes with attached garages. The crowd of people standing in the street and on the sidewalks, surrounding several police and fire department vehicles, stared forlornly at the charred ruins of the burned-out home. People from TV stations and several newspapers, including The Herald and The Daily Press, stood discussing the situation with the suburban fire chief.

"This is not good!..It is an awful shame!" the fire chief declared, loudly. "Here it is almost Christmas and everything these people had...is gone!..All the kids' presents, books, new clothes, toys...everything is gone!"

"I'd like to find the bastards who are responsible for this!" Max said, angrily.

Marcy was remorseful as she observed the entire scene with tears in her eyes. "Maybe...maybe this wouldn't have happened if I hadn't featured them in our newspaper!..Maybe this is all my fault."

"No...don't say that," Gene II whispered, "that was a wonderful human interest story you wrote...I think good stories like that should be told...You can't blame yourself for the actions of some fanatical nuts!"

"Where's the family now?" Max asked the fire chief.

"We got 'em all out...not a scratch," the fire chief replied, proudly. "They're sitting over in that busvan in that driveway right across the street from what's left of their home...that's all they got now. The neighbors have been helpin' out some...they brought 'em some hot chocolate, coffee and donuts...If there was just one or two children the neighbors would take 'em in...but with ten children...all we can do is contact the shelter at the Salvation Army."

"A shelter at the Salvation Army?" Gene II asked in disgust. "That's no way for a family to spend the Christmas holidays."

"How do they know it was the Nazis and the Skinheads?" Max asked, "Did anyone see them do it?"

A policeman listening to the conversation, walked closer and handed Max a neatly folded flag. Gene II looked at it, puzzled, as Max held it out in front of him and let it unfurl.

"A damn swastika!" Gene II grumbled.

"It was draped across the front porch when we got the family out," the policeman said, grimly. "They wanted to make sure they got the credit for their dirty work!..I'd like to give 'em somethin' else!"

Several photographers from The Herald and other newspapers began snapping pictures of the flag and the entire grisly scene as Gene II, Marcy and Max walked over to the bus-van parked in the driveway across the street from the burned out home. Several other people were crowded around the van and they quickly made room for the three when they saw the "press" card pinned to their coats. Marcy took the lead as she leaned into one of the front windows of the van...

"Dr. Kramer...Mrs. Kramer...remember me?..I'm Marcy Dugas from The Herald...I'm so sorry this happened!..Is everybody OK?"

"As good as can be expected," Dr. Kramer said. "How you doin, Marcy?"

"Hi, Marcy," Mrs. Kramer said, cheerfully, as she turned to the kids in the back seats. "Kids...look who's here...it's Marcy from The Detroit Herald!"

"Hi, Marcy!" the kids all shouted, happily.

Marcy introduced Gene II and Max to the Kramers who all seemed to be in good spirits, bearing up well under the dreadful conditions...Some of the children played with a puppy in the back of the van. Gene II poked his head in the window next to Marcy..."Dr. Kramer...you have any idea where you're gonna stay tonight?" Gene II asked.

"With this brood?" Dr. Kramer asked, chuckling. "Probably some shelter I guess...What about that, Betty?"

Betty Kramer looked at her husband and shrugged her shoulders. "We don't have any relatives in Michigan," Betty Kramer answered, "so I guess we'll try to get into some shelter...we don't wanna be separated...The police mentioned something about the Salvation Army shelter...it may not be the best but beggars can't be choosers...can they?"

Marcy continued talking to the Kramers as Gene II motioned for Max to step away from the van. Max followed Gene II a short distance away.

"What's up?" Max asked.

"Let's take 'em all back to The Herald and feed 'em lunch in the cafeteria, "Gene II whispered, "you get on your car phone and set it all up as soon as the Kramers agree."

"But the police are trying to line up some shelter for them at the Salvation Army," Max answered.

"Forget that...would you wanna spend the holidays at some shelter?" Gene II asked, annoyed. "When we get back to The Herald I'm sure we'll think of something better than that...just look at those poor children...who wants to spend the holidays in a place like that?..They've got children from ages two to thirteen...they want a real Christmas!"

Max walked back over to his car and got inside as Marcy and Gene II continued to talk with the Kramer family.

"Dr. Kramer...Mrs. Kramer...will you do us the honor and follow us back to The Herald?" Gene II asked "They're setting up a big lunch for your family in our cafeteria."

"We were told to stay put until we hear from the Salvation Army, Mr. Stanton," Dr. Kramer replied, "it'll be a week or so before our insurance company can arrange any temporary housing for us."

"I'm sure The Herald can find you better accommodations than that," Gene II answered. "Will you follow us?..Cheeseburgers, fries and milk shakes for the entire family...all on The Herald!"

The Kramers all looked at each other with big grins on their faces. The parents looked back at the children who were anxiously waiting with hopeful expressions on their small, little faces. The Kramers turned back to Gene II and Marcy, beaming...

"It looks like they're all voting for you, Mr. Stanton," Dr. Kramer answered, grinning.

"Mr. Stanton's my dad," Gene II said, smiling. "Just call me, Gene...We'll let the police know where you can be reached and you can call your insurance company from our office."

Gene II waived his hand, signaling Max, as he and Marcy walked towards the car. In a few minutes they drove off with the Kramer's bus-van following them...

The large cafeteria at The Detroit Herald Newspaper was known for it's high quality of food. All of the cooks and attendants helped serve the Kramer family, playing with all of the children and generally making everybody feel at home. The entire Kramer family, all twelve of them, ate heartily. Gene Stanton came down from the publisher's office and met all of the family as they enjoyed cheeseburgers, french fries and milk shakes. Gene sat in between Doctor and Mrs. Kramer as they finished their lunches. They all smiled at each other as the kids began asking for dessert. Gene quickly summoned chocolate cake and ice cream from the kitchen attendants who eagerly obliged...

"We haven't had any luck finding a place for your family as yet," Gene said, "most of the hotels that do have some rooms left don't have enough space...the Christmas holidays have filled up most of the hotels and motels in the entire metro Detroit area."

"We figured it would be too difficult to find that many rooms just before the holidays," Betty Kramer said.

"Sure...we understand," Dr. Kramer agreed, "and we really appreciate what you've done for us, Mr. Stanton."

"I spoke to my wife...she wants you and your family to stay at our home for the holidays the next three weeks." Gene said, grinning broadly, "It's all decorated...the tree is up...plenty of room...and we're overstocked with food."

Both of the Kramers almost choked while drinking their coffee!..They stared at Gene, stunned by his offer!..

"You serious?..All twelve of us?" Dr. Kramer gulped. "You willing to put up with all of these people...that long?"

Gene laughed. "Of course!..We'll be happy to have you."

"You got enough room?" Betty Kramer asked, unbelieving. "This is a lot of people!"

"We've got twenty-eight rooms," Gene replied, chuckling, "Of course some of my six kids plan to be here for the holidays, but you'll still have plenty of room...our home is on a few acres so the kids will have the space they need to run around...besides, if you and your wife can adopt all of these wonderful children...this is the least we can do."

"How could we ever repay you?" Dr. Kramer asked.

"We need more people like you and your wife," Gene answered. "Your story has been picked up by the national news services all across the country...you both are very important people!"

"Wow!..That's awfully nice of you, Mr. Stanton," Betty Kramer said, still in shock. "You and your family are...are just wonderful to do something like this for us!"

"There's just one more thing...we've only got a few more shopping days until Christmas," Gene said, "as soon as you two get your family settled in our place, I think you better make up a shopping list so we can replace all of the gifts and toys you lost in the fire...We'll all go on a shopping spree at one of the malls...and charge it to The Herald."

Gene looked up across the cafeteria as Gene II, Max and Marcy joined them at the table. Max was beaming with pride as he showed Gene a typewritten sheet of paper...

"This is the editorial for Sunday's paper," Max said, smiling, "let me read it out loud so everyone can hear it;

"Neo-Nazis, Skinheads and the Gerogie-Peorgie Syndrome... Come Home to roost."

"The Neo-Nazis and Skinheads are racist cowards!.. They sneak through innocent and peaceful neighborhoods at night and plant burning crosses on front lawns, scribble the words "nigger" and "Jew" on garage doors... desecrate graves of the dead, and taunt old women and children... A few days ago one of these brave groups burned down the home of Dr. and Mrs.

Kramer in the Detroit suburb of Stonebrook... You remember the Kramers, don't you?... They are the pediatrician and psychologist who adopted ten multi-racial homeless children to provide them with the love, protection, care and education these children never would have gotten elsewhere. The Kramers are building ten good Americans who will become the future leaders of this country... What in the hell are these punk Nazis and cowardly Skinheads building other than criminal records?... What good are they doing?... If they truly believed in the erratic rhetoric they espouse, why don't they confront the men who oppose them instead of sneaking though the night to attack defenseless women and children while wearing antiquated uniforms, leather jackets and armbands that signify nothing but the failure of psychotic ego maniacs more than fifty years ago!... We believe it is significant that the Skinheads wear the same style haircut reminiscent of Curly of The Three Stooges comedy team... and that Neo-Nazis groups are always neo (new) because usually, by the time the various Nazi groups become old, they no longer exist... It is obvious that the Nazis represent the frustration of ignorant and powerless pimple-faced teenagers who lose this "Mein Kempf" demeanor as soon as they grow past puberty.... The few who remain only represent the mentally deficient who lack the intellect to move past that stage of mental growth.... consequently, The Herald is issuing a challenge to the Nazis and the Skinheads to come out and confront the men they oppose instead of hiding in closets like frightened little people... Maybe they would confront them in a neutral territory.... like an inner-city basketball court or a Detroit high school football field... Until then we will look upon them as mere cowards who only remind us of that old nursery rhyme.... Georgie Peorgie, puddin' and pie, kissed the girls and made them cry, but when the boys came out to play, Georgie-Peorgie ran away!... So here's to the Neo-Nazis and Skinheads who so boldly displayed their hate and bigotry by burning down the Kramer's home and running away... they were seeking attention and publicity... well they just got it!..."

When Max finished reading he quickly glanced at everyone sitting at the table. They all grinned at him and nodded their heads in agreement. Marcy put an arm around his shoulder.

"Oh, Max!" Marcy said, staring into his eyes, "I think that was just perfect!"

Everyone stood up and applauded as Max continued to beam, proudly. Marcy reached over and kissed him on the cheek.

Roger Carlson drove the sedan up into the driveway next to his home and parked. The doors to the car all opened and Roger, Janet, Michelle and a nurse got out. Michelle smiled confidently as they went inside the front door.

Michelle and her nurse, Ruth, sat in the living room and quietly sipped coffee

THE WINDS OF TOMORROW

while both Janet and Roger smiled at Michelle, shaking their heads in disbelief...

"It's good to have you home again," Janet said, "are you sure you're feeling alright?"

"That's the main reason why I'm here, Mrs. Carlson," Ruth said, "it is important that Michelle be re-connected to her family as soon as possible to insure a successful rehabilitation... It is very hard for the families who have experienced such a traumatic behavior as Michelle exhibited the last time she was here... It may be difficult to understand, but you must realize... that this Michelle... this Michelle doesn't remember anything that happened that day."

"According to my therapist... this is why I... had been forgetting so many things," Michelle said, calmly, "it wasn't really me."

"Each personality takes full control of a person's behavior," Ruth said, "each usually has little or no knowledge of the other's activities. It seems to be a built-in safety valve to allow someone to dissociate from an unpleasant present, lapse into a state of amnesia or altered consciousness... It's an example of spontaneous dissociation... a coping mechanism."

Roger looked skeptical. "Will she be OK around others?" Roger asked, cautiously. "We've been invited out to dinner on Christmas Day and there will be a lot of people and children there."

"That's good... she needs to be around a lot of people and I'll be with her," Ruth answered. "The last few weeks she has had no bad episodes at all... She's been completely at peace with herself and everybody else... I think it'll be good to have her around a lot of happy people."

"That's fine... she will be," Janet said, smiling. "Michelle.... you look great."

"It's been quite some trip," Ruth said. "As the subject grows, this psychological mechanism may become ingrained, an almost automatic response to stress or trauma... thus, a new personality will show up, one better able to deal with the situation at hand... In this case, that seems to have happened with a positive result."

"I see... how does something like this begin?" Roger asked, thoughtfully. "I've heard of plenty of incest victims... but... but those victims never reacted like this."

"When a small child is the incest victim... they become confused and terrified by the threats of pain from supposedly loving adults," Ruth explained, "A child may become, figuratively, two people... One of the people that the child becomes may absorb the abuse and lock away any memory of it... another person, whose conscious thoughts and recollections and purged of the horror... If the abuse is severe enough, the child may parcel out the pain even further, becoming three or four people... Dr. Willingham, Michelle's therapist, fells she may have as many as fifteen different personalities."

"That is so sad," Janet whispered sympathetically.

"In some cases, the victims of M.P.D. have been approached in bars by strange men who begin to negotiate the price of sex," Ruth said, analytically," It is clear to the victim that these men know her, but only as a prostitute."

"How awful!" Janet exclaimed.

"I was asked to tell you both all of this information because I understand from Dr. Willinham that there's some questions about continuing her pregnancy," Ruth said, concerned.

"That's because we feel the pregnancy may have triggered that violent personality," Roger answered, "and we do not want a repeat performance if the pregnancy presents continued pressure on her."

"I suspected you may have thought this could possibly be genetic," Ruth said, "it definitely is not."

"The doctor assured us that is wasn't," Janet said, "besides, the embryo is a derivative form Roger and me... not Michelle... we just didn't want to be responsible for damaging her psyche any further."

Ruth turned to Michelle, watching her carefully. "Well, that's your call, Michelle... How do you feel about carrying their baby full term?"

"I am extremely happy to be able to do this for them," Michelle replied, calmly. "They are very nice people... I've never been treated this good in my entire life... and this way I can repay their kindness."

"Then why was that violent personality unleashed?" Roger asked, puzzled.

Dr. Willingham feels that personality is the direct result of some form of rejection," Ruth replied, "If one personality suffers a severe form of rejection that related to a past severe rejection... that could happen."

"What kind of rejection could you have suffered, Michelle?" Janet asked, "Do you remember anything like that?"

"No... no I don't... but it could've happened to one of the others," Michelle replied, thoughtfully. "I just can't remember."

Roger turned and walked over to the window, remembering Michelle standing by his bed in a sexy teddy!... He recalled her slipping into bed next to him and pressing her body against his... and the look on her face when he rejected her advances and demanded that she get out of the bedroom!... Then he remembered what Michelle's father had said when he was asked if he wanted Michelle to come back home... his answer was simply, "no"...

Roger was brought back to the present when he heard the complete innocence in Michelle's voice when she broke the silence in the room with one whispered question...

"Roger... Janet... where's my little furry friend?" she asked in a tiny voice. "I haven't seen him today."

"Who?" Janet asked.

"Bosco."

Chapter Thirty-Four

It was snowing heavily at the Stanton mansion as the Christmas decorations and lights lit up the bushes and trees surrounding the spacious home. The long, circular driveway was covered with fresh snow as the rays of moonlight filtered through the tall trees. Several lights were on throughout the house but the center of attention was the tall, heavily decorated and strategically lighted Christmas tree standing in the big window of the living room. Inside the home, all of the Kramer children sat on the thick carpet in the spacious living room admiring the gigantic tree which was loaded with blinking candles, candy canes and decorations while the flickering lights from the great fireplace cast long shadows that danced on the walls.

Across the wide center hallway, in the richly paneled library, Gene Stanton discussed Father McCarthy's dilemma with Eric and Betty Kramer. Patricia brought in a large tray of coffee and set it on the cocktail table. They all smiled as they heard the children in the living room began to sing Christmas carols and laughing in the background...

"That's really good to hear, Betty." Gene said, chuckling. "I love to listen to children singing and laughing around the holidays... that's what Christmas is all about."

"You hear that, Eric?" Betty laughed, "Let's see if he feels that way in a week."

"He'll probably evict us," Eric chuckled.

"I don't think so... Gene loves children," Patricia said. "And with what you two are doing... that's a direct line to his heart."

"That's why I mentioned this priest," Gene said, seriously, "he's between a rock and hard place... if he chooses the students he wants to choose to star in this Christmas Pageant these parents of the other students are threatening to charge him with child molestation."

"Has it occured to you that he may be guilty?" Eric asked.

"Not a chance... we checked him out," Gene replied. "This is a dedicated and religious teacher who only wants to do his job."

"Some of these ambitious parents would try something like that," Betty said. "Remember the cheerleader's mother who hired a hit man to take out her daughter's competition to get on the high school's cheerleading team?"

"That's true... some of those parents have almost ruined little league sports teams," Patricia said.

"Is there anyway he could get those girls to admit the truth before he announces his choices?" Betty asked, thoughtfully.

Gene leaned back in his chair and stroked his chin for a minute. "I don't know... I guess it's possible."

"How much time do we have?" Betty asked.

"Oh, oh!... I smell wood burning," Eric said, laughing. "She's thinking again!"

"No... I'm serious," Betty said, "we might be on to something."

"He plans to make the announcement in a few days," Gene answered. "The pageant is right after that...just before the holiday break."

"As a psychologist, I could arrange a special interview for those five girls to get an honest commitment from them," Betty volunteered.

"I don't follow you," Eric said, " what would that prove?"

"I could arrange the interview to include some borderline questions about sex," Betty answered. "These are all teenaged girls...this could test the strength of their characters."

"What kind of questions?" Gene asked.

"Questions about self-respect, their families, their boyfriends," Betty replied, "and if they've ever been sexually molested by anyone."

"I don't think we should go that far," Gene said, thoughtfully.

"Why not?" Patricia asked. "Their parents will be there, the priest will be there...Maybe we could arrange to have a policewoman present for more authenticity."

"That's good...it'll be kinda hard for them to deny ever being molested before the announcement and then suddenly change their minds because their friend wasn't selected as one of the two best actors," Betty said, smiling.

"Especially with the high profile witnesses who will be sitting in on the interviews...A pediatrician, a psychologist, a newspaper publisher, an attorney, a priest and a policewoman."

"It works for me," Patricia said, smiling.

"But isn't that kinda sneaky?" Eric asked.

Gene laughed, slightly relieved at the plan Betty had concocted. "In politics they call it tact and diplomacy...getting the truth out front before anybody can change it...this just might work...let's try it."

They all looked at each other and smiled, toasting the plan with a sip of coffee...

"If they wanna play hardball...we'll go them one better," Betty said, determined, "we'll play tackle football...with no pads!"

Gene grinned confidently. "Sounds like a winner...I'll contact Father McCarthy and set up these interviews right away."

St. Anthony's Academy was renowned for producing fine, young dramatic actors. The credit for this outstanding reputation had to be given to Father McCarthy, a diligent and hard working professional who was dedicated to the success of his students. As a result, people from all over the midwest tried to get their aspiring child actors enrolled at the academy. When Father McCarthy suggested the psychological interviews to his superiors they jumped at the opportunity to show the lengths the faculty at the academy were willing to go to improve their drama curricula and increase the academy's enrollment for the next semester...especially since there was no cost involved.

The hallowed halls of the century old academy were adorned with pictures of successful child stars who had become Hollywood actors. With an ivey covered exterior and tall, lead glass windows from floor to ceiling contrasting sharply with the dark oak paneled walls, the academy had the facade of an old, imposing and established learning institution which is exactly what it was.

The large conference room on the first floor of the academy was extremely active this day as anxious parents accompanied their actor/students for the interviews which were being conducted prior to the selection of the two leading actors for the Christmas Pageant. Mrs. Betty Kramer, a psychologist, chaired the open interviews in the conference room observed by a panel of well known and established professionals to insure that the interviews were properly administered. Mrs. Kramer wore a pair of heavy rimmed eyeglasses and a dark business suit as she sat at the end of the long conference table. Father McCarthy sat on her right and Gene Stanton sat on her left. Police Sergeant Driscoll sat next to Gene and Attorney Roger Carlson sat directly across the table from the policewoman. On the far end of the table sat a female student between her two parents. The atmosphere was cold and professional as Betty Kramer turned to Father McCarthy

"How many more do we have, father?" Betty asked.

"This is the last one," Fr. McCarthy replied, whispering, "and the most difficult...You're doing a fine job, Mrs. Kramer."

Betty introduced everyone at the table while the student and her parents waited nervously. She studied the student's academic records briefly before looking up and staring at the girl and her parents, critically peering over her glasses which were resting on her nose. Betty began to speak in a solemn and serious manner....

"You are...Lou Ann Spencer...and these are your parents, Harry and Sarah Spencer, is that correct?..Before we begin I'd like to explain what this interview is all about...First, if either of you object to these proceedings we are holding today we will stop the interview immediately...This interview is being recorded on video tape for future reference in selecting lead roles for the pageant...does anyone object to that?..Father McCarthy has reached an impasse in making his selections and he has asked me to impanel these prominent citizens to observe as I conduct a psychological examination and interview to determine which students are best qualified and suited in character to represent St. Anthony's in these acting roles...We want to make sure that we have the best, all-around candidates...Do you understand?"

Lou Ann glanced at her mother and father before answering, meekly. "Yes...yes, ma'am."

"Do either of your parents have any questions before we begin?" Betty asked in a brisk manner.

The parents shook their heads, no.

"Fine...let's get started," Betty said, firmly. "First, place your hand on the bible and swear to tell the truth, the whole truth and nothing but the truth."

"I do."

"Do you have a boyfriend, Lou Ann?"

"No...I had one but we split up."

"How far did you go with him?"

Lou Ann was puzzled..."Pardon me?"

"Did you ever go further than just necking?"

"No...I never have."

"Then you are a virgin?"

She looked around at her parents, nervously. "Yes...of course I am," Lou Ann replied.

"Have you ever cheated on a test?"

"Certainly not."

"Have you ever been a victim of incest?"

"Never!" Lou Ann was on a roll.

"Have you ever been molested by anyone?"

"Nope...I've never been touched," Lou Ann snapped, smiling at both of her parents proudly.

Betty Kramer smiled back at her and quickly completed the interview. After everyone had left except Gene, Betty and Father McCarthy, Betty turned to the priest and smiled.

"Well, father...according to all of these signed affidavits and our video tapes...all of these girls have unequivocably stated that they have never been molested by anyone...and that includes you!"

"I think you're off the proverbial hook, father," Gene said, smiling broadly.

"Will this stand up in court?" Fr. McCarthy asked.

"I couldn't say for certain whether it would or not," Gene replied, "but at least you now have a video and signed and witnessed documents stating that you're innocent...I think that ends that threat."

"I don't know how I can ever thank you all," Fr. McCarthy said, gratefully, "especially you, Mr. Stanton...I realize that you are an extremely busy man running that newspaper and running for mayor...but you still took the time out to help me and I deeply appreciate it...I knew you'd figure out some way to do it."

Gene motioned to Betty Kramer. "Don't thank me, father, this was all her idea, not mine...and I think it's gonna work."

Father McCarthy turned to Betty, smiling. "I've seen you before, Mrs. Kramer...aren't you the same lady who's adopted all of those multi-racial children?"

"The one and the same," Gene said, smiling.

"GOD bless you, my child," Father McCarthy said, proudly. "It seems that you've just saved the career of another lost child."

It was Christmas Eve and the heavily decorated shopping mall was packed and jammed with last minute Christmas shoppers bustling back and forth with large, brightly colored shopping bags stuffed with toys and merchandise. The sounds of continuous Christmas carols could be heard in the background along with the jingle of overworked cash registers ringing up sales. Gene and Patricia, along with Eric and Betty Kramer, Susan and Gene II, all carried huge shopping bags and looked exhausted as they quickly walked through the mall and out into the heavily falling snow, making their way to the Kramer's bus-van in the crowded parking lot. They wearly loaded all of the packages into the back of the van, climbed aboard and relaxed as the van slowly crept out of the jammed parking lot and onto the slippery, snowy roads...

As night fell on the Stanton mansion the sounds of Christmas carols softly floated throughout the house from strategically placed stereo speakers. The giant fireplace in the living room burned brightly, casting giant, flickering shadows on the walls and sending out the warm aroma of burning white birch logs. The gigantic Christmas tree stood proudly in front of the frosty windows with it's heavily decorated branches reaching out to touch each person with the spirit of the season. Twenty red stockings hung from the mantle above the fireplace. Most of the children in the house, caught up in the mystery of Christmas, sat quietly in front of the majestic tree, hypnotized by it's grandeur. The aroma that drifted through the mansion was a combination of all of the delightful foods that Connie and her army of helpers were preparing for the big Christmas dinner.

The peacefulness of the evening was suddenly interrupted as Connie's voice echoed throughout the hallway and several children scrambled out of the kitchen door!..

"Get out of my kitchen and don't you dare come back here until tomorrow!" Connie shouted, angrily. "All of you cookie stealin' crumbsnatchers!"

In a few minutes the sounds of carolers could be heard just outside of the front door. Everyone flocked to the front door to see the singers. Gene II opened the door and discovered Liz, Ze-Ze, Kim, Vic, Joe, Mel, Kelly, Karen, Robert and their three children, all covered with snow and singing at the top of their voices with their arms filled with presents...They all began shouting in unison and seperately..."Merry Christmas!..Merry Christmas!.."

As the large group came into the home laughing, shouting and shaking the snow off their coats and stomping their feet, they all suddenly stopped in shock as they stared back at all the multi-racial little children staring at them!..Mel looked at the children and then at Patricia in stark surprise!..He paused a moment as he patted Kelly's swollen and pregnant stomach...

"Mom!..I thought Kelly and I were doin' something having this baby...but you...you and dad are something else!..You been holding out on us!"

At that, everybody began laughing loudly and hugging each other as the holiday spirit touched everyone...

Later that evening, after some of the guests had left and the children had all gone to bed, Gene and Gene II went up to the butler's quarters on the third floor and pulled out a Santa Clause costume from a trunk stored in the closet. Gene II looked at the suit and shook his head slowly from side to side in a negative manner. He blew dust off of the costume.

"Naw...naw, pop," Gene II said, sadly, "that ain't gonna work."

"What do you mean, it's not gonna work?" Gene asked.

"You can't get into that."

"Me?..Not me...you!"

"I'm not wearin' that thing," Gene II said, flatly.

"Why not?..It's perfectly good."

"No way!..Get Mel or Joe...I ain't wearin' no Santa Claus costume and makin' a fool out of myself!"

Gene remained calm as he glared at his son. "Listen...Joe and Mel don't have any kids waitin' for Santa Claus...you do!..Just think of all those little kids down there... they've been burned out of their home at Christmas time and now they're laying in bed waitin' to see Santa Claus come down the chimney...You gonna let them down?"

"I'm not coming down any chimney, dad!"

"Take it easy...relax...I know that...just a figure of speech...We got so many chimneys in this house you'd probably get lost and be stuck up there 'til March!"

"C'mon, dad!"

"Don't worry about that chimney business...we'll just say you came down the fireplace where the fire wasn't lit. That makes sense doesn't it?"

"OK...OK!..You made your point...I'll put on the costume...but...but you're gonna owe me one."

"Me...owe you?..Who do you think wore this thing when you were a little boy?..Santa Claus?" Gene asked, indignantly,.

Gene II was surprised. He looked at his father and then back to the costume as he held it up in front of himself.

"This...this the same costume you use to wear for...for me?"

"The very same."

Well I'll be damned!" Gene II mumbled, smiling. He put on the cap and looked at himself in the mirror. "Well I'll be damned!"

Gene quickly began dusting off the rest of the costume. He pulled out a pair of black boots and wiped them off, carefully. Gene II took off his sweater and picked up the costume's jacket. He automatically began searching the pockets. He pulled out a inspector's slip and stared at it. He stopped and looked at Gene who was still wiping off the boots...

I thought you said this was the same costume you wore when I was a kid, dad." Gene II said, "this slip is dated 1988!..This ain't the same costume!"

Gene became irritated..."Well I lied!..Now put on that damn costume and hurry up before some of these kids start sneakin' back downstairs!"

It was late Christmas Eve night when Gene II, dressed completely in the Santa Claus costume, waited impatiently outside of the library window. He carried a large bag full of toys and gifts. The strong whistling winds and the heavy snowfall created blizzard like conditions. Gene II rubbed his hands together and stomped his feet, trying to keep warm. He reached up and tried to lift the window again...Nothing!..He was about to give up when a light came on in the library. He peeped above the window ledge slowly and saw his brother, Mel, close and lock the library door. Mel stealthily slipped over to the window, unlocked it and partly lifted the window up. Mel bent down and whispered..."Santa!..Santa, you big fool!..What the hell you doin' out there?"

"Yo mamma!" Gene II snapped, angrily. "Let me in you big nut I'm freezin' my ass off out here!"

Mel laughed. "Be careful...that's not the Christmas spirit to be talkin' bout my mamma."

"OK!..OK!..Big deal...Please let me in, dear little brother...or I'll throw you and this bag of toys through the damn window!"

Still laughing heartily, Mel finally opened the window all the way. He reached out and pulled in the big heavy bag. He then reached down and pulled Gene II up. Just as Gene II climbed into the window he slipped off the ledge and twisted his ankle!..He cursed in bitter pain as he rubbed his ankle...He looked all around the room, limped over and quietly opened the door..."Is it safe?"

"I think so," Mel replied, still chuckling. "C'mon I'll help you."

"No...no...I'll do it alone...No use going through all of this if you're gonna help me...Santa works by himself!"

Mel slowly opened the door. The living room was completely empty. He checked the long, dark hallway. All clear...He turned back to Gene II and grinned as he whispered softly. "OK, Santa...the coast is clear...I'll cover ya!"

Gene II, with the bag of toys on his shoulder, limped across the hallway to the tall Christmas tree and began to strategically place the toys and gifts under the tree. Mel watched him from the library doorway with a big smile on his face...

On Christmas Day the great room in the Stanton mansion was converted to a spacious dining room with an elongated dining table to accommodate all of the people they had invited for dinner. Everyone sat at the table in a very happy mood, excited about the holiday and beaming with joy and laughter. Three chairs remained empty as Gene glanced at his watch. He looked at Patricia, puzzled.

"Where's Liz?" Gene asked.

"I don't know," Patricia replied, "she said she'd be here."

Kim overheard her parent's conversation and joined in with a big grin on her face. "Oh, I forgot to tell you, mom...Liz and Ze-Ze are going to be a little late...Liz is doing me a favor."

"What kind of favor?" Patricia asked.

"I spoke to Adrian Grant this morning to let her know I was in town," Kim said, casually. "She was all by herself today and since her place wasn't too far from Liz's...I invited her to dinner and Liz said she'd pick her up...Is that alright with you, mom?"

Gene almost choked on his food. He could feel Patricia's eyes penetrating his forehead. He tried to ignore her by sipping his wine. She finally answered Kim's question.

"Yes...I guess," Patricia said, reluctantly.

"Adrain Grant?..She's a great reporter," Gene II said, "she's gonna be dad's campaign manager...I'm gonna miss her in editorial."

Gene II got up from the table and limped over to the buffet to get more food. One of the Kramer's kids began shouting in alarm..."Hey...look, mommie!..He's limpin' just like Santa Claus...even on the same leg!" the boy shouted.

Gene II glanced at Mel and Joe who were doubled up with laughter!..

When the dinner was almost over most of the children had left the great room. Liz talked with Roger, Janet, Michelle and her nurse, Ruth Sanders...

"Well, Michelle...it's good to see you again," Liz said, smiling, "you're looking absolutely beautiful."

"It's good to see you again, too." Michelle answered, "how's the paper doing?..I wish I could go back to work...I miss it."

"That'll be a while yet," Janet said, "Michelle's in a family way...work may not be the best thing for her."

"Are you having any trouble carrying the baby?" Ze-Ze asked Michelle.

THE WINDS OF TOMORROW

"No...the doctor said everything is just fine," Michelle replied.

"You know," Ze-Ze said, "we're interested in this...in vitro fertilization, too."

At that remark Hattie angrily got up from the table and left, mumbling under her breath..."Heavens no!"

Liz ignored Hattie's mumbling. "In fact, Janet...if you and Roger should change your minds about Michelle's baby...Ze-Ze and I would be interested in assuming your responsibilities," Liz said, concerned.

Everyone at the table stared at Liz and Ze-Ze in stunned silence as Liz calmly sipped her coffee...Kim, sensing the awkward moment, came to the rescue.

"Kelly's about done," Kim chuckled. "She's due any day now."

"Yeah...I wish she'd quit stalling," Mel said, beaming. "If she gets any bigger I'm changing her name to Twiddly-Dee."

"Oh, shuddup," Kelly quickly said, "you act like you've never seen a pregnant woman before."

"Not naked!" Mel laughed.

"When are you due, Kelly?" Roger asked.

"Last week!" Mel answered.

"You better keep her away from pins and needles, " Joe said, grinning.

"Pins and needles?..why?" Adrian asked.

"If she sticks herself...she might burst," Joe replied, laughing..

"Adrian...I understand you're Gene's campaign manager, "Vic Martin said. "Congratulations...I think that's a great move."

"Me too," Kim said, "if anybody can do it...Adrian can."

"That was an excellent press conference," Eric Kramer said, "the best I've seen on a local level for years...if you had anything to do with that, you're doing an excellent job, Adrian."

"Thank you," Adrian replied, "we're just beginning and we've got a lot of hard work ahead."

Later on in the evening, Gene sat behind his desk in the library discussing strategy for the upcoming primary campaign as Adrian jotted down notes in a notebook. Just as they were about finished, they noticed Patricia standing in the library door staring at them, disapprovingly. Adrian quickly snapped the notebook closed and got up, ready to leave the room. Patricia stood in her way for a second, then reluctantly stepped aside, allowing Adrian to leave...When Adrian was out of earshot, Patricia angrily slammed the door closed and turned to Gene with fire in her eyes!..

"The nerve of that bitch!" Patricia snapped, angrily. "Coming over here on Christmas Day!"

"She was invited, remember?" Gene shot back. "You better cool down!..What in the hell are you raving about?..She's my campaign manager and we were setting up the campaign schedule and strategy for after the holidays."

"Well, you're gonna have to change your plans!"

"Why?"

"Running for mayor or not...you're going to get another campaign manager or...or I'll file for divorce!' Patricia screamed, "then we'll see what happens to your campaign!"

Patricia angrily marched out of the library and slammed the door behind her!..She failed to notice Karen sitting in the living room near the door to the library. Karen quickly got up and followed her mother into the kitchen. Patricia, sensing someone behind her, turned to face Karen with her eyes still smouldering in anger!..

"What do you want, Karen?"

"Just hold on, mother!" Karen shot back, angrily. "I heard what you just said to dad and I'm not having any of it!"

"You're not having any of it?..Just who in the hell are you?" Patricia snarled.

"Dad's the best thing to happen to this city in many years and I'm not about to let you or anybody else ruin it with this holier than thou attitude you've suddenly adopted!"

"I can't believe my ears," Patricia said, stunned. "Who died and put you in charge?"

"I'm warning you, mother!"

"About what?"

"You know damn well...what!"

"What are you talkin' about?"

"If you do anything to sabotage dad's campaign...I swear...I'll tell dad and the whole damn world who my father really is!"

Patricia was shakened by Karen's threatening words...She stepped backwards, steadying herself as she glared at her oldest daughter who didn't back down one inch!..

It was a few days after Christmas and Gloria StantonThompson stood in the lobby of The Detroit Herald Newspaper building with several other people and stared out of the large lobby windows at several young white men walking back and forth on the sidewalk in front of the entrance to the building, holding signs charging The Herald with yellow journalism and discrimination against the Aryan race. In a few minutes Adrian Grant stepped off of the elevator at the rear of the lobby, walked over and stood next to Gloria and joined her in looking out at the picket line.

"Hi, have you been waiting long?" Adrian asked.

"Oh, hi...No...I just got here," Gloria replied.

"What's going on?"

"It's the neo-Nazis and the Skinheads," Gloria answered, "they're picketing the newspaper because of that editorial about them burning down the Kramer's home."

"Oh, that...Gene told me they've been making threatening calls the last few days," Adrian said, "after what they did...they have their nerve!"

Gloria glanced at her watch. "We'd better leave...you don't wanna be late."

"What about this picket line?"

"Have no fear," Gloria answered, smiling, "there's a police squad car parked on the corner."

Adrian was happy that Gloria had decided to go to the doctor's office with her and she remained silent as Gloria maneuvered the car through the heavy traffic. A slight snowfall dusted the windshield just enough to warrant the use of the windshield wipers. Adrian laid back in her deep cushioned seat and listened to the soft, easy music on the radio. She opened her eyes and glanced at Gloria who was deeply engrossed in her driving. What a godsend Gloria had turned out to be, Adrian mused. She had been a stalwart supporter ever since Adrian had discovered this thing in her breast...She had arranged the mammogram and explained the biopsy process...All of this while knowing Adrian was in love with her brother and was about to disrupt his long-time marriage...and Gloria had never mentioned it since having their little talk in Gloria's office that day...What a wonderful person she was, Adrian thought. What a fine big sister she would be!..

Adrian reached over and put her hand on top of Gloria's hand. Gloria looked at her and smiled..."Hey, c'mon now... it's gonna be alright," Gloria reassured her.

"Well...regardless...I want you to know how much I appreciate you," Adrian said, softly. "Gene is really lucky to have a sister like you."

"He's lucky to have a woman like you!" Gloria said. "You've made him a completely new person...he's happy and I've never seen him so charged up...running for mayor...I think it's just great and it's all because of you."

"He'll make a good mayor, too," Adrian said. "Your brother is the most diligent person I've ever met,"

"Your opinion doesn't count, dear...you're too much in love to be objective."

Adrian laughed. "Yeah...I am...he means the world to me!..You should've seen him at that news conference."

"I did...I was there."

"I didn't see you."

"That's because you only had eyes for Gene," Gloria chuckled. "They could've landed a 747 in that lobby and you wouldn't have noticed it."

"Yes...I guess you're right."

Adrian and Gloria sat uneasily in the doctor's office waiting for him to return. Gloria looked at Adrian and smiled, cheerfully. "You alright?" she asked.

"Yes...I'm OK,": Adrian replied. "What's taking him so long?"

"Relax...he'll be here in a few minutes."

The doctor's receptionist stuck her head in the doorway. "Would either of you care for some coffee?..Dr. Greenway should be here in a minute."

Adrian looked at Gloria and nodded her head. "Yes...we both would like a cup...black, thank you."

"Good idea...it sure can't hurt," Gloria said.

In a few minutes Dr. Greenway hurried into the office carrying two cups of steaming hot coffee. He handed one to each of the women. "Here you are ladies...I'm sorry...I was tied up in a conference."

The doctor sat down behind his desk and flipped open a large manila folder, laying it in the middle of his desk. He studied it for a while and looked up at Adrian over his glasses, with a frown on his face. "How are you feeling today, Adrian?"

"I'm alright," Adrian answered, "just a little tense waiting for your verdict."

"Verdict?" he asked, glancing at Gloria. "It's not a verdict...it's the results of your tests...haven't you felt some discomfort or even a slight swelling under you arms?"

"Well...yes, but I jog a mile, two..maybe three days out of the week," Adrian replied, "sometimes my muscles tighten up."

The doctor stared at her thoughtfully. "What I'm about to tell you isn't good...I'm glad you brought Mrs. Thompson with you."

"Was it malignant?" Adrian asked in a whisper.

Gloria tightened her grip on Adrian's hand and squeezed

"Adrian...the lab analysis of your biopsy and your last physical examination have indicated that you are suffering from an invasive kind of breast cancer that has already spread to your lymph nodes," the doctor said, sadly. "You have an especially aggressive cancer that usually is only found in young women in their late twenties or early thirties who have never had any children...We have performed several tests to determine the severity of your disease and to cross-check our findings...The tests all reached the same conclusions...one confirming the findings of the other."

"Are you telling me that I'll have to have a breast removed?..Or...maybe...both?"

"No...first let me explain to make sure you understand that a mammogram is a breast x-ray that is able to find early signs of breast cancer, often before it can be felt as a lump in the breast."

"Yes...I understand that."

"After your mammogram, we performed a biopsy to determine if the lump you discovered through self-examination and confirmed by the mammogram was actually malignant," Dr. Greenway explained. "The biopsy results not only showed that it was malignant but also that it was a particularly insideous and invasive disease that spreads rapidly."

"Are you saying that because this kind of cancer spreads so fast...I will have to have a double mastectomy?" Adrian asked, nervously.

"No...there would be no beneficial results from such an operation," the doctor replied. "I'm afraid that when the cancer has matastisized to that extent...the cancer has spread too far for that."

"Chemotherapy?"

"No...It would be useless."

"Then...what are you telling me, doctor?"

The doctor leaned back in his chair, took off his glasses and rubbed his eyes, wearily. "I'm telling you that mine is not the final word...As your primary physician, I would suggest that you get a second opinion before you accept my prognosis."

"Which is?"

"Terminal."

"Oh, my GOD!" Gloria exclaimed, squeezing Adrian's hand.

"How...how much time do I have?" Adrian whispered, stunned by the doctor's words.

"At the most...with the disease spreading throughout your body as rapidly as it is," Dr. Greenway said, reluctantly, "I'm sorry...but...the most time I feel you have left...is three to six months."

Chapter Thirty-Five

Mel giggled as he stared through the plate glass window at his new born son. He was a proud father. Kelly had delivered a perfect baby boy. The baby was a beautiful soft brown and all he seemed to do was sleep. Mel smiled as the baby made a face and clinched his little fist. Mel clinched his in response. He turned when he felt a hand on his shoulder. He found himself face to face with Gene who was beaming with pride.

"Is that him?" Gene asked.

"That's him, dad," Mel whispered, softly. "The heir to the Stanton throne."

"Hey... he looks like me," Gene said, "what a cute little guy."

"He's gonna have your name too, pops."

"Really?"

"Yup... Melvin Eugene Stanton... I'm gonna call him "Mes" for short."

"And Kelly will kill you... dead!" Gene said. "How's she doin?"

"Just great... she was here just a minute ago," Mel replied, "but she got tired and went back to bed... her mom and mom were about to talk her to death."

"I'll look in on her after I check out my new grandson... what did he weigh in at?"

"Eight pounds even... twenty-one inches long... a power forward," Mel answered, handing Gene a cigar.

"Has he opened his eyes yet?" Gene asked, "and what's that he's doin' with his hands?"

"He's signaling for a time out."

Gene turned and stared at Mel. "You need psychiatric help, son."

"This baby represents a new life for me and Kelly, dad," Mel said, earnestly.

"A who new world has opened up for us."

"It looks like we're all starting a new life."

"You mean running for mayor?"

"Yes... that and a few other things that are going on," Gene answered, thoughtfully.

Mel looked at his father for a moment and turned back to the nursery. "I know you're havin' problems with mom... I didn't want to interfere."

"Thanks."

"Is there anything I can do?"

"You just did it... this little boy has lifted up my spirits... I'll stop in and see Kelly before I go back to the office."

"I understand the paper's being picketed."

"No sweat... that's an American way to protest."

"Not what those jerks did to the Kramers," Mel said, angrily, "they belong in prison!"

Gene thumbed through his messages as he walked into his office. He was surprised to see no messages form Adrian. He hadn't heard from her all day and he was anxious to tell her about his new grandson. He sat in his big leather executive chair behind his desk and dialed Adrian's number. In a few moments he heard that soft, warm voice... only this time something was different...

"Hello," she answered.

"Honey... are you alright?"

"Why?"

"You sound ... a little different."

"I'm OK..."

"Are you coming back to the office today?"

"I hadn't planned to."

"Is something wrong?"

"No."

"Did you get a chance to approve those changes on the mock-up of Belle Isle?" he asked.

"I meant to speak to you about that and a few other things," she said, cooly.

"Like what?"

"About me being your campaign manager," Adrian replied.

"I thought we had that all settled."

"It's not settled with your wife... I know how upset she was on Christmas."

"Don't worry about that."

"I think she might be right, Gene."

"What... what are you saying?"

"I'm saying that... maybe... maybe you ought to listen to her."

"What's going on with you, Adrian?" Gene asked, concerned. "Are you telling me you want to resign as my campaign manager?"

"I think it would be best."

"C'mon, Adrian!"

"No... I mean it."

"I'll be over there in ten minutes."

"No... don't come over."

"Wh... what?"

"What did you call me about?"

"I don't like the way you're acting!... What's going on?"

"I asked you.. why did you call?"

Gene rubbed his brow in frustration. He hoped a new subject might bring back the old Adrian. "I called to tell you that I have a new grandson... Kelly delivered a boy this morning."

"That's nice," Adrian said, indifferently. "Listen, I'm going to have to cut this conversation short."

"That's nice?... Is that all?" Gene asked, surprised. "Am I missing something?"

"I'm going to be off for the next few days... I'll talk to you then."

"Wait... I want to... "

He was interrupted by the click of Adrian hanging up the phone. Gene was stunned!.. What was this all about, he mused. She had never acted like this before. This was the first time they've talked on the phone and she didn't say she loved him!... Hell, she didn't even want him to come over!... Now, she wanted to resign from being his campaign manager!..

Gene got up and walked over to the window, jamming his hands into his trouser pockets and staring down at the traffic building up in the street. He couldn't get Adrian off of his mind!.. Had he done something without realizing it?... Had Patricia gotten to her?... That's it... that must be it!... Making Adrian feel guilty!... That had to be it!..

He sat back down and quickly dialed her number. When she answered he quickly replied.. "Don't hang up... please!.. We've got to talk!"

"I told you I'd talk to you later," Adrian insisted.

"You'll talk to me now!" Gene demanded.

"Now you're getting upset."

"What did you expect me to do?... I love you, Adrian and you speak to me like I'm some delivery man."

"I'm sorry."

"Have you been talking to Patricia?"

"Patricia?.. I haven't seen or heard from her since Christmas... why?... You really believe she'd contact me?"

"I'm only trying to understand why you're acting the way that you are," Gene said, calmly, "I'm not going to bug you and I won't call you anymore... only, I thought you loved me... and I deserved and explanation."

"Well, to be honest with you... I wasn't too comfortable being named your campaign manager in the first place... I knew your wife would resent it."

"She'd resent anything you did."

"And then there's Roger... I think he expected to named your campaign manager... He was hurt when you selected me."

"He understands."

"No... I think you should have him as your campaign manager," Adrian said, firmly, "just explain that we both felt he was more qualified."

"Is that what you want me to do?"

"Yes."

"I understand about you being off for a few days," Gene said. "I wanted to spend some time with you up at the island... When will I see you?"

"The island... yes, that would be nice."

"I could pick you up this weekend and we could spend a few days up there."

"No... I'm going to be out of town for a few days... I'll call you when I get back," Adrian said.

"Out of town?... Isn't this rather sudden?... You never mentioned anything like that before."

"It'll only be for a few days."

"Where are you going?"

"I'm being interviewed for a professorship in Los Angeles," she lied.

"You'd leave here?" Gene asked, stunned.

"It's just a job interview, Gene."

"But... what about us?"

"We'll talk about that when I get back."

"OK... I see... apparently something is wrong with our relationship and you're not ready to discuss it," Gene said with resignation in his voice, "I'm sorry, Adrian... I didn't know... I'll back off and give you all the space you need."

"That would be best."

"I love you, baby.. I want us to spend the rest of our lives together."

"We'll talk when I get back... I gotta go now.. and... please don't worry... remember.. I still like pine trees, wild berries and black bears."

"I'll be waiting... Call me as soon as you get back."

"Bye, love." she whispered.

Gene placed the phone back on it's receiver and slowly turned the chair around, facing the huge window behind him. He placed his right index finger to the side of his face, thoughtfully... Something's not right.. maybe she really is having second thoughts about their relationship. I'm gonna miss her, he mused... I'm gonna miss her like hell!..

He felt an empty sensation deep within his chest as he thought of life without her... He couldn't conceive of not having her in his arms and holding her... loving her...

Willard liked the idea of being able to walk into the Daily Press offices and ask to see the publisher. Most of the downtown Daily Press offices were vacant now and he knew that F. Walton Dugas expected to be completely out of the old offices by the first of the year. The security guard accompanied him up to Dugas' offices and turned him over to Dugas' secretary.

"Is Mr. Dugas expecting you, Mr. Thompson?" the secretary asked. "We're all packing up to move."

"I spoke to him on the phone... he knew I was coming over."

"Just a minute, please," the woman said as she buzzed the inner office phone. "Mr. Dugas... Mr. Thompson is here."

"Send him right in," Dugas replied curtly.

"The secretary looked up at Willard and smiled. "Go right in sir."

Dugas' office suite was one big mess. Willard was surprised to see Dugas in blue jeans and shirt sleeves as he stacked up boxes behind the desk. Dugas stared at him with an annoyed expression on his face. He sat a stack of boxes on his desk and dabbed at the perspiration on his forehead.

"Did we have an appointment?" Dugas asked.

"Well.. no, not really," Willard replied, "I just wanted to know if you have reached a decision on.. my offer to set up an advertising arrangement."

"Listen... maybe we're got a little misunderstanding here... I never agreed to anything like that and I'm surprised that you're persisting with such a ridiculous idea!" Dugas said in a harsh manner.

"Ridiculous?"

"Yes, it's ridiculous... and it's illegal!" Dugas said, angrily. "The government calls it industrial espionage and if you're not careful both you and Karen Stanton-Whyte might land in prison!"

"I thought you'd be interested in destroying The Herald and establishing our relationship," Willard said, surprised at Dugas' reaction.

"What relationship?" Dugas snapped. "You think you're the only child I've had by some other woman?... Join the club!"

"Well, like it or not... I'm still your son!"

"Big deal!... That and a buck might get you a cup of coffee!"

"And do I really have stock in this newspaper?" Willard asked, suspiciously.

"Yes... and it's only valid upon my death," Dugas shot back, "and to tell you the truth that was only done to keep you out of court... when I'm dead I really wouldn't give a good goddamn who owns this newspaper!"

Willard got up angrily. "Then why in the hell did you send for me in the first place?"

"To see if you really were my offspring," Dugas shouted, "that and the DNA tests convinced me that you are... but it stops there!"

"What do you mean by that?"

"Just this... no matter what's happened to bring us together... I'm still White and you're still Black!... I don't have any Black friends or associates and I don't want any!... Do you understand?"

Willard picked up his briefcase and walked towards the door, hurriedly. He turned back to Dugas with a disgusted look on his face... "It was just my damn luck to be born to a bigoted bastard like you!... The only thing I really hope for is to be able to cash in that stock as soon as possible! Two good things can come from that... I'll be rich and the world will be a helluva lot better without a sonofabitch like you!"

Willard stormed out of the office, slamming the door with a loud, echoing bang!.. The secretary looked up in shock as Willard marched by her desk!"..

When Willard parked his car at a metered parking space on the street in front of the Herald he was still upset from the meeting with Dugas and he failed to notice two of the Skinheads step away from the picket line and approach his car from both sides before he could get out. The man on the driver's side gently tapped on the car window. Willard rolled the window down and stared at the man angrily.

"What do you want, man?" Willard growled.

"Aren't you on the advertising staff at The Detroit Herald?" the man asked, calmly.

"Yeah... I am," Willard shot back, "what's it to ya?"

"Well, let me congratulate you, niggah!" the man shouted, pulling out a liquor bottle, "Here... have a drink on me!"

Before Willard could respond the man quickly doused the contents of the bottle all over Willard's clothes and backed away form the car, laughing!... Willard smelled gasoline and started to get out when the man at the passenger side, snatched open the door drawing Willard's attention...

"Here, you Black sonofabitch!" the man screamed," Have a light!"

The man quckly tossed a lighted match onto Willard's lap, igniting the gasoline!.. The entire interior of the car burst into flames as Willard screamed for help!.. A Detroit Herald newspaper truck screeched to a stop in the middle of the street and the driver and his rider rushed to Willard's rescue!... Fighting the smoke, flames and heat, the two truckers managed to pull the now unconscious Willard from the burning vehicle as other truckers following the first truck also stopped, got out and subdued all of the Nazis and Skinheads on the picket line including the two who had attacked Willard!...

Willard was hospitalized at the University of Michigan Burn Center in Ann Arbor, Michigan, with burns over nearly thirty percent of his body. The two men who were responsible for the attack were locked up in the Wayne County Jail and charged with attempted murder. Prosecutors were seeking life sentences because of the racist nature of the attack and the extreme physical trauma to the victim, who was lucky to escape the incident alive!... The Detroit Herald Newspaper commended The Herald truckers who saved Willard's life and managed to stifle any further racial unrest by clearly noting that all of the rescuers, like Willard's attackers, were also White. The rest of the Nazis and Skinheads who were picketing The Detroit Herald were locked up and held separately in Wayne County Jail overnight where they were all savagely beatened up by Black inmates. When they were released the next morning, some to City Hospital, they all swore vengeance against The Detroit Herald Newspaper...

The following day, Gene and Gloria sat in the waiting room at University of Michigan's Burn Center as Willard's doctor, Dr. Waldeck, explained the status of his condition.

"Your son's a very lucky man, Mrs. Thompson," The doctor said, "if those truckers hadn't pulled him out of that car when they did... he wouldn't have made it!"

"How bad is it?" Gloria asked, sobbing.

"He's burned over thirty percent of this body," Dr. Waldeck said, "but there's no smoke damage and his lungs are clear... he's a healthy young man... when the fire started he automatically covered his eyes and face from normal reflexes. Since he was wearing a top coat and blazer, the fire didn't get a chance to do too much damage. He has a few blisters on his face, his hands and arms are severely burned and he's lost some of his facial hair but that'll grow back... His most severe damage is to his legs and thighs... we may have to do skin graft in those areas... it depends on how well he heals... the good thing is there's no loss of limbs or joints and he should mend quickly."

"Thank GOD for that!" Gene said, "Can we see him?"

"Oh, sure... he'll look worse than he actually is," the doctor replied, "he's all wrapped in bandages... looks like an escapee from an Egyptian tomb but he's doing alright... When I just left him he was reading this morning's Herald."

"How long do you expect him to be laid up?" Gloria asked.

"Not too long... believe me... he's out of the woods," the doctor answered, smiling. "Burns take a while to completely heal but we ought to be able to allow him to go home within the next few weeks."

Gene and Gloria visited with Willard most of the morning. As they were leaving they met Liz and Mel in the hallway and explained to them that Willard was in no danger. Both Liz and Mel were relieved and anxious to see their cousin.

Gloria rode with Gene back to The Herald. She looked at her brother and studied him carefully as he drove the car... "You alright, Gene?" Gloria asked. "I don't think we'll have to worry about Willard... he seems to be doing just fine."

Gene smiled. "I'm not worried about Willard... it's just all of this hate we're seeing today... I expected race relations to be better than what they are."

"I know... I did too," Gloria said, "but I think whenever the country is going through a recession like we are today... hate groups flourish."

"That's true... maybe it'll get better with the economy."

Gloria quickly glanced at Gene. "I plan on being out of town for a few days next week... will you look in on Willard for me?"

"Of course I will.. with all of these relatives he's got here, you won't have to worry about that," Gene chuckled. "Where are you going... back to Wisconsin?"

"No... I'm just lending support to a friend with breast cancer," Gloria answered in a whisper, "there's been rumors that she might find some help in Mexico."

"No operation can help her?"

"No."

"Chemotherapy?"

"No... she's terminal."

Mel Stanton wrote out several autographs to nurses and hospital attendants while he and Liz sat next to Willard's hospital bed as he ate his lunch. Willard's entire face was wrapped in bandages with small, round holes for his eyes, nose and mouth. His arms and hands were also completely wrapped and heavily bandaged. Willard caught Liz staring at him with a smile on her face. He stared back at her, puzzled. "What?" he asked.

"Huh?... You talkin' to me?" Liz asked.

"What are you looking at, Liz?" Willard asked again.

"She's probably thinking you look better with your bandages on than you do with 'em off," Mel laughed.

"Huh!... You can't talk... you're lucky your baby looks more like Kelly than you!" Willard shot back.

"Listen, Willard," Liz said, "I got a call from United Department Stores and they asked me to pass it on to the advertising department."

"What's that?" Willard asked, slurping his soup.

"They've been expecting the proofs on their anniversary tabloid section they gave you."

"I don't have it," Willard said, "I gave it to Karen when I brought it in."

"Karen?" Liz asked, surprised. "Why would you give it to her?"

Willard realized he had said the wrong words to the wrong person... "I... I don't know... I was showing it to her and she said she wanted to look it over."

"Why would Karen get involved in advertising, Liz?" Mel asked, suspiciously. "You'd better check it out... no tellin' what she's up to."

Liz bit her lip, thoughtfully. "You're right... I'll take care of it when I get back to the newspaper."

"Leave me out of it," Willard said, "I just do what I'm told."

"Don't worry... I'll get to the bottom of it," Liz said, calmly, "you just get well... I'll try to get up here a few more times before they kick you out."

Mel glanced at Liz and smiled, knowingly... "And keep your greasy little hands off those nurses, Willard... we got enough problems without you gettin' thrown in jail for molesting one of these pretty little nurses."

"Yeah, right," Willard replied, sarcastically.

By the time Liz returned to The Herald she was furious at what Karen had done. She stormed into her studio office and dialed Karen's number before she even sat down. She waited anxiously, thumbing her fingers on the desk... In a few moments, Karen came on the line... "Hello."

"Can you come down here right away?" Liz asked, angrily.

"Liz?.. What's going on?" Karen asked.

"Can you come down here?... It's important!"

"Ok.... Ok... I'll come right down."

"And one other thing, Karen."

"Yes?"

"Bring that United Tabloid advertising material with you!" Liz demanded, roughly.

"Who told you I had the United tabloid?"

"Damn that!... Just bring it with you!"

It was after five in the afternoon and most of the employees had gone home when Karen marched into Liz's studio office and stood in the middle of the floor with her hands on her hips, angrily!... She impatiently waited for Liz to finish speaking on the phone. When Liz finished, Karen leaned across her desk with fury in her eyes!... "What do you mean speaking to me like that over the phone?"

"What the hell are you doing with that United tabloid advertising section?" Liz demanded, angrily.

"What the hell do you think I'm doing with it?" Karen shot back.

"I think you're plannin' some kind of sell-out!... That's what I think!"

"Oh, go to hell, Liz!... I'm not impressed with your bullshit!"

"You're not gettin' off the hook that easily!" Liz shouted. "I remember how you threatened to sell your stock to Dugas when you were trying to stop dad from converting from a weekly to a daily!... I vowed then to watch you because I knew you'd try something!"

"Watch me?... There's not a damn thing you could do if I did decide to sell out!" Karen shouted.

Liz slowly walked around her desk and faced Karen eye to eye... "I'm warning you... if you ever try anything like that...I'll... I'll..."

"You'll what, little sister?" Karen asked, sarcastically. "Go home and tell mommie and daddy?"

"The first thing I'll do... is kick your goddamn ass!" Liz warned. "Now give me that United tabloid material and get the hell out of my office!"

"You want this?" Karen asked, throwing the United envelope on the floor in front of Liz's desk. "Well there it is!"

Just as Liz bent over to pickup the envelope, Karen kicked her square in her butt, sending Liz flying across the room, sprawling on the floor!.. Karen shrugged her shoulders and laughed as she swaggered towards the door to the studio. Before she could reach it Liz quickly got up and socked her in the back of her head, knocking Karen into a row of undressed mannequins!.. As soon as Karen hit the floor, Liz sprang on top of her, clawing at her clothes and hair!... The two women fought crazily as they cried, cursed, kicked, scratched and screamed at each other!...

In a few minutes Gene II and Max strolled into the studio and they were shocked at the scene of two exhausted women with their clothes in complete disarray, still trying to fight each other!... The two men quickly pulled them apart as they continued screaming and cursing!... Gene II forced Karen towards the door of the office as Max restrained Liz behind her desk!.. Liz was furious as she screamed at Karen!.. "You stupid, dumb bitch!.. Why don't you grow up and act like you got some sense!... Get a life!"

"Get a life?" Karen screamed back. "Why in the hell don't you... get a man!"

The days without any word from Adrian were torturous for Gene. Everytime his phone rang he hoped it was her... It had been more that a week since they had last spoken on the phone... He knew she was back in town from information he had accidently gotten from Max and Marcy. Why she refused to call him was the big mystery... Finally, tonight, he could wait no longer. His heart ached to hold her in his arms again, to hear her voice and her laughter. He flatly refused to even entertain the notion that she had stopped loving him... He made up his mind that he was going to see he tonight!

When Gene pulled his car into the parking lot of Adrian's townhouse apartment complex the guard waved at him and smiled as he always had done in the past. Gene walked down the sidewalk to Adrian's unit as the January wind brought on a slight chill. He pulled up his coat collar and walked up to the door. He knocked gently and waited. No response. He knocked a second time, this time a little harder. He heard a slight stirring inside and then her soft voice... "Use your key... I've been expecting you."

Gene used his key and slowly walked into the darkened living room. He could barely see the outline of Adrian laying on the living room couch. He could hear the soft music playing on the stereo as the flickering light from the fireplace danced across the walls. Gene closed the door and stood in the vestibule as she sat up on the sofa.

"Adrian," Gene said, softly, "are you alright?"

"Yes... I was sleeping... but I knew you'd come," she said.

"I thought you said you were going to call me ... and I've been waiting. When did you get back?"

"A few days ago."

"How did your interview go?"

"I'm not going to leave... I decided to stay here."

"What did you decide about us?"

"That's a problem."

"Why?... Because I love you so much?" Gene asked. "Can I turn on a light... I can barely see you."

Adrian reached over and switched on a table lamp. Gene looked at her and smiled.

"GOD, you're beautiful!"

"We've got to talk, Gene."

"I know."

"You're reaching a major crossroad in your life and I'm standing in your way," Adrian said, almost in a whisper.

"That's nonsense."

"No... it's true.. you know what will happen if your wife files for a divorce before the election."

"Then I won't run."

"That's not fair to the people of this city."

"To hell with the people of this city!... I love you!"

"That's just being selfish... you're not thinking clearly."

"Damn it, Adrian!... Don't you love me anymore?"

"I didn't say that."

"Then what are you saying?" Gene asked, fretfully. "You've been playing this game with me ever since Christmas!... I haven't held you or kissed you!... You won't call me!... Dammit I haven't seen you in almost two weeks and it's tearing me apart!... Tell me the truth.. why are you doing this to us?"

"I'm sorry."

"Don't be sorry.. be my lover again!.... Be my whole world that makes my life worth living!.."

"I think we should suspend our relationship until after the primary election," she said, quietly.

"That's six months away!" Gene protested.

"But when we resume our relationship, you would've been nominated and they couldn't take it back away from you."

"If I can't have you now... I will not run, Adrian."

"Then we're at a stalemate."

"No, we're not... something's not right here and I intend to find out what it is," Gene said, looking all around the room.

Gene walked around the room carefully examining the tables, the walls, looking for anything that would give him a clue... He looked back at Adrian who still laid on the sofa, her eyes following him as she smiled...

"What is it?" she asked.

"Can... can I have a drink?"

"Yes, of course... I'll get it for you," Adrian replied as she started to get up.

"No... no... I'll get it," Gene said, "I know where everything is."

"There's cold water in the fridge."

"Thanks... I'll be right back."

Gene walked into the kitchen and turned on the light. Everything was neatly in place. He saw several prescription bottles on the counter. He picked them up and examined them. Morphine and Demerol... two powerful pain killers!.. He picked up the two prescription bottles and started back into the living room just as the phone began ringing. He stopped in the hallway and listened...

"Hello... Hi, Gloria.. yes... yes, I promise you I will. I know... I know... Yes, he's here now... Yes... I love him so!... I will... you're very kind... thanks... bye, bye."

Just as she hung up the phone, she saw Gene standing in the doorway holding the two prescription bottles. He motioned to the telephone, puzzled... "That was my sister wasn't it."

"Yes."

"Why is she calling you and why are you taking these powerful pain killers?"

He sat down on the arm of the sofa as it all began to come together. He placed the two prescription bottles on the cocktail table and sat down on the sofa, facing Adrian as tears filled her eyes... He placed both hands on her shoulders and stared tenderly into her eyes... "Oh, baby!... My sweet, sweet baby!... Is that what this is all about?... I'm not in love with your breasts... I'm in love with you!"

His arms embraced her, bringing her trembling body close to his heart.. "Why didn't you tell me, honey?" he cried. "I don't care if it's a lumpectomy or double mastectomy... I love you, baby... no matter what happens with any operation!"

He kissed her feverishly, all over her face as tears streamed down both of their faces... She tried to speak but he wouldn't let her...

"Gene... Gene!.. please honey.. there's more," she cried out between sobs.

"OK... OK... tell me everything," Gene said as he continued kissing her passionately, "no matter what the cost or how many operations.... we'll face this thing together and beat it!"

"They won't operate, Gene... they all have said... it's too late."

"No!... I won't accept that!" Gene protested, angrily, "We'll get a second opinion!"

"We've already had second, third and fourth opinions," Adrian whispered, sadly, "and they all agree, honey... they say I have six months at the most."

"No!... No!... There must something we can do!"

"I'm so sorry, baby... I love you so much," Adrian said, crying softly.

Gene held her tightly as tears streamed down his cheeks. He kissed her neck and her wet face... "We'll never be apart again... I'll drop out of the race... I'll spend all of my time with you."

"No... I don't want you to do that."

He leaned back and stared into her eyes... "What do you want me to do, baby?"

"I want you to love me forever."

"Would you like to move up to the island?"

"And live among the pine trees, wild berries and black bears?... Yes, I'd like that!"

"Can I come up there and live with you?"

Adrian smiled, broadly. "Oh, Gene... would you?... That would be wonderful!"

"How much does Gloria know?"

"She's been with me form the beginning."

"Then you were the friend she escorted to Mexico."

"Yes... but don't blame her... I made her promise not to tell you."

"What a fool I've been!... All of these precious days I could've been with you... I've been blaming you... I should have known it was something beyond your control."

"Please don't torture yourself," she pleaded, "it's just something that is out of our hands... I have an extremely invasive disease that spreads rapidly. It usually occurs in women between 25 and 35 who have never had any children... I seem to fill the bill."

"I'm not leaving you tonight."

"I don't want you to ever leave me."

"And tomorrow... I'll arrange for us to move up to the island in a few days," Gene said, thoughtfully.

"What about your wife?... I really want you to stay in the race and I know she'll file for a divorce if you leave her."

"I'll have to talk to her... but you've got to understand one thing," Gene said, firmly, "I'm not totally convinced there is nothing we can do about this illness... I'm still in shock now... I was devastated trying to face each day without you.. and now this... Just the thought is overwhelming... but we'll face it together, baby... As GOD is my witness... I'll do everything I can to beat this thing!... Will you cooperate, Adrian?"

"I'm putting myself completely in your custody."

He put his arms around her and pulled her closer to him, lightly kissing her ear and throat as the tears came down his cheeks. "I'll be there with you every morning, every day and every evening... you are my whole world, Adrian, and I am committed to you more than anything or any person on this planet!"

"When Gloria and I were in Mexico... an old Mexican woman saw me... and for no particular reason... she just started talking to me in broken English... She said the strangest things to me... At first we thought it was kinda weird... but she must have known something."

"What did she say?"

"She explained that there are three main stages of the grieving process... shock and denial.. anger and depression... and reconciliation."

"Are you saying I'm in shock and denial?"

"We've got to have our anger, Gene," Adrian whispered. "And we've got to recall all of our beautiful memories together... and..."

"And what?"

"You've got to learn to live in the world... without ever forgetting the person who..."

"No!... Never!"

Chapter Thirty-Six

Walton Dugas proudly took his daughter, Marcy, on a tour of the new offices of The Daily Press Newspaper. The entire building was built in the style of modern architecture with wide, spacious offices and endless parking lots. The business offices were adorned with thick, plush carpeting, luxurious paneling and window walls covered in vertical venetian blinds, framed with heavy drapery.

After the brief tour Dugas led Marcy back into his enormous office suite. He sat behind his long, executive desk, looked at Marcy and smiled..."Well, what do you think?"

"It's marvelous, dad," Marcy answered, "I can see you didn't spare any money in the materials."

"All of this...could eventually be all yours and Doug's."

"I don't think so."

"Listen...I know I haven't been the easiest person to have as a father," Dugas said, calmly, "I've made a lot of mistakes with you and Doug."

"I'm surprised to hear you admit it."

"Since Douglas has joined my staff...I am amazed at the changes he has made...not only on the job where he has made tremendous strides, but also in his personal life...He has become more stable and self-confident...hell, I'm actually proud of him."

"All he needed was a chance," Marcy said, "but in the past...you never gave him the time of day."

"That's my point...I've changed...this thing with Doug has shown me that I can have a good relationship with my children...both personal and in business."

"C'mon, dad...what're you driving at?"

"I want you here at The Press."

"No way!"

"Look...all I'm asking is a chance," Dugas said, "just like I finally gave your brother a chance...Why can't you give me one?"

"It's more than that and you know it," Marcy replied. "I am thoroughly against your editorial policies of racism and sexism...I couldn't possibly represent this newspaper."

"What if it changed and became more like your precious Herald?"

"If you could do that...I would certainly consider it."

"Listen, Marcy...you're planning to get married...settle down and have children," Dugas said. "I love that idea...to know that the blood line is going to continue through you and Doug...Don't you think that the future of your family would be more secured if you were working here...about to become the editor and publisher?"

"Of course it would, but there's a principle involved here," Marcy answered, "and I'm not willing to sacrifice my principles to secure my family's future."

"OK...I understand that," Dugas shot back, "but what happens if I could work out a plan that would incorporate some of the virtues of the Detroit Herald that you admire so much?"

"Such as?"

"When I committed to building this plant out here in the suburbs a few years ago, I underestimated it's final cost and overestimated our yearly profits...as a result I am facing a financial deficit that presents and uphill battle I could lose."

"Whose fault is that?" Marcy snapped. "The only reason you moved out here was to get away from the heavily Black population that's in Detroit!...Prejudice and bigotry can be expensive!"

"And with The Herald cutting into our advertising revenue...it help compound the problem also."

"Don't blame the Herald."

"Blame and fault are not the point...It's how to resolve this financial problem that is," Dugas said.

"What's that got to do with The Daily Press incorporating some of the virtues of The Herald?" Marcy asked, concerned.

Dugas leaned back in his chair and stared at Marcy, thoughtfully..."Are you familiar with the term, J.O.A.?"

"J.O.A.?"

"Joint Operating Agreement," Dugas said. "It allows two major daily newspapers in the same metropolitan area who are both suffering great financial losses which threaten the jobs of thousand of employees, to combine all but editorial functions in order to reduce their operating expenditures to survive."

"How does it work?"

"Essentially anti-trust exemptions under the Federal Newspaper Preservation

Act of 1970, allows a J.O.A. to maintain control over expenses and prices to deliver fat profits to each entity," Dugas explained.

"This would mean that both newspapers, The Herald and The Daily Press, would become business partners?" she asked.

"Exactly...both newspapers would be ran by one newspaper agency. During the week both newspapers would publish it's own newspaper...but on Saturdays, Sundays and holidays, they would publish a single newspaper with the mastheads of both newspapers on the front page...In our case it would read; The Detroit Daily Press and The Detroit Herald."

"Or The Detroit Herald and The Detroit Daily Press."

"Whatever."

"That's interesting," Marcy said, thoughtfully.

"I thought you'd feel that way," Dugas said, smiling. "So you can see that if that happens...you and your future husband could wind up working for The Daily Press...indirectly anyhow."

"Do you think Gene Stanton would go alone with that?" Marcy asked, thoughtfully.

"I think he might if he knew you'd be one of the principles representing The Daily Press," Dugas replied, smiling. "He may not care too much for me...but he thinks the world of you and your...Max Jenkins."

"You'd want us both over here?"

"Definitely!"

Gene was surprised at Patricia's amiable response to his request to meet with her at their home. This was one of the first times he had stayed out all night and she had to have some idea of what the meeting was going to be about. She always seemed to have a second sense when the subject was Adrian. She had resented her from the start, even before she met her. Although she never objected to Kim's friendship with Adrian, she never expressed a positive notion in her regards and she would remain silent at the mention of her name rather than speak negatively about her. Adrian's reactions to Patricia were similar in that she too refrained from trying to debase the quality of Patricia's character, realizing that any slam against Patricia was also a slam against Gene that could possibly cast Adrian in a negative profile from Gene's point of view. She was simply too intelligent to become caught up in such a trap and Gene, out of loyalty to a long time relationship with his wife, appreciated Adrian's consideration in that regard.

However, today the time has come to set the priorities straight in Gene's life and being the forthright man that he was and bound by the time restraints of Adrian's illness, he knew what he had to do...After Patricia's outbust on Christmas Day about Adrian being named Gene's campaign manager, he wasn't sure what reaction he could expect...

It was a warm winter afternoon when he reached the Stanton home. He saw Patricia's car in the driveway and the large amount of snow on the car indicated that she had not been to the Community Affairs Offices. His absence overnight was certain to have provoked her. Although they had not slept together in many years, he knew that the pretense of a normal marriage was important to her. Especially now that he was running for mayor.

As he walked across the wide, vine covered front porch of the mansion he was surprised to see the front door slowly open and Patricia, dressed in a dark business suit, standing there holding a cup of coffee. She offered him the cup and smiled..."Hi...you're right on time...I'm in the library."

Gene followed his wife into the huge paneled library. She took his coat and hung it up in the vestibule closet as Gene glanced at his mail and a handful of messages. Patricia quietly walked back into the room, remaining silent as Gene studied his messages. He stopped and looked up at her..."You alright?"

"Oh, yes," she answered, "I'm doin' just fine."

He stared at her, admiringly. She still had the model's figure and the tight fitting suit was sexy but still business. "You look great in that outfit."

"Thank you...I'm surprised you noticed," she said.

"You have something special planned today?"

"Sorta."

He laid the mail and the handful of messages down, slowly and walked around to the front of the desk and sat down on the corner. Patricia took a seat on the sofa, waiting for him to continue.

"I'm sorry about upsetting you on Christmas, but Adrian was recommended to be my campaign manager by Congressman Ghetts," Gene explained. "She was well qualified and was familiar with most of the city and state politicians, so I asked her and she accepted."

"Of course she would."

"Well, she's changed her mind now," Gene continued. "She resigned as my campaign manager yesterday."

"Why?"

"She agreed with you...she didn't think it was appropriate. She feels that Roger would be better qualified."

"Well...if she did that to try to placate me...it's too late."

"Too late?..Too late for what?"

"I had been waiting for us to have this frank talk for months now," Patricia said, "I'm sure you have, too...You and I have had a good marriage and we have raised six wonderful children...but I think it's time for both of us to be honest with each other...and...and end this charade...without rancor."

"Charade?"

"Gene...be honest now...one of your best characteristics has been your ability to remain candid in any situation. Please don't change now."

"Go on."

She stood up and calmly walked over to the wide front window, staring out over the spacious, snow covered front lawn and the huge trees that proudly guarded the Stanton estate. Patricia's voice became unsteady as she continued..

"You know...when two people first get married...they are two individuals who really have no idea what the future might hold for them. After twenty-five or thirty years of marriage, six children and the ups and downs of life in general...those two people who originally married each other 25 or 30 years eariler are usually, in most cases, no longer the same people."

"Sometimes they grow closer."

"Sometimes they may make it appear that they've grown closer," she said, calmly, "it's a practice that long married couples automatically develop to perfection in order to dissuade others from knowing the truth and to conform to the acceptable standards of an outmoded society...But today, our lives are changing so rapidly most of those standards do not necessarily apply."

"That's true...which accounts for so many unhappy couples remaining in a marriage that is squeezing the life out of both of them. It's a known fact that there is a definite connection between depression and major illnesses," Gene said, thoughtfully, "A lot of unhappy marriages contribute to that."

"Exactly...that's why, if the average person in this country can maintain their health with a good exercise program and stay away from devastating diseases like AIDS, cancer, heart conditions...eliminate the excessive use of improper diets, drugs, booze and cigarettes...they could live a long time, especially if they are generally happy and in a positive state of mind," Patricia said, analytically. "At the turn of the century our life expectancy in this country was estimated between 45 and 60...now, it's been expanded almost to 75 and 80. With the prospect of a much longer life span and stimulated sexual desires, our whole life styles are changing...Drugs like estrogen, tetostorone and the new smart drugs are making men and women who were at one time considered old at 50 in the past, much more vibrant and virile today and similar to being in their 20s and 30s instead of in their 50s...It's like our lives today are divided like a movie and it's sequel...into part one and part two...Part one is growing up, going to school, getting married and raising a family...and part two is the beginning of a second life with a new love-mate, new career or a new business."

"That doesn't necessarily apply in all cases," Gene said.

"It does in our case," Patricia responded. "We have always been more progressive than most people...You've started an ambitiously new business and now you're running for mayor."

"And you're beginning your law career...I think that's great!"

"Don't you see?..It all fits the pattern I was talking about," Patricia said. "I've often wondered what kind of woman you would choose if something ever happened to me...I knew she would be exceptionally beautiful, young, intelligent and extremely sexy...I had envisioned her many times before Kim ever introduced her to me...Adrian just put a face on the vision...but I knew it would be her."

"And you...you have Bill Clark," Gene said, smiling.

"You know about Bill Clark?" Patricia was shocked.

"From the beginning...it was hard to accept at first," Gene answered, casually, "I even followed you to Washington. In fact I just missed you at the airport."

"Why didn't you ever mention it?"

"I knew this day was coming...there was nothing I could do," Gene replied. "I was surprised that he nominated me for mayor."

Patricia turned to face Gene and walked back over and sat down on the sofa. "That's why I said it was too late for Adrian to resign as your campaign manager and think it would affect me...I'm moving out, Gene."

"You're going to Bill?"

"No...I've leased my own apartment downtown...I'll be by myself for a while."

Gene turned and walked back behind his desk, throughtfully. He sat down in his chair in disgust. "I really can't blame you, Pat...maybe I shouldn't have accepted the nomination for mayor."

"Don't worry about the election," Patricia said, quickly, "I think you'll make an exceptional mayor...and be good for the city, so I've decided to maintain my address here. We'll continue the facade until after the primary or the election itself...As long as you're in the race I'll stand behind you at the podium at all of the political rallies, holding your hand and punching holes in air with my fist."

"When it's all over...we'll work out a fair settlement," Gene said, sadly, "just let me know what you want."

"You can tell Adrian...she's getting a wonderful man."

"She's having a difficult time right now."

"Oh?..Is anything wrong?"

"I'd rather not get into it," Gene replied. "Is there anything you want me to do?"

"No...not really," Patricia answered as she stood up and walked over towards Gene. She leaned across the desk and kissed him on his cheek. "They were all wonderful years, Gene...we may have had a little trouble after we first got married, but we managed to work it out...And I think you'll be the best mayor this city ever had."

"Thanks for the marriage," Gene whispered.

"You're welcome...and thank you, too."

Patricia quickly turned and walked out of the library. In a few minutes she came out of the home with several pieces of luggage. She hurriedly stacked the luggage in the trunk of her car. Although she could feel Gene's eyes watching her, she refused to look back at him for fear he would see the tears streaming down her face. As she drove the car down the long, circular driveway, she looked into the rear view mirror and saw the front door to the mansion open as Gene stepped out on the porch and watched her drive away. Patricia drove the car to the most desolate part of Palmer Park, about a mile south of the Stanton Estate. She parked the car and turned off the ignition. She placed both of her arms on the top of the steering wheel and leaned her head on her hands...She sobbed hysterically as her shoulders convulsed in a deeply passionate anguish!..

The security around The Detroit Herald Newspaper building and it's executive garage and employee parking lots had been bolstered late at night by cruising Detroit Police squad cars ever since the attack on Willard Thompson by the neo-Nazis and the Skinheads. Since that time, almost one week ago, carloads of screaming Nazis and Skinheads would drive by the building late at night waving swastika flags and shouting racial epitaths at the security guards, who would usually retaliate by giving the night riders a distinguished finger extended high into the air.

Tonight, it was bitterly cold as a police car pulled up to the security guard's station at the front of the executive garage at midnight. Two policemen slowly got out and walked over to the security guard's office and tapped on the window. The security guard inside the office looked up from his pocket book and smiled..."Eddie...how ya doin', man?" the guard asked.

"Hi, Joe," Eddie answered, grinning, "you got any hot coffee in there?"

"Yeah, c'mon in...help yourself to coffee and doughnuts," Joe replied, "It's colder than a well-digger's ass out there!"

Just as the two policemen strolled into the security guard's office they heard the screeching of tires as three carloads of Skinheads and Nazis streaked around the corner and zoomed down the street as the vehicle's occupants screamed and hollered, waving flags and trying to taunt the policemen and the security guards!..

"Those friggin' nuts!" the security guard grumbled, "don't they ever sleep?"

"They're like vampires," Eddie said, chuckling as he poured some coffee, "they only come out at night...ain't that right, Harry?"

Harry had a smirk on his face as he quickly devoured a jelly doughnut. He slowly took off his police cap and rubbed his brow. "I don't like it...there's too many of em'...when they run in a pack like that, they're usually up to no good."

"They been doin' that for ... for the last couple of nights," Joe said, concerned, "ain't nuthin' happened since they lit up that advertising guy."

Yeah, but that's what's been eatin' 'em," Harry said. "They got their butts kicked pretty bad in the country jail and they didn't like it...they want some revenge for that ass-kickin' they took!"

Eddie stood up and walked over to the window, looking up into the sky above the building. He stopped, suddenly, looking above the building's skyline..."Hey...what the hell is that bright red light over there?"

Joe walked over and stood next to Eddie. "I dunno...never seen anything like that before!"

"Hell, that ain't no light!" Harry shouted, spilling his coffee, "the goddam building's on fire! Call 911, Joe!..Those bastards have set the newspaper building on fire!..C'mon, Eddie...let's get 'em!"

The two policemen rushed out to their squad car as Joe quickly dialed 911!..By the time the fire engines arrived the building was in a raging inferno!..Crowds of people quickly gathered around the building as several fire units fought the giant blazes!..All through the night the firemen were severely hampered by the cold weather that caused ice to form on the sidewalks and froze up their equipment, which created a difficult and almost impossible task to control and put out the fire!..

It was after five in the morning when Gene and Roger walked slowly down the sidewalk, observing all of the fire equipment and vehicles in the street and all of the damage to The Herald Newspaper building. Firemen walked through the smouldering ashes checking for any late flare-ups. The building had been damaged severely, destroying over fifty percent of the business offices and production facilities. A disheveled fire chief walked over to Gene and Roger and shook his head, sadly..."Morning, Mr. Stanton...it looks like they must've threw firebombs through a lot of the office windows...normally, since our station was only a few blocks away...we could have stopped it before it spread so much...but this damn weather froze up some of our hoses."

"Anybody hurt?" Gene asked, sadly.

"No, suh...everybody got out...nobody hurt, they just mad as hell!" the fire chief answered.

"They know who did this?" Roger asked.

"Know who did it?..Hell, they caught 'em before they could make their getaway!" the fire chief replied. "Two cops were over here when it happened and they got 'em before they could reach the freeway...had gasoline all over their clothes, too!"

"Skinheads or Nazis?" Gene asked in disgust.

"Both!" the fire chief snapped, angrily. "They ought to fry 'em in hell!"

Gene motioned for Roger to follow him a short ways. The two men huddled together in front of the shattered glass windows in the lobby. Roger looked at Gene sadly.

"We'll ol' buddy...they've put us out of business for a while," Roger said, bitterly.

"Yeah, it looks like it," Gene said, "but it may not be for as long as you might think."

"Gene!..It's gonna take time to rebuild and this weather won't be decent for a couple of more months!"

"I realize that," Gene said, "we've got to find some place to set up temporary offices in the meantime."

"Like where?"

Gene looked across the street at the building directly facing The Herald. "Right there...check with the owner and tell him we're interested in leasing as much space as we can get for the next few months...We might have to shut down for a while but as soon as we get everything in place, we'll start publishing an interim daily newspaper."

"What about the printing plant?" Roger asked.

"We'll contract with the biggest printing company in the area...they'll be happy to get the work."

Roger smiled at Gene as Gene II, Max and Marcy rushed up!..They stared at the partially burned out building in horror!

"Aw, dad!" Gene II groaned, "What the hell happened?"

"Oh, my GOD!" Marcy cried. "This is awful!"

"Is there anything we can do, Mr. Stanton?" Max asked.

"Yes, there is...Roger's going to check out the availability of that building across the street and try to arrange a printing contract with a local printing company," Gene said, anxiously, "I want you guys to organize an emergency staff of your most efficient employees to contact all of our personnel and tell 'em to stand by...I'm sure they've heard about the fire by now, but tell them they won't miss one day's pay and we're planning to resume publishing in a matter of days!..The Herald ain't dead yet!"

"Can you be more specific when we'll resume publishing, dad?" Gene II asked, "That's what they'll all be asking."

"Give us a few days," Gene replied, "it depends on how fast everyone can move...our building's about fifty percent damaged and I don't want any of you to try to get in there until the fire department gives the OK."

"Mr. Stanton," Marcy said, softly, "I think we should talk."

The Detroit Herald Newspaper resumed publishing a daily newspaper three days after the fire. Although most of the business offices were destroyed, the majority of records were salvaged since the southern part of the building was virtually untouched. The loading docks and trucks were not damaged. The carpenters and engineers had arranged for part of the building to be used while the front part was being rebuilt. Between the usable space at The Herald, the temporary business and editorial offices in the building across the street and several local printing companies who were anxious to please the executives at The Herald...they had managed to resume publishing within a short period of time, but Gene realized they would have to be ready with their own facilities in the very near future if they expected to survive!..

Gene was also surprised by Marcy's proposal for a Joint Operating Agreement with The Daily Press. He couldn't imagine this coming from the mouth of F. Walton Dugas, but Gene was a wise business man and he didn't turn it down. He calmly explained to Marcy that he would have to examine all of the parameters involved in such a proposal and check with other daily newspapers in a J.O.A. partnership before he could give them an answer...

Roger and Janet Carlson arrived in Duluth, Minnesota with Michelle Matthews late in the morning. They were met at the airport by Michelle's two sisters, Erin 17 and Inga, who was 13. Both girls were happy to see their older sister and overjoyed at her pregnancy through in vitro fertilization. The three sisters chatted excitedly as Roger and Janet led them to a cafeteria in the airport. They had coffee and hot chocolate as the three sisters reacquainted themselves. Both Roger and Janet were surprised by the cordiality between the sisters. Roger explained the situation to them in a very gentle manner...

"Janet and I discovered Michelle living in the streets of Detroit, homeless, so we took her into our home," Roger said.

"We got her a clerical job at The Detroit Herald Newspaper," Janet said, "and she's been staying with us ever since."

"You should see their home!" Michelle said, excitedly. "It is absolutely gorgeous!..It's just beautiful!"

"And you got...pregnant by this in vitro fertilization?" Erin asked in a little girl's voice.

"Yeah...who's he?" Inga giggled. "Does he have any brothers?"

They all laughed, relieving the tension. Janet quickly began to explain..."Roger and I have always wanted a baby but due to a physical problem we could never conceive...however, we could create an embryo. Michelle volunteered to be our host mother so the embryo was implanted in her...and that's how she became pregnant."

"But...but what happened to the other pregnancy?" Erin asked, softly. "You were pregnant when you ran away."

"I lost it...I had a miscarriage," Michelle answered.

"Gosh...that's too bad," Erin said, "but you sure are lucky...I wish I could run away."

"Me too," Inga said, solemnly.

"Why?" Roger asked. "Is something wrong at home?"

Erin looked up at Roger and Janet suspiciously. "Didn't Michelle tell you?..Isn't that why you're here?"

"Yes...she did," Janet replied, "but we want to hear it from you and Inga."

"It's gotten worse since Michelle left," Erin said, sadly, "before...he'd come into our room in the middle of the night...and take Michelle downstairs when we were real small...they'd be gone for a long time and then Michelle would come back in the room crying...she'd cry until she fell asleep."

"Didn't your mother ever say anything?" Roger asked.

"No...she's afraid of daddy," Inga answered.

"Then...as we got bigger...he'd take turns with me and Michelle," Erin continued, "it hurt so much...and I was sore all the time...but if I ever complained or anything...he'd hit me!"

"That bastard!" Roger snarled, angrily.

"Then...when Michelle became pregnant...he ordered her to leave!..He called her a whore and told her to get out!" Erin cried. "After she left...he began to get in my bed every night!"

"He would get me in the bathroom," Inga volunteered, as tears streamed down her face, "he would make me open the door when I was in the bathroom...he would come in there and close the door...and stick his thing in my mouth and he would do it...right in my mouth!..He said it was the same thing that babies did with their mothers when they were breast feeding...only this is what they did with their fathers."

Janet was disgusted and Roger became furious. He got up and walked away, extremely upset!..Janet remained sitting with the three girls..."Are you girls all willing to tell this to the police?" Janet asked, calmly.

"Yes, ma'ma...I just want it stopped," Inga said, sobbing quietly, "it makes me feel so dirty!"

Roger walked back over and put both arms around Inga and Erin..."We understand, girls...and we'll put an end to this," Roger said, comforting them both.

"You all realize...your father will go to jail, don't you?" Janet asked, searching the girls' facial expressions.

"After all he's done to us...that's where he belongs," Michelle replied, angrily.

Erin looked at Michelle, confused. "There's just one thing...daddy said that some football player knocked you up and that's why you ran away...is that true?"

"No, it's not true!" Michelle snapped, angrily. "He's told everyone that lie...but the truth is...he put me out because I was pregnant...but with his child!"

The penthouse offices of the National Steel Corporation were plush with deep, thick carpeting and rich, cherry paneling. The sophisticated business atmosphere reeked of wealth and power. Roger sat in the outer office with Deputy Sheriff Christine West and Deputy Sheriff Ben Williams as Walter Matthew's secretary kept glancing at the trio and the woman and three young girls sitting across the room from the man and the two deputy sheriffs. The three girls with the woman looked vaguely familiar but since the oldest girl was obviously pregnant, she dismissed any chance of having known any of them in the past. However, her curiosity got the best of her and she turned to Roger with a puzzled look on her face...

"You say you have important personal business with Mr. Matthews, Mr. Carlson?" the secretary asked. "He's a very busy executive and he says he doesn't even know you."

"Just inform Mr. Matthews that Mr. Carlson is an attorney who represents his three daughters," Deputy West angrily interrupted, "and if he doesn't come out of that meeting in the next five minutes we're going in there!"

THE WINDS OF TOMORROW

The secretary's face turned a bright red. She quickly got up and marched into the conference room. In a few minutes she opened the conference room door and motioned for them to come in. The two deputies followed Roger into the conference room. They were surprised to see a long conference table with sixteen people sitting at the table who all turned to face them as they walked into the spacious room. A gray haired man, tall and handsome, who was sitting at the head of the table stood up...

"I'm Walter Matthews," the man said in a commanding voice, "what's this all about?"

"Mr. Matthews...I'm Deputy Sheriff Christine West and this my partner, Deputy Sheriff Ben Williams...We're from the Criminal Sex Crimes Bureau of the County Sheriff's Office," she said, officially, "this is Mr. Roger Carson, your three daughters' attorney... he has a signed complaint charging you with incest and criminal sexual abuse against a minor!"

"That's an outright lie!" Matthews angrily shouted, becoming obviously upset and shaking. "You better get the hell outta here!... Disrupting my meeting with some bullshit rubbish like that!... You have no proof of such ridiculous charges so get the hell out of here before I call security and sue you for slander!"

"You want your security, Mr. Matthews?" Roger shot back as he motioned to the doorway.

In a few moments the door slowly opened and two of National Steel's security guards walked into the conference room followed by Janet Carlson and the three girls... Mr. Matthews was surprised to see his three daughters, especially Michelle, who stepped forward with her swollen and protruding stomach conspicuously in view...

"Hello, daddy," Michelle said, softly, "you're going to jail!"

Matthews was startled at the sight of Michelle and he immediately began to defend himself. "That's not my baby!" Matthews shouted in protest. "I haven't touched her in over a year!... I mean... I haven't seen her in over a year!"

Everyone in the large conference room including all of the executives sitting at the table were stunned by the words Matthews had blurted out!... He stepped backwards, momentarily, realizing the drastic mistake he had made. Deputy Sheriff West smiled knowingly as she walked up to him, blocking his path. The anger in her voice could not be mistakened as she turned back to her partner and ordered, in a terse command...

"Read him his rights while I cuff him!"

Chapter Thirty-Seven

In the winter, Grand Island offers a dance in an icy wonderland and a trip back in time. A silent glide through frozen wilderness after the last fall leaves are buried under blankets of silvery snow. The island's mysterious spiderweb of wilderness trails disappear into the frosty white nights, across frozen lakes and over river channels with only moonlight to guide the way. There is nothing around for miles but tall, elegant pine trees heavily ladened with snow and the deep sounds of silence. All through the hills and by lookouts over the lakes, it is silent and peaceful.

It was dusk when Harry and Marie Jones met Gene and Adrian in a horse-drawn sleigh carriage at the helicopter landing pad. They quickly loaded up the carriage and climbed aboard the vehicle of ancient vintage. Adrian cuddled in Gene's arms as snowflakes floated down out of the pale gray skies that blended into the bleak, white landscape. The air was bitter cold, nipping at the exposed areas of their faces. Gene leaned down and kissed Adrian on her cold nose. She looked up at him and smiled.

"This is just beautiful," she sighed.

"Yeah, it's beautiful and cold," Gene chuckled.

"Where are all of the animals?" Adrian asked.

"You won't see as much wildlife as you did in the fall," Gene answered, "but everything is so still and quiet in this cold climate...you can actually hear the woodpeckers hard at work...still, you'll see so many tracks, you know the animals are there."

"This is great...I've never had a sleigh ride before."

"That's the only way to travel on these roads with this much snow...a car wouldn't make it...Are you alright?"

"As long as I'm with you...I'm doin' just fine."

He kissed her long and passionately. Harry and Marie glanced back at them and smiled.

"I got a surprise for you," Gene said.

"What?"

"Not what...who."

"Well...who?"

"Gloria's flying up here tomorrow...Willard's out of the hospital and she wants to spend a few days with you," Gene replied. "You don't mind do you?"

"Mind?..No...I love your sister."

"I know."

"Have you made up your mind about running for mayor?"

"I'm not sure," Gene answered, thoughtfully, "it will take more time away from you."

"But I want you to run...Detroit needs you!" she urged.

"So do you."

"Gene, please!"

"Now, since the newspaper's been racked by that fire...it may be too much for them to deal with...especially with Roger becoming my campaign manager."

"They resumed publishing a few days after the fire," Adrian said, "from what I hear from Marcy...they're doing alright."

"And that's another thing...I've got to answer Dugas' proposal."

"You mean the Joint Operating Agreement?"

"Yes...on paper it looks good."

"Then what's the problem?"

"I think I can get more out of Dugas."

"Like what?"

"I've got a few ideas...I'll think about it for a while before I answer her."

"Marcy's excited about it," Adrian said. "She thinks it's gonna happen."

"How do you feel about it?"

"I like the idea...it'll leave you more time to concentrate on the primary while it almost guarantees The Herald's continued success," Adrian replied, thoughtfully. "To be in partnership with The Daily Press...a publisher with two newspaper offices and two production plants!"

Gene leaned over and kissed her again as the carriage pulled up onto the horseshoe driveway leading to the main lodge house...He stared at her and smiled, hungrily...

"It'll leave me more time to make love to you, too."

"Yeah, that too," she said, crinckling her nose at him.

"I'll call her tomorrow with my counter-offer."

"You've reached a decision?"

"You just gave it to me."

Gene and Adrian had a memorable evening after they moved all of their belongings and luggage into the main cabin at the lodge. From making a giant snowman in the front yard of the lodge, snowmobiling down through the winding winter trails in the thick forest, an impromptu snowball fight and finally making endless love in front of the huge fireplace in the living room. When they snuggled up together, wrapped in each other's arms and drifted off to sleep in the king-sized bed in the master bedroom, they both wished this dream would never end...

The next morning at ten Gene was on the phone with Marcy Dugas while Marie and Adrian were banging pots and pans in the spacious, stone-walled kitchen, supposedly preparing breakfast.

Adrian showed Marie a hand woven Indian artifact she found tied to the headboard of their king-sized bed in the master bedroom. Marie looked at it and smiled.

"That's a dreamcatcher," Marie said, "Indian folklore says it keeps out the bad dreams. The hole in the center allows only the good dreams to come through."

"Where'd it come from?" Adrian asked.

"Harry put it there for you...it will help ease the pain," Marie answered.

Adrian put her arms around Marie and hugged her.

"Thank you...thank you both," Adrian said, "you and harry are such wonderful friends!"

Gene continued talking to Marcy as adrian placed a steaming hot cup of coffee in front of him on the dining room table. Gene looked up at her and smiled as he continued speaking over the phone..."Yes...Adrian's doin' alright...just a little sassy."

"Have you had a chance to think over the J.O.A. proposal?" Marcy asked.

"Yes...yes, I have."

"Well?"

"I'll do this on one additional condition," Gene replied.

""What's that?" Marcy asked.

Adrian sat down across from Gene sipping her coffee and waiting for Gene's answer with a puzzled look on her face.

"Listen, Marcy" Gene replied, "your dad...The Daily Press has two newspaper offices and two production plants...all with the latest equipment."

"I'm listening," Marcy said, "go on..."

"The Herald has one-half of a burned out building," Gene continued. "The Daily Press can show their good faith in this Joint Operating Agreement by allowing The Detroit Herald to move in and take over their old offices and production facilities in downtown Detroit for the total sum of one dollar...This will give us first rate equipment and offices while we're waiting for the reconstruction of our building and the new equipment we've had on order."

"That makes sense," Marcy replied, thoughtfully. "I'll pass it by my dad and see if that dog can hunt."

Adrian reached across the table and squeezed Gene's hand as she smiled broadly..."Hey!..I think that's neat, honey!.."

"Call me as soon as you find out," Gene spoke into the phone. "If he agrees tell him I'll have my attorneys meet with his as soon as possible to get this ball rolling. We'll want to move in to those offices right away."

"I sure will, Mr. Stanton," Marcy replied, anxiously, "And I think it will show Washington D.C. that The Herald and The Press are already working together."

As soon as Gene hung up the phone they heard the jingles of the horse drawn sleigh pulling into the parking lot. Adrian rushed to the front window and looked out...

"It's Gloria!" Adrian cried, happily. "Harry just brought her in from the landing pad!"

Adrian and Gene grabbed their jackets and went out to greet Gloria and Harry. Gene helped Harry with Gloria's luggage as Adrian and Gloria talked excitedly. Gloria was startled by the size of the lodge and the many surrounding cabins.

"My goodness this place is big!" Gloria shouted. "I had no idea it was this spread out!"

Adrian was confused. "When is the last time you were up here?"

"When she was about eight or nine," Gene laughed, "She's a city girl...can't stand any place without sidewalks."

"Oh, shuddup," Gloria chided Gene, smiling. "I brought you something if you've been a good girl, Adrian."

"A present...for me?" Adrian screamed, excitedly. "What is it?..Where is it?"

"Has she been good?" Gloria asked Gene, laughing.

"She pushed me out of a snowmobile and hit me in the head with a snowball!..What do you think?" Gene asked.

"Then she's been good," Gloria answered. "I've got your present out in the carriage...I'll be right back."

Gloria quickly went back outside to the carriage.

Adrian looked at Harry and Gene. They both shrugged their shoulders, helplessly. In a few minutes Gloria came back in carrying a small, insulated box with air holes. Adrian cautiously took the box from her, looking back at Gene.

"What's in there?" she asked.

"Open it up and see," Gloria answered, smiling.

"Probably a rattlesnake," Gene said, jokingly.

"Maybe a boa constrictor," Harry chuckled.

Everyone remained quiet as Adrian slowly lifted up the lid. Her face suddenly brightened as a huge smile crossed her face!.."Oh, he's just beautiful!..Thank you, Gloria!..Thank you so much!" Adrian threw her arms around Gloria and hugged her. "It's something I've always wanted!"

Adrian gently placed the box on the cocktail table and lifted out a small cocker spaniel puppy, who looked like a little ball of golden fur, trembling in Adrian's hands. Everyone smiled broadly as Adrian played with the puppy.

"Hey...he's a cute little guy," Gene laughed, "his ears are bigger than he is... He's the perfect gift for her, Gloria...Thank you."

"He's not yours!" Adrian said. "He's all mine...and I got to think of a name for him...a newspaperish name."

"What'cha gonna call him, Newsprint?" Harry asked, chuckling.

"What about deadline?" Marie asked from the kitchen.

"No...I don't like Deadline," Gloria said.

"What about Byline?" Gene asked.

"I like that," Adrian answered, smiling at Gene, "that's what we'll call him...Byline...Here, Byline...come to mommie."

Gene looked at Gloria and smiled. He walked over to her and kissed her on the cheek as he whispered in her ear. "You're wonderful and very thoughtful...I think Byline will make her very happy...Did you send off that letter?"

"Direct to Moscow," Gloria whispered back.

"Thanks, sis."

"What are you two whispering about?" Adrian asked.

"No problem," Gloria said, turning back to Adrian. "You know how to housebreak a puppy?..He didn't come with a list of instructions, you know."

Suddenly, the sound of the telephone ringing attracted their attention. Gene quickly answered it. He smiled at Adrian as he covered the mouthpiece..."It's Marcy...they bought it!"

"Bought what?" Gloria asked.

"The personnel at The Herald are going to take over the offices and the production facilities of The Daily Press in downtown Detroit," Adrian answered, happily.

"How soon can we move in?" Gene asked Marcy.

"Whenever you're ready," Marcy replied, "he said to have your attorneys draw up the lease and as soon as it's fully signed...you can move in."

"That's great, Marcy...you've done a super job!"

"There's just one thing it's gonna cost you."

""What's that?"

"The best damn reporter you ever had?"

"Who?"

"Me!"

"Why?"

"It's part of the deal...he wants me over there as editor," Marcy answered.

"What about Max?"

"He's stayin' at The Herald...but that's OK...he may have The Herald but I got him!"

"I guess this really is going to be a Joint Operating Agreement," Gene chuckled.

Spring came to Grand Island like a will-o'-the-wisp, deceptively changing the entire island in a magic transformation enhanced in a technicolor dream and accompanied with the delightful sounds of singing birds and curious animals. Deer frolicked throughout the forest as black bears wondered aimlessly, searching for food. Frozen river beds became bubbling brooks. The vast unspoiled woodlands suddenly began to sprout the wonders of nature in the form of greenery that seemed to be painted by an artist's brush. The internal lakes flowed again with clear, blue water as the activity along the great lakes was stimulated by the lonesome sounds of the moody horns of giant freighters gliding their way through the deep waters.

The months had passed by fast. Gene jockeyed back and forth between Detroit and Grand Island as Adrian's illness seemed to be holding in place with only slight indications in the form of less energy and a slight loss of weight...Although he had been in constant communications with the doctors in Moscow they had rendered no definitive answer that would possible offer the slightest hope to disprove the prognosis of the other medical experts. Meanwhile, Gene's political supporters grew anxious at his failure to constantly campaign with a stringent ongoing program to defeat the other primary candidates. Although he was still considered far out front of the rest of the pack in the opinion polls, rumors had surfaced that supported speculation that he might withdraw from the race because of the pending Joint Operation Agreement, a possible split with his wife and a purported ongoing romantic affair he was involved in.

Gloria's visits to the island became more frequent and lasted longer. When Gene was on one of his extended visits back to Detroit, Gloria would always be there, taking long walks with Adrian and Byline while Harry would inadvertently show up, following them with a video camera. Although nothing was ever said, they all realized that Harry was only doing what he had been told to do...

Today, when they walked along the rocky shoreline of the island enjoying the deep blue waters of Lake Superior and the comfort of the sun kissing their faces, Adrian and Gloria became excited as Gene's helicopter floated above them, heading towards the landing pad. The two women quickly walked back to their Range Rover parked on the dirt road and happily drove off. When they reached the landing pad Gene was waiting for them with a big smile on his face. He quickly climbed in next to Adrian and passionately kissed her.

"Did you miss me?" Gene asked as he settled next to her squeezing her shoulders.

"Of course I did," Adrian answered, "you've been gone for two whole days...you forget about me?"

"Oh, you two!" Gloria laughed. "Two whole days...big deal!"

Gene kissed Adrian again as Byline tried to lick his face. He looked at Adrian and smiled..."Hey, honey...how come you're so damn sexy?"

"I had to be...I was custom ordered just for you."

"You two want me and Byline to get out and walk?" Gloria asked, chuckling. "What are we...chopped liver?"

"Hi, Gloria," Gene said, "you been taking care of my love?"

"She's doin' OK."

"You alright, hon?" Gene asked Adrian.

"Just a little tired," Adrian replied.

Gene kissed Adrian again, his tongue gently exploring her open mouth. His right hand quickly slipped Gloria a letter that she stuck inside her breast pocket. Gene continued to study Adrian carefully..."You wanna take an afternoon nap?..I'm, kinda tired, too."

"I know what kinda nap that'll be," Gloria laughed, as she maneuvered the truck over the steep inclines of the dirt road.

"With all that flying back and forth...you oughta be tired," Adrian said. "You gonna be here for a while?"

"I gotta go back tomorrow for that big UAW rally...but I won't go if you don't want me to," Gene answered, concerned.

"No...I want you to go," Adrian said, anxiously, "I've been reading the newspaper everyday...a lot of people think you may withdraw and that's an important rally!"

"They may be right."

"No...I don't want you to withdraw!" Adrian protested, becoming upset. "The city needs you!..You're the only candidate who can bring Detroit back!"

"OK..Alright...don't get upset!..You've got to be more mature about this," Gene said, calmly. "Let's go home and get some rest...we'll talk about it later."

"It seems I've matured more than you in the last few months."

"I guess we all have...You more than anyone."

"That's true...but life is so fragile, my love...No one has ever got out of it alive."

"It doesn't seem fair...you won't be there when I go."

"That's nonsense...I'll always be with you...even when you give your big speech before the election. Just study every face in the audience...I'll be there."

Gene reached over and gently placed two fingers over her lips. "Shhhh...don't talk like that."

He embraced her tightly, feeling her body tremble.

Chapter Thirty-Eight

Gloria remained downstairs as Gene and Adrian went up to their bedroom. She pulled out the letter Gene had slipped her and quickly read it. It was from the Russian doctors in Moscow. They had turned Adrian's case down because they agreed with the earlier terminal prognosis. Gloria's eyes filled with tears as Byline whined at her feet. She gently picked him up in her arms and took him outside to the long, wooden porch and released him. Gloria leaned back against the porch pillar and stared into the deep blue skies as a flood of tears streamed down her cheeks...

The next morning Gene left early to go back to Detroit before Adrian was awake. When she came downstairs Gloria was having coffee with Harry and Marie in the kitchen. Adrian looked at them, puzzled..."Why didn't someone wake me up when Gene left?"

"He wouldn't let us," Marie said, "he wanted you to get your rest."

"Oh, my goodness...I'm not an invalid," Adrian said.

"That's good," Harry said, chuckling, "then you can plant those trees you ordered."

"They're here?" Adrian asked, excited.

"Yes...they came yesterday afternoon while you were sleeping," Harry answered, smiling, "I knew you'd be happy."

"That's great!" Adrian exclaimed. "Gloria, you gonna help me plant them?"

"I'll do the best I can," Gloria said, laughing. "I don't have a green thumb...but I know how to dig a hole."

"Where you gonna plant them?" Marie asked.

"Right on top of Gene's hill," Adrian replied.

"Gene's hill?..Where's that at?" Gloria asked.

Adrian walked over to the picture window and pointed to the hill..."Over there...that's Gene's hill...he told me all about it."

"That's Big Bertha's hill!" Gloria shouted, laughing. "It used to be Gene's hill until Big Bertha beat him up and took it."

"Who's Big Bertha?" Adrian asked, smiling.

"She was a big, fat girl who use to like Gene," Gloria said. "Her parents brought her up here one Sunday when Gene was about nine and he was struttin' around here like a barnyard rooster, sayin' he was King of the Hill...Big Bertha whupped his ass and took his hill."

"He told me it was his hill, too!" Harry said, laughing loudly.

"Don't say anything about it," Gloria said, "he doesn't think I know...but Big Bertha is now a Police Commander with the Detroit Police Department...now she's kickin' everybody's butt!"

That afternoon Adrian and Gloria worked diligently planting the two pine trees on top of the hill while Byline barked at the birds flying by. When they were finished they both were exhausted. They stepped back and admired the two small evergreen trees standing side by side.

"I still think you planted them too close," Gloria said, thoughtfully, "it looks like their branches will touch as they grow up and spread out."

"That's what I wanted," Adrian said, smiling, "these two trees represent me and Gene. The smaller one is the Adrian Tree and the other one is the Gene Tree...as they grow bigger their branches will touch and intermingle, knocking their seeds to the ground...and..."

"I get the picture," Gloria interrupted, smiling.

"Thanks for helping me," Adrian said, "I've always wanted a big sister like you."

"You've got a big sister like me," Gloria corrected her as she suddenly turned, stopped and pointed in the direction where Byline was barking furiously..."Adrain look!"

Adrian turned around and saw Byline standing face to face with a black bear cub!..The cub stared at Byline and moved towards him!..Adrian quickly ran down the hill to get Byline just as Gloria began screaming!.."Adrian...No...lookout!"

Adrian looked further down the trail where a huge black bear sow stood up on her hind legs staring at them!..

"Adrian STOP!" Gloria screamed, "Don't go any closer!"

Adrian stared the bear sow directly in the eye as she slowly walked closer to Byline, who's hair was standing up behind his neck as he continued to bark and snarl at the bear cub!..

THE WINDS OF TOMORROW

"No, Adrian!..Don't move!" Gloria screamed again.

When Adrian quickly bent down and scooped up Byline the two bears just stood, frozen to the ground!..Adrian hugged Byline to her chest as she slowly backed up. When she finally reached the Range Rover, Gloria joined her as they quickly climbed inside the vehicle and locked the doors, relieved!..

"Wow!" Gloria sighed, breathing deeply. "That scared the hell out of me!..Are you brave or what?"

"I wasn't gonna let them get hold of Byline!" Adrian answered, determined.

"That's funny...I always heard that mother bears would attack if anyone ever came near their cubs...that one didn't even growl!"

"It's Byline," Adrian said, laughing and kissing his wet nose, "he strikes fear in every bear's heart!"

"Yeah, right."

Gene realized that the United Auto Worker's Union was an important endorsement to have if he was going to stay in the race for mayor. The turnout for tonight's rally was much greater than they had all anticipated. All of the candidates were present and everyone recognized Gene as the front runner...What they didn't know was if Gene was going to stay in the race or withdraw as so many political experts had predicted.

Crowds of people continued to come into the Riverview Room at Cobo Hall in downtown Detroit. Gene and the other seven candidates sat behind a long dias waiting for the proceedings to begin. Congressman Ghetts walked up behind Gene's chair and whispered in his ear. "Can I speak to you for a minute?..This is very important.!"

Gene got up and followed Ghetts to a small room just off the main floor. When he entered the room Gene found himself confronted with the major players of several church and grass roots groups who had came out early with their support of his candidacy. Gene greeted them all as they anxiously crowded around him.

"We have to know if these damn rumors we've been hearing about you are true!" Ghetts said in a somber tone. "We went way out on a limb to support you and your economic plans...Now we're hearin' you may withdraw your candidacy."

"Yeah, Stanton!" someone shouted from the rear. "What the hell's goin' on?"

"Are you still with your wife?" another person asked.

Gene spread out his arms to quiet everyone down. "I can understand your concern but I've got to be honest with you...I plan to run and win the mayorship of this city!"

"Then why are we hearing all of these damn rumors?" a labor leader asked. "You've either got to run or get off of the pot, Gene Stanton!"

"When The Herald's building was almost destroyed by that fire...it threw a monkey wrench into my plans," Gene explained, "but now that we've got that resolved, I'm ready to move forward."

"What about your wife...are you two still together?" a concerned woman asked. "That could hurt our chances if you are divorced before the election."

Gene spotted Bill Clark in the background and he refused to look Gene in the eye. Gene carefully looked over the crowd until he spotted Patricia on the other side of the room, standing with the Stanton family. Gene smiled at them...

"Why don't you ask my wife...there she is in the back...Pat?" Gene motioned for Patricia to come forward.

Patricia made her way next to Gene and held his hand high up in the air, firmly. She quickly kissed him on the cheek. "Somebody said we're splitting up?..I don't think so...We're still at the same address in Palmer Woods and everything is just fine...Sure we've had problems in the past like most of you have...but he's still my husband and I'm still his wife...just ask our kids, here."

All six of the Stanton children lined up behind Gene and Patricia as everyone clapped loudly...Roger Carlson stood by the door, grinning from ear to ear. He winked at Gene slyly as he turned and walked back out to the ballroom.

After a question and answer period with all of the candidates, they each were allowed a five minute speech.

Gene Stanton was the last to speak and the only one to receive a standing ovation. When he finished and the applause had subsided, the president of the United Auto Worker's Union took the podium and proudly announced his union's unanimous endorsement of Gene Stanton for mayor!..

As Gene stood behind the long dias shaking hands and accepting congratulations from people lined up to meet him, he was suddenly interrupted when Roger tapped him on the shoulder. Gene turned and looked at Roger whose face was ashen with fear!..

"Gene!..Gene!..Gloria's on the line...it's urgent!" Roger said, his voice shaking.

Gene and Roger quickly rushed back to the room just off from the main floor. As he walked into the room Roger pointed to a phone setting on the bar. Gene quickly picked it up and answered..."Hello."

Gloria's voice was tense. "Gene!..You'd better come home!"

"What's happened?..Is she alright?"

"I've already called the doctor...she exhausted herself today...and now...she's not doing well at all, Gene!"

"Where is she?"

"Upstairs in bed...but it doesn't look good, Gene!..She's so weak!"

"I'll be right there!"

"I'm so sorry!"

"Just hold on...I'm on my way!"

When Gene turned back to Roger he was standing there with Gene's raincoat in his hand. "I've already got the helicopter standing by and waiting for us...I'm going

THE WINDS OF TOMORROW

with you."

"OK...let's go!"

It was pouring down raining outside as Gene and Roger climbed into the limousine in front of Cobo Hall. The thunder and lightning from the rainstorm played a symphony of music backed by the thumping of the windshield wipers and the beating of raindrops on the roof. Gene sat back in the rear set, staring out of the window without saying a work.

Pictures of Adrian floated through his head a she remembered when he first saw her almost two years ago, sitting in his receptionist's office with Kim and smiling at him...He recalled their first kiss in her apartment...it was raining then, too...He thought about that day in his bedroom when he was recuperating from the shooting and she swaggered across the bedroom towards him. She said she wanted to make love to him without touching him and when she left, she said she spelled sex with a capital 's'...She sure did, he thought!..He remembered the first time they had made love...the whole world had been shut out as they clung to each other, his body firmly implanted in her's...her soft moans of pleasure and all of those hot, wet kisses...He could actually taste the sensation of her warm tongue in his mouth, searching for his...He remembered her smiling at him from her hospital bed when she and Marcy exposed that baby selling ring...He kept thinking about the way they would make love in the woods, in the car, by the river...and how stunning she was at Mel's wedding and how he just could not resist her charms and almost made love to her right there in the library before the wedding!..GOD, he thought!..He couldn't lose her...he refused to accept that!

The trip in the helicopter was scary as the storm increased rocking the ship from side to side!..It was early morning when they finally arrived at Grand Island. Harry was waiting for them at the helicopter landing pad. Gene and Roger ran from the helicopter and the rain continued coming down in sheets as lightning cracked across the surrounding forest. None of the three men said a word as Harry drove the Range Rover like a madman, splashing through huge puddles of water, crashing down the steep, hilly roads, throwing mud up on both sides!..When they pulled into the lodge parking lot Gene was out of the car before it stopped moving. Roger was close behind him as Gene barged into the living room!..

Gloria rushed into his arms, disregarding the water dripping from his raincoat. She sobbed continuously as she tried to speak. Marie stood in the kitchen doorway, dabbing at her eyes...

"Is she OK?" Gene asked, standing in the middle of the room, dripping with rain. "Is the doctor still here?"

"She's resting," Gloria sobbed, "but...the doctor said there's not too much time...he's up there with her, now."

Gene quickly ran up the stairway, two steps at a time! Roger walked over and embraced Gloria..."Where's Byline?"

"He ran away this evening," Marie sobbed, quietly.

"Animals can sense these things," Harry mumbled.

Gloria looked at Roger..."That's true...the strangest thing happened today...there were these two bears..."

When Gene rushed into the room, the doctor stepped back from the bed. Adrian looked up at Gene and smiled. The doctor looked at Gene sadly as he quickly walked out of the room. Gene sat down on the bed and embraced Adrian tenderly. He kissed her face over and over as he rocked back and forth, holding her in his strong arms, tightly. He stopped rocking and looked into her face. "Hey, honey...how come you're so damn sexy?"

"I had to be," she answered, weakly, "because I was custom made just for you."

"Oh, my baby!..My sweet, sweet Adrian!..I love you so much!"

"I love you too, Gene," she whispered, "I...I planted our trees on your hill...they'll always be there...and I'm so happy you're here with me...our love will always be there, too."

"I'll always be here with you."

"Gene...please open the drapes and take me to the window."

Gene slowly got up and walked over to the window and opened the drapes. The rain had slowed down now and the first glimpse of dawn was coming over the horizon. He went back to Adrian and picked her up, burying his face in her bosom as he cried, softly. He sat down in front of the window, holding her tightly in his arms as the sounds of raindrops splattered against the window pane. She looked up at him and smiled..."Whether it's in a snowfall or a heavy rain...our two souls shall meet again...I really believe that, Gene...you are my soul-mate and we were meant to be together."

"I know...I think I've known that from the beginning."

"Can you see the two trees I planted on your hill?"

At that very moment there was a crack of lightning that illuminated the entire area. Gene saw the two trees.

"Yes...I can see them...they're beautiful."

"The Gene Tree and the Adrian Tree," she whispered softly, "and will you make me a promise?"

"Anything."

"Please, Gene...never...never let me leave this island."

"Never...I'll change it's name to Adrian's Island."

"I'd love that...pine trees, wild berries and black bears," she said, smiling and closing her eyes. "I'm so tired, Gene."

"Rest, my dear...remember, I'll always love you...look out over your island and watch this beautiful dawn...it's a new day, Adrian...it's your day."

THE WINDS OF TOMORROW

Adrian didn't answer. He picked her up and carried her back to the bed. He laid her down and gently pulled the covers up over her shoulders. He looked down at her beautiful face, partially hidden in the morning shadows. He bent down to kiss her lips as his tears fell upon her cheeks. He knew in his heart that her fight was finally over...From somewhere in his mind the refrains of an old poem repeatedly went through his head:　　　"And so the night has ended,
>   The worldly problems are gone,
>   And there will be peace forever,
>   For those who die at dawn."

Epilogue

It was a month after Adrian's death and a few days before the mayoral primary election. The rumors of Gene's eventual withdrawal had been fueled again...this time by his lack of personal appearances on the campaign trail. Television newscasters all across the country were asking the same question..."Where is Gene Stanton?"

Roger Carlson, Gene's campaign manager, steadfastly maintained that Gene was still in the race but his task began to lack credibility without Gene's personal appearance. Tonight's scheduled speech at The Michigan Education Association was considered crucial for any primary candidate, especially one who had not made a public appearance in weeks. Opinion polls were now showing Gene with only a five percentage point lead over his closest opponent and that five percent was in jeopardy if he failed to show up at tonight's scheduled meeting.

Reporters from national news services were stationed at the Stanton mansion in Palmer Woods, at the old Detroit Herald offices, at the new Detroit Herald offices and at Gene's campaign headquarters.

One lone woman reporter from Newsmonth Magazine showed up early in the morning and waited impatiently at the receptionist's desk at The Detroit Herald newspaper offices in the former Daily Press' publisher's suite. She jumped up in surprise when Gene Stanton casually walked out of the office and spoke to the nervous secretary.

"Is that speech for tonight all set, Mrs. Cunningham?" Gene asked solemnly, without noticing the woman reporter who was staring at him.

"Yessir...I put it on your son's desk," the secretary answered, "do you want another copy?"

"No...it's probably still there," Gene replied. "What about Roger Carlson...did you reach him?"

"He's on his way over here...I'll buzz you when he gets in."

"Thank you," Gene said, turning to go back into the office.

"Er...ah...Mr. Stanton...do you have a minute?" the reporter asked, anxiously.

"I'm sorry...I'm kind of tied up right now...later maybe," Gene mumbled, going back inside the office.

The Newsmonth reporter sat back down and looked at the secretary who smiled back at her. "Gosh, he's handsome!..Where's he been?..Everybody's looking for him...is he going to stay in the race?"

"I really don't know," Mrs. Cunningham answered, "I don't think anyone knows but him."

"Where has he been?"

"He has an island in upper Michigan...he just lost a close friend and he's been spending a lot of time up there."

"Who was the close friend?"

"A reporter who worked here for a while."

"A man or a woman?"

Mrs. Cunningham smiled, knowingly. "A brilliant young woman...she was a natural beauty."

"Was she Black or White?"

"Why?"

"Just curious...no harm intended."

"Yeah...right."

"So that's what's been going on!"

"I can't tell you anymore than that."

"What was so special about that island?"

Mrs. Cunningham smiled secretively just as Roger Carlson walked up to her desk.

"Is he here?" Roger asked, impatiently.

Mrs. Cunningham buzzed Gene's office and smiled at Roger. "He's waiting for you, Mr. Carlson...go right in."

The woman reporter waited until Roger went into the office. She turned back to Mrs. Cunningham..."What was so special about that island?"

"I don't really know," Mrs. Cunningham replied. "Pine trees, wild berries and black bears."

"Pine trees, wild berries and black bears?" the reporter repeated, not seeing Gene standing in the doorway to the office.

"What did you say?" Gene snapped at the reporter, angrily. "Where did you get that from?"

The reporter became nervously confused..."Pine trees, wild berries and black bears?..Why?"

"Forget it," Gene answered, turning to the receptionist. "We're going to the Michigan Education Association...I'm gonna make a few changes in that speech...if anybody wants us...we'll be over there."

"Mr. Stanton," the reporter said quickly, standing up, "can I use that line?"

Gene looked at her as moisture filled his eyes..."Be my guest...you got it."

Later that evening, the spacious auditorium at the headquarters of the Michigan Education Association was jammed packed with people. It was a standing room only crowd as Gene Stanton and Roger Carlson slowly made their way through the throng of supporters and down the aisle in the center of the enormous auditorium as flashbulbs popped and Gene patiently tried to shake the hands of his excited constituents who were all shouting for him to stay in the race. As they neared the front row of seats, Gene saw many members of his family, close friends and Herald employees, all urging him on...Gene shook hands and returned quick hugs. He stopped when he reached his sister, Gloria, who stared at him, smiling with tears running down her cheeks. They quickly embraced as Gene whispered in her ear..

"Do you think she's watching?" Gene asked.

"Yes...I'm sure she's up there, smiling," Gloria answered, "whatever you decide to do...I know she'll understand."

"Thanks...I sure hope so."

The huge audience in the auditorium was tense with anticipation as the time drew near for Gene to speak. As always before, Gene was the last candidate to address the restless crowd. The question was on everyone's lips...Was Gene Stanton going to remain in the race?..Gene's mannerism and the poise he displayed as he sat on the stage behind the dias gave no indication of what he intended to do. When he was finally introduced by the master of ceremony, the crowd roared their approval with a standing ovation and left no doubt that Gene Stanton was the unanimous favorite. The master of ceremony beat on the podium with his gavel several times before the audience settled down with only a few sparse shouts from the rear, echoing the chant for Gene to stay in the race...Gene raised both arms to quiet the crowd before he began speaking...

"Fellow Detroiters, citizens...I thank you," Gene began, in a solemn voice, "thank you for such a warm welcome. I know that many of you may have questions on your minds that I will try to answer tonight...The answer may not satisfy all of you...but please bear with me as I explain how I feel about running for mayor of this great city...For the last twenty years, prior to the Clinton Administration and with the exception of four years during the Carter Administration, our country has endured the indifferent attitudes of conservative administrations in Washington, D.C. who have ignored the plight of our cities and our major urban areas simply because of their majority Black populations and minority leadership...As a result, many programs that were implemented to help the poverty stricken in these cities have been cut-off and suspended with no regards for the people who were enduring this poverty...Today, we have more people and children

THE WINDS OF TOMORROW

living below the poverty level than we have had since the mid 1960s...unemployment in skyrocketing, crime is rising, drug abuse has increased and violence is racking our country...consequently, today we are witnessing a modern American apartheid as the nation's cities are now almost 85 percent Black and Hispanic, surrounded by suburban areas that are almost 85 percent White!...This has happened because most minorities lack a clearcut political and business agenda to compete with other special interest groups...Now, it is imperative that all minorities, including Whites, Blacks, Hispanics and Asians, form a mass mobilization and coalition building across racial lines, and fight to rebuild our cities with new economic innovations that will create employment, stimulate business, double our police force to reduce crime, and provide a better qualityof life for all Detroiters...for as Detroit goes...so does the suburbs!..Most minorities do not control the financial institutions, the retail industy, manufacturing or the major businesses in the service section that provide jobs and contribute to the economy of our cities...This is why such a coalition across racial lines is mandatory...The Belle Isle Theme Park I have proposed offers Detroit and the entire metropolitan Detroit, six county area, an opportunity to resolve this economic chaos we are now going through!..Previous conservative presidents abhored government involvement in the creation of jobs and relied on a "trickle down" economy and the "Free Market" to do so...This has resulted in the worse poverty in thirty years!..The unity of a massive coalition, across racial lines and including the federal, state and city governments and all of our citizens to support the Belle Isle Theme Park, could create a "trickle - up" economy and bring Detroit back to Detroiters, providing a better quality of life for every citizen in the metropolitan Detroit area!..Those conservatives who are the Free Market extremists should visit the foreign countries who are slowly but surely moving ahead of the United States in various fields of new technology such as high-speed rail transportation, computer networks, biotechnology and fiber optic communications systems...Contrary to Free Market thinking, these foreign countries are practicing a combination of Free Market formula in partnership with the people, government, businesses, and labor...This same kind of partnership could become the catalyst to accomplish the construction of the Belle Isle Theme Park which could eventually play a major role in resolving most of Detroit's and the metropolitan area's financial problems...This is why it is time for Detroit to elect a mayor who can bring about new, dramatic innovations to stimulate business, create employment and make the City of Detroit a leader in our nation once again!..My fellow Detroiters...it is up to you, for you have the opportunity to set Detroit on a course that will save our city!..You must elect a mayor who is committed, willing and able to devote all of his time to bringing the city back to economic stability...A mayor who has shown in the past that he is not afraid to implement new innovations!.. This coming November...you will elect a new mayor for the City of Detroit...and with your help, support and prayers...I intend to be that mayor!"

    The huge audience suddenly broke out into a thundering and spontaneous applause as everyone stood up, waving their "STANTON FOR MAYOR" signs, whistling, shouting and screaming their approval and satisfaction in a resounding and standing ovation!..The entire Stanton family and many of their supporters all crowded behind the podium, next to Gene, holding their arms high up in the air!..

In the balcony, the shadow of a lone woman was cast upon the wall when she stood up and watched the gathering on stage as the audience continued to applaud and cheer.

Many people surged on to the stage, surrounding Gene, and displayed their enthusiasm as they all joined hands with the Stanton family and began singing.

Suddenly, a strange compulsion made Gene look up into the balcony where he recognized the familiar shadow of the woman on the wall as she slowly turned to leave. Startled, his pulse quickened and he became speechless as the woman's shadow disappeared from view among the dispersing crowd.